TO LOVE
A
PRINCE

Endorsements for Rachel Hauck

TO LOVE A PRINCE

"Another compelling royal story by the master of princely tales!"
—Susan May Warren, *USA Today* bestselling,
RITA award–winning novelist

"*To Love a Prince* is breathtaking and enchanting! Rachel Hauck is the queen of inspirational royal romance."
—Teri Wilson, bestselling author of
Unleashing Mr. Darcy and *Christmas Charms*

"Hauck has taken elements we love from fairy tales and given them a fresh twist in a modern setting. A delightful read!"
—Becky Wade, bestselling and Christy Award winning author

THE FIFTH AVENUE STORY SOCIETY

"Hauck intertwines the stories of five New Yorkers who each receive a mysterious invitation to join a "story society" in this exhilarating inspirational… Hauck inspires and uplifts with this mix of tales. Readers who enjoy Karen Kingsbury will love this."
—Publishers Weekly

"Rachel Hauck's rich characterization and deft hand with plotting and setting had me enthralled until I turned the last page of this superb novel. *Fifth Avenue Story Society* is truly a masterpiece—a one-of-a-kind novel that lingers long after the last page is turned. This is one I'll reread often, and it should garner Hauck much well-deserved acclaim. This should be on everyone's shelf
—Colleen Coble, *USA Today* bestselling author

THE WEDDING SHOP

"I adored *The Wedding Shop*! Rachel Hauck has created a tender, nostalgic story, weaving together two pairs of star-crossed lovers from the present and the past with the magical space that connects them. So full of heart and heartache and redemption, this book is one you'll read long into the night, until the characters become your friends, and Heart's Bend, Tennessee, your second hometown."

—Beatriz Williams, *New York Times* bestselling author

THE WEDDING CHAPEL

"Hauck tells another gorgeously rendered story. The raw, hidden emotions of Taylor and Jack are incredibly realistic and will resonate with readers. The way the entire tale comes together with the image of the chapel as holding the heartbeat of God is breathtaking and complements the romance of the story."

—*RT Book Reviews*, 4.5 stars, TOP PICK!

THE WEDDING DRESS

"Hauck weaves an intricately beautiful story centering around a wedding dress passed down through the years. Taken at face value, the tale is superlative, but considering the spiritual message on the surface and between the lines, this novel is incredible. Readers will laugh, cry and treasure this book."

—RT Book Reviews, TOP PICK!

THE ROYAL WEDDING SERIES

"Perfect for Valentine's Day, Hauck's latest inspirational romance offers an uplifting and emotionally rewarding tale that will delight her growing fan base."

—Library Journal, starred review of *How To Catch A Prince*

"Hauck spins a surprisingly believable royal-meets-commoner love story. This is a modern and engaging tale with well-developed secondary characters that are entertaining and add a quirky touch. Hauck fans will find a gem of a tale."

—Publishers Weekly starred review of *Once Upon a Prince*

Also by Rachel Hauck

Visit www.rachelhauck.com

Stand Alone
This Time
Hurricane Allie
Georgia on Her Mind

Nashville Series
Nashville Dreams
Nashville Sweetheart

Lowcountry Series
Sweet Caroline
Love Starts with Elle
Dining with Joy

Songbird Novels with Sara Evans
The Sweet By and By
Softly and Tenderly
Love Lifted Me

The Wedding Collection
The Wedding Dress
The Wedding Chapel
The Wedding Shop
The Wedding Dress Christmas

The Royal Wedding Series
Once Upon a Prince
A March Bride (novella)
Princess Ever After
How to Catch a Prince
A Royal Christmas Wedding (novella)

Stand Alone
The Writing Desk
The Love Letter
The Memory House
The Fifth Avenue Story Society

To Love A Prince

RACHEL HAUCK

To Colleen Coble for all the years of friendship and cheerleading.

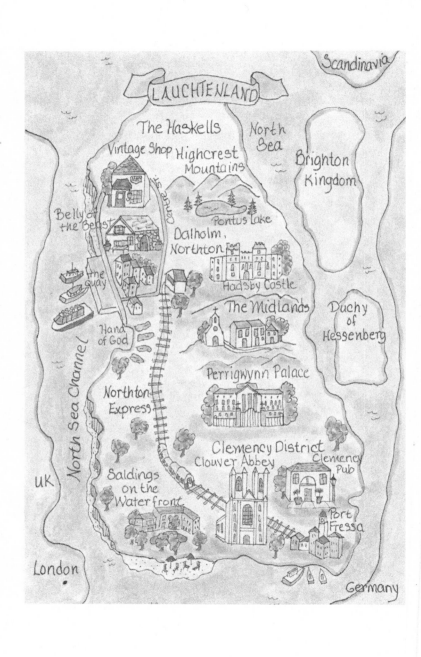

LET'S BEGIN HERE...

1938
DALHOLM, NORTHTON, LAUCHTENLAND

I t's said in the north country of Lauchtenland that the sea has a song and love blooms from the earth the same as flora and fauna. It perfumes the air and touches lives in ways no one quite understands.

Beware then, if you travel north to Dalholm, County Northton, where the wind sings through the Highcrest Mountains. Expect a bit of fairy dust on your heart. Expect to fall in love. Yes, even you.

For Taffron Björk, love saved him. If the tales of love amounted to nothing more than folklore, he'd still be a believer. He'd be forever grateful to his hometown's legend of love. To his wife, Eileen, and their sixty years of marriage.

Where would he be without her?

On this fine morning of his eighty-second birthday, Taffron woke with a dagger of sunlight in his eye and the song of spring birds in his ears. Eileen had let him slumber too long, lounge in bed like a lazybones.

Will something good happen today?

He moved from his bed to the water closet with a spring in his step. Showered and shaved, nicking his jiggling jowls as he hurried over his whiskers with a straight edge. Tended the wound with a bit of cotton, and dressed in slacks, pressed shirt, and tie.

He may be nothing more than a simple tailor, but he must always give the appearance of a man of means, like the designer he'd wanted to be. The designer he'd once been. A shooting star across the world of fashion—ever so briefly.

Checking his nick before heading downstairs—the aroma of breakfast teased his senses—he regarded his lined reflection.

Age and time hadn't dulled his blue-eyed sparkle. Well, not much. And the unruly mop of gray hair atop his head remained full.

Thanks to Eileen's pestering about brushing, he still had a good set of teeth. Some might laugh, but these things mattered to the aged. His hearing lacked for nothing either.

Still, what had he done important in life? Did his existence matter? Had he made a difference? Touched someone's life in a way that they would remember him?

Eileen would insist, "Of course, you silly jester. You made *her* gown. Princess Louisa's." His wife was only indulging him. Seems she'd pledged to do so in their wedding vows.

Yes, he'd designed a wedding gown for a princess, but he'd not seen her since the wedding. She was a mother herself with a married princess daughter. Yet Taffron's phone did not ring. He'd not been invited to be a part of the daughter's day.

Taffron wagged a finger at his reflection. "Get over yourself, old man. You had your chance. Your one day."

What a day it was too. Chosen in 1898 to design the wedding gown for Princess Louisa, eldest daughter of King Rein III of the House of Blue. Together they created a unique and timeless dress. And for a brief moment, the poor boy from Dalholm, County Northton, Lauchtenland, was a star.

But he'd been reminded stars don't shine forever. They burn with all their might, then *poof!* Vanish into nothing.

Taffron blazed onto the fashion scene with a stunning gown for a royal wedding, convinced he'd finally, *finally* arrived. Made his mark. Yet within a year of the princess's wedding, his name and face faded from the fashion world's view.

For the past forty years he put food on the table by marking and penning men's suits and sewing ladies' dress hems.

"Morning, wife." He kissed Eileen, who hovered over the cooker in the warm and bright kitchen.

Her eyes laughed as she picked away his cotton swab and handed him his cup of tea. "Sharpen your razor, love. That's the third time this week." She combed her slender fingers through his hair. "Happy birthday. Eighty-two and still as handsome as ever."

"Eighty-two and old, you mean. Love, where's the time gone?" Setting his tea aside, he stepped from the kitchen onto the porch and faced the wind and the North Sea channel.

His gaze drifted along the rim of a shredded red sky toward the foothills, then around to the cliffs high above the water, to the cleft known as the Hand of God, carved into the stone by time, wind, and rain.

The last time he navigated the steep pathway cut into the granite wall to sit in the grassy cleft, he'd been a much younger man. A desperate man.

But he'd found answers. If he could, he'd climb again. But his legs were too shaky. His knees too weak.

Behind him the screen door creaked. "Birthdays tend to make us all reflect, do they not?"

Eileen rested her head on his shoulder. "You're remembering the day you climbed the rocks?"

"Emmanuel came shortly after. Next thing I know, I'm designing a wedding gown for Princess Louisa. I thought we'd arrive, Eily. Believed I'd achieved my dream. One lucky break with a princess orchestrated by a man we'd never seen, nor would see again, and we were destined for Milan, Paris, New York. I thought I'd be designing haute couture for movie stars and aristocrats the rest of my life."

"I know you don't mean to sound ungrateful, Taff, but has our life in Dalholm been so terrible? So unfulfilling?"

"No, love, no." He wrapped his arm about her and kissed the top of her head. "You are the light of my life. It's just... Eighty-two and what've I done of any importance? What legacy do I leave behind? Besides one princess wedding gown?"

"One that remains a standard, even today. Brides still want a gown like the *Louisa*."

He peered down at her. Even with age, she was as beautiful as the day they'd met. The laugh lines stretching from the corners of her hazel eyes were evidence he'd been a decent husband, if not a good one, despite all of his disappointments and failures.

"I'll try to be cheery today. After all, a man only turns eighty-two once."

"I see what you're thinking, old man, and I'm telling you now, your life has value. Look at how you've loved and cared for me. It may not be something tangible one can leave behind like money or a house, or furniture, a painting, or—"

"A gown that sings when the wearer moves."

"I'm not sure it sang, darling, but yes, it was spectacular. I just believe our love and life are as good as a royal wedding dress. After we're long gone, our goodwill toward mankind will remain."

"You are right, my love, as always. Except that gown did sing. Like the song in the hills."

That's what they said when Princess Louisa appeared in the nave of Clouver Abbey. "Her gown seems to sing as she moves."

"I stand corrected. I remember what the *News-Leader* reporter wrote. 'She was like a living and breathing melody. I've never before seen music, or a woman, more beautiful.'" Eileen leaned against him.

"You are my forever champion, Eileen." Taffron kissed her head. "I adore you for it. You still capture my heart with a single glance."

She laughed and patted his breeze-tousled hair. "You're under a Dalholm spring spell. I'm sure I've not captured anyone's heart with a single glance in decades—if ever."

"Not true, darling, not true." Taffron lowered his lips to hers and kissed her with a young man's vigor. "I'm still under the spell of Mrs. Eileen Björk, neé Hinkley."

"Have I been enough?" she whispered, grazing the razor nick with her fingertips and brushing away the remaining cotton fibers. "Did I hold you back from your dream? From Milan and Paris?"

"Never. You saw what happened. I tried to take us to Milan, then Paris. Even New York. Every door closed."

"What about children? Aren't they the best legacy? And here we are, more than well down the path, childless."

"Now look at what I've done." He held her hands to his thick chest. "I've made you brood as well. Pay no mind to this doddering old fool who's feeling sorry for himself. I've lived a blessed life, and you have been more than enough. We have our health. We have each other. Our old shop above the quay. Why, we couldn't afford to buy this today. Did I tell you an estate agent rang and offered me more than I ever imagined?"

Eileen's eyes widened. "You turned him down, I hope."

"Of course, love. This is our home, where we and our memories live."

"Where you made *the* dress. Taffron, most men dream of things they never, ever achieve. Not even a little. But look at you. Chosen from all the designers in the world by Princess Louisa to make her wedding gown. The poor lass never looked so beautiful. She was incredibly grateful, remember? Saying how you made her feel special, like a real princess. Imagine. A princess wanting to *feel* like a princess. But you have a way, Taff. A way of making everyone feel special. It's a gift, I say, a gift."

"She was lovely. I so enjoyed working with her. But that was a long time ago. Let's not think of it any longer. I'm ruining my day. What's past is past."

"Taffron, look at me." Eileen's tone was as firm as her grip on his hands. "What if you were put on this earth to create one extraordinary gown for an ordinary, insecure princess? You can count on one hand how many designers dressed a royal on her wedding day. Even less if they made someone like Louisa shine at her most critical hour. That is who you are, love. You make gowns for women who need to know who they are, who need to feel beautiful, accepted. She needed to feel she was a princess. Not just know she was one because her father was the king."

"You are wise, my wife." Taffron turned his attention once again to the cliff that held the Hand of God.

Shipwrecked sailors named the cliff-top, carved-out nook over three hundred years ago when their vessel shattered on the channel rocks during a storm. Miraculously, they somehow survived the sea, scaled the rough, sheer rock face, and found shelter.

When asked how they survived, they said, "The Hand of God."

"Do you think some are born for one solitary purpose and no other?"

"The good Lord only had one purpose. Do you suppose you are better than He?"

Taffron laughed. "I can't quarrel with you now. You've trumped me with the Almighty."

"I'll have to tell the other wives my secret for besting my husband. Now let me get on with your breakfast."

Taffron gave her bottom a loving tap as she turned to go. Eileen swished her behind from side to side, her flirtatious wink tossed over her shoulder causing his heart to quicken.

She paused at the kitchen door. "Taffron Björk, you are somebody to me. You made a difference in my life. I don't know where I'd be without you. Isn't that more enduring and lasting than if you'd designed the most beautiful gowns in Europe?"

Taffron gazed again toward the Hand of God as Eileen's words cut through him. How selfish to long for what he never achieved while disregarding what he had—a beautiful life with his beautiful wife. But still...

"I'm still here. Use me."

Despite his speech about letting go of the past, he tripped backward to the time of Princess Louisa. For one glorious season, he'd been a somebody. Or so it seemed. Worthy. The fashion world raved over him. Lords and ladies called upon him.

Then without warning or reason, it all ended. The letters and inquiries stopped. His calling card meant nothing. So he climbed the Hand of God again because it was after his first ascent that Emmanuel came with the opportunity of a lifetime.

But the old man never appeared again.

Now it was too late. While Taffron had his sight and his teeth and a full head of hair, arthritis and tremors gripped his fingers, preventing a steady grip on his scissors and needle. If Emmanuel somehow appeared today, Taffron would have to turn him aside.

In the distance, a horn bellowed, signaling a ferry leaving the dock, headed toward England. From inside, Eileen called him to the table.

He'd just picked his cup up from its saucer when the shop doorbell chimed. Taffron glanced toward the passageway leading from the seaside cottage kitchen into his workshop and storefront.

"Are you expecting someone?" He regarded his wife. Had she planned some sort of birthday tomfoolery?

"I bet it's Mrs. Gunter. She inquired of your birthday last week, hinting she had something for you." Eileen motioned for him to sit. "I hope it's not cake. I'm making your favorite."

"Chocolate caramel? You do love me, don't you?" Taffron snapped his napkin over his lap and took up his utensils. A chocolate caramel cake. Well then, he'd welcome eighty-two with open arms. No one bested his Eileen in baking.

But first, he'd take his wife out to dinner, celebrate like a man who'd lived a good long while. Drink a pint or two and *then* come home for cake.

He'd just cracked open his three-minute egg when Eileen reappeared, her eyes wide, her face pale.

Taffron was on his feet. "What is it?"

"*He's* here," she whispered. "In the workshop." She pointed toward the doorway, her words rushed and breathless. "My goodness, he doesn't look a day older. How can that be?"

"Who's here?"

"*Him.* Emmanuel."

"What?" Taffron toppled his chair as he moved around the table. "Surely not. He was an old man forty years ago."

"He's the same old man. Exact same. And in our shop."

Taffron took a wobbly step then steadied himself on the adjacent chair. "What do you think he wants?"

"I've no idea. Perhaps another glorious assignment." Eileen glanced toward the exit then at her husband. "He is as kind as ever too."

"What assignment? There are no princesses to be married. Why me? I'm nothing more than a common tailor."

"Perhaps there's a duchess or a marchioness marrying? Didn't I read in the paper that the prime minister's daughter was engaged?"

"I can't," Taffron whispered more to himself than Eileen, rubbing his crooked sewing fingers with this thumb. "The last time I looked at fashions, the *Titanic* had just sailed."

"Go." Eileen urged him forward. "What if he just wants to wish you a happy birthday?"

"How would he know it's my birthday?"

"Everyone in the hamlet knows it's your birthday. Now go."

With a tug at his tie, Taffron slicked back his hair and headed into the shop.

"Good morning, sir." Good. He sounded casual. Confident. "How can I help you?"

Emmanuel stood in the center of the shop, filling it with his large frame and seeming to bring a light all his own.

He wore a long, woolen anorak and a broadbrim hat over sleek, white hair. But it was his eyes that arrested Taffron. The way they moved, searched, and saw, as if straight into his soul.

"It's been a long time," Emmanuel said.

"Indeed. Forty years." Taffron raised the lights, unsure if he should treat the man like a lord or a bloke he'd met down at the pub. He was both sorts. One and the same. "Please, have a seat."

But he remained standing, so Taffron did as well. "I've a final task for you," he said.

"For me?" Taffron schooled his features, tossing the statement off with a quick laugh. "Surely not a royal gown or a fancy frock. I am old, sir. Out of touch. My fingers are bent. My hands shake."

"I'm confident you are equipped for the task. But you do not have to accept." Emmanuel reached back for the door. "I assure you it is a worthy endeavor."

"What am I creating?"

"Another gown."

"Another gown? For whom?"

"Another young woman who needs to know she's a princess."

"A princess. Emmanuel, you're old so you may not know but Princess Louisa's daughter is already married. And Princess Lore is too young. There are no more princesses to be married. Not in Lauchtenland anyway."

"Taffron, this particular lass needs to *feel* like a princess. To believe who she is on the inside whether she bears a title or not. Do you accept?"

"Won't you tell me who?"

Emmanuel glanced out the window and for a moment, Taffron thought he heard him mumbling. Then he reached for the nearest chair.

"Actually, there are two young women, Taffron. One born a princess and one who will become a princess. But you must keep this between us. Only we can know."

"Tell me more, m'lord." Taffron sank into the squeaky rocker by the window. The light was perfect no matter what time of day for doing delicate work. "What will you have me to do?"

"With the royal wedding ball two months away, we have to ask, where is Prince Gus?"

—TWEET FROM @NEWSLEADER

"Prince Gus made his great escape. Will he have the courage to return? Tweet your thoughts. We'll read them tomorrow on the show."
#maddyandhyliveshow #princegus

—BRIGHTON KINGDOM'S MADELINE
AND HYACINTH LIVE!

"He may be a prince but I think he's the king of the broken hearts."

—STONE BRUBAKER, THE MORNING SHOW
ON PRINCE AUGUSTUS

CHAPTER ONE

DAFFY

This was the life. A girl on holiday with her mates. Surely something memorable was bound to happen.

Standing on the water's edge, Daffy washed her weary soul with the low rumble of the waves, raised her face to the sun, and pretended she was more than an ordinary girl.

Time away was so needed. After graduating with her master's degree, she jumped straight into work, striving to prove herself with barely a moment to breathe.

Two years in she needed a break. Then while online Christmas shopping she stumbled across the sweet blue cottage on the American coast and booked a week in February without even checking her diary. Then she coaxed her little sister along with her best friend, Leslie Ann, to join in the fun.

The three had arrived on the central Florida private beach around midnight and slept until the sun filled their rented beachfront cottage with glorious light. The sights, sounds, and sun filled her with expectation. This week was going to be amazing. She just knew it.

"I think I'll emmigrate to America," she said.

"Surely not." Little sister Ella splashed through the winter-chilled waves. While the sun was warm, the breeze still nipped with a southern chill. "Why would you?"

"Why not? I always said I wanted to live abroad."

"You never." Ella paused beside Daffy as she tied her rich dark hair into a floppy topknot.

"You wanted to marry the prince and *rule* Lauchtenland. Besides, you joined the Royal Trust to work for Mum. She'd be put out if you left."

"Dream killer." Nevertheless, Ella was right. Well, partially right. Daffy couldn't leave the Royal Trust after Mum went out on a limb to secure her position. Not very far out on the limb, but far enough. "But I do love my job."

With her master's degree in restorative arts, she wanted nothing more than to knock around historic artifacts, furniture, clothing, paintings, photographs and literature. The House of Blue had acquired such things for the last, oh, five hundred years. Longer, if the Hadsby Castle fire in 1595 hadn't destroyed nearly everything the royal family owned.

But *the chair* had been saved. The *King Titus*. Constructed by Lauchtenland's first king after the Norman conquest. It had been the royal throne for almost a century before King Louis II replaced it in 1881.

"What are we talking about?" Leslie Ann Parker, stunning, talented—and the latest sensation of Lauchtenland's national *Morning Show,* reporting on all things royal—arrived at the waves.

"Daffy wants to immigrate to America," Ella said.

"Surely not." Leslie Ann dismissed the idea with a flick of her hand.

"That's what I said." Ella slapped Leslie Ann a high five then bent to inspect a rather large conch shell.

"Thanks, you two. Your vote of confidence in me is touching."

Why couldn't she move to America? She was educated and confident—well, most of the time. Surely American museums and historic societies needed curators. Lately corporations had been hiring curators to acquire fine art. Others to build a museum of the company's history. Daffy would love such an opportunity.

"When did you ever want to live in America?" Leslie Ann repeated Ella's question. "I've known you since A-levels and never once did you express a desire to live abroad. Darling, don't you remember the time it took a month of talking to get you off on a London weekend?"

"Maybe I said it more to myself than out loud. Look, we're standing on a Florida beach, aren't we? This whole holiday was my idea. And the weekend to London was during final exams. Of course I didn't want to go." Daffy kicked at a small foaming wave as if to make her point.

"She also never said out loud that she wants to marry a prince. But she does." Ella was simply on a wild, fantastical roll this morning.

"*Wanted to* marry a prince," Daffy said. "Past tense. Present tense makes me sound like a silly little girl." Which was the purpose of sisters, no? "And if I never said it out loud, how do you know?"

"Fine. Not *wants* but *wanted*." Ella ran the shell up to their beach chairs and returned with more on the prince topic. "I suppose I can tell you now. When I was little, I used to sneak into your room and read your diary."

"You read my diary?" Daffy laughed, then sobered. "Please say you're joking."

"Yeah, the one titled *My Life with the Prince by Daffodil Caron.* I thought it was fiction at first. You went on and on about this beautiful, sweet girl who married a prince. It couldn't have been you." Daffy splashed her laughing sister. "But in the end, you started writing your names. Daffy and Gus. You wanted to marry Prince Gus."

"And you never did?" Daffy said. Both sisters grew up in the halls of the palace. For a while anyway. Before the great departure.

"Marry Prince Gus?" Leslie Ann moved away from a seagull that touched down a little too close. "Where is this tome? I want to read it."

"Don't tell me you never had visions of marrying one of the Blue princes?" Daffy faced her friend. "Half the girls in my class wanted to be my friend so I'd invite them to the palace after school." Where she went every afternoon while Mum worked. She'd been the queen's private secretary before taking on the direction of the Royal Trust.

"You'd get a jolly laugh, I tell you." Ella pressed her hands to her cheeks and batted her eyelashes. "'I just love him so much. He's *sooooo* cute.'"

"Now I *have* to read it," Leslie Ann said. "What a great feature idea. An exposé on all the girls who grew up with Prince John or Prince Gus as their dream date. I'd use your diary as a starting point."

"I've never been so glad in my life the diary is gone." Daffy turned away from the flocking seagulls who sought for something she didn't possess. "I was ten when I started the diary, and Gus was my friend. Not some cute chap I admired from afar."

Was being the operative word. She'd not spoken to him in eighteen years, except in passing. A "Your Royal Highness" here, a "Prince Gus" there. She saw him when she helped serve at state dinners. Then once or twice a year after university when Mum had transitioned from the queen's personal secretary to the head of the Royal Trust.

"You mean *My Life with the Prince* doesn't exist?" Leslie Ann again.

"Not anymore." Daffy said. *Thank God.* There was more in that book than a dreamy-eyed ten-year-old's fairytale. "Now what should we do with our day? Our first day at the beach?"

"I'd always wondered about the missing pages, Daff." Ella refused to let the topic alone. "Torn out. Then toward the middle, you stopped writing. You didn't finish your love story."

"Because there was no ending. It was all make-believe." And the torn-out pages? Hidden between the endpaper and the leather cover. "How do you remember so much? You were only eight."

"I'm brilliant. I remember everything."

True. There was no denying her little sister's savvy intelligence. A graduate of the prestigious Byhurst College with honors in engineering, she was now a software developer with an international tech company based in Lauchtenland's capital, Port Fressa.

"Ella." Leslie Ann shivered as the sun went behind a cloud. Her barely there bikini provided no warmth. "Obviously Daffy doesn't want the book. So if you ever find it, give it to me."

"Lucky for me Mum threw it away in one of her big clean outs." Daffy headed for their beach chairs, hoping the sun would burn off the chill by lunch time. "Why would you want to do a story on it, Leslie Ann? Besides embarrass ten-year-old me? No one cares about Daffy Caron."

"I would never embarrass you, Daff. But think of how every girl wants to be a princess at one point in her life. You actually had access to the palace. To the House of Blue. Or..." Leslie paused and stared off, thinking. "I could do a piece on Prince Gus's love life. We could write his happily ever after ending. If your diary came true, what would his life look like today? Maybe married with a baby in his arms? The poor chap was left at the altar. A year later, goes through a second broken engagement. All while the world watches."

"Leave it be, Les." Reclining in a wooden Adirondack, Daffy draped a towel over her legs and dug her feet into the cool sand. "You'll only remind him of his pain. Besides, you're the one who started rumors something must be wrong with him for losing two amazing women."

"It was a valid question." Leslie Ann chose a chair and sat, legs outstretched toward the emerging sunlight. "I'm a journalist. I'm paid to think deep." Both Ella and Daffy laughed. For real. Not the fake kind. "Besides, we don't even know where the man is so how could I remind him of his pain? No one's seen His Royal Highness in over a year. He's pulled a Prince Harry and run away from the royal family."

"Run away from the press is more like it." Daffy couldn't resist defending the man. So what they weren't chummy anymore, he was still her friend. "The media showed no mercy when Coral Winthrop never showed up for their wedding. And you sacrificed him on your altar of headlines and money when Lady Robbi broke off their engagement."

"Can you blame us? It was downright scandalous." Leslie Ann dug in her rucksack for her phone. "I think I'll text my boss about this. And, Ella, I'm serious. If you find Daff's diary, hand it over."

"She won't, but even if she does, you'll be gravely disappointed, Les." Daffy closed her eyes and sank into the peaceful sunlight and the repeating drum of the crashing waves. When the wind wasn't blowing, the sunlight was glorious, almost hot. "Besides writing how cute he was, I only dared dream of holding his hand."

Well, maybe there was the one teeny-tiny kissing scene. All very G-rated. Something like, "The prince scooped her up in his arms and kissed her on the cheek." What did she know of kissing at ten? And she was done discussing her journal.

After she was banned from the palace—another story no one else needed to know—she wrote her final entry and tossed the book under her mattress. Then in a drawer. Then in a box in the back of her closet.

She'd forgotten about it as best she could—with time, lots and lots of time—and went happily, successfully, through secondary school, A-levels, and university. Somewhere in the midst of all those days, months, and years, maybe during Mum's great decluttering of '09, the box with the diary became rubbish.

A few years ago, she'd decided to look for it and that's when Mum broke the news. *"We figured if you wanted it, you'd have taken it with you."*

More than a decade later, Daffy was grateful. Because there was more in that diary than a silly prince romance.

There was a secret. She and Mum were the only ones who knew. And there was no one more loyal to the queen than Morwena Caron. Based on her reaction to Daffy's inquiry, Mum had also done a splendid job of forgetting the diary's contents.

Losing a few mementos along with the little book was the price she gladly paid.

Her thoughts intertwined with bits and pieces of Ella and Les's conversation. What was Ella saying? Something about the Space Center.

"If I get this close and don't go, my colleagues will never let me live it down."

"Sounds good." Daffy mumbled, drifting toward a warm, beachy rest.

My Life with the Prince.

Gus. With his tangle of dark hair, almond-shaped blue eyes, world-renowned smile. She could see him. Breathe him in. The Pudgy Prince grew into Prince Charming. And—

"Did I tell you?" Leslie Ann's voice interrupted. "I'll be presenting outside Clouver Abbey the day of Prince John's wedding?"

"Only the entire plane ride over." Ella.

"If I see Prince Gus at his brother's wedding, I'm going to pounce."

Daffy sat up and squinted through the sunlight at Leslie Ann. "You will not. Leave him alone. He's been through enough."

"Leave him alone? Are you kidding me? He's the story everyone wants—if he even shows up for his brother's wedding. Which would be a whole other scandal. But we need to know, Daff. Why did the American heiress abandon him at the altar? No one knows. Not really. She gave some flimsy interview with *Good Morning New York*. They let her off easy."

"Focus on Prince John and Lady Holland, Les." Daffy dug through her Melbourne Beach tote she bought at a souvenir shop they'd passed in the airport. "Or the queen. Her silver jubilee is coming up. Do a retrospective on her life." Daffy set the bag and her towel aside. "I'm going inside for my sunglasses. Anyone want anything?"

"Grapes." Ella.

"Crisps." This from Leslie Ann. "And water."

Grapes, crisps, and water. Daffy started for the cottage's deck. "Ella, put on sunscreen. Your white legs are starting to beam."

"Thanks, *Mum*, but I'm fine."

Daffy approached the back of the blue cottage which was pinned between the beach and highway A1A.

All this talk of Prince Gus raised old thoughts, old feelings, distant dreams. She absolutely had wanted to marry the prince when she was a girl. Because of their friendship, she believed she would one day.

But not all dreams come true. They weren't supposed to, she'd decided. Besides, she had an amazing life. A new downtown Port Fressa flat. An advanced university degree. A good position with the Royal Trust, which was a dream opportunity. A handsome, marriageable boyfriend. Yes, she'd done well for herself.

Still... Was this it? Was this all she'd hoped for her life? Was this how she'd make her little mark in this world?

When she asked these questions, *he* definitely came to mind, but seriously, Prince Gus was way out of her league and had been out of her life for years.

Inside the cottage, she searched for the sunglasses, then gathered the requested snacks for the beach.

As she headed back out, balancing the food items in her arms, she slipped on her shades and reversed her thoughts of Prince Gus. He was not her future. Thomas was her future. Or so it seemed anyway. They'd been together for a year and he was a solid match. Kind, loyal, successful, and very good looking.

They'd developed a good routine. Friday nights at the pub with their mates. Saturday night dinner and a movie at her place. Sunday afternoons they visited his family for lunch and hers for dinner. Then it was back to the weekly grind where they met for lunch on Tuesdays and shared a virtual dinner on Wednesdays.

Thomas had taught Daffy how to invest and save. He'd be disappointed to learn she'd blown what little she'd put by on this trip, so no need to tell him.

And to her recollection, he'd whispered "*I love you*" at least once the past year during a particularly romantic evening.

Did she want Thomas to be her future?

As she reached the edge of the deck, Daffy remembered her phone was on the charger and ran back to retrieve it. She'd missed a call from Mum and a text from Thomas.

Miss you. Send photos.

She'd save Mum's voice message for later. She was on holiday and didn't want to think about work. If it was family related, she'd text or call Ella too.

Heading back out, Daffy spied the barbecue. Ooo, they could grill out. Maybe tonight.

Stepping off the deck, she raised her voice. "Hey, Ella, Leslie Ann, why don't we—"

Something hard and fast thwacked her on the side of her head. "Hey!" She jerked sideways as her sunglasses, the grapes and crisps, a lime-green Frisbee, and a golden retriever landed at her feet.

Rubbing the side of her head, she stooped for her glasses and addressed the panting dog. "You throw a mean Frisbee, pup."

"Adler, good girl. Come." The man's American accent enchanted Daffy as he jogged over the sand. "Sorry about that."

Blimey. He was something to behold. Shirtless, tan, and wrapped in taut abs, his arm muscles evident as he jogged slowly toward her.

"Are you all right? Again, my apologies." He bent for the Frisbee. "The wind caught the darn thing at just the right moment."

"I'm fine, really." She slipped on her sunglasses and rubbed her head again. The sting was nearly gone.

"Are you sure? I'd better have a look." The dog, Adler, remained at her feet and swept the sand with her tail.

"It's not necessary, really, but thank you."

"I heard it hit from twenty yards out." She winced as he gently touched her chin and tilted her head. He smelled of soap, sun, and surf. "Adler goes a bit crazy when I bring out the Frisbee." He stepped a bit closer. "No blood. Not even a bump."

"I'd hate to think I could be dented by a dog's toy." Daffy pulled away and gave him a slight once-over. Very nice. America was looking better and better all the time.

She liked the sound of his laugh, which felt oddly familiar. Besides his rather well-crafted physique, which he showed off proudly, the chap sported a thick beard and a mass of wavy, dark-brown hair knotted on his head. A few loose tendrils curled around his neck.

"Let me help." He gathered the dropped snack items and handed them to her.

"Thank you." She clutched the items to her chest and extended her hand. "I'm Daffy."

Their eyes met as he raised his hand to hers. But only for a moment. Then he jerked around and walked away. "Come, Adler, now."

But the dog hesitated with a whine and rested her nose on Daffy's foot.

"Adler, come." He added a whistle to his command.

Twenty yards way, Leslie Ann and Ella peered over the back of their chairs, watching the entire scene.

Adler glanced at Daffy, twitching her fluffy eyebrows up and down and shifting her gaze between her owner and Daffy.

"Adler. Now." The American returned, flashing the chewed plastic disc. "Come, girl."

But she refused to move and added a quick lick to Daffy's toes.

"Go." Daffy pointed to Adler's owner. "Go on now." She looked at the American chap who had yet to give his name. "Perhaps if I throw the Frisbee."

"No, thank you. Adler, I said come." He softened his tone as he crouched down. "Are you all right, girl? I don't know what's gotten into her."

Poor bloke seemed rather frustrated now. "Dogs like me." Daffy ruffled Adler's ears. "But not this much. Do you think she's hurt?" She inspected her forward paws.

"Here, let me." He inspected her back paws with his back to Daffy. "No, nothing." When he started to move, Adler bounced up and tripped his step, causing him to crash into Daffy.

Together they stumbled backward and fell into an awkward dance as they attempted to stay upright.

"Adler," he said. "What in the world? I am so, so sorry. She's never—"

Their eyes locked. Daffy gasped as he looked away.

"Your Royal Highness." She released him, a warm blush creeping across her cheeks. "W-what are you doing here?"

Really? After eighteen years? He still made her blush?

"Shhh. Don't give me away." He put his back to the beach, to Leslie Ann and Ella, and positioned Daffy in front of him. "I'm an American named Pete George. Are you sure you're all right? You look flushed."

"I'm fine." Daffy rubbed her hand over the rosy warmth. "Your Highness, you're not an American. You're Prince Augustus Carwyn George of Lauchtenland's House of Blue."

"Yes, of course, of course, but for now... Say, remember when we used to play pirate in the crow's nest at Hadsby?"

"Once. I only went to Hadsby two summers." When Mum was the queen's secretary.

"I was Pirate Pete."

"And now you're American Pete?"

He tipped his head slightly toward Leslie Ann and Ella. "Is that your party there? Please tell me that is not Leslie Ann Parker." His American accent was brilliant. Perfect.

"That's not Leslie Ann Parker, sir. *Pete*." She leaned close, catching more of his clean scent. "But it is."

Now that she was face-to-face with him, she saw everything about his appearance that made him Prince Gus. Above his beard and tanned cheeks sat a pair of unmistakable cerulean blue eyes. They were jewels mounted into a smooth piece of gleaming and golden wood.

His smile, which he'd not flashed at her quite yet, was perfection. Before the media dubbed him "Prince Pathetic" and "Prince of the Heartbreak"—or was it "King of the Heartbreak"— he was Prince Charming. The prince with the world-famous smile. It was more than his white, even teeth or full lips. It was something beyond the physical. Something true, in his heart.

"Don't give me away, Daffy, please."

"To Leslie Ann? She's harmless, really. I'm sure she wouldn't—"

"*Daffy*. I've managed a year on this quiet, private beach without press or paparazzi. The respite has nearly restored my lost dignity. I can hold my head up when I return home for John's wedding."

"I'm so glad you're going home."

"Of course. Why would I not?"

"I don't know… I suppose we all wondered." She locked eyes with him once again. It was him. *Her* prince. "I'm sure if you just said hello, she'd—"

"Have me splashed all over the news within an hour. When and if I ever go to the press again, I want it to be on my terms, with my story. Can you understand? I beg of you, keep my secret. For old times' sake. For the laughter we shared as children."

"Then I will. Whatever you ask." She glanced around Prince Gus again to see Les and Ella bottoms down on their chairs, white legs stretched across the beige beach. "They're not watching. So…this is where you've been hiding for the last year?" She kept her voice low. "Your American accent is astounding. I would've never recognized you had you not looked right at me."

"A mate from uni offered me his beach house here, and after a week I landed a job, if you can believe it, and decided to stay awhile."

"You've changed." Her gaze drifted down to his toned legs and up again. He caught her perusal, and her face tingled again with heat. She never blushed. Never. Except around this man. "I mean, before…after Lady Robbi, you were, well—"

"Portly? Pathetic? King of the Heartbreak?" He scratched Adler behind the ears. She sighed and lay down by Daffy's feet again. "Gained two stones?"

"I never said those things. I never even *thought* them."

"Maybe not, but they were headlines. Almost daily. I did eat my way through two devastating breakups. I admit it. Then I arrived here and found some inner strength."

"You look, um, well… Good for you, sir. Pete."

"Daff, aren't you going to introduce us to your friend?" Leslie Ann called from her chair.

"Shake my hand." Prince Gus slipped his hand into hers, his skin warm. "Pat the dog's head and I'll be off. Tell them I was inquiring about your cottage. Possible future rental. Actually, it is quite lovely." He peered at her for a long moment, then in a surprise of tenderness, brushed the back of his fingers over her cheek. "Be careful. I think you're burning. The winter sun is deceiving."

With a whistle to the dog, he was off, and this time Adler loped along behind him. Ella and Les peeked around their chairs to watch him leave.

Daffy tried to move, but her legs wobbled. She took a deep breath and collected herself. Guard up, or Leslie Ann would know something was amiss.

But goodness. Prince Gus. Here. On this beach. She pressed her palm to her cheek still warm from his touch.

Shake it off. She wasn't a girl running 'round the castle with a crush on her friend. She was an adult. Mature. Practically spoken for by another. Note to self: *Confirm with Thomas that we are officially a couple.*

"Here we are." Daffy handed out the snacks then headed for the water. "Thomas texted he wanted pictures."

"Who were you talking to for so long?"

"Just a bloke who thought he might rent the cottage next year. The dog was sweet."

"A long conversation for 'Hello, is this cottage suitable?'" Just as Daffy feared, Leslie Ann's reporter radar was honing in.

"I asked about his dog." Daffy snapped another picture. Her face should be back to normal by now. "I love golden retrievers."

"Why is your face all blotchy?" Leslie Ann squinted at Daffy as she twisted the cap from a bottle of water.

"I'm hot. All that running to the cottage and back." Daffy gave Ella *the sister* eye.

Change the conversation.

"All that running? It's what, twenty yards? Please."

"Ella, what were you saying about the Space Center?" Daffy sat in her chair and took her book from her bag. "Do we need tickets?"

"I'll look when we go in. Let's try that pub down the beach tonight. The Captain's Hideaway. The sign said something about the best American food on the Space Coast."

"I was going to suggest barbecuing." Daffy texted her pictures to Thomas but in her mind, she only saw Prince Gus. That gorgeous chap was here. In Florida. On her beach. What were the odds? The idea sent a chill down her arms. "But we can do it another night. We have all week."

Would she see him again? Should she try? If she got up early and started hanging out on the beach, Leslie Ann would get wise to her. *No, Daff, just leave it alone.* Leave him be. He's found some peace and dignity.

Meanwhile, she'd read the first line of her book ten times. She looked up when Leslie Ann interrupted. "So, did the love of your life text you back yet? Did he like the pictures?"

Daffy peered down the beach in the direction Prince Gus, rather *Pete George*, had gone.

"No, the love of my life has not texted." She ducked down behind her book. "I'm not sure he ever will."

CHAPTER TWO

GUS

I t's possible for a prince to hide. Though he'd known that sooner or later the paparazzi, or *someone* would find him out, he never imagined it would be the beautiful Daffodil Caron.

Looking up from his station behind the bar at the Captain's Hideaway, he wondered if he'd see her again.

She was more lovely than he remembered. Then again he'd not seen in her in quite a while. Seeing her made him long for his family and the comforts of home. Even if his home was a palace.

But running into her—or hitting her with a Frisbee—again would be unwise. Too many encounters would risk his secret. Nevertheless, he held onto the sweet, warm sentiment that had filled his chest since their eyes met in recognition.

When she said, *"You're Prince Augustus Carwyn George of Lauchtenland's House of Blue"* he felt the words rattle in his bones. For the first time in well over two years, he wanted to be that chap again.

It was time to go home. Not that Dad or Mum or John would let him get away with missing the wedding ball and the ceremony. And after his year of healing, he almost looked forward to it.

25

Still there remained a certain dread about hosting John's wedding ball, as all royal House of Blue siblings did for one another, in light of his own wedding fiasco.

Buck up, lad. Don't travel the worn roads of pain and despair. Been there. But had taken the exit off during his time in Florida. He must carry home his renewed mind and heart. His hope. The press would be bored with his trials by now. Surely, the lot of them had moved on to John's successful marriage match. Lady Holland was an outstanding woman.

He didn't care much for Leslie Ann Parker—how did Daffy know her so well? She was the telly presenter who raised the question: "Why do good women leave him?"

Excellent question. He'd spent the first six months of his Florida getaway pondering that very thing. First to scamper was Coral Winthrop, the beautiful, poised American heiress and owner of CCW Cosmetics. Then Lady Robbi De Smet, daughter of an ancient Lauchtenland family. Never mind their breakup had been mutual. Still, he'd failed to capture her heart.

"Hey, Pete." Helene, his boss and owner of this quaint little pub, a thatched-hut tiki bar with a wraparound deck edging up to the Atlantic, waved her hand in front of his face. "Where were you? Land far, far away?"

"No, just, um…what can I do for you?" He'd been staring into a bin of limes waiting to be sliced.

Helene Simmons, a fifty-something-year-old woman, with flowing, sun-kissed hair and mischievous green eyes, gave him purpose the day she offered him a job.

He'd come in twice for a bite to eat. The second time she sat at his table announcing, *"I like the look of you. Want to work here?"*

If she knew his true identity, she'd never let on. Didn't say a word when he handed over his diplomatic papers to satisfy payroll. Knowing her as he did now, however, the last thing she wanted was the attention caused by a royal prince pouring pints. Which was fine with Gus.

"Carmen called in sick again. You'll have to bus tables tonight."

"I thought you fired him." Gus—preferably known as Pete—lined up limes for slicing.

"Three times but he boomerangs back." She turned to the man who sat on the stool in front of her. "Ike, how're you doing? What'll you have?"

"Same." Ike reached for the beer nuts. "Pete, how you doing?"

"Can't complain."

In fact, he was grateful. It was in the daily routine of this bar that he'd found relief from his shame. How the one person he loved more than anything, the one he believed would share his life, the one to whom he'd given his heart, had humiliated him in front of millions.

It took him over a year to abandon the idea she did it on purpose. As if performing the world's most elaborate prank. Then Robbi came along and proved to be a good boost to his confidence.

In the last year, Gus had mellowed. During the slump between lunch and happy hour, he listened to the old guys tell wild, exaggerated tales of surfing the "big one," or of wrestling with a swordfish. *En garde.* And he found a rhythm that healed his scarred heart.

When the singer arrived at night with her guitar, he served drinks and wiped down the bar, letting the lyrics of hope and love seep in.

Maybe, just maybe... One day. Years from now. He'd fall in love again. Truth be told, there were enough love songs in the world—including the entire Beatles' collection—to win him back to romance. To trust another woman with his heart. He just needed gobs of time.

By the time he'd sliced the pile of limes then lemons for happy hour, the first wave of spring breakers arrived, sunburned and shivering.

"Helene, I'm going to bus some tables." Filling a bucket with hot water and soap, Gus grabbed a clean towel and an empty bin for the dirties and headed out to the tables.

Out on the deck, he collected dishes and wiped the tables, his mind drifting back to Daffy, his true identity and duty, and the reality that John's wedding was a mere eight weeks away. The ball? Seven weeks. Gus must do a smashing job for John because his brother did nothing less for him.

His past must not continue to impact the future—especially his brother's future. Gus must take back control of his life.

Wringing out his towel, Gus looked out over the beach toward the ocean and the pinkish red sunset. He'd miss this place but it was time—

"You want to tell me what's going on?" Helene reached for the tub and began clearing the last table. "How was Adler this morning?"

"Delirious with joy, chasing the Frisbee up and down the beach."

"Don't make her like you more than me. She is my dog." Her deep chuckle carried the rasp of a former smoker.

"She adores you." Gus moved to wipe down the table.

Helene anchored the loaded bin on her hip. "You have something to tell me, Pete? Or should I say, Prince Augustus?"

He paused in mid-motion, then went back to wiping the table. "How long have you known?"

"Since you handed me your papers."

"Why didn't you say something?"

"I read up on you. I understood why you were here. I wanted to give you space."

"Thank you." He dropped the dish towel in the bucket with a splash. "I almost feel myself again."

"But?"

"My brother's getting married and I need to be there for him." Gus reached for the bucket as a group of bikini-clad girls approached the deck. "I've shirked too many duties. It's tradition for the brother or sister of the groom to host a wedding ball, which takes place the week before the ceremony. More than host really, I'm responsible for the entire event. From planning to execution. To make it all about the happy couple. My brother was there for me when I was getting married. Never complained that his little brother would stand at the altar before him. I should have gone home sooner. But I wasn't ready. Told myself I didn't want to leave you in a bind."

He still wasn't ready to face the media, but he was ready to see his family and friends.

A clatter sounded from the kitchen. Helene called toward the kitchen. "Roswell, everything all right?" The old cook answered like a drunken sailor. Helene grinned and turned for the door. "I'd better get in there. When do you want to leave?"

And just like that, his time in Florida was over.

"Next week, I reckon."

Helene hesitated, then walked over for a one-arm embrace. "I'm going to miss you. I'd like to say you were the son I never had, but even I couldn't believe I'd ever give birth to a prince."

"A prince is nothing more than a son, a brother, a friend." Gus rested his chin on the top of her frizzy hair. "You and my mum would get along just fine."

"Stop or you'll make me cry." Helene pulled away as another crash echoed from the bowels of the Hideaway. "What is going on in there?"

Gus laughed, his eyes misting. What was it his grandfather used to say? *"If you didn't miss where you've been, it didn't mean that much to you."*

He wished he'd known his grandfather King Rein IV better. He died just after Gus's fifth birthday.

Finishing outside, Gus dumped the dirty dish water and headed to load the dishwasher, surprised, yet not surprised, to see Carmen standing there.

"I thought you called off."

"I changed my mind." The man-child of twenty-two loaded the dishes.

"Carmen, I'm leaving soon. I've business elsewhere. Try to step it up for Helene."

He looked at Gus with surprise. "Where're you going?"

"Home." To stand on precious Lauchtenland soil once again. The nation in the North Sea that defeated the Normans. That held off the Nazis when threatened, and that was becoming the Silicon Valley of Europe.

Now that he'd made up his mind, a tightness he didn't know he had eased. He'd call John on his break. Let him know he'd be there for him.

Just like you were for me.

A lot of things had changed in the last year. He'd lost weight, muscled up, and become a regular Joe. Or a regular Pete as it were.

But it was time to be a prince again. To put the past behind him. Once and for all.

CHAPTER
THREE

DAFFY

S he was lost in a romance novel when Leslie Ann knocked on her door. They'd come in after lunch for naps and for assessing their sunburns.

Leslie Ann was burned but Ella was roasted. Daffy refrained from saying, "I told you so." She, on the other hand, was a golden color with a touch of pink on her nose.

"I'm starving," Leslie Ann said, smelling of aloe lotion. "Let's go eat."

Daffy closed her book. "How's the burn victim?"

"Moaning. I just lathered her with lotion. She needs to get dressed." Leslie Ann disappeared down the hall. "Ella, come on, we're going to the Hideaway."

"Just leave me for dead." Ella's response was muffled and pitiful.

Daffy stepped around Leslie Ann and eased open Ella's door. "You'll feel better if you get moving. After you eat."

"Thank you for not saying 'I told you so.'"

"You're welcome."

While Ella dressed to a constant chorus of "Ouch, ouch," and "ooh, ooh," Leslie Ann sorted the contents of her crossbody bag.

Daffy took a seat on the couch to check her email and listened to Mum's voice message.

"Do you want to stage the wedding dresses at Hadsby for the ball?"

Stage the royal wedding dresses? At Hadsby Castle? For the ball? *Mum, why are you even asking? Of course!* Daffy answered with a text. Mum and Dad would be getting ready for bed.

> Mum, yes!!!! I'll stage the dresses. You know I'm dying to see the Princess Louisa.

> Good. Are you sure? You'll have to go straight up after your holiday. Won't you miss Thomas?

> He'll understand. Seeing the Princess Louisa in person? I'm in.

"Ella, sometime this century, love." Leslie Ann joined Daffy on the couch. "What was your mum's message? Something about Hadsby?"

"Mum assigned me to the wedding dress parade at Hadsby."

"You'll finally get to see the *Louisa*?" Leslie Ann gripped Daffy's arm and gave her the look—the one that said, *"Get me in to do a feature."*

"You know the RT has strict media rules. You want to see the dress, go through the office."

"What's the benefit of having a friend with the Royal Trust if she won't do me favors?" Leslie Ann tapped on her phone. "I have so many stories developing I won't have time anyway. Ella! Coming or not?"

The *Princess Louisa* had set the standard in late nineteenth- and early twentieth-century wedding gowns. At least with the aristocracy and wealthy. Designed by an obscure Dalholm designer, Taffron Björk, the gown remained timeless. Taffron quickly faded from the fashion world, and the *Louisa* was his only known gown.

As for Daffy, both the gown and Björk fascinated her. She wrote her dissertation on its unique mark in the fashion world and how the RT maintained the gown one hundred twenty years later. She also recapped the life of the man who designed a wedding dress for a princess and was never heard of again.

He died in '48 at the age of ninety-two. In her research, Daffy stumbled upon a quote from his beloved wife, who died in '55, claiming he'd designed one last special gown before his death. If he had, no one had ever seen it.

"Help." Ella appeared in the lounge wearing a yellow sundress, which only accentuated her radiating skin. She held her arms out to the side, her steps mimicking a bowlegged American cowboy. A bottle of Bactine dangling from her finger tips. "Spray me. I'm dying."

"Come here, love. You're not dying." Daffy reached for the bottle and coated her sister's skin with the liquid contents.

"I'm wondering why Ella and I look like Rudolph's nose," Leslie Ann said. "While Daffy looks like 'The Girl from Ipanema.' All golden and brown."

"I inherited the Italian blood."

"Italian blood? With your mass of red curls and blue eyes? Ella's the one with dark hair and eyes."

"Take it up with the Almighty." Daffy applied another layer of Bactine. For good measure. Ella winced with every touch. "I got the Lauchten and Italian side of Dad's family. Ella is stuck with Mum's Lauchten and Irish. I had no choice in the matter."

"Interesting." Leslie Ann moved to the sliding glass door and stepped onto the deck. A saline breeze brushed through the cottage. "Well, you may have Italian blood and an enviable tan, but your face glowed this morning after talking to that shirtless chap with the abs."

"So? I was warm from my errand. And what abs? He had abs?" Daffy capped the Bactine and walked with Ella out to the deck.

"Warm? The breeze was like ice. And don't even tell me you didn't see his abs. Lying doesn't suit you."

"No, that's your thing." With a laugh, Daffy linked her arm through her friend's. "We're in Florida on holiday. How glorious!"

"You lovelies go ahead." Ella's pace matched that of a hermit crab. "I'll be along. Save me a seat."

"We can't leave you behind." Daffy and Leslie Ann flanked Ella and headed down the beach.

The evening was stunning, cool and salty, full of sounds only God could create. Above them, the pinkish sunset swallowed the blue sky, and the scene demanded contemplation.

Daffy sank into the silence as the three of them walked to the pub. Any more questions from Leslie Ann about the shirtless chap, and she'd blush again. This time she couldn't blame the sun or a jog to the cottage and back.

She didn't understand the blushing. She wasn't one to do so easily. But it started when she was a girl. Whenever the prince came round. Well, no worry. She'd not see him again.

The Captain's Hideaway was packed on this Monday night. A group of uni students hovered on the deck, the lads in Ohio State shirts and caps, the girls in tops adorned with Greek letters.

"Excuse us. Pardon us." Leslie Ann pushed inside, past the picnic tables to the high tops on the other side of the dining area. "Broadcast presenter coming through."

"They have no idea who you are, Leslie Ann," Ella said as they cut through the crowd. "I thought this was a quiet, private beach. Where did these people come from?"

"Probably on holiday, like us." Daffy chose the only vacant seating and passed out the table menus. She liked the feel of this place. Peaceful, homey, as if one could come here to raise a pint and laugh with one's mates.

That's what they did at home. The three of them along with their friends. They migrated to Pub Clemency on Friday nights to hang out with Kayle and Frank, Tonya and Marlow, Albert, Rick, Jones, and Thomas. If she moved to America, she'd miss those nights.

"I'm having a cheeseburger." Ella slapped her menu closed.

"Same." Leslie Ann shoved her menu aside and took out her phone. "Snapping a picture for the mates at home. Our Florida Pub Clemency."

Daffy smiled as the server, a young man with a surfer vibe, set down tall tumblers of water and asked if they were ready to order.

Three for three. Cheeseburger, fries, and a diet fizzy.

"If you see the chap who hit you with a Frisbee, point him out." Leslie Ann scanned the room. "You might have a boyfriend, but I don't."

Daffy rested her cheek in her hand as a warm blush bloomed on her cheeks. *Don't think about him.* Prince Augustus had to stop turning her cheeks into candied apples. He was a friend—no, more like an acquaintance. An HRH. Royalty. Out of her league, no matter what their past.

"Did you see the puddings?" Daffy reached for her menu again "What do you think of sharing the chocolate molten cake?"

"Daff, your face is all blotchy." Leslie Ann pressed her hand on the menu. "I barely mention the chap on the beach and look, we could fly a sleigh by your light."

"You exaggerate. Ella, cake for pudding?" Daffy put the menu away. "Really, LA, I'm not one of your interviewees on the *Morning Show.*

"Did he ask you out?" Leslie Ann came at her again with her deep, controlled reporter voice. The one she'd used when she broke the university cheating scandal. "Is that why you're blushing?"

"Les, why are you making a deal of it?" Ella to the rescue. About time. "So she blushes?"

"Yes, yes, he *did* ask me out." Thank you, Leslie Ann, for the excuse. "After he inquired of the cottage. We're madly in love. Going to get married as soon as the law allows." Daffy leaned to see down the aisle. "Where is our server with those fizzies? I'm parched."

"Okay, fine, but don't be a smarty." Leslie Ann shoved Daffy's tumbler of water toward her. "Drink this if you're thirsty. Look, I've known you for thirteen years. I can't recall you ever blushing. Well, except when Sprite Crandall dumped out your handbag and a tampon landed on his foot."

"He turned into a flaming bush." Daffy slipped from her chair. "I think I'll go to the loo." She shot Ella a look. *Not another word!*

Ella knew Daffy blushed when Prince Gus was around. It began during the writing of *My Life with the Prince.* Mum noticed it whenever Gus was around and teased her. The more she teased, the redder Daffy beamed. However, in the last eighteen years she'd not blushed once over the prince. Well, maybe a few times when she passed him at the palace. When she helped Mum with some Royal Trust function.

Following the neon light to the loo, Daffy rounded a corner just as a chap came in from the deck toting a loaded bin of dishes. She cried out, but too late. The whole lot slipped from his hands and crashed on the floor.

"I am *so* sorry." Daffy dropped to clean up the mess at the exact same time as he, and their foreheads conked.

She moaned. He swore. Then hollered for someone named Carmen to bring a mop and broom.

"Please." He raised his hand to stop her efforts to help. "I've got this. Go."

"It's my fault. I wasn't paying attention."

He tossed a broken piece of glass into the bin as he reached for the broom and mop brought 'round by another chap. "You should go," he said.

"I insist—" When she looked up to plead her case, her eyes met his. "Your Highness."

"Pete, remember?"

"You work here?" She lowered her voice to a raspy whisper.

"Are you here with your mates?" He abandoned his American accent and spoke with the full lilt of home.

"Leslie Ann insisted we come for burgers."

"But you've kept my secret?"

"Of course. She knows nothing. Nor does Ella. They asked about the man on the beach and I told them you were interested in renting the cottage. Leslie Ann thinks you asked me on a date. I told her we were getting married to shut her up. You really hid *here* all year?"

"Amazingly, yes." His fingers grazed hers as they reached for the same glass. Daffy pulled away from the heat of his touch.

"Rather brilliant, I say." She reached for the broom. "I'll sweep, you mop."

After they cleaned up the mess, Prince Gus started for the kitchen, then hesitated. "I've avoided the Lauchtenland media for over a year. Do people wonder where I am?"

"At first, you were all they talked about. But once your brother became engaged, the news focused on him."

"As it should. Is Lady Holland being embraced?" He set the bin on a counter just inside the kitchen entry.

"I believe so. She's very charming and classy. Well suited for the job of future queen."

"What do you think of her?"

"Me?" She shrugged. "She seems very real and sweet. Beautiful and poised. Prince John seems to adore her."

"But how is she in person? She seems a grand choice but I only remember her from school days. And at a distance."

"I've never met her. Why and where would I?"

Gus's attention lingered on her. "With the Royal Trust, of course. At the portraiture. You attended my, my, you know…" He studied his worn black trainers. "Mum adores her and she and John have been friends for years. I guess Cupid finally fired his arrow and hit my brother."

So, it still bothered him. His story. How the American heiress ran off. Daffy had represented the Royal Trust during their wedding portrait, taking notes, describing the scene, documenting the marriage that would become part of Lauchtenland and House of Blue history for the generations to come. However, two months later, she removed the portrait from the frame and, along with her notes, stored the lot in the trust office's attic.

"You'll be at the wedding, of course." Her words were an attempt to fill the void.

"Naturally. In fact, I must get home to arrange John's wedding ball. The planners have done most of the work without me. But I should be there to tie all the ribbons and bows, make sure the affair is about John and Holland."

"Good, good. He'll be glad, I'm sure."

"And you? What are you up to, besides preserving royal artifacts and helping me clean up dirty dishes?" He turned her face to see where the Frisbee hit. "And getting hit with runaway Frisbees."

"I'm well. Fantastic. Just bought a flat in the Clemency district."

"In one of those new lofts? I'd live there myself if I weren't required to live at the palace." He cupped his hand beside his mouth. "Free rent, you know."

She laughed. "I have a lovely view of the city. Even part of the bay."

A shout came from the kitchen, then someone called, "Pete!"

"I'd better go." He turned back into an American, though it did little to cover his princely stature. Did he know? The light of his identity, his essence, his famous smile never burnt out. "Good to see you, Daffy. We've not clapped eyes on one another in eons and now here we are, twice in one day. In another country to boot."

"Pete, dude, need you at the bar." A narrow woman with sunbaked skin and flyaway blonde hair approached with a frustrated and drawn expression.

"On my way." Gus paused. "Helene, this is Daffy Caron. An old friend." He smiled, and the sights and sounds of the pub simply faded. She saw and heard nothing but Prince Gus.

In an instant, she was young again, running through the palace gardens, playing hide-n-seek with Prince Gus, Prince John, and their cousin, Princess Rachel.

"Take my hand. Quick, in here." He led her to one of the *gardener's sheds. "John says it smells like manure. He'll never look here."*

But when he opened the door, Prince John burst through and charged at them with a growl like a hungry winter bear.

Daffy screamed, and with a laugh, Gus snatched her hand and led her away.

"I found you." Prince John's protest hounded them. "I found you. Rachel, ollie, ollie oxen free."

"Daffy?" Gus said. "Are you all right? You zoned out and your face is flushed."

"Too much sun." Helene nodded. "Drink a lot of water. Pete, let's go."

"If I don't see you again, Daffy, good luck on your holiday. Have fun."

"Your High—Pete." She rose up to meet his gaze, the memory of his ten-year-old hand still on hers. "You want to know if Lauchtenland thinks of you? Yes. We miss you. We feel your absence every day."

"Are you sure it's not just because they're bored, looking for someone to pick on?"

"The media can do their worst, but the people love you. We feel a bit adrift when you're away."

"Adrift?" His expression softened. "Because they've no one to tease and mock? Your friend Leslie Ann run out of princes to psychoanalyze?"

"Forget Leslie Ann. She loves the sound of her own voice. The people felt for you, they're for you. They don't see Prince Pathetic or Pudgy Prince or whatever else they can alliterate. They see Prince Charming, the spare heir who won us over with his brilliant smile and prowess on the football field. The prince who served his country in the Royal Army alongside every other chap called up for duty."

"How nice to see the world from your eyes."

"Then listen to what I say. Make my picture your picture."

"I'll try. But I still see the pathetic chap, the fool waiting for his bride who never showed."

"I see a chap who loved with all his heart." She touched his hand, then pulled away. "Everyone will be so glad to see you. I promise."

"Pete." Helene appeared again. "Either ask her out or cut her loose. You're needed behind the bar."

"You heard the boss." He gave her a quick salute. "I must go. But please, keep my secret? I'm not ready to be in the public eye yet. Not from here. Helene would not thank you or me, or Ms. Parker, if her place was overrun with the press and royal seekers."

"Mum's the word." She mimed locking her lips and tossing away the key. "I've got your back."

By the time she made it to the loo and returned to her table, her burger had arrived.

"Where have you been? I was about to call for rescuers." Leslie Ann set down her half-eaten burger.

"Long line at the loo." Daffy peeked at the bar where the bearded prince laughed with a patron and poured a pint.

"Will you look at this?" Leslie Ann held up her phone. "I am missing all the juicy news at home. Celebrities breaking up, royal wedding details. Lady Holland announced who was making the wedding cake. Still no word on her dress though." Leslie Ann sighed. "Daffy, are you sure you don't know anything?"

"About her dress? How on earth would I? Now, Ella, what about the Space Center? Did you get tickets?"

"Hold on a moment." Leslie Ann turned her phone's flashlight on Daffy. "You're blushing. Again."

CHAPTER
FOUR

GUS

What in the world? A constant pinging sound drew him from a sound, deep sleep. The night maintenance man called in sick, so Gus stayed to clean the vats and hose down the kitchen. It was after 3:00 a.m. before he crawled into bed.

But what did his phone care? Text after text pulled him from a sound sleep. Gus slapped the side table, feeling for his phone.

"All right. What? What?" Sometimes his mates from home included him in a funny meme text. Five lads sending smiley face icons or *LOL* replies got old quickly. "This better be good."

Focusing on his screen as the mid-morning light edged the drawn shades of his second-story room, Gus scanned the most recent text.

It was from John with a link to the *Morning Show*. What was this? Yawning, Gus ran his hand through his tangled hair then tapped the link. As it opened, another video link arrived from his friend Charles Larrabee.

Did you see this?

Same one John sent. What could possibly be so interesting on the *Morning Show*?

Gus pressed the play icon. But the screen remained dark and silent. He upped the volume. After a second, a voice sounded.

"I'm standing outside a pub on the beach in central Florida. The

Captain's Hideaway. Viewers, you are not going to believe—"

Gus tumbled out of bed. *No, no, no.*

A light flashed across a face. Leslie Ann Parker. Standing on Helene's deck.

"...is serving pints and clearing tables. Imagine, the man we bow and curtsy to is taking orders from a frizzy-haired, American hippy. It's incredible. I'm stunned."

The voice of the lead anchor, Stone Brubaker, broke in. "Can you get closer, Leslie Ann? I can't quite make him out."

"The pub is closed so I can't go in, but I see him showering down the kitchen. Let me climb up here—" She stood on the outer deck railing and raised the phone to the window.

The image faded and bobbled, but after a few seconds, she captured HRH Prince Augustus Carwyn George, shirtless, aiming a hose at the greasy kitchen floors.

"My, my, my. Our prince. How do you like that?" Surprised laughter elevated Stone's voice. "Leslie Ann, you've captured the story of the year. Our spare heir—a kitchen yeoman."

"I rather like his beard." This from a female voice Gus couldn't place. "And those abs. Leslie Ann, get closer. Our Prince Pudgy has been working out."

He felt sick as the clip zoomed, catching the dirt on the windows as well as Gus's hard-earned eight pack.

The time stamp proved she'd been filming him live. Two in the morning in Florida was the second hour of Lauchtenland's most popular wake-up show.

Then while he slept, Lauchtenland—*the world*—woke up to a House of Blue royal wielding a mop. Well, so what? Royals weren't above honest, hard work. But she identified the Captain's Hideaway.

Helene's quaint little business just hit the global map. Gus skimmed the rest of his texts. Most were of the same clip. A few were links to royal reporters' or royal watchers' social media accounts.

How did this— Daffy. She'd outed him to her friend. The girl who'd locked her lips and thrown away the key must have picked it up on her way back to her table. One night. She didn't keep his secret for one night.

Gus yanked on a T-shirt and shorts and headed out by way of the pool deck, steam fueling his every move. Crossing the pool deck, he exited the gate and cut through the tall, waving sea grass toward the beach.

Lauchtenland headlines were one thing. The press portrayed him as they wanted. He was used to it. But betrayal from a friend? No. He'd not tolerate it. *Not one more betrayal.*

He'd hid his head in the sand when Coral left and again when Robbi confessed she'd been spending time with her ex. But not this time. Fighting words brewed as he stormed down the beach, sand kicking up in his wake.

A new text arrived from John with a link to Daffy's Instagram. She'd posted three pictures of him in various stages of disarray as he cleaned.

> Our Prince Pudgy has abs, ladies. Catch Leslie Ann Parker's Morning Show YouTube if you missed the story. #royalwatcher #houseofblue #princegus @leslieannparker

The wind raced with him, pushing from behind while swirling ahead of him. Seagulls soared on the current, cawing their approval. Even the sun burned bold and warm.

His jog burst into a run when the blue cottage came into view. The seagulls dropped down in front of him and landed on the deck, squawking his arrival.

Gus hammered the sliding glass door. "Daffy, open up. Now." He cupped his hands about his eyes and peered inside. "Daffodil Caron!"

Leslie Ann dashed into the lounge from the hallway, her posture one of surprise, then determination as she opened the door.

"Your Royal Highness, how can I help?"

Gus shoved past her. "Where's Daffy?"

"Sleeping. What do you want?"

He flashed his phone. "You know what I want." He stationed

himself at the top of the short bedroom passage. "Daffy Caron, I need to speak to you!"

"What's all the commotion?" Ella emerged from her quarters with disheveled hair, her sunburnt legs protruding from a short sleeping shirt. "Prince Gus... Your Royal Highness." She tugged on the hem of her top and offered a wobbly curtsy.

"Your sister, if you please." Stiff-backed, he folded his arms and waited.

"Yes, sir." Ella whirled toward the remaining closed door, knocking once, then entering. Muffled voices carried through the wall.

"Would you like some tea?" Leslie Ann offered him a cordial smile. "I brought some from home."

Gus didn't answer.

"Are you angry?" He heard the clank of the kettle against the burner. "I'm sorry, but I did my job, Your Royal Highness. I'd do it again."

"How is it your job to spy on a private citizen?"

Her laugh was the mocking he loathed about the media. As if their right to a story trumped everyone else's rights. Especially members of the House of Blue.

"You may be on a humble, private beach in Florida, but you are an international citizen and senior member of one of the world's oldest royal families. By the way, where is your protection officer? Was it the skinny chap with the baggy apron? Doesn't seem like he could put up much of a fight but—"

"Daffodil Caron, please, may I speak with you?"

Daffy's door jerked open and Gus changed his stance. To battle stations. She appeared in shorts and a T-shirt, her hair in a neat ponytail, her clear blue gaze darting from Gus to Leslie Ann.

"What's going on?" She sighed. "Oh, Les, what did you do?"

"You *know* what she did. You told her. What happened to keeping secrets?"

"I said nothing. I promise."

He waved his phone. "Then why am I on the *Morning Show* and splashed all over social media?"

"What?" Daffy watched the live feed of Leslie Ann reporting on Gus as he swabbed the decks. "Oh my gosh, Leslie Ann. Why? How did you find out?"

Gus took back his phone. "Clearly you told her."

"I never." Daffy braced herself against the kitchen island. "Leslie Ann, explain this."

"I've been here over a year in complete anonymity, which is somewhat of a miracle, then the lot of you show up and bam! I'm back in the news. Couldn't you leave well enough alone? Is that why you're here? Did you find out my location? Did you come seeking me out?"

"We didn't know. I found this place online while Christmas shopping. How would we know you were here?"

"That's why my story is the scoop of the year," Leslie Ann said, standing behind the kitchen island, waiting for the kettle to boil. "You heard Stone say it. You're my witnesses if he ever denies it." The kettle blew, and Leslie Ann methodically, with a smirk on her face, filled her cup. "Unless I discover an even *bigger* story."

"Leslie Ann, tell him." Daffy's cheeks flamed red. "How you found out. You know it wasn't me."

"Actually, it *was* you, Daff." Leslie Ann carried her tea to a club chair and curled up. "You have a *tell* whenever you're around the prince."

"What's this?" Gus glanced from Leslie Ann to Daffy.

"No, I don't." Daffy sank into one of kitchen chairs with a weak laugh and pressed her hands to her cheeks. "It's a story, a fable Mum made up."

But her reply lacked conviction.

"Daffy, it's my fault. I told her." Ella's confession came from the corner by the sliding glass doors. "I thought it was funny, if not a bit odd, since you rarely blush. I never imagined Prince Gus would actually be in Florida."

"Would someone fill me in on this 'tell'?" His anger faded somewhat. Yet, couldn't he be a normal chap, run his own life, not have someone else deciding things for him? Like where he'd been living for the past year? Or if he married the woman he loved or not?

Coral decided they weren't marrying without a word to him. Not even a chance to plead his case or make it right. Now Leslie Ann reported his whereabouts for her professional gain, not caring about how it affected him.

"Apparently, whenever Daffy is around you, she blushes." Leslie Ann grinned. "Not a subtle, pinkish hue, but a steamy, blotchy red. I could see it from our chairs on the beach yesterday morning when you two spoke."

"How did you know it was— Never mind." Gus turned to Daffy. "Is this true?"

"No." Daffy cradled her head in her hands. "It's a joke, truly."

"Admit it, Daffy, you blush when he's around." Leslie Ann sipped her tea. "Yesterday you blushed more in a day than the last twelve years of our friendship. So, being the good journalist that I am, I investigated. First getting Ella to tell me why you blush. Then following up on the chap at the pub. I saw you talking to him. Recognized him from the beach."

"Why are there photos on her Instagram?" Gus sat in the nearest chair, his legs weak from the drop of adrenaline.

"I posted them. She left her phone on the kitchen island."

"You posted on my Insta?" Daffy retrieved her phone, the swim of tears in her eyes unmistakable.

"Yes, and you're welcome. You're at *ten thousand* followers and climbing."

Daffy tapped on the screen. "Oh my gosh, Les, you put down the location? The Captain's Hideaway. I'm deleting this."

"Why wouldn't I put down the location? What great promo for the owner. It's on my Instagram too."

"Except she doesn't want that kind of promo." Gus started for the door. He'd had enough. Besides, he must warn Helene. "Hear this, the lot of you, and make no mistake. *Leave me alone.* All of you." He pointed to Daffy. "Especially *you.*"

This betrayal, innocent or not, called to those of days gone by. He didn't like it. Not one bit. But at the moment he seemed powerless to move beyond them. They still ached deep in his bones.

Was he so unworthy of loyalty? Of friendship? Of any devotion?

Down the beach, he dialed Helene. "Brace yourself but—"

"Prince Gus, wait. Please."

He swung round to see Daffy racing toward him. "I'll call you back. But it's out. My identity."

"Please, sir, don't be angry." Daffy skirted alongside him. "I don't know why I blush. It's silly really. I never took it seriously. Thought it a joke. I never imagined Leslie Ann would stalk you at your job."

"But you do *blush?* When you're around me?" He gazed into her eyes and thought how a man could get lost in the white and the blue under the shade of long dark lashes.

She stepped back, hands to her face. "I don't know. Maybe."

He lowered one of her hands. "Did you know you're blushing now?" He leaned for a closer inspection. "A very bright red."

"I just ran down the beach after you burst into my house and accused me of betrayal. Of course, I'm blushing."

"Daffy?"

"Yes. All right! I blush, but I don't know why. I can't stop it. It's embarrassing. And if you want to blame someone, blame my little sister. She's the one who gave me away."

"You can't possibly have a crush on me. Not after all these years."

"Of course not. I have a boyfriend. Thomas Dune."

"Do you blush around him?"

She paused, her brow furrowing as she considered his question. "I don't know." She covered a low laugh with her fingers. "I suppose I should, but I don't."

Standing next to her, his home world connected to his *now* world and he felt hope, of all things, and an eagerness to return to Lauchtenland.

"Well, then, I'm sorry about back there. It's just betrayal... It feels so—"

"Painful? I understand. Believe me."

"You don't have to be so kind to me, Daffy."

"Why not? You're trying to apologize."

Gus watched the waves for a second. "I don't blush around you, but I had a crush on you."

"Really? You never said."

"During my pudgy prince days. You were the cute girl who beat me in a foot race."

"One time, and only because you fell."

"I seem to remember several times." The tension he'd carried from his place to hers began to evaporate. He kicked at the sand and let the wind comb through his hair. "So are you and this Thomas serious?"

"I'm not sure. But we enjoy each other's company. We have a routine."

"I'm sorry I barged into your place like a raging lunatic."

"I'm sorry Leslie Ann exposed your hideaway." The wind blew her auburn hair about her face and shoulders. "I'd not tell your secret unless you were dying and maybe not then. I know how to keep a Blue family secret."

"A Blue family secret?" He peered past her shoulder toward the cottage. They were being watched. "And what would that be?"

If he remembered correctly, he was about twelve when the queen's security introduced new measures and the children of staff, even those of her personal secretary, were no longer allowed in the palace. Not above stairs, anyway. Not in the royal quarters.

That's why they'd lost touch and he didn't see her again, save for the occasional state dinner where she helped out the dining staff.

"Look, you should go. I'm sure your boss—Helene, is it?— needs fair warning."

"You didn't answer my question. Do you have a Blue secret?"

"Forget what I said."

Gus regarded her for a moment. Other than himself and John, Daffy had only been around his parents. In fact, she'd been rather close with his mother. Until security changed everything. But she couldn't have anything on the queen and king consort. They were above reproach. Especially the queen.

"If you had a secret since you were a girl, you'd have told someone by now."

"Not necessarily. What if I did have a secret? What if I understood, even as a girl, the importance of holding my tongue? I am a loyal royalist and a secret keeper."

"Then tell me. I am a loyal royalist as well. What do you know?" He squinted at her. "You can't be referencing Queen Catherine II. She's the greatest regent Lauchtenland's ever known. A virtuous leader. So, are you hinting at something about my father?"

"Don't listen to me. I say foolish things. The queen is a virtuous leader and, Prince Gus, I've no secret. But if I did, I'd not tell you." She offered him a slow smile. "Then it wouldn't be a secret."

"You're having me on. You're being Daffy the trickster."

"I should go. We're touring the cape this morning. So, if I don't see you here, or at home, I wish you all the best, Prince Gus. Or shall I say Pete?"

"Daffy, again, I'm sorry." He motioned to the cottage where Leslie Ann and Ella sat on the deck, chins in their hands, watching. "I was angry. It gets old, you see, everyone criticizing, mocking, waiting for me to fail. Me feeling like I let the Family down."

"No one is waiting for you to fail. You didn't let your family down. Forget the Leslie Anns of the world. She's only out for herself. I love her, but it's true. You know she never remembers my birthday? Never. And at Christmas she sends a cheap bauble she found on Amazon. I can't think of a time she did something for me or gave me something that was actually meaningful. It's just who she is. Do forgive her."

"I forgive you. She may take some time."

"Fine but do yourself a favor, sir. Stop seeing yourself as the one prince in all of royal history who was jilted at the altar. Begin to see yourself as a man worthy of love. Of a life."

"You make it sound so simple. Frankly, I'm not sure I am."

"Of course you are, and it is simple."

"You almost make me believe."

"Good. I know you have questions, but if you keep doubting, you'll never find the one who *will* fall head over heels in love with you. The one who will be devoted to you. Who will let you love her in return?" She squeezed his arm. "Stop mourning the past. Wake up. It's a new day. Time to dance. Literally, at your brother's wedding ball. Whatever you learned here, take it with you and be the man, the prince, you want to be."

He squared off with her for one, two, three seconds under the endless blue sky and a golden grip of sunlight.

"How'd you get so wise?"

"I used to be friends with a prince. He taught me."

He laughed. "If only that were true."

"See you, Prince Gus."

"See you, Daffodil Caron."

Gus walked along the water's edge, wishing everything she said about him and love were true. But deep down he doubted. He feared. Let his brother be the one who found true love and bore the House of Blue heirs.

Gus would watch from the sidelines as the bachelor uncle. The man who struggled to trust his heart again.

CHAPTER
FIVE

GUS

He'd been summoned by the queen. She'd left him alone when he first returned five days ago on the heels of the *Morning Show*'s breaking story.

After leaving Daffy on the beach, he'd warned Helene of the storm to come and resigned. Nevertheless, by early afternoon, A1A was backed up with traffic to the Melbourne Causeway.

Floridana Beach was overrun with royal seekers, most of them women, the local media, and a few curious pelicans.

At his gated rental, he stayed clear of windows and prepared for a midnight escape to Orlando, checking in at the airport hotel until his flight home late Wednesday.

Meanwhile, Helene updated him every few hours.

We're out of everything.

We've done a month's business in a night.

She sent a picture of an overflowing, shoulder-to-shoulder crowd.

New barback is a joke. Carmen is only coming in to flirt with the ladies but at least he's here.

51

She sent a final message as he boarded his flight to Port Fressa. A selfie of her beleaguered expression, sticking out her tongue.

> You just had to be a real prince and now, I'm exhausted. Richer. But exhausted. I'll miss you, my friend.

He arrived at Perrigwynn Palace Thursday morning and slept until Friday. Unpacked and reacquainted himself with his staff on Saturday then said a quick hello to Mum and Dad.

Sunday he braved a fresh wave of Lauchtenland's winter and in the evening, as the snow piled high in the city streets, Gus dined with John and Holland.

To his delight, he found he was at rest in the palace and returning to his place as a member of an ancient, royal family. A year and a half ago, he'd felt foreign, rooted in a slough of melancholy. What was his way forward?

He'd shut down after Coral. When he took up with Lady Robbi, he never truly opened up. In hindsight, a wise choice, since the lady was still in love with her ex.

After dinner and a game of billiards with John, he retired early, slept through the night, and rose with just enough time to shower, eat, and make his way through the royal corridors to the queen's office.

After his meeting with Mum, he was scheduled to meet his new protection officer, organize his diary with his private secretary, Stern, before meeting John tonight, along with school chums Charles, Turner, and Lute, at Pub Clemency. He was looking forward to seeing them again.

The opulence of the palace he called home was an ornate and extravagant contrast to the dull board floor, exposed beams, and beat-up bar of the *Captain's Hideaway*.

Dressed in suffocating layers—slacks, blue button-down under a darker blue jumper, regular shoes (not flip-flops,) and socks—Gus looked like his former self. Almost. He'd trimmed his beard close but left his hair long, brushed to a sheen, the waves combed back, yet falling loose about his face.

Down the Queen's Corridor, he passed under the portraits of his ancestors. Past monarchs whose painted eyes seemed to follow him. What would they say if they were alive today?

"Buck up, lad. Stiff upper lip."

"Tally ho, into the breach."

Or worse, recite the ancient, unwritten Blue motto.

"Take heart. Marriage is a must for every royal Blue. Love is not."

The tradition began when Great-great-great-great-grandfather Louis, the crown prince, would not decide on a wife. And so his father, the king, decided for him.

"You must marry and produce an heir. Falling in love is a luxury."

While the saying was refined over the centuries, the sentiment remained the same. Royal Blues married. All of them. Heir or not.

Gus peered up at the portrait of King Louis V. "Thanks, Gramps. What do you do if you're unlucky in love? Like me?"

Try as he might, Gus could not see himself living fifty, sixty years with someone he merely liked. Call him a romantic, but he wanted heart-pounding love. Memories of passionate nights, giving themselves to one another, exhausted at the end of it all.

He wanted a woman with whom he could relax in the library, reading, breaking the silence every now and then with, "Listen to this line."

He wanted to romp with their children, to tell them how loved and wanted they were. Teach them football, how to ride horses, and struggle to understand their new math homework.

He was grateful Mum wouldn't force him into anything. It wasn't in her modern royal nature. He was confident if he couldn't find a woman to fit the bill, he'd remain alone.

Confident, yes. Eager about his future? No.

Approaching Mum's office, Gus braced for a surge of negative sensations that had plagued him the year before he hopscotched over the Atlantic.

He'd had no peace back then. No sense of normalcy. One evening he couldn't bring himself to drive through the palace gates, so he parked down by the port and slept in his car—much to Mum's dismay.

Gus had to go to bat for his protection officer, keep him from getting sacked. But he'd sent the man home that night, promising he was going to his apartment. But he never made it.

Mum's secretary nodded as Gus approached. "She's expecting you, sir. Welcome home."

"Good to be home, Mason."

Mum stood when he entered, removing her reading glasses. If there was a classic "queen" smile, she possessed it. Some said his "world-famous" smile began with her.

"My prodigal has returned." She reached for his hands as she angled to kiss his cheek, then brought him close for a hug. Her familiar perfume reminded him of the goodness of home. "I've missed you."

"I've missed you," he said. "But I'm hardly a prodigal, Mum."

Queen Catherine II was a modern royal. When she found herself queen twenty-five years ago, decades before her time, she brought the House of Blue and every tending service into the technological age.

She'd studied and learned, visited tech companies in the city and around the world. To this day, technical magazines sat on her bedside table. When social media boomed, she was one of the first monarchs to dip her royal oar into the waters.

She modernized policy and procedure, the staff pay, uniforms, and customs, all the while skillfully keeping the valued traditions that made Lauchtenland an ancient European treasure.

East of England, west of Brighton Kingdom, Lauchtenland was a vital ally to the Brits and Brightonians, as well as Sweden, Denmark, and Norway.

A graduate of both Haxton University and Yale, Mum earned degrees in politics, as well as the law. She studied military strategy and knew a good deal about how the economy worked. She kept Lauchtenland leaders and the privy council on their toes.

"You're tan. I'm a bit jealous." Mum held him back for inspection, her gaze drifting to his hair and beard.

"The hair stays." Gus answered her unspoken request. "And the beard."

"Did I say anything? I'm taking it all in, this new look of yours."

"Tell me the news." Gus backed toward the tea trolley. "Are you looking forward to your crown prince's wedding?"

"Very much. I heard you dined with them last night. What did you think? You've known of Holland for a long time, but now that she's your future sister-in-law, does she come up to the mark?"

"She does. Mostly she makes John happy." Gus poured two cups of tea, sweetening them both with cream. "I'm only just getting to know the real Lady Holland, but she seems prepared for the life she's marrying into." Gone was his American accent. He spoke with the tone and formality of the House of Blue.

Mum reclined in her favorite winged chair while Gus stationed himself by the window. The snow had stopped, but low-flying gray clouds promised a dreary day.

"You're situated with Stern?" Mum's teacup was poised by her lips. "He should've given you the spring schedule. You've a lot to catch up on."

"He said he's missed me. Spent the past year twiddling his thumbs. He was more than eager to get to work. We're meeting this afternoon, but really, Mum, you should've reassigned him while I was away."

"I tried, but he wanted to wait for you."

"How'd you know I'd come home?"

"Because you're my son. You may have been knocked down, but you were not out for the count. When John proposed to Holland, it was only a matter of time."

"Am I so predictable?"

"If by predictable you mean a man who loves his family, a man who is bound by his duty, then yes, you're predictable, and all the better for it. You saw we have a family dinner tomorrow night and a portrait sitting on Friday?"

"I assume Granny will be at dinner."

Mum arched her brow. "Unless I want to incur her wrath, yes."

"Will we have to dissect my life? Starting with being left at the altar?"

Granny kept her royal roots buried in the old days and the old ways. She resented and complained about Mum's modernizations. She preferred the rules and rigidity of her day when Grandfather was king and she his queen.

"One day we Blues won't be any different from the people. We'll be extraneous."

"I've already told her dinner is a celebration, not an inquisition."

"You think that will stop her?" Gus raised his cup. The hot and creamy tea served in the familiar family china was another bit of home anchoring him in place. He never found a good tea in Florida. Especially at the Captain's Hideaway. Helene had the most horrid brand.

"Probably not, but you don't have to answer her."

"Why not? I've nothing to hide. Coral left for her own reasons, and there we are. Robbi and I weren't right in the end. Then John suggested I go away to recuperate. Charles offered his Florida place. I couldn't see a reason to turn him down."

"You didn't have to stay away so long. You missed the entire renovation of Hadsby Castle, which was your brainchild, by the way."

"My part was done. I lent nothing to the actual work. You said so yourself. But it's complete now, sparkling new for John's wedding ball." Hopefully any residue of Gus's wedding ball was removed by hammers then swept away. "I've seen pictures. The renovations look spectacular."

"You can see for yourself. I'm sending you up there next week."

Gus startled away from the window. "Serious? I just returned and you're shipping me off? What happened to 'the prodigal has returned'?"

"You're not a prodigal. I thought going north would be a simple way to ease you back into your duties. Besides, you love Hadsby. Why not enjoy it before it's overrun with ball guests and the media?" She set her teacup on a side table and retrieved a folder. "This was just finalized this morning. A copy has been sent to Stern. It's a list of appearances and visits while in Dalholm. The Youth League and the Berkshire School are very excited you're coming this year. They've missed their patron."

Gus flipped through the folder. Mum had respectfully filled his diary with weekday duties, leaving his weekends free. A walkabout through the old city, a visit to a new tech company, meetings with the mayor and police commissioner over the influx of guests and tourists arriving for the ball. A day with the Youth League and another with the Berkshire School.

And the crème de la crème. Wedding ball planning. This would be his true test. Had he really healed in Florida? Or would memories of his wedding ball surface?

"Are the planners the same as, well, mine?" He sat in the chair opposite Mum's desk.

"Yes. The Northton Planners. It's all there. They've done all the preliminary work. You just have to—"

"Make it about John and Holland."

"Are you okay with this?" Mum's gaze softened. "It's been two years since your ball. But no one can demand a heart move on if it's not ready."

"I'm fine. I can do this. Have the invitations gone out?"

"Just. I worked with the designer on them but everything else will be up to you. Music, food, wine, flowers, lighting, the china and crystal."

"I'll need to inspect the rooms since they've all been redone."

The dining halls, media rooms, drawing rooms, libraries, and the suites. As the host, he was the one to ensure everything went off without a hitch. Another House of Blue tradition.

"John did a smashing job for me. I won't let him down." Gus settled the folder under his chair and finished his tea. "Funny though, I can't seem to remember much of anything except standing there in Clouver Abbey like a chump."

"You weren't a chump. Not now, not then. And isn't that a good thing to not remember?"

"I suppose, though I have questions and doubts."

"You should talk to Coral, Gus. She can answer all of those questions. She's the only one who can set the story straight."

Leaving the abbey the same way he came in was the most difficult moment of his life. He shut down. Refused to talk to his ex-fiancée. He didn't care about her *reasons*. Two years later he couldn't bring himself to ask. In the meantime, she'd moved on. Recently married.

"I'm not sure I want to hear how I let her down. Or that she never loved me. I've put so much behind me I think it's best to keep it buried."

"All right, you've made your decision, now stand by it," Mum said. "So off to Dalholm and Hadsby. It will be refreshing. You know how much the hamlet loves you. When I visit, the crowds are modest. When you go up, the crowds are so large they have to bring out the volunteer mounted police."

"Yet I can walk down Centre Street without being accosted. Dine in a pub, shop without security."

"But you will have security." Mum used her queen voice to drive her point home.

Gus did love the small, coastal hamlet that faced the North Sea Channel and the eastern edge of England.

When he and John were young, Mum spent the summers at Hadsby and enrolled them in sports leagues. For their teen years, she put them to work on construction and grounds crews. As far as Gus knew, the beam he'd helped install at the Belly of the Beast, Dalholm's oldest public house, was still holding the place up.

"One more thing." Mum reached for another folder. "This is the final guest list for the ball."

Gus scanned the list of confirmed guests. The ball was a pre-wedding celebration attended by family, close friends, and a few political allies.

"You can't be serious." He glanced up, having finished his inspection, and tossed the folder onto the heavy, hand-carved desk commissioned by King Titus VIII in the nineteenth century.

"I'm afraid so."

"I'm to host a ball with my two ex-fiancées and their husbands?" He modulated his tone. "I don't mind Robbi. While it was painful to part, we were on good terms. And I like her husband, Bennett. But Coral? No, Mum, no. She humiliated the entire House of Blue and all of Lauchtenland." He shot to his feet. "Why is she even on the list?"

"I understand, Gus. The thing is, Coral and Robbie are very good friends of Holland."

"What about the brother of the groom? Do his feelings matter?" He was more than willing to step up to his brotherly duty. But to live, dine, and sleep in the same castle, no matter how spacious and grand, with the woman who'd obliterated his heart? Who humiliated him and the entire family?

No. Just no.

"Holland should've talked to you last night. When she became involved with your brother, many of her friends showed their true colors and proved untrustworthy. Some even abandoned her. Said she was too high and mighty for them. Meanwhile, Coral and Robbi have been a huge support. Holland is concerned about your feelings, but, Gus, love, this is her wedding." Mum reached back for her cup and saucer and stared at the fine bone china as if it contained some mythical wisdom and courage. "When Coral lived here, they became quite close. Now Holland's marketing firm represents CCW Cosmetics in Europe."

Another downside of being a royal. Their world was very small. Everyone knew everyone else. Billionaires and world leaders were their friends. Of course Coral, an heiress to one of America's richest families, would be a friend to Lady Holland.

This moment called for cinnamon puffs. Gus retreated to the tea trolley and filled a plate with his favorite pastry. A light, airy donut dipped in cinnamon.

"Do you know about Coral's husband? Her mother tells me he's an Uber driver, but he's growing on her."

"I may have read that somewhere." Gus popped puff after puff in his mouth and instead of a comforting sweetness, the cinnamon tasted bland. Flat. He didn't work hard all last year to get in shape only to lose it because Coral Winthrop might come to town.

"You don't still love Coral, do you?" Mum's question was laced with compassion.

"Love? No. I only recently stopped hating her." Gus set his plate on the cart and dusted cinnamon from his fingers, then ran his hand over his hair. The long locks weren't as fun here as they were on the beach, behind the bar. "But think about what it takes to unravel all the love you've given someone. All your hopes and dreams. Gone in a moment." Gus dropped down to the thick, leather couch.

"Believe it or not, I'm not unfamiliar with a broken heart." Mum sat next to him. Her hand was soft and warm on his. "You're almost twenty-nine years old. Very much a man, not a boy. I think seeing Coral will bring closure."

"What do you know of a broken heart? You met Dad, fell in love, and married six months later."

"Take it from me, Gus, love is worth your effort. Don't give up, darling."

"On love? Too late, I'm afraid. At least for the time being. I've tangled up myself twice with disastrous results. For now, I'll remain unencumbered. And I won't walk the Blue family line either. Marriage without love."

Mum brushed her hand over his head. "In case I've not said it in a while, I'm proud of you and how you've weathered your romantic recent storms."

He leaned to kiss her cheek. "You're all right, Mum. For a queen."

"Well, isn't that high praise."

"I'll leave on that note. I've got to meet my new protection officer. Stern set up a meeting at eleven."

"What about the newsbreak by Leslie Ann Parker? Do we need to discuss it?"

"What's to discuss? She found me out. I heard their ratings went through the roof. And you are the royal champion of the press and free speech. More than any of your predecessors. I think we have to live with it."

"Very well. I agree. One more thing. The Royal Trust is setting up the wedding dress display at Hadsby next week. A treat for our guests, then to remain as we reopen the newly renovated castle for tourists during spring and summer."

"Very good."

"Daffy Caron will be heading it up."

Gus paused at the door. "Daffy? You know she outed me to Leslie Ann Parker. Not on purpose but—" He gave the queen the short version of the story, ending with the mystery of how she blushed whenever he was around.

"Then be on your guard, Gus. I'm mistrustful of Daffy. Ever since she was a girl."

"That doesn't sound like you."

"It does when people overstep their bounds. Daffy ran around Perrigwynn so much she thought she had the run of the place. I found her in my dressing room once trying on clothes."

"So she's why we had new security protocols?" Why hadn't anyone said before now? "Trying on your frock is hardly a breach of national security."

"It was a violation of my privacy, and frankly, her access to the Family was setting her up for huge disappointment." His mother's tone cooled. "She was not, nor ever would be, a royal princess. She needed to grow up in *her* world, not ours."

"Put your mind at ease. I have no intentions toward Daffy Caron. The royal wing is on the other side of the castle from the servant and guest quarters. I doubt we'll see one another." He started to leave then remembered something Daffy said on the beach. "Mum, does Daffy know a Blue family secret? She implied she did but when I questioned her, she put me off. She doesn't know anything, does she?" Gus regarded his mum, searching for a flicker of truth.

"Certainly not. What could she possibly know? Now I must get on. I'm part of the judges' panel for the woman who left her child in a hot motor last summer. Dreadful case. Gives me nightmares."

As Lauchtenland's sovereign, Mum sat in on certain legal cases. Ones with constitutional ramifications—she was Lauchtenland's living constitution—and capital cases. Once in a while, she was part of the judges' panel, along with a twelve-person jury, on high profile cases. It was the reason all crown princes or princesses studied the law. Why Mum spent three years at Yale.

"Horrid case," Gus said. "Are deliberations nearing an end?" He'd read the story online while in Florida.

"No, we're in the middle of things." Mum shuddered.

A text sounded on Gus's phone. "It's Stern. I should go. Don't want to keep the new protection officer waiting."

As he departed, he heard Mum muttering. "She claimed a secret? Now I ask you…"

CHAPTER SIX

DAFFY

She had a grand task ahead of her. Preparing the royal wedding gowns for a trip north to Hadsby Castle in the hamlet Dalholm, County Northton.

But she was caught between time zones, her body not sure if it should be awake or asleep, thanks to their delayed flight home—one postponement after another. Their flight landed early Sunday morning instead of Saturday afternoon.

Yet when Daffy unlocked the door to the Hall of Dresses, inspiration sparked. The massive, windowless room housed a sentry of armoires and chests of drawers, each one labeled with a princess's name and the year she married.

Inside, the gowns were stored in muslin and unbuffered acid-free tissue within a cedar drawer. Daffy had until Friday to box all the gowns and carefully transfer them to the Royal Trust lorry headed to Dalholm and Hadsby Castle.

She would train up that same day and await their arrival.

Removing her blue uniform jacket with the House of Blue cypher over her breast pocket, Daffy stood between the decades 1790 and 1800 and launched the wedding gown inventory on her tablet.

The very idea of arranging these historic gowns made her heart swirl. This room—the one-of-a-kind treasures within each armoire—was one of the main reasons she joined the Royal Trust.

To preserve the story of Lauchtenland and the House of Blue. To see the *Princess Louisa.*

This was her first, in-person glance of the famous royal wedding dress. She'd been fascinated with the gown since reading about it in grammar school. When she wrote her master's thesis, the gown had been on an around-the-world tour so she wasn't able to inspect it firsthand.

Daffy told others that she loved the *Louisa* for its history, its unique beginning. The fact it was more art than clothing. Even the story of the designer, Taffron Björk, fascinated her.

But being in the Hall of Dresses...somehow affirmed her. Touched her with a sense of romance. Of distinctiveness. As if her dreams were within reach. That the girl who penned *My Life with the Prince* wasn't forgotten.

She had a wedding dress in her someday future. And while her gown would not be placed in the Hall of Dresses, she'd feel like a princess bride on her wedding day. Chosen. Special.

Daffy focused on her tablet. She was here to work, not daydream.

Reviewing her inventory and the map of the cabinets, she eyed the stack of boxes to be put together. She'd start with Queen Catherine II's dress and work backward in time. The oldest gown belonged to Queen Aribella, wife of King Rein I, and weighed twenty-five pounds. Fashioned in 1510 from a heavy, damask textile—because the princess feared she'd catch a cold during her winter wedding—and decorated with a thousand diamonds and two thousand gold studs. Her extravagance put her father into debt from which he never recovered.

Daffy texted her counterpart, Lucy Melrose.

I'm here. Starting to assemble boxes.

"May I come in?" Daffy turned to see Lady Holland just inside the door.

"Yes, please." Daffy bobbed in a quick curtsy. "How may I help you?"

"I wanted to see how you handle the dresses." She stood straight, her shoulders back, her tall frame wrapped in a pink, light wool suit, the jacket cut to her waist, the skirt extending to mid-calf, just above a gorgeous pair of Louboutin heels.

The recessed lighting bounced off her golden hair and caught the sparkle in her glorious diamond engagement ring.

"I'm a bit in awe my gown will be here one day," she said.

"We can't wait to see it." Daffy set one of the boxes on the worktable. "I expect it will set a new trend in bridal gowns. There's no family more watched and documented than the royal family."

"Goodness, I hadn't thought of that." Holland exhaled, a hand pressed to her stomach. "I mean I knew I'd be watched and followed. The Chamber Office said there are three hundred social media accounts about me. But being a part of history feels...awe-inspiring."

"You're making history by marrying a crown prince." Daffy liked the future queen. She was both regal and everyday. She'd fit in with Daffy's mates at Pub Clemency as easily as with world leaders during a state dinner.

"For me it's just about marrying the man I love." Lady Holland twisted her engagement ring around her finger. "It's a conundrum—he's a crown prince."

"Aren't you glad they've done away with old traditions like arranged marriages and bedding ceremonies?"

Holland laughed with a heavy exhale. "Yes. Very much so." She extended her hand. "I'm Holland by the way."

"Yes, of course you are," Daffy said. "I'm—"

"Daffodil Caron. I know you." Lady Holland joined hands with her. "And then I saw your Instagram post."

"Not mine, I assure you. Leslie Ann Parker pirated my account." She refused to go down for something Les did.

"I heard about it from John. He was quite angry at first. Said you used to be mates with the princes when you were children, but changes in palace policy put you below stairs."

"Please tell him how sorry I am. I had no idea—"

Lady Holland's smile offered her grace. "He knows. Gus set him straight. And he shared some fond memories of you."

Gus defended her? "I have many fond memories of the princes—"

Just then Lucy barged into the room. "Daff, did you remember we need a gown for the *Unknown Bride*? Oh, hello." Lucy stopped short and curtsied to Lady Holland with a side glance at Daffy. *What's she doing here?*

"Lady Holland came to see the dresses," Daffy said.

"I don't want to take up your time," Lady Holland said. "I know you have work to do. But would it be possible to see the *Princess Louisa*? Do I even have the right to ask?" She glanced between Daffy and Lucy, stepping closer. "My designer modeled my gown like the *Lousia* and I'd like a peek at the original."

"Of course." If a member of the royal family, or almost a member, wanted to see an artifact, they could. "I've no dress forms in here, but I can retrieve the gown and spread it out on the worktable. Lucy, would you please cover the table with a cloth?"

Daffy opened the cabinet marked *Princess Louisa*. For a moment, only a moment, she feared it'd gone missing—a silly thought, really. The gowns were all safe in this room. And the cream-and-ivory gown lay sleeping in its linen bag.

With slow, measured motions, she and Lucy removed the gown from the protective cloth and arranged it across the table one layer at a time.

"Stunning." Lady Holland leaned close, her hands clasped behind her back. "Is it all chiffon?"

"With organza and layers of French lace." Lucy added additional details.

"This gown, along with the *King Titus I* chair, which I probably may never see, were my spark into curating," Daffy said. "Their history and beginnings fascinate me."

And now she was in charge of one of them. Life did offer sweet surprises.

"The *King Titus* chair?" Lady Holland smiled. "This is your lucky day. John told me this morning the queen is setting out the chair for the ball. So you'll see it after all."

"But I won't be attending the ball, milady."

"They're releasing it from storage this week, I believe."

Lucy whistled, a high, soft sound. "The chair has only been out of its room twice in the last twenty-five years. The queen is so protective of it."

The chair was stored in a controlled environment at Hadsby Castle and only seen for rare and special occasions.

But, back to the star of the moment. The *Louisa*. The three of them admired the dress with its princess collar, long, tight sleeves ending with a subtle Tudor flare. A pattern of pearls decorated the bodice that connected to a pleated skirt of chiffon and organza. The pleats released just above the hips, and the creamy fabric flowed, boosted by layers of muslin and tulle.

"Well? Is your gown very similar?" Daffy straightened the collar.

Lady Holland stepped away from the table and offered Daffy a cunning smile. "We'll just have to see."

Lucy waited to say anything until the future queen of Lauchtenland had exited the room. "I'm sorry. But a gown modeled after the *Louisa* is not unique at all. Lots of aristocrats have been inspired by this gown. If she wanted to be unique, she should've designed her gown after the *Queen Arabella*. Or even the *Queen Catherine II*."

"She'd never make it down the aisle in an *Arabella*. Besides, it's hideous. And if you ever quote me, I'll deny it. And the *Queen Catherine* is too new. She was the last princess to marry. Holland had to make her own mark. We shall see how her designer modified Taffron Björk's pattern."

"Makes me wonder if Björk faded from the fashion scene because everyone copied his design," Lucy said.

"Maybe. But isn't it lovely that a common girl could wear something like a princess?" An image flashed from her past of when she'd stepped into one of the queen's gowns. The blue fabric was so rich and elegant. Even at the age of ten, she knew she'd touched something special.

She shouldn't have been in the queen's dressing room, but once she saw the dress, everything else faded.

Carefully and methodically, Daffy and Lucy packed the dresses for their moving day. Upon inspection, they noted those that needed slight repairs before being placed on the display dress forms. And goodness, the skirt and long train of the *Queen Catherine II* practically required its own postal code.

Late in the afternoon, Lucy ran to the corner shop and back for sandwiches and crisps—which they ate in the courtyard.

They'd boxed seven gowns with eighteen to go when their bellies rumbled. After the gowns, they'd tackle the dress forms and stands, sewing kits, and repair tools. Last but not least, plan the staging.

Daffy had just finished boxing up the simple drop waist dress of Princess Amelia from 1922 while Lucy prepared the next gown when Mum entered.

"I see you're making progress."

"Four hundred years of wedding gowns, three to seven princess brides per century, plus the two from the medieval era... We should be done on time. Oh, we had a special guest earlier. Lady Holland came by to see the *Princess Louisa*."

"Did she? Any particular reason?" Mum inspected the *Arabella* gown. Not as a casual observer, but as a curator. "Check the seams on this, Daffy. They seem weak."

"Lucy and I will go over everything when we set up the dresses." The work would be slow and tedious, but worth it. She would do Mum proud. Prove she was worthy.

"You'll be ready to leave on Friday?"

"I haven't booked my passage on the Northton Express yet, but I plan to take the early train. The dresses will go up in the lorry. I'll be there to welcome them."

"Well, I've a surprise." A sweet twinkle lit Mum's eyes. "The Royal Travel Porter has booked you in the royal car."

Daffy made a face. "Really?" Such a treat didn't seem likely. "Thank you."

"He mentioned the car would be empty, so I suggested you could keep the plush purple chairs company. He agreed." Mum turned to Lucy. "You can book first class but I didn't want to push my luck with the royal car."

"I love first class. Wouldn't know what to do with myself in the royal car."

Daffy selected a box for the gown Lucy brought from a deep cedar drawer. "I thought you were here to scold me about last week."

Mum's twinkle sharpened to a laser. "The queen knows it was Leslie Ann's doing. Which Prince Gus confirmed."

"He spoke to her about me?" First Prince John and now the queen. Lucy took over assembling the box while Daffy arranged the gown—the Princess Dauphine from 1924—on the worktable. Dauphine was the younger sister of Princess Amelia. "I'm sorry about Leslie Ann, Mum. I had no idea—"

"I know." Mum patted her hand. "It's over. Let's move on."

The same words she'd said eighteen years ago when Daffy, and thus Ella, had been removed from Perrigwynn's upstairs and thus the company of the princes.

"The queen and her security team deemed it necessary."

Mum knew Daffy had been caught in the queen's dressing room. In hindsight, a rather poor choice for a hiding place. She also knew that she'd tried on one of the queen's gowns. And that Daffy had stumbled upon a secret.

From that day to this, they never spoke of it.

"Do you really blush around the prince?" Lucy looked at Mum, then Daffy. "Your Mum told me."

"So it seems. Though I don't know why I only blush around him. Seems a rather odd quirk. Mum, you started it with your teasing. Created a Pavlov's dog sort of thing."

"Then create a new *dog*. Think of something else when you see him." Mum laughed. "And I did not make it up. You blushed the first time you saw him—and every time after. Have you sorted things out with Leslie Ann?"

"A little. She can be so self-focused." Daffy began folding the Princess Dauphine's simple skirt. "The whole blooming mess ruined our holiday. Every time I thought of Prince Gus barging into our cottage, I wanted to tear her to strips all over again. She was proud of herself. You should've seen her smirking, sipping her tea, lording her scoop over us."

"What about your sister? She's quite repented of her part in it all."

"She's naïve—and a geek. I don't blame her, except she blindly admires Leslie Ann. But I've forgiven her."

"Work it out with Leslie Ann." Mum smoothed a wrinkle Daffy missed. "She's one of your oldest friends, and good friends are a treasure. Even selfish ones."

"There's always Blink," Daffy said. Another one of her friends from A-levels. Blinky, the exuberant one of their group. But a flake, according to Mum.

"I'm not sure I'd put my eggs in Blinky's basket. You never know what she's going to do."

"I know she'd never betray me." Lucy helped Daffy settle the dress in the box and folded the bodice and sleeves. "Mum, you should've seen Gus's face. One of absolute betrayal. And after what he's been through, with not one, but two women, I don't blame him."

"He's an adult, Daffy. And a royal. He's grown up in a world where the paparazzi is always pointing a camera at him or trying to find the next story. Preferably something negative. Scandals sell papers. I'm sure he's used to it."

"Why should he have to be used to it, Mum? It's a crummy world to live in, if you ask me."

When she was a girl, the palace was a marvelous playground with real-life princes as her mates. She had no need for fairytales. She'd lived in one.

Until she was discovered. Then she learned not all fairytales had a happy ending.

"There's one more thing." Mum aided the packing by stuffing tissue around the dress, stabilizing it for travel. "Prince Gus will also be at Hadsby. He has several things on his diary, as well as finalizing wedding ball details."

"What?" Was the drumming of her heart echoing in the room as loudly as in her ears?

Try as she might, Daffy couldn't get Prince Gus out of her head. Up until the day they'd lugged their packed bags to the motor and locked the cottage door, she watched for him on the beach. Or Adler. Or him with Adler.

She'd even wandered, oh-so-casually, past the Captain's Hideaway's back deck, customers overflowing and spilling out onto the beach, where Helene had set up plastic tables.

It wasn't until she returned home, to her world, that she'd begun in earnest to scrub that man out of her hair. Her mind. Her heart.

"He's on assignment for the queen and his brother." Mum gave her a quick glance. "Shouldn't be a problem, should it?"

"Of course not." Daffy fitted the lid on the Dauphine and stood back while Lucy sealed it. "Hadsby's a big place, and the staff quarters are on the opposite side of the royal apartments. I doubt I'll see him."

"Good." Mum glanced at her watch. "I'm late. I'll see you later. Good work, ladies. Oh, Daff, I hear you're meeting your mates at Pub Clemency tonight."

"How'd you hear?"

Mum hesitated then fired out, "Ella."

"Naturally. It's not our usual Friday night but Thomas insisted. Everyone else seemed keen. To be honest, I think I'll cancel. I'm still worn out from the trip home."

"Go." Mum nodded as if the pub waited outside. "Show off your tan. I'd let you take a personal day tomorrow, but you've a lot to do."

"True." Daffy sighed and looked around the room. "But the more I think about it, I'm going to beg off. I'd rather rest for the week ahead."

"Don't, love. Thomas missed you. You can always make it an early night. What do you say, Lucy?"

"I'm always game for a night out with my mates."

"Exactly." Mum's jolly laugh escorted her to the door. "Daff, call me after the pub if you want."

"Why would I call? I'll see you tomorrow."

"I don't know—just if you want."

CHAPTER
SEVEN

DAFFY

Ten of the gowns were boxed and ready to ship. Ten more tomorrow and then the final few on Wednesday. Followed by packing and planning for staging, Daffy would just make her Friday morning train time.

However, she was an hour late for her date with her friends at Pub Clemency. Thomas texted, as well as Ella and Leslie Ann.

Are you coming?

Where are you?

Love, I've saved you a seat.

She needed to go home first and change. She wasn't allowed to wear her RT uniform to a pub. Plus she was exhausted, and hot from working in a windowless room all day. And then the footmen assigned to carry down the crates forgot so that she had to run all over to find them.

All it took was a quick shower to renew her spirits. She changed into jeans and trainers, and breezed into Pub Clemency— established 1742—hungry and eager to see everyone.

The Clemency District marked the cultural crossroads of Port Fressa. One block south, on Clemency Street, was the home of the media. A hundred years ago there were no less than five newspapers competing for the nation's, if not the world's, attention.

Now there were two, along with three tabloids, four television stations, and, in one building, the north European offices of Twitter, Facebook, and Instagram. Half of Port Fressa expected that place to implode at any moment.

North of the district was the Royal Plaza. Over three square kilometers of royal offices and dwellings, including Perrigwynn Palace and the Chambers Office. Just north of the Royal Plaza was Republic Boulevard, home of the Royal Republic Parliament and the Supreme Court.

To the west sat the financial district, where Thomas worked. Modern office structures were mixed in with the enormous, old world mansions, creating a tableau of the past and the future.

To the east were the brownstones, walk-up flats, and simple homes of the staff and servants who tended the rich, the royal, and the elected.

This was Daffy's world. Where she grew up in a three-bedroom, two-bath home on good ole Waverly Street, a mere stone's throw from Perrigwynn.

As much as she loved Florida, this was home. As she made her way around the tables, Thomas greeted her halfway.

"You made it." He kissed her cheek and led her to their regular large booth in the corner, under the shuttered windows.

The pub buzzed with voices, white collar and blue collar mingling together. In the far-left corner, a singer tuned his guitar and tested his mike.

"Hello, everyone." Daffy squeezed into the circular booth next to Ella. "Sorry I'm late. Lucy and I were packing wedding dresses."

"Are you still going to Hadsby next week?" Thomas said.

"Friday actually."

"What? No. Since when?"

"Since we realized how much we had to do. I'm sorry. I won't be gone long. Promise. Two or three weeks."

"We'll keep him company." Sitting on the other side of Ella with a tall glass of wine, Leslie Ann inserted herself into Daffy's private conversation. No surprise. "Why don't we all go up to Dalholm on the weekend? For some late winter skiing?"

Frank and Kayle, who sat on the other side of Leslie Ann, said they were game. So did Marlow, Tonya, and the three single lads at the end of the table. Albert, Rick, and Jones.

"Let me get up there and see how much work I have to do, please." Daffy shot Leslie Ann a look. *Stop controlling things.*

In Florida, she and Leslie Ann hashed out their differences, but the sting of her betrayal hadn't quite faded.

"Where's Blinky?" Daffy smiled at the server who set a pint in front of her then eyed the already started plate of sausage rolls. "Tonya, can you dish me a few of those? I'm famished."

"Blink is still working," Thomas said, moving closer to Daffy, slipping his arm behind her on the back of the booth.

"Daff, you can't still be mad at me?" Leslie Ann angled around Ella.

"Leslie Ann, just drop it." Daffy bit into a sausage roll.

"I'm so jealous of your tan, Daffy." Gracious Kayle steered the conversation to a lighter topic. "Frank, take me to Florida." She nudged her husband of two years.

"Now see what you've done, Daff?"

"Not my fault you never take your wife on vacation."

"Who can afford it?"

"Daffy." Leslie Ann rapped her knuckles on the table. "You have to forgive me sometime." She pleaded her case to the table. "I was just doing my job."

"What you did was pretty rotten, Les." Thomas came to Daffy's defense. "You highjacked her social media account."

Apparently at this table "drop it" meant talk about it.

"There's laws against that, you know." Tonya sounded every bit like a Port Fressa prosecutor.

"I've apologized." Leslie Ann slumped against the back of the booth. "Whatever happened to forgiveness?"

"I've had enough. You two are ruining *my* fun." Ella grabbed Leslie Ann's hand, then Daffy's. "Leslie Ann, do you promise to never involve Daffy in one of your stories again?"

"Especially anything related to the royal family." Daffy pulled her hand free as she twisted toward her friend. "I work for them."

"I promise." Leslie Ann crossed her heart, sending a kiss toward heaven. "I will never involve you again."

"Then I forgive you. Again. But don't ever—"

Leslie Ann crossed her heart again. "Never, ever. Unless the story is—"

The entire table chorused, "*Leslie Ann!*"

"Fine, fine." Leslie Ann raised her wine goblet. "Never, ever."

In the distance, the singer with a guitar began a James Taylor song, one Mum used to play when she wanted Dad to dance with her.

"Just yesterday morning..."

As he pulled the notes from the guitar strings, he pulled a few more thorns from Daffy's holiday. She smiled at Leslie Ann. Yes, all was well. Mum was right. Good friends were a treasure.

The blonde presenter with porcelain skin and apple-green eyes reached around Ella to hug Daffy.

"All this emotion." Jones feigned tears, dabbing his eyes with his napkin. "I can't take it. So much love."

"Jones, what is it about emotion you can't handle?" Albert, the psychiatrist of the group. Always analyzing.

"No more pints for him." Rick slid Jones's glass to the center of the table. "And I have an announcement. I closed on the estate I'd listed last month. Finally. My commission will keep me well into next year."

Applause and hoots circled the table.

And just like that, their *normal* resumed. Teasing banter, laughter mixed with serious news, and job details.

Daffy snuggled against Thomas, relaxed, half-awake and half-listening as Tonya detailed what she could of her day in court. With a long inhale, Daffy breathed in the woodsy notes of Thomas's cologne. Most of it had faded, but what remained lingered in his shirt threads. She nestled a little closer and he gently stroked her arm.

The table talk moved to a debate over food. Just when they worked out which starters to order next, the pub door opened, escorting in the sounds of the streets along with three tall, broad men with the chiseled profiles of aristocracy.

One bearded bloke bore the undeniable kiss of the sun on his high cheeks.

Prince Gus.

Daffy looked away too late. The warmth of her *tell* spread across her face.

Dressed in a chocolate-brown coat and gray slacks with his dark hair wavy and loose around his face, he was no longer Pete George, the man toting a bin of dirty dishes.

He was the chap who rode into every girl's dream on a white horse. Daffy's blush burned hotter.

"Blimey, the princes are here with their friends." Big, burly Frank, a former rugby player, rose from his chair. "Come in, lads. Shut the door."

The first man removed his hat as he scanned the overstuffed room. Charles Larrabee, a longtime friend of the princes. He pointed to a man in the far back corner—Lute, yet another longtime friend.

Walking three abreast through the semi-silent pub, the trio made their way to the large table reserved for them, their regal confidence sparking the atmosphere.

Daffy watched Prince Gus, thinking she should look away. Not be caught staring. But *he* was here. She rubbed the tingling chill from her arm. As the men passed their booth, the prince's gaze met hers and he nodded. Daffy just might implode.

Once they were seated, the pub chatter resumed normal volume and the singer covered another song. Daffy yanked up her jumper sleeves, loosened her scarf, and fanned herself with her hand.

"Are you warm, love?" Thomas flashed her a saucy grin. "From being so close to me."

"See, I told you. She's blushing." Leslie Ann all but shouted as she pointed to Daffy. "That's how I knew the prince was in Florida. Daffy blushes—"

"Will you be quiet?" Ella clapped her hand over Leslie Ann's mouth. "Do you want him to hear you?"

Leslie Ann yanked Ella's hand away, her eyes narrowed. "Don't ever do that again."

"Then stop shouting about blushing."

"I never shout."

"Then don't say everything that wanders into your head." Under the table, Ella squeezed Daffy's hand. "The world doesn't revolve around you, LA."

"I beg your pardon—"

"Ladies, can we give it a rest?" Thomas nodded toward the royal party. "Les, we know you scooped the prince. Bravo, good for you, and well done. We have other things to talk about tonight."

With that, he scooted off the bench and stood, his smile a bit wobbly. "Daffodil Daisy Caron—"

"Your middle name is Daisy?" This from Jones. "Were your parents into gardening when you came along?"

"Mum was delirious on pain meds." Ella supplied the explanation as if she'd been present at her older sister's birth. "Dad stepped out for some lunch when the nurse arrived with the birth certificate. By the time he returned, the deed was done."

"Lads, ladies, please…a moment?" Thomas brushed his hand down the side of his trousers. Perspiration dotted his high, smooth brow. What was he up to? "Daffodil Daisy Caron—" He pointed at Jones with a narrowed gaze. "Not a word." Then he removed something from his pocket. Slowly he lowered to one knee. "Will you marry me?"

"W-what?" She sat back as a cavernous hole seemed to open up in the pub and swallow all the lights and sounds.

"Love, will you marry me?" Thomas opened the ring box to reveal a beautiful, round solitaire. His voice echoed as if calling to her from the other side of a chasm. *Marrryyyy…meeee.*

A hand gripped her arm. Rick's voice broke through. "Mate, what are you doing?"

"Daffy?" Thomas lifted the ring higher, his gaze locked on her face. "Will you?"

"Thomas, um…" She closed her eyes, trying to focus as her brief response clung to her dry lips. "I mean, w-what are you… You want to marry me?"

They'd barely declared any sort of love let alone a life partnership. And a public proposal was so unlike him. Daffy twisted her fingers together and leaned toward him, lowering her voice to gain a sense of privacy. "Thomas...are you sure? We've not talked about—"

"Yes, I'm very sure."

Very sure? "We've never talked much about marriage."

"Well, I love you. I think you love me. We're good together, don't you think?" The perspiration beads on his brow multiplied.

Slowly the cavernous space closed, and she became aware of their friends watching and waiting, heard the song from the stage and clanking pints.

"I-um, wow, darling, goodness." She smiled, supposing her relationship with Thomas had been leading up to this moment. But of all the ways to get a proposal, this was not what she had in mind. "You're sure? How long have you been planning this?"

"When you went on holiday I realized how much you meant to me. How we could build a life together." He covered her hands with his. "What do you say?"

"I guess I say yes. Sure. Why not? I'll marry you."

With that, Thomas took her trembling hand and slipped on the ring. When he looked up, he drew her in for a kiss.

"Wait, wait!" Elizabeth "Blinky" Cox dashed through the pub, twisting and squeezing between patrons and tables. "Did I miss it? Did I miss it?"

She landed at their table like a 747, dropping the suitcase she used for a handbag in the middle, knocking over an empty pint.

"Oh my word! Thomas asked you already. Daff, you said yes. Of course you did. Isn't the ring gorgeous? Let me see. Tell me everything. How'd you propose, Thomas? Move over, Jones." When he scooted back from the table, Blinky plopped down in his lap. "Someone order me a pint. Daffy, go. Tell me everything."

The vivacious chestnut blonde with bright red lips and blue eye shadow reclined against Jones, who rolled his eyes and complained she'd gained another stone or two, even as he settled his hand comfortably about her waist.

Thomas returned to his seat next to Daffy, brushed the pub floor grime from his slacks, and recounted his simple proposal.

"And she said yes?" Blinky reached for Daffy's hand. "I knew it would fit. Well done." Blinky stood and faced the pub. "Couple over here engaged, everyone!"

The patrons cheered, and someone ordered the table a round. Caught up in it all, Thomas jumped up with his arms overhead. "I'm engaged! She said yes!" He dragged Daffy to her feet and together they stood on the booth seat.

Daffy smiled as the voices raised in a triple "Hip, hip, hurray." Then the singer began a soft rendition of *"You Are So Beautiful."* Thomas helped Daffy down and held in her in a slow, romantic sway, his legs bumping the chair behind him.

So this was it. Love. Her story. Her prince. The next chapter of *My Life with the Prince* by Daffodil Caron began with a new hero.

"Are you happy?" he whispered when the attention dialed down. His warm breath tickled her ear.

"Surprised. And yes, happy."

"I decided to be spontaneous." He pressed a soft kiss to her lips.

"You mean you didn't even plot this on your spreadsheet?"

He laughed and gripped her closer, still turning in the slow dance. "Well, maybe a little. But I knew you'd want something spontaneous, so—here we are."

When the song ended, they returned to their table as the server arrived with a round of pints.

"From the princes." She nodded toward the corner.

When Daffy looked over, Gus raised his pint to her. She willed her blush to *not* creep across her cheeks, but the heat singed her skin.

She'd have to get over this...this...*thing*. She could not go through life with a *tell* that indicated affection for a man not her husband.

For now, she would celebrate. Kayle and Tonya launched into tales of their engagements. Frank and Marlow kept interrupting to "set the record straight."

"But tonight," Thomas said with a puff of pride, "you've been outdone by a master."

"Master? You're mad. I promise I thought she was going to turn you down flat."

"Where are the flowers, mate? You didn't even bring flowers."

"If I ever get engaged—"

And so it went. Daffy tucked herself between the conversations to assess. She was engaged. A bride-to-be. To a man she'd declared love for once, maybe twice.

"Mum wants you to call," Ella whispered.

"Now I know why she was acting funny this afternoon," Daffy said. "Do you know if Thomas talked to Dad?"

"While we were on holiday." Ella's eyes glistened. "Are you happy? I'm so thrilled for you. He's a catch, Daff. Truly."

"I know, and yes, I'm happy."

Give her another hour or two and she would feel her confession and profession. After all, she'd given her word. And wasn't a promise where love really started?

CHAPTER
EIGHT

GUS

The sun and sand of Florida still flowed through his bones Friday morning as he waited in the royal lounge at Port Fressa Authority for the train to Dalholm, Northton.

He wasn't scheduled to leave until Monday, but a mate from uni rang, inviting him to a housewarming.

"The wife and I just built the place and need to show it off. Every raise we get until we're retired will go to paying it off, save the children's education. But who cares? It's only money."

Easy to say when one had money. Gus doubted very seriously Melvin Ludwig, who was to inherit his father's fortune, would be house poor. Nevertheless, the invitation warmed Gus, prompting him to leave Perrigwynn early so he could attend. Seeing old friends, touching base with his life before the humiliation would help erase more shadows from the last two years.

Besides, he was rather anxious to see Hadsby, the renovations, and the rolling green hills surrounding the castle where he'd lived his best summer memories.

His parents worked very hard to give Gus and John as normal a childhood as possible. The laid-back hamlet and Hadsby were their staging area.

Gus stared across the lounge. His secretary, Stern, read, while his new protection officer, Hemstead, stood outside the door, scanning the platform.

While he was glad to be home, truly, he missed being free of his security shadow. He tried to convince Mum he didn't need a PO, but she wouldn't hear of it.

If he had to have a man watching his back, Hemstead would do. Gus liked the brisk, formal demeanor of the former special forces officer.

Gus texted Helene last night to see how she was getting on and asked after Adler. She replied with a short video of the crew and a few of the regulars giving him a shout-out.

"Come on back, buddy. Not the same without you."

"Helene said you had family business. I thought we were your family." Old Ike. Gus missed him. Even teared up a bit at the sound of his voice.

Hemstead stepped inside. "The train is arriving any second."

Gus finished his bottle of water and gathered his coat and satchel. Dressed in trousers and a tailored button-down shirt, a coat and scarf, he met the PO on the platform as the train whistle pierced the soggy sky.

Passengers—businessmen and women, travelers, tourists, mothers with young children—gathered, hunched against the late February cold.

As the speeding train pulled into the station, the porter arrived with Gus's suitcases. Yes, everything was as it should be. Very proper and royal.

Once on the royal car, Gus settled into one of the plush, purple reclining chairs and pulled out his laptop. He must catch up on his patronages. And maybe reminisce about Florida by going through photos.

The train engine rumbled beneath him. The platform cleared. The whistle blew.

"All aboard!"

The coach's steward, a chap called Alex, dashed into the car. "Sorry, Your Royal Highness." He delivered a box of snacks to the serving counter. "I had to wait for these."

"It's only two hours north, Alex. I'm sure we won't starve."

The whistle blew for the final time. Three short but shrill blasts. Gus had just opened the update on the Dalholm Youth

Sports League when a distinct, feminine voice called from the platform.

"Wait… I'm coming! Wait!"

He glanced up just as the doors eased closed. Someone was terribly late. Maybe one of the station's porters could assist her. But this express train waited for no one. Not even the royal family.

"Wait…please!" Running footsteps echoed over the cold concrete. The breathless call was desperate.

Gus moved to the door just as it clamped closed on Daffy Caron, who struggled along with her large suitcase.

Stern stood next to him. "What is she doing? She acts as if she belongs in this car."

"Open the door, please." She rapped on the window as the hydraulics sighed and the train inched forward. "Prince Gus, I'm supposed to be in this car."

"I can't." He raised his hands, palms up. "The train is moving. Stern, can't we do anything?" Though Gus knew the answer.

"She'll have to catch the next one." The private secretary returned to his chair, snapping open the *News Leader*. "But I daresay she's not to ride in the royal coach."

"She's with the Royal Trust. Someone must've granted her permission." Gus moved to the back of the car and waved with a shrug, watching her for as long as he could.

DAFFY

Halfway to midnight, when a thick darkness settled over the hamlet of Dalholm, Daffy arrived at Hadsby Castle. She was tired, hungry, and beyond agitated.

"I'm here." She dropped her suitcase in the middle of the sitting room of her suite and collapsed on the love seat, holding up her phone as she talked to her mum. "I caught the eight o'clock. There was nothing else. Everyone's heading north for the final weekends of skiing. Lucy arrived on time, however, met the crates, and had the footmen bring them to the second floor Grand Gallery."

"Daffy, what happened? After I booked you in the royal car."

"I left my flat in plenty of time. Made a quick stop." To say goodbye to Thomas. He'd sent her the most beautiful roses before she left. "Then sat in a jam by the port for an hour."

If she didn't have a suitcase full of clothes and her laptop case, she'd have hopped out and sprinted the five miles to Port Fressa Authority.

But she was here now. Ready to work. And this dreadful day was only minutes from ending.

"Get some sleep. You'll feel better in the morning." Mum yawned, her speech softening to sound more like a mother than a boss. The two of them were still working out how to be boss and staff while also being mother and daughter. In the background Dad called, "Love you, sweetheart."

"Love you too, Dad."

Ringing off, Daffy rolled her suitcase to the bedroom, retrieved the chargers for her watch and phone, then hung her coat in the dressing room that was almost as large as her flat's bedroom.

Kicking off her shoes, she flopped on the bed and sank into the mattress. She might just stay like this all night.

Eyes closed, she drifted through various stored memories. The purple hue of Highcrest Mountains. The sunrise over the channel. The honk of the ferry horns as they crossed the channel, and the low lap of Pontus Lake against the shore. Then she saw roses, two dozen beautiful roses. Thomas's roses.

She sat up. She forgot to tell someone to water them. Reaching for her phone she texted Ella.

Please go by my place. Water the roses. Xo

Thomas suggested a ski weekend next week when she'd popped in to say goodbye and show off her ring to his colleagues. He'd get it organized, he said. So the lot of them might descend on the lodge. Daffy hoped she and Lucy had progressed far enough with the gowns to take time off.

Not that she could ski anyway, not after breaking her ankle two years ago falling down an icy slope. But she could sit around the fire and drink hot cocoa with the rest of them.

Opening her suitcase, she retrieved her toiletries as a small door chime sounded from the front room. Daffy listened at the bedroom door. The chime sounded again, followed by a muffled, "Daffy, are you awake?"

"Prince Gus?" When she opened the door, he stood on the other side, and the unwanted invasive warmth spread across her cheeks. Daffy stepped back, inviting him in. "What are you doing here?"

"Is it too late? I've been waiting for you. I am sorry about this morning, truly I am. I didn't see you coming until it was too late."

"The fault was entirely mine—and the ridiculous traffic in Port Fressa. Even if you knew I was coming, you couldn't have stopped the train."

"You looked so forlorn standing on the platform as we pulled away." He tilted his head, his dark hair falling over his forehead.

"Did I? More like mad. But Lucy arrived to receive the dresses, so all is well."

Silence fell between them for a moment. Then he pointed to her left hand. "Quite a proposal from your chap. You looked surprised."

"I—I was very surprised. Thomas and I never talked about marriage. Not really. Just casual things like 'When I marry I want…'"

"He seemed rather sure of himself."

"That's Thomas."

The prince walked farther into the room. "Cranston let you in? Is everything shipshape?"

Cranston was Hadsby's butler and house manager.

"He did. As for shipshape, I'll know more in the morning." She joined Prince Gus in the larger room.

"I think there's a dining schedule around here somewhere," he said.

"I'll find it," Daffy said. "So, what about you? Did you find everything in shipshape?"

"I think so. The renovations exceed my expectations. I've

dinner tomorrow night with a mate. A busy diary next week plus the Aegean task of choosing the wine, food, puddings, music, flowers, lighting, guest gifts, and on and on for John's ball." He rubbed his hand against his bearded jaw. "I'd fooled myself into believing I'd just stand at the door and greet everyone. If I had my way, we'd order pizza and pints, put bowls of crisps and dip on standing tables. Hire a DJ to play oldies."

She laughed. "Sounds perfect. But then, John threw you a very elegant bash."

"Did he?" Gus stopped by a portrait of his great-grandmother wearing her bridal gown. "I can't remember. At least, I try not to. But yes, he hosted a rather lavish affair."

"I'm rather busy with the parade of wedding gowns, but if you need help with the ball, just ask."

"Do you mean it?" He swerved from the painting to face her. "After the way I came after you in Florida, I'm not sure I'm worthy of your friendship."

"Your Royal Highness—"

"Gus. Please call me Gus. Not Prince Gus either. Just Gus. Even Pete if you dare." His famous smile beamed right through her as he came near, moving with the ease and grace she'd witnessed on the beach.

"Gus, you always have my friendship." She took a step back. What was it about his smile that made her feel welcomed? Wanted? What did it reflect from his soul that she understood?

"When I saw your Instagram post, I didn't think clearly. I reacted based on past experiences, past betrayals. Not at all fair."

"You thought I'd betrayed you too. Because you were betrayed so cruelly by someone you loved. *Not* that you love *me*. Or I you. I mean— Not, um, in *that* way." It was hard to pedal when one's foot was in one's mouth.

His smile dropped her into the nearest chair, hand to her warm cheek.

"I should have all that mess behind me by now. Should be ready to move on." He pumped the air with his fist. "Not everyone will betray me the way Coral did. It's just—"

"You get a knot in your belly every time something smacks of it? Or breach of trust? I get it. Been there. Nothing feels right. There are no comforts. Not even food or the telly."

"Exactly. And I hope you've not been through what I've been through."

"Well, I wasn't left at the altar—not yet anyway." She made a face and flashed her ring finger. "But I've been let down by others, by myself even. I was turned inside out over what Leslie Ann did."

Gus's light faded. "Have you two made up? If you haven't, you won't get a speech from me."

"We were stuck in that cottage together. We have the same friends. So yes, I've forgiven her. She's promised not to include me in any more royal family stories. Not that I have anything to contribute."

"I suppose we all need our friends. To forgive." He hesitated, then sat on the edge of the love seat. "To be honest, I'm not sure how to forgive Coral. We're not friends, so I don't have to navigate that breach." He said her name without a hiccup. "Mum asked me if I still loved her. I said I'd only stopped hating her."

"Hate only costs you, Gus. Doesn't harm her at all." From the hallway, one of the six grandfather clocks chimed the midnight hour.

"No, but hating her made me feel good." He shook his head. "That's a lie. I felt horrible. I'm just not sure she deserves my forgiveness."

Daffy eased down deeper into the club chair. "Do any of us deserve forgiveness?"

"Ah, now you're going philosophical on me, and meanwhile, the clock is telling me I shall turn from a handsome prince into a chubby mouse. I should go."

"You're not a Disney animated mouse." His nickname as a kid was Gus-Gus. When he gained weight, tabloids posted images of Cinderella's chubby friend with Gus's face. "Or the Pudgy Prince."

"But I do love cheese." His grin teased the rosy hue to her face again.

She laughed as he said goodnight, closing the door before Gus asked about her tell. Maybe it was because she was so tired. Or newly engaged. Or that the memories of her two summers at Hadsby with John and Gus, the adventures and laughter, came back so easily. But their brief conversation seeped into some of the cracks of her soul. Places she hadn't known were dry and thirsty. Places where she'd missed her old friend.

GUS

He had a good weekend. Met with old and good friends. Had a blast. He needed to forget himself and laugh. On Saturday and Sunday, he explored the castle renovations, which were more impressive than he realized.

The old family homestead was set for the next generation, and the one after. Despite being constructed of stone and timber, Hadsby had always been a place of elegance and luxury. Every regent from the sixteenth century on had found a way to put his or her mark on the old fortification. Especially since flaming arrows and ballista stones no longer threatened the high walls.

Monday morning, Gus met with Dalholm's mayor and police commissioner to discuss the influx of visitors and tourists for the ball and thank them on behalf of the queen for all their hard work.

In the afternoon, he visited one of the hamlet's new tech companies, Smart Life, where their young CEO, Callie Porter, outlined a way to turn Hadsby into a smart castle. One day the staff at Perrigwynn would be able to manage security, lighting, even some cleaning aspects of Hadsby from Port Fressa.

In the evening, he ate a solitary dinner with a footman waiting on him. On the credenza, silver tureens warmed salmon, roasted potatoes, asparagus, and an apple tart pudding.

"And what is your name?" Gus reached for his wine.

"Miles, sir."

"Is everyone else in the servants' hall? The staff? The members of the Royal Trust?"

"Yes, sir."

"Then I'll join them there tomorrow. Let Cranston and Chef Charles know." It seemed he had a bit of Pete George left in him.

Hadsby ran a lean staff, especially in the winter months. No more than thirty lived in and maintained the house. When it reopened in the spring and summer for tours, the staff tripled.

"Yes, sir. They warned me, sir, that you—" The footman, all of twenty, clipped his words.

"That I what?" Gus carried his plate to his seat.

"That you weren't so pleasant, sir. On account of being left at the altar."

"They warned you I wasn't nice?"

"More like sad…and maybe impatient." His pale expression implied he'd said too much.

"Then I'll have to watch myself," Gus said, taking a bit of his salmon. "Do you have a girlfriend, Miles?"

"Yes, sir, I do. Getting married in June, sir. I'm sorry if I said too much."

"I appreciate the honesty. And congratulations." Gus stood to shake the man's hand, breaking all the rules dividing staff and family.

Do not discuss your personal life.

Do not discuss their personal life.

Never mind Gus's personal life was all over the media.

From then on Miles tended Gus with an easy smile though the conversation faded into the silence of eating alone. The loneliness seemed to echo through him. He ate breakfast alone in Florida after a run. Dinner was at the pub, usually with Helene in her office. On weekends, he explored the Florida coast, grabbing a bite here and there on the run.

But he'd not eat alone when thirty or so people dined one floor below, laughing and talking.

In truth, he wanted to see Daffy. Talking to her last night was easy. Like it'd always been. Since she was an engaged woman and he a confirmed bachelor, a friendship with her was perfectly safe. Just what the doctor ordered.

When Miles cleared away his dishes, Gus retreated to his apartment. There was nothing on the telly. And though there were thousands of books at Hadsby, he didn't feel like reading.

He stared out his lounge window toward the lights of the Old Hamlet. What he needed was a night with his old mate Ernst at the Belly of the Beast.

Collecting his wallet and keys, Gus exited his apartment, down the hall to a small, hidden door that led him down a winding staircase to a narrow door. Cutting through covering ivy and a couple of hedges, he escaped over the grounds toward the woods and the gate leading to Centre Street.

He could've just gone down the Grand Stairs and out the front door, but why be normal when he could be clandestine? Besides, he wanted to sneak off without Hemstead.

Centre Street, the heart of the Old Hamlet side of town, with its ancient shops and cottages, was sleeping and quiet. The only sound in the cold night air were his footsteps.

However, on the other side of a low row of buildings and the Centre Park was the New Hamlet, loud, bright, modern with tall edifices, flashing lights, revving motors, and car horns.

Gus was in his element in the Old Hamlet. So peaceful and enveloping, full of his childhood memories. Being fifteen seemed like eons ago.

Down the old cobblestone, past the thatched roof shops and flickering Victorian lamps, he turned down Wells Line and aimed for the Belly of the Beast, one of the region's oldest pubs that overlooked the quay.

"Ah, look who." Ernst, the owner, greeted Gus with a bow and hearty backslap. Royal protocol took an unusual form in the Beast. "Your Royalness, come. Too long, too long. Betsy, love, prince pint. Lads, your prince. Shape up, sail right." Ernst motioned to the table by the fireplace. "Food? Stella! Fish chips."

"No, thank you, Ernst. I've had my dinner. Just a pint. One." Gus thanked the smiling and curtsying Betsy, Ernst's daughter—

or was it his niece?—and drifted easily into the welcoming and familiar atmosphere of the stone floor and rough beam pub. As well as the humorous and curtailed dialect of County Northton natives.

Maybe it was because of the extreme winters in seaside Dalholm or the sloppy, rainy summers, maybe it all started with the hardworking, seafaring founders, but Northtonians shorthanded their speech. Complete sentences not required. Only the words that mattered.

One year the queen allowed the mayor to give a national speech. She thought he'd be prepared to address the entire nation. Instead one would've thought he stood on a hamlet corner, speaking to his neighbor. He delivered the whole thing in Dalholm-speak as news presenters frantically called for translators.

"How's doing? Florida?" Ernst pulled up a chair.

"Florida was good. But I'm home now. The queen sends her regards."

"Ah, what love. My regards." Ernst twirled his hand and bowed his head. "Sure? No eats?"

If he didn't say yes, Ernst would offer all night. "Thank you, yes, I think I'll have a very small serving of chips."

"Chips. Northton grown. Can't beat." Ernst shoved away from the table and called to his wife. "Stella, chips."

"You prince?" The man at the table next to Gus leaned toward him.

"So it says on my birth certificate."

"Sorry. Women." He shook his head. "Can't figure. Those lasses. Running. You a good man." He clapped Gus's arm. "Don't give up. Right one." He patted his heart. "Love is worth it."

"T-thank you." Gus buried his face in his pint, his eyes stinging from the man's sincere encouragement. But was it true that love was worth...what? Everything he'd been through? All the grief? The mortification? The nights he wondered who he was—if all the headlines were true? Pudgy? Pathetic? That there was something wrong with him that caused women to leave?

Maybe love was for everyone else, just not him. Never mind.

He was in no mood for a pity party, but two broken engagements in less than two years? One had to work to shrug it off.

Gus's phone pinged. Hemstead.

> Where are you?

> In town. Perfectly fine. Be home soon.

> Please, sir, do not leave the castle without me.

Ernst burst from the kitchen with a *large* plate of fries and set them in front of Gus. "Stella. No small. Only large." He reached into his apron for a bottle of ketchup. "America." His big laugh tickled Gus. "Betsy, more pint."

Ernst returned to his chair and rested his thick, muscled arm on the table. "Now, tell Ernst about it."

"About what?"

"The lass. The love." He twirled his finger in front of Gus's eyes. "I see."

Gus batted the man's hand away. "You see nothing. There's no love. Why don't you tell about the Belly of the Beast and life in Dalholm?"

Ernst's rapid, broken speech was its own kind of poetry, and Gus's mind automatically filled in the vacant parts of the story with proper grammar. Nevertheless, he understood life for Ernst was "supersplendous."

The tech companies caused the hamlet to prosper with a surge of young career folks who then met, fell in love, *ah, only in Dalholm*, and married. Ernst stressed *married* with a narrowed gaze at Gus.

"You. Marry."

"Not for me, my friend. Not for a long, long time."

Ernst huffed at the answer but carried on with his update. After they married, the youngsters bought the older homes on the east side, in the Old Hamlet, and began restoring them.

"New? *Pffbbt*." Ernst swiped the air with his broad hand. "Restore old. Better. You?" He clapped his hands. "Dalholm is love. Catch you, prince, will catch you."

"Noooo…" Gus shoved the plate of chips away—he couldn't eat one more bite—and spoke in shorthand. "Wrong. Miss by long shot. Big."

Ernst laughed. "Me wrong? You wrong. Very wrong."

Well, that started a debate as Betsy angled a pitcher over his glass. Love? What did Ernst know about Gus's love life? Past, present, or future?

"Listen up, Ernst," he said, reaching for the frothy pint and speaking in the queen's dialect. "Let me tell you what you didn't read in the press. Let me set the record straight."

CHAPTER
NINE

QUEEN CATHERINE II

Today was one of those Mondays that stretched the limits of her royal demeanor.

She woke up early, agitated instead of refreshed. Regrets from years gone by crept from behind long-ago closed doors and haunted her dreams.

She wanted to cancel her appointments, but calling in sick was not a luxury for a queen. Not unless she was truly, actually ill. Poor sleep and bad dreams did not qualify.

She snapped at her secretary twice before nine and had to apologize. After a lunch meeting with the Prime Minister, she spent the afternoon reviewing the case of the child left in a hot motor, followed by a review of the Finance Minister's lengthy, laborious economic report. He was new to the post and seemed to think if one word would suffice, why not use ten?

She'd been reading ministry reports for twenty-five years, and this was the first time she wanted to toss her computer through the window.

That would make for a nice headline, wouldn't it?

QUEEN CAUSES DAMAGE TO PALACE WINDOW AND
COMPUTER AMOUNTING TO SEVERAL THOUSAND POUNDS.

But she mustn't complain. She was so blessed, healthy with a living parent, a sister who'd become a friend, an adoring husband, and two stellar, handsome sons. One was about to marry the exceptional Lady Holland and the other, her broken, wounded baby boy, Gus, had returned home calmer, more resolved, more healed than when he'd left.

She'd contemplated ringing him while he was away and telling him her story. The one of her own hard-earned lesson in love. How she'd endured, overcome, and risen above. How the painful lessons of the past had made her a better wife, mother, and queen. Above all, how she'd forgiven herself.

But she was not free to speak. And some lessons had to be learned for oneself. Besides, if she confessed her story, which to this day Edric, her beloved King Consort, did not know in detail, she might suddenly appear less in her husband and sons' eyes, and *that* she could not bear.

With a glance at her watch, she closed her laptop and made her way to apartment 1A where she'd lived since her father's passing twenty-five years ago.

She wasn't hungry after all that dull reading, but the palace's Chef George always prepared a delicious dinner. The aroma might awaken her appetite.

"Dinner is served, Your Majesty." Pablo, Perrigwynn's butler, greeted her in the dining room holding out her chair. He'd replaced her long-time butler, Greenly, three years ago, and she and Edric were still getting used to him. Handsome, kind, even-keeled, exceptional at his post, she could find no fault. Perhaps there was the rub. Ole Greenly had a bit of mischief about him. Pablo was so perfectly perfect. As if he could go rogue at any moment and belt out a show tune in the middle of a state dinner.

"I'll wait for His Royal Highness." She nodded as she passed the table. "Let me put my computer away."

Down the hallway to her bedroom, she set the laptop on her desk and settled into the worn reading chair, turning on the table lamp. The winter days were growing a bit longer as spring approached, and the golden hue of sunset still rested on the horizon beyond her window.

With a glance toward her dressing room, Catherine stepped inside. She'd rearranged it a dozen times over the years, updated it once, but through it all, she still carried the memory of Daffy staring up at her, wearing the blue gown. How she regretted her response. So harsh. She'd never made it right. Never. She was too afraid.

In the moment, she'd seemed so exposed. As if the girl had discovered all the secrets hidden in that dress.

But Daffy didn't know. She'd been playing with the boys. And how many times had Catherine invited her into her room to try on a scarf or a splash of perfume?

She also didn't know that five minutes before Catherine walked in the dressing room she'd been on a call that brought up *those* memories.

Catherine caught her reflection in the mirror. She looked matronly, wise and queenly, with her trim suit and neat, coiffed hair, colored a dark brown.

Her eye flitted to her dresses. She half expected a brilliant blue sheen to leap out at her, but the gown was gone. She'd disposed of it years ago, never been seen again.

So what brought all this on? Why think about it now? Catherine closed her eyes and pressed her fingertips to her bowed forehead. She wished the drift down memory lane was due to the minister's wordy report, but it was the dream. Well, she'd get over this like she did in years past. But if time healed all wounds, it was taking its sweet time with her.

On top of it all, she still tangled with postmenopausal symptoms. Combined with John's wedding and Gus's return, her feminine sensibilities drove in their own lane.

"Kate, are you here?" Edric's voice called from their bedroom. "Shall we eat? Pablo looks on edge. I think he's counting the seconds the food is warming in the tureens. I'm starved. How was your day?"

"Both awful and boring."

"The child case?" He joined her at her dressing room door. "What are we doing? Staring at your shoes?"

She smiled and patted his chest. "Just thinking."

"About?"

"Nothing really."

He bent to see her face. "Doesn't look like nothing."

She squeezed his arm. "I'm glad Gus is home, aren't you?"

"Very much. I was worried since he'd stayed away too long. Sending him to Hadsby was a good move."

"Dalholm and Hadsby are his places."

If she could tell Edric what crept past her in the night, then maybe she'd find her way clear to tell her sons. But in thirty years of marriage, this particular secret was one she could not bring herself to tell. Even to the man she loved with every fiber of her being. The man who'd rescued her.

"Come, let's eat." She linked her arm through his, thankful for how he always anchored her. "Edric, could you look over the Finance Minister's report? I need someone to boil it down. His lengthy sentences with economic terms I've never heard of are giving me a headache."

"Anything for you, love."

Edric, her sweet Edric. So kind and giving. Her wise rock. One of these days she *must* unburden herself to him. *One* of these days. But that day was not today.

DAFFY

Crates lined the gallery and debris littered the royal red carpet. By Monday evening, Daffy and Lucy had assembled the dress forms, stationed them according to their design plan, and unboxed the first gown—the oldest, from the fifteenth century—of burgundy velvet, cream silk, and lined with white fur.

It was well preserved, but under inspection, they found it needed some delicate repairs.

The hall clock struck ten as Daffy stretched, her low back aching, and surveyed the gallery.

"I'm starting to think we don't have enough room."

Lucy looked up from stitching a layer of silk. "It's a big gallery, Daff. We've not yet used half the space."

"I know, but we have at least six dresses with cathedral trains. They'll run the width of the gallery, through the rails, and over the sides if we're not careful."

"True. The *Arabella* train is twenty feet." Lucy stood and stepped around the unboxed crate. "I'm off to get some silk remnants to finish this."

"It's late. Wait until morning."

"I just want to tend it while I'm thinking of it." Lucy leaned in for a hug goodnight. "I'll see you at breakfast. Seven-thirty."

"You're making me feel guilty." Daffy lifted the lid from the next box. Inside was another beautiful, but heavy, gown from a House of Blue bride. Worn by Princess Georgianna in 1588, the dress required some careful assembling. Many of the embellishments had fallen off or loosened, and some of the tapestry threads on the bodice needed repair. Tedious work. Any modern touches must appear the way the original dressmaker intended.

"Don't," Lucy said. "I'll bug out early on you one night. Sleep well."

Collecting her tablet, Daffy started for her suite, the Princess Charlotte, but when she passed the stairs, she saw a light in the foyer spilling out from what could only be the Queen's Library.

At lunch Cranston announced he was bringing down the *King Titus* chair in the afternoon. While he wasn't officially a member of the Royal Trust, he had jurisdiction since the ancient piece was stored at Hadsby. And the less handling the better.

The idea of seeing it in person renewed Daffy's energy. Enough to head down the bronze and gold double balustrade staircase for a quick peek. With the castle so quiet, now was the time.

She tiptoed over the marble floor to the library's open doors and passed under the light from an etched glass dome to catch a glimpse of the chair.

The room was long and narrow, scattered with leather club chairs, thin-legged desks, and gilded floor lamps with broad shades. Where would Cranston have put the chair? And truly, the doors should be closed and locked.

"Beg pardon, but have you seen the prince?"

Daffy jerked around. "Hemstead, you scared me. The prince? No, I've not seen him. Is he lost?"

"He's run off. I thought he'd be back by now." The broad and muscled protection officer stepped into the room. "Do you need my help?"

"I was just sneaking in to see the *King Titus*." Daffy lit the lamp on an end table and found the ancient chair situated in the front corner, hidden by the open door.

"The *Titus*?" Hemstead stiffened, arms folded. "Don't see the fuss over a thousand-year-old chair, former royal throne or not. I'd rather see the prince. Give him a piece of my mind."

"Check his apartment."

"What do you think I've been doing? He's gone to some pub, but I can't remember what he said. I've never been here before."

"Don't look at me, I've not been here since I was a girl. Well, to ski but we were at the lodge." She pointed to her foot. "Broke my ankle the last time."

"Yeah, I don't ski either." Hemstead sighed and glanced out the window. "I've been to six places in New Hamlet, but no one had seen him. Do you think he'd stay in the old part? Don't see the appeal there."

"Maybe."

With a harrumph, Hemstead said good night, his heavy exit echoing in the foyer.

Closing the left side door, Daffy faced the ancient, hand-carved chair. "Beautiful."

Her intrigue over this artifact was an unexplainable curiosity. The wedding gowns and other textiles made sense, but an old chair? Once she joined the Royal Trust, heard the older members wax on about the first time they'd seen the former royal throne—made by the first king of Lauchtenland, Titus, after conquering the Normans—she knew she was somehow destined to be a part of its historic preservation. She'd be a part of the team that made sure it survived for the next generation.

She knelt to inspect the thick, square legs that held up the broad seat with intricate carvings. The arms were flat and wide. The ends were smooth and round where royal hands had rested for centuries. The tall back flared at the top like wings, and a carved crown was attached to the top. The trees the king cut to fashion the structure had been extinct for three hundred years. And the upholstery fabric was a rich purple that experts in the RT could not duplicate.

"You're still working?"

The unexpected question caused Daffy to rise up. Prince Gus stood just at the threshold.

"I saw a light from the library and came down to see the *Titus*." She tucked her tablet under her arm. "Hemstead was looking for you."

Gus closed the other door, finger to his lips. "*Shhh*. I've been to the pub."

Indeed, he had.

"Apparently not the ones where he looked."

"It's my secret place. The Belly of the Beast." He wobbled from side to side. "But don't tell."

"How many pints did you down?"

"One." He raised his chin and breathed deep. Brushed back his wavy locks.

"One? Plus…"

He held up one hand, fingers spread. Then two fingers, no three, on the other. "I think. Ernst kept talking while his sneaky little waitress filled my glass. One pint I said. Never thought they'd refill it seven"—he hiccupped—"eight times."

"You should go to bed."

"How mad was he?" The prince jammed his hands in his pockets as if to anchor himself. "Hemstead?"

"Six on a scale of ten."

"I've been warned." Gus saluted, then stepped toward the chair. "Hello, old Titus."

"Have you seen it before, then?"

"Once. As a kid. I tried to sit in it. Mum came flying across the room, almost knocked over the American Ambassador, just as my trousers touched the seat. 'Don't sit down, Augustus. Don't sit down.'" He swayed from side to side. "I'm talking too loud?"

"No, but you should sit down before you fall."

Despite his current state, he was extraordinarily appealing, the look in his almond-shaped eyes a soft blue instead of the usual piercing hue. And he sported a fixed, saucy grin.

"Should I sit here?" Before she could answer, Gus plopped down in the *Titus* and slapped his hands on the broad arms. "Long live the House of Blue." He sat back, crossing his legs, rubbing his hand over his beard as if he was about to make a royal decree when a soft crack snapped through the air.

"What was that?" Daffy said, stooping to see the leg joints.

"I'm not sure." Gus wiggled in the chair side to side. "Do you still hear it?"

Daffy gasped, and for a moment, blacked out. Not really, but a crack in the *Titus*? Never was there a worthier blackout moment.

"Gus, stop moving." She grabbed his wrist. "You'll make it worse. Get up. Let me look."

"Wait." He pulled free. "Listen. Where is the sound coming from?" He raised up a few inches, walked the chair forward, and then sat back down. Daffy almost fainted. Again, not really. But what was he doing to her?

The chair moaned and squeaked as he jiggled in his seat. "Feels like the right side."

"Gus... Your Royal Highness...as a representative of the Royal Trust I must *insist* you get out of that chair. Now." Her deep voice was weak with anxiety. If he broke the *Titus*, it'd be her job. Sacked without a plea.

He leaned over the arm to see under the seat, still moving and listening. "As a member of the Royal Family, I insist I find the weakness in my ancestor's throne."

"As a member of the Royal Trust, I remind you that all artifacts are under our jurisdiction, not the House of Blue's."

"As a member of the royal family—House of Blue, as you say—I remind *you* that all royal departments and staff are subject to Her Majesty, the Queen, and thus so funded."

Daffy clung to her tablet, eyes closed, inhaling, exhaling. Good grief. How was she caught up in such an absurd argument?

"As a member of the Royal Trust, I remind you the House of Blue, and thus the Royal Trust, are also funded by Parliament and the people of Lauchtenland. Now get out of that chair!"

Gus held up one hand. "Simmer down, lass. Give me a moment. I've fixed chairs before." Again, he scooted the chair forward. But not with any care or concern. No, his senses were dulled by seven, eight pints. "There. Do you hear it?"

Rising up, Gus dropped down on the seat with force, then rocked against the chair's back. Not once but twice. Three times.

The cracking was unmistakable. Like ice breaking during the first spring thaw. Just one fault on the surface and the whole blooming block shattered across the water.

"*Gus*—" But Daffy was too late. The right side legs splintered under his weight. The back broke away, pulling the rare purple fabric from the seat and *kaboom*! Prince Augustus Carwyn George Blue, along with the chair, landed in a heap on the hard, polished pinewood.

CHAPTER
TEN

GUS

Next time he went to the Belly of the Beast—how fitting the name come morning time—he'd insist Ernst serve him no more than one pint. *One.* Not one glass filled many times over, thank you. Nevertheless, Ernst was an all-too-gracious host.

He'd avoided drink during the "great humiliations," choosing to stifle his pain with ice cream, puffs, and pizza. Yet Ernst meant no harm. To him it was a crime for any man to sit long in his pub, catching up with his mates, and not raise a pint.

In the bathroom, Gus splashed his face with cold water and remembered he had a meeting with the wedding ball planners this morning.

But something nagged at him...something more than the dull ache over his left eye from too much ale. Something in his belly. Like a twisting regret.

Wandering into his living lounge where the blazing sun rudely splashed through the high windows, he collapsed on the couch with a sigh. What happened last night that...

He sat up. The *Titus.* Daffy. The crack. Carrying the splintered chair up the Grand Stairs. *Oh no. Oh no.* The twisting regret became a clear reality. He'd broken the chair.

"Your Highness?" He turned at the knock on his door. Hemstead. "Gym. Ten minutes."

Gus toppled over and landed face first on a brocade cushion. Why did he ask his protection officer to act as his trainer?

Even worse, he'd have to face Hemstead and deal with the consequences of leaving him behind. Then face Daffy and the problem—no, disaster—of the chair.

"Sir?"

"On my way." Gus paused at the snack station on his kitchen island. Better not. It'd only come up after the first set of Hemstead's mountain climbers.

As expected, the former special forces officer put the prince through a brutal workout, as if penalizing him for disappearing last night. It took all Gus had to remain upright. When Hem released him, he stumbled back to his apartment, showered, and blended a protein shake.

He felt surprisingly renewed and focused enough for the planning meeting. But first, he had to find Daffy. Down the back stairs to the servants' hall, he inquired of Cranston.

"Have you seen Miss Caron?"

"I imagine she's in the Grand Gallery. With the dresses."

"Of course. If you'll excuse me."

"Your Royal Highness, I wanted to apologize for not locking the Queen's Library door last night. I remembered in the middle of the night and came down straightaway." Cranston smiled. "She's locked and secure now."

"Yes, no worry." Gus braced for more. Like how Cranston looked for the *Titus* but it was not in its corner. "Anything else?"

"No, sir. Should there be?"

"No. All good here. Thank you, Cranston."

He took the stairs two at a time. They must repair that chair. He found Daffy in the gallery hoisting a monstrous gown over a mannequin. "Careful of the sleeves, Lucy."

He hid behind a wide column until they'd completed their task. "Daffy, may I have a word?"

If looks could kill...

"Lucy, will you excuse me?"

The woman inspected Gus, then Daffy. "I'll go for the gold

thread." She curtsied to Gus then backed down the wide, carpeted gallery.

"Can we talk in your suite?" he said.

She started for the Princess Charlotte without a word. Gus tried to fashion his opening statement, but the dull throb over his eye troubled his concentration.

"About last night," he said the moment the door closed. "I am so sorry."

"You broke the *King Titus*." Her voice rose and fell with his heartbeat. "The *King Titus*. Gus, I don't…" She paced, hands flexing in and out of a fist. "One of the world's oldest artifacts. Not just Lauchtenland's but the world's." She swung her arm toward the dressing room where they'd carried the broken pieces, wrapped them in a pink blanket, and hid them in the corner. "Disaster."

"Yes, we have a problem but—"

"We?"

"Okay, I have a problem. Me."

"No, no, you're right. We. It'll be my job not yours. Ha. You don't even have a job. You *are* the job. I want it on record I told you to get out of the chair."

"Fine. Though I don't remember much of anything but a cracking sound. Daffy, is there any chance the chair was one of the remakes?"

"Not a snowball's. The real *King Titus* is very distinct. The fabric, the wood, the markings. The wood is from the forest lost in the mid-eighteenth century when the hamlet cut down every tree during the brutal winter. The fabric color is unique. The scuffs on the legs, the smoothness of the arms are all very distinct and very documented. Besides, Cranston personally carried it down to the library. He knows it's the original."

"I saw him this morning. He apologized for not locking the doors. Said he came down in the middle of the night to do so."

Daffy gasped and dropped to the arm of a chair. "Did he see it was missing? Please, tell me he didn't."

"No, no, I don't think so. If he did, he said nothing."

"I'm going to pass out." She bent forward, panting.

"Shush, lass, it's all right. We'll figure this out." Gus patted her back, angling to see her face. A red hue crept across her cheeks and around her eyes. He had a feeling this "blush" wasn't about him. Not in the sweet, she-had-a-crush way.

"I have an idea." She sat up, eyes glistening. "Is turning back time one of your princely powers?"

"I'm serious and you're joking."

"It's the only way to keep from *freaking out!*" She shook out her hands and sort of hyperventilated. "This will be my position. My reputation. I'll be lucky to get a post recycling rubbish."

"Stop. You won't lose your job. We can work this out." The plural pronoun here comforted him. He'd take the heat if it came to it, but he liked teaming with a friend.

"Gus, we broke a thousand-year-old chair the queen has kept in storage for twenty-five years except for two world tours in '98 and '08. There is *no* air in this room." Daffy stumbled to the window, drew up the sash and pressed her face against the cold screen.

"*We* did nothing. This is all on me, Daffy." It was his turn to flex his hands and pace. "What we need is a plan."

"W-what we need...is a *miracle.*" Daffy swerved from the window with a hint of tears in her words.

"The replicas." Gus stopped beside her. "We'll use a replica."

Now she just looked mad. "Every curator knows that chair. And several reporters. Never mind your mum as well as mine. A replica would be spotted in a second. *Wait.* Did you say you'd fixed a few chairs in your life?"

"Hammered a nail. Tightened a screw. Nothing like what that blooming chair needs. We'd fare better with the replica."

Daffy returned to her chair, tugging at the cuffs of her blue uniform. "I should call Mum. Tell her the news."

"Not yet, Daffy. We have time to figure this out. If anyone makes a call, it's me to Her Majesty. I'll shoulder the blame. As far as I'm concerned, I was the only one in the room."

"But you weren't. I know the truth." She twisted her fingers together. "If I lie about what happened, what kind of integrity do I have?"

"Keeping a secret isn't a lie, is it? Don't you have one about the queen?"

She glared up at him. "Keeping a *confidence* is not the same as pretending I wasn't there when the *Titus* was destroyed—which I was. If I'm asked outright, I'll have to tell the truth."

Her red hair waved and curled about her face, giving her a wild, free look. For the first time Gus saw she carried a bit of a lioness inside. For a moment, his thoughts drifted from the current dilemma to the woman in front of him. And what it might be like to kiss her.

Now he was blushing. Clearing his throat, Gus turned for the open window. He needed a breath of cold morning air himself. Best to focus on the trial at hand and not how she'd feel in his arms. *Friends, mate. She's just a friend.*

"Tell your maid not to go into the dressing room," he said, taking command of himself and the situation.

"She won't. There's nothing in there besides my coat and an empty suitcase."

"Is there a key? Can you lock it?" Gus knelt next to Daffy and placed a hand on her knee. "I have an idea. My friend Ernst will know how to help. How to find a skilled craftsman."

"We cannot tell him about the chair."

"He won't ask."

For the first time since they'd been talking, Daffy brightened and rested her hand on his. "We need someone good, Gus. More than a man or woman with a hammer and carpenter's glue. And someone with discretion."

Gus's phone pinged. He knew without looking Stern was reminding him of their planning meeting.

"I've a meeting in twenty minutes in the New Hamlet so I've got to go. But meet by my apartment tonight. Eight o'clock." Gus rose to his feet and stepped back.

"Make it nine. Most of the servants have gone home or retired to their quarters by then. We won't be seen."

"Look at you with your espionage plan." Gus offered her a grin and a salute. "See you at nine."

Out of the suite, Daffy went one way, Gus another. He met Stern in the Grand Foyer, who motioned to their waiting car.

Sunlight flooded the streets as the motor jostled over old Dalholm cobblestones to the smooth asphalt of the modern side of the hamlet.

Stern ran down the meeting agenda, but Gus barely listened. Instead he pictured the redhead who seemed to bring her whole soul with her wherever she went.

Daffy was both beautiful and easy to be around. Too bad he didn't meet her two years ago. After Coral. Even better, before Coral. Their reconnection was too late for him.

Besides, she was engaged which stuffed any musings of a "them" back into the box where it belonged.

DAFFY

A snowstorm gobbled up the sunlight as it rolled over Dalholm midafternoon, burying the hamlet in white. By teatime, windblown drifts collected along the castle walls. By dinner, the kitchen staff had to push against the doors to carry out the rubbish.

Gus appeared in the servants' hall doorway just as they sat down. "May I join you?"

A chorus of chairs scraped over stone as everyone stood. Cranston made a place for him at the end of the table.

"We eat buffet style, sir."

"I'm used to eating my dinner while standing in a kitchen." Gus shot a look toward Daffy. She gave him a low smile. "This is rather nice."

His arrival shifted the atmosphere of the room. Instead of talking in pocket conversations or leaning in as someone told the whole table a story, the staff ate in pleasant silence broken only by a football inquiry or how it was already the first of March and everyone longed for spring.

From his seat, Gus listened, laughed, predicted Dalholm

would make it to the FA Cup, and declared the snow was rather refreshing.

"Didn't see any of this in Florida."

"I'd take that any day, sir." This from Miles, the footman, who seemed rather comfortable with the prince.

While working on the dresses, Daffy had put the *King Titus* out of her mind. Unboxing royal wedding gowns, draping them over dress forms, and inspecting them for repairs was almost calming. But when she thought of what was wrapped on the bottom of her dressing room floor, she felt ill.

Gus finished his dinner rather quickly and left the dining hall. Daffy followed a few minutes later. As she started up the stairs, she heard Cranston bragging about carrying the *King Titus* down to the Queen's Library and she lost her battle with anxiety. The nasty beggar had moved in and settled down with a good book.

She'd not sleep a wink if worry lingered. It could be days before the chair was repaired and back in the library—if she and Gus even managed to accomplish such an impossible task. Hearing Cranston boast, she realized she and Gus needed a plan to keep Cranston out of the library.

To meet Gus, Daffy changed into jeans, a warm jumper, and her lined boots. A few minutes before nine, she grabbed her coat and scarf from the dressing room and eyed the corner to make sure the chair was still there. Then she hurried to the royal wing of the castle.

Prince Gus opened the door before she knocked. "This way." He led her down a side corridor where a single bookshelf sat against the wall. Gus pulled on a dark spine and the shelf snapped open.

"You're kidding."

"Nope." Gus took her hand as they started down a narrow, spiraling staircase.

"What is this?" The stone space was dark and cold, held together by rugged beams.

"The secret passageway, of course. Every castle has one. Didn't John and I ever show you?"

"I'd have remembered this."

Didn't John and I... Gus spoke as if she were one of *them*. Maybe in his mind, she was, at least when she was a girl. But she was *not* one of them. Which was why *My Life with the Prince* had no ending.

Launching from the last step, Gus shoved open a plain, slab door and together they stepped into the falling, twisting snow.

"Blimey, it's a blizzard." He kicked through the drifts, cutting a path toward the woods.

"Gus, where's Hemstead?"

He stopped short. "Blast, I keep forgetting him."

"Shouldn't you text him? Tell him to come?"

He shook his head. "Do we want him on this mission? If I'm lucky, he won't check on me. I told him I was going to turn in early. Besides, I have you to watch my back."

Did she? He made her sound like an intimate friend, but they barely knew each other as adults.

"Who will watch mine? I don't even know where we're going."

Gus pulled up, turning to her, the white lights of the grounds' lamps haloing his face. His breath billowed when he spoke.

"I will have your back." His breath mingled with hers. "You've got mine."

"Are you sure you trust me after Florida?"

Gus stepped back into the shadows and resumed his trek toward the trees. "Are you done throwing that in my face?"

"Almost."

His warm laugh defied the cold, thin-air night as he led her into the trees on the northern perimeter.

"Wait. Is this your big plan? Hide me in the dark forest? Maybe have your friend Ernst off me and then claim I'm on the lam with the *King Titus*?"

"You've quite an imagination."

"I blame my father. He was our bedtime storyteller." She startled and ducked low when something grabbed at her hair.

"Almost there, love."

The off-hand endearment caused Daffy's too-easy blush to

bloom, but Gus wouldn't know, thanks to the cover of night. And he'd not meant it, calling her *love* with such an affectionate tone. Probably didn't even realize he'd said it. But yet somehow it rested on her, in her, and filled her.

"And this is not the dark forest. It's just a lump of trees. The forest is a kilometer northwest. *Oomph*." Gus stumbled forward, taking Daffy with him. "Careful, something reached up and grabbed me." He swung around with a growl, his raised hand curled into a claw. "*A-hahaha!*"

Daffy screamed. Then ran. Blindly. Around trees. Into trees. Through trees. Low hanging limbs clutched at her hair. Ice crystals filled her lungs.

"Daffy, wait." Laughter chased her. "I was only joking. *Daff!*"

She broke from the woods into a clearing, tripping over one last snow-covered root, and landed face-first in the snow.

Gus knelt next to her. "Love, are you all right? Daff?" He brought her to her feet, his laugh muffled, but evident. "I am so sorry."

"No, you're not." She popped him in the chest. Hard, too. "You're laughing." She turned for the stone wall.

"Come on, that was funny." He followed, brushing snow from her coat. "I don't remember you scaring so easily."

"Well, I do." She stopped at the gate. "Are we doing this pub thing or not?" Her heart still thumped in her chest. What was he thinking? She punched his arm—just because.

He laughed, gripping his arm as if in pain. Though she was sure he couldn't feel a thing through his thick jacket. "Are we even now?"

"Maybe."

Gus opened the gate with a code and closed it behind him. When Daffy moved for the sidewalk, he caught her arm.

"You're covered in snow." He drew her closer, dusting off her shoulders, her hair, her nose, her eyes.

Through the dim street light, their gazes tangled. "Daffy, I—" He was hesitant, breathless, but intent. As if he truly had something to say. "I, um, I—" He stepped back. "We...we should go." He started down the amber-lit street. "Ernst. Waiting."

"Of course." He'd been going to kiss her. She knew it. Felt the desire that soaked the air between them.

Falling in step with him, hands in her coat pockets, she sorted her thoughts. Did she want him to kiss her? Yes. She couldn't deny the truth. But she must remember Thomas. She'd said yes to his proposal. Wore his ring.

She scoffed at the fairytale stories of Dalholm's magic love spells. That if one wanted to fall in love, one must go to Dalholm. But hadn't she fallen in love with Thomas here on a ski weekend? She did love him, didn't she?

Never mind. She'd said yes to his proposal. Thomas was a solid chap. She'd not be untrue to him. Wanting to kiss Gus was not the same as kissing him. Meanwhile, Gus was on a love hiatus. Any dalliance with romance was foolish and shortsighted.

"W-where are we going again?" She braced against the slippery downhill slope of the cobblestone avenue. Mum liked to say the hamlet itself could be part of the Royal Trust. Founded in 1074 by the Duke of Northton, much of the old world charm remained. At least in the Old Hamlet.

"The Belly of the Beast. Just off Wells Line."

Walking settled her down and her breathing returned to normal. They turned down the narrow lane. "It's as if we're in a snow globe."

"Yes, with the city lights and all the snow." He stopped short, facing her. "I wanted to kiss you back there."

His confession shook the snow globe and knocked her off-balance. "What?"

"I forgot myself for a moment. Forgot that you're engaged. Forgot I'm a confirmed bachelor for now."

"We should be careful. Mindful of our respective boundaries." Should she confess she wanted him to kiss her? When Gus stepped closer, desire bloomed again. Even through the cold, she could feel his warmth. What she couldn't feel was Thomas's ring.

"Agreed. Because Daffy, you're not a lass a man can kiss and forget. You deserve a bloke who can give you his heart. Not one who only wants one thing."

She warmed at his compliment. "Do you only want one thing?"

"From you? No. Not from anyone really. Never was one of those lads who could love them and leave them. But I'm alone now. My own commander, sailing through life by myself."

"Gus, don't you see what you're doing? Really?" Daffy risked touching him, placing her hands on his arms. "Letting an American heiress and an uppity Lauchtenland aristocrat dictate your life. You're letting their decisions define you. Don't let their choices steer you. Not only are you rejecting a chance at love, you're rejecting yourself."

"Rejecting myself? I'm *protecting* myself."

"Is that what it is? Sailing alone. Not trusting anyone with your heart, including yourself. Blimey, Gus, be honest. Any girl would be lucky, blessed to have you. Not just because you have a title and a crown. She'd be amazingly blessed by you." She poked his chest. "The man who lives in here."

"You don't hold back, do you?"

"Not when you're being stupid."

He stared past her head, his thoughts twisting behind his eyes. Had she gone too far? Said too much? But she'd only spoken the truth. He had to get over himself if he ever wanted a chance at happiness.

"Thank you," he said, tipping his head toward the bright light at the end of the lane. "Come on. Ernst. Waiting."

At the last establishment, Gus opened the door and stood aside for Daffy to enter. "Welcome to the Belly of the Beast."

The pub, with wide plank floors and hefty beams, was fragrant with a wood-burning fireplace. Almost every table was full, but no one looked up when the Lauchtenland prince darkened the doorway.

From behind the bar, a bear of a man with more girth than height leaned on his elbows and nodded as he listened to a skinny chap wearing a woolen ferry cap tell a tale.

Above the mirror, a sign read "Enter the Belly of the Beast with Sword in Hand."

"What does that mean?" Daffy tugged on Gus's sleeve and pointed to the sign.

"Whatever Ernst wants. Come on, over here."

CHAPTER ELEVEN

GUS

"Well, Prince." Ernst looked up from the bloke with the story and came around the bar, his stained apron barely covering his equally stained white shirt and faded black trousers. He'd braided his goatee tonight and Gus noticed when he walked, his feet spilled over the sides of his scuffed and battered leather shoes. "On a night. Beasts face beast."

The proprietor embraced Gus with no royal reservation. But that was his way. His version of respect. "And this?" He held Daffy by her shoulders. "A blue for the Blue." His cackle resonated in his chest. "Can't resist ladies."

"Ernst, this is Daffy Caron. She's part of the Royal Trust and setting up a historical wedding gown display at Hadsby. For the wedding ball. Daffy, this is Ernst, proprietor, and if he has a last name, I don't know it."

"Ernst of the pub, that's me." He pulled Daffy to his chest in an exuberant hug. "Nice to meet." Clapped his hand on Gus's back. "Sit. Pints! Fish and chips."

"We've had our dinner—" Daffy raised her voice over the pub's clamor.

"Don't waste your words. He won't listen." Gus held her chair, then sat next to her, facing the fire.

Should he just pretend he'd not confess what he confessed? What was he thinking? The whole kissing thing? He blamed the snow and the romance of the street lamps. He'd argued with himself as they trekked carefully down Centre Street, told himself to say nothing, then the moment they turned on Wells Line, out it came.

"I wanted to kiss you."

Worse, he still wanted to kiss her. He gazed down at her ring finger where a respectable diamond proclaimed "Off limits. She belongs to another."

Having been the chap left at the altar, then left for the man his betrothed still loved, he'd never move in on another lad's territory. He respected what that ring stood for.

Ernst returned, smiling, very pleased with himself. "Prince and a blue."

"A blue?" Daffy leaned close.

"A blue." The old man wiggled his eyebrows. "You. Girl. Love."

"Ernst, no. She's a friend."

"I work for the Royal Trust." Daffy rushed past Ernst's presumption despite the soft blush on her cheeks. "Gus believes you can help us with a sensitive project."

Betsy arrived with two foaming pints. "One and done, okay?" Gus peered up at her. "Listen to me, not your uncle. One pint only." He turned to Ernst. "I need a carpenter."

Before Ernst could answer, a couple of the blokes from two tables over moved in to shake his hand.

"Your Royalness. Welcome."

"Don't stay away."

"Good to see you, lads," Gus said, taking the first man's hand, then the next.

"Sorry for troubles, sir. Things sort out."

"Indeed they do. Oh, hello. Dylan, yes, of course I remember you. From the Youth League a few years back. How are you getting on?"

Meanwhile, Ernst excused himself to tend a customer. After a few more pleasantries, the lads trotted off and Gus returned his attention to Daffy.

"I'd forgotten how much I liked the cadence of the locals."

Daffy sipped from her glass, then stretched her hands toward the glow of the fire.

"Before you know it, you'll be doing it too."

"I'm not sure I understand the rules."

"There are no rules. Just say the necessary words and leave the rest." When she smiled, Gus sank a bit further into her charm.

"Ah, well. You. Popular. Here."

He laughed. "Less robotic and you've got it." He pointed to the ceiling beams. "Helped install it."

"Look at you." Her smile conveyed respect. "But you can't fix a chair?"

"*Ha.* A beam is nothing like repairing a chair where no one sees it was broken."

"Here we are." The feminine version of Ernst arrived with a large platter of fish and chips. She kissed Gus on the cheek, then Daffy, and hurried away.

"That was Stella, Ernst's wife." Gus regarded the overflowing platter. "Do they still think I'm Prince Pudgy?"

"Not if they have eyes." Daffy selected a small slice of fish. "This smells too good not to try."

He liked her cloaked compliment. Even approval. She didn't see him as the fat Gus-Gus prince. Just as a chap who might be worthy of a good woman. He wished he could see life through her eyes.

As he took some fish and chips for his plate, Hemstead texted.

Not again.

"Busted." He held up the screen for Daffy to see. "What's he doing, checking on me at nine-thirty? I told him I was going to bed."

"You know the castle has cameras everywhere outside."

"Right. I forgot."

Daffy ate while Gus text-groveled to his protection officer.

Just down at the Belly of the Beast with Daffy Caron. All is well. Home soon.

I'm coming down.

No need. I'll text when I'm back.

But he knew Hemstead would barge through the pub's heavy door before he finished his pint.

"Good?" Ernst returned and pulled round a chair. "Well? Whatcha?"

"Right, down to business." Gus exchanged a look with Daffy. "I'm looking for a craftsman. A furniture maker who's more an artisan than anything. We have a delicate repair. You know everyone in the Old Hamlet. Does anyone have those ancient carpentry skills? Could you introduce me?"

"Old Emmanuel. But..." Ernst tugged on his goatee. "Old as Methuselah. Ain't seen."

"He's a carpenter? A craftsman?"

"Best round. But..."

"Is he still alive?"

"Do'no. Lives up mountain. Two peaks above lodge." Ernst leaned back in his chair and bellowed toward the kitchen. "Stella? Old Emmanuel? Seen him?"

"Goodness." She matched his bellow. "Eight."

Ernst sat forward. "Eight years since, Yer Royal. Chance he's with Almighty."

"Can you find out? Or do you know of another skilled carpenter? This is *very* important and detailed work. Work done in the name of Her Majesty."

Gus typically loved the shorthand gait of the Dalholmian speech. But tonight, he wanted lengthy, clear answers. For Daffy. For the queen.

"Well, well. Everything high tech. Let me see." He tapped the side of his nose, as if he had some mystical powers. "Word out."

"What if you can't find this Emmanuel?" Daffy said. "Do you have any other names?"

Ernst stood, indicating he was done talking. "Another pint?"

"No, thanks. Ernst, when do you think we'll hear about this chap?"

Ernst pressed his thumb to his ear. "Ring. Tell you."

Gus jotted down his number and swore the man to secrecy—though he had no doubts. When Ernst walked away, Gus slumped forward, his forearms resting on the worn tabletop. "I'm not too hopeful."

"To be honest, I'm not either, but he's our only lead." Daffy cupped her slender hand around her cold mug. "If we don't hear anything by the end of the week, we have to tell the Trust."

Gus shoved a hot, greasy fry in his mouth. "End of the week. We'll give it until then."

"Why does Ernst call you Yer Royalness?"

"He also calls me Your Magistrate, Prince Sir, Prince Royalness." Gus couldn't hold back a grin. "His way of being my friend, as well as honoring the title to which I was born."

"Do you ever resent it? Being a royal?"

"Not really. I don't know anything else. I sometimes envy Prince Harry, married to an American, getting a taste of another life."

"What about King Nathaniel and Prince Stephen? They married Americans, but their wives dedicated their lives to Brighton."

"Susanna had no choice. She married the king. Stephen's wife was an heiress, already very global."

"Like Coral?"

"Yes, like Coral."

"Would you have gone to America with her?"

"We talked about it. She had a business, of course, but she understood I had royal obligations. We'd planned for her to work out of the Port Fressa office with trips to New York as needed. But that's all— Enough about me. What about you? Ever want to do something different? Achieve the unachievable?"

"Doesn't everyone?" She buried her answer in a gulp of beer. "Does it bother you? Being teased in headlines?"

"You're full of questions."

Daffy propped her chin in her hand, a contemplative expression softening the curve of her face. "I remember the year you came home from school because the lads teased you so much. Fifth grade, I think."

"Brock Chancellor saw my stash of junk food and started calling me Gus-Gus."

"And John didn't defend you."

"He tried, but even princes want to be accepted by their peers."

"What made you finally ask to come home?"

Gus paused, recalling the scene he considered the worst in his life. Little had he known back then what the future held for him.

"We were coming out of evening vespers when Brock and his mates called me over. This was spring term, and for some reason, they'd let up on the teasing after Christmas."

"Can I ask why you had so much junk food?"

"Why does anyone have chocolate and biscuits and sweets? For comfort. I never liked boarding school, Daffy. If I ever have children—and that's a big if—I won't send them away. I missed Mum and Dad." He raised his gaze to hers. "You."

The color on her cheeks deepened. "What happened when Brock called you over?"

"This movie started playing on the side of the building. Me. My face...on the body of Gus-Gus, the fat mouse in the animated *Cinderella*. Brock's older brother was a film student. The scene was the one where Gus had all the corn in his hands and couldn't get away from the cat."

"What? You're serious?"

"Everyone laughed. *Ha, ha*, Gus-Gus the fat prince." His smile was more of a grimace. "The worst part was John laughing with them."

"Want me to slap him for you?"

"Would you?" He sat back, shoving his pint aside. "Mum brought me home the next year. We tried to keep it quiet, but the news went on about me having issues, raising questions about my intelligence."

"I remember."

"Yes. We played a lot of video games together, didn't we?" His eyes warmed at the memory.

"We did." Daffy finished her pint and watched the fire. "I never saw you as Prince Pudgy. You were always...my friend."

"I was really upset when the new security measures changed your privileges. I begged Mum to make an exception, but she claimed she must adhere to the new protocol."

Daffy's soft smile communicated something he couldn't understand. "I hated it too. But I think the queen did what she thought was best."

Silence stretched between them for a few moments, broken only by the sounds of the fire popping and a burnt log cracking. Gus felt completely and utterly safe. At peace. Home. As if all the people surrounding them formed a barricade, sheltering him, and Daffy, from the outside world, allowing him to just be who he was on the inside.

"So who was your childhood nemesis?" Gus's question pulled her gaze to his. "Wait. Let me guess. You didn't have one."

Daffy shook her head. "No, not really, but when I was ten and banned from the upstairs, that was really, really hard. I felt like I was being punished for something I didn't... Well, whatever."

"I'm sorry. I never really considered it from your side. Did the queen ever speak to you about it? Tell you why?"

She made a face and shook her head. "No."

Gus waited, sensing there was more. Daffy traced the grain of the table, avoiding Gus's intense gaze. "The pain of it stayed with me for a long time. I... I'd lost my best friend. I thought you all were my friends, like family really."

Her lips twisted around her confession, and though she tried to smile and bat them away, tears collected in her eyes.

"Daffy, I'm so sorry." He smiled. "I've been saying that a lot lately. Sorry."

"Either way, all of *that* was a long time ago. We've grown up. Moved on."

Hemstead crashed through the pub door. Ah, there he was. Slower than Gus imagined. He stalked through the tables filled with patrons and, with a determined scowl, sat in the nearest chair, his steely eyes pinned on Gus.

"Something tells me I won't be sneaking out alone again."

Daffy covered her laugh with her hand. "Well, give the chap a break. It's his job to mind you."

"*Mind me*? I'm not two."

"But you are a royal. And that changes things."

"It always does." Gus closed his eyes and sighed. Shifted his shoulders, as if settling a weight on them again. "Shall we go?"

They waved goodbye to Ernst and Betsy and the lads lingering at the tables, motioned for Hemstead to follow, and stepped into the cold. The storm had passed, and the northern stars spread across the night sky.

"Up in the mountains, you can see twice as many stars." Gus crossed over to Canal Street and leaned on the railing to overlook the quay. Hemstead stood a few feet away.

"I know." Daffy joined him, shivering, folding her arms over her torso. "I came up here with friends to ski two years ago. Broke my ankle. Haven't tried since."

"Ankle breaks are the worst." He put his arm around her and turned her slightly to the south, pointing. "Can you see the Hand of God?"

"The cleft in the cliff?" She brushed her hair away from her face. "Too dark."

"Not if you look just right. The rocks reflect the light. See?" He pointed again, telling her to follow the line of his arm.

Daffy squinted. "I'm not sure. Is it there?" She pointed in the direction of the cleft.

Gus stepped in closer. Too close. But just this once he wanted to feel like he was her man. He was letting Dalholm's spell cloud his judgment. "That's it. Ever climb up?"

"I haven't. Too high."

"We'll climb sometime. I can lead you up. Can your ankle handle a steep climb?"

"I think so. It hurts still from time to time, but it's probably more in my head than my bones."

"Can I ask you a personal question?" Gus drew his arms to himself and leaned on the railing. From the corner of his eye, he could see Hemstead staring out over the channel. "Why Thomas? What made you pick him?"

"Why does anyone pick another person to love?" she said. "We get on well. Started meeting up at the pub. Ran into him at church one Sunday. Then he suggested a movie night at his flat and things took off from there. He's sweet and funny, talented and smart."

"And?"

"And what?" He couldn't make out her expression in the shadows of the amber street lamps.

"Is that enough?" The dark made it easy to ask questions one wouldn't pursue in the light.

"Shouldn't it be? Why'd you pick Coral? Or Lady Robbi?"

"Robbi and I were both on the rebound when we saw each other at a party. We were what we needed in the moment. I got carried away and proposed. But Coral? She was a different story." And one he wasn't ready to share. "Do you love him? Thomas?"

"Yes, I suppose so." She turned for the street. "We should go. It's getting cold."

As they walked, Gus tucked his hands into his pockets, resisting the urge to reach for her. This *feeling* was getting a bit out of hand. But he'd get over the newness of her in a few days. Over the infatuation. In fact, maybe this meant he was more healed up than he realized.

"We're not very mushy, Thomas and me," she said through the quiet. "More practical. Especially him. But we're a good match."

They'd just arrived at the castle's front steps—no running through the woods and climbing secret stairwells to get back in—when she faced him.

"What happened?" Her question was straightforward. "Why do you let the press go on and on about how this amazing woman left you? How *two* amazing women dumped you. Why didn't you share your side of the story rather than letting the press tell theirs? Why did Coral leave?"

"Whoa, lass, there's about a thousand details in those few questions. First, with the press, what would I say?" He moved around her for the high, granite steps. "I didn't want to slam either

Coral or Robbi, and until a few months ago, I wasn't sure their assessment of me wasn't wrong."

"Of course they're wrong. Gus, tell them your side—the truth. In Florida, you said you wanted to be in command of your story. To tell it on your terms. Choose someone and tell it."

"I can't, Daffy. Robbi, yes. We knew we weren't right for one another. We'd rushed in. But Coral?" Talking about it dug up some residual anger. And he'd been feeling so free. Gus jogged up the steps and then swung around so fast he nearly knocked Daffy back. "I can't, Daffy, because I don't know why she left. I blooming don't know."

CHAPTER
TWELVE

DAFFY

By Friday evening, ten of the twenty-five gowns graced the Grand Gallery, their elegant trains flowing over the carpet like luminous rivers of ethereal dust across a red moon.

Lucy looked up from the hem she tacked into place, peeking through strands of her sandy-blonde hair falling from random hair clips.

"Done." She timbered to one side, tried to catch herself, and then crashed to the floor. "Every muscle in my neck is knotted. I need a massage. I hate to say it, Daff, but these gowns were not as cared for as we were led to believe. Two of them had stains—bad ones. The legendary Ilsa, grand dame of royal wedding gowns, was a fraud."

"Let's keep the truth to ourselves. Ilsa served the crown for fifty years." Upon inspection, each gown had something to be repaired or cleaned. A torn corner of lace. Missing pearl buttons. Scuff marks on some trains caused by careless tourists.

The veil for the *Queen Ambrosia* was missing. Daffy had had to call the office and sweet-talk Goody into searching for it. Of course, Goody told Mum, who called straightaway and wanted to know why Daffy hadn't noticed the missing inventory before she left.

"I know you don't mean it, Mum, but it sounds as if you're accusing me."

"Well…" Mum sighed. *"I suppose I am. But I know you'll sort it out. No worries."*

Easy for her to say. *No worries indeed.* And she still felt more like a daughter than a staff member. They'd work it out. Just took time. The next day Goody found the veil and drove it up Friday morning, then checked into the ski lodge for the weekend.

But Daffy wasn't here on vacation. She had a job to do, even if she struggled with wanting to live up to Mum's expectations—and fearing she wasn't.

Then there was the dread of the chair. She'd not seen much of Gus since Tuesday evening. He'd texted her one night from a local youth symphony concert.

> Help! ☺ The planner wants to use them for the ball. Says it will bring a sense of heart and community. While I'm very proud of the youngsters' accomplishments, and am a fan of community, they are not quite up to the task of a royal wedding ball.

> The first chair violinist shot her bow over her instrument and into the eye of the cello chap behind her. I am not kidding. P.S. Still no word from Ernst.

Last night she considered his youth symphony dilemma and texted a suggestion to place various quartets or quintets about the castle Friday night before the Saturday ball.

> You're a genius.

"Daffy, I can book in at Spa Delight at eleven tomorrow. For an hour." Lucy jumped to her feet. "Want to come? Please say we're not working. I could use a break."

"A spa day? You go ahead. I might go to Port Fressa for the weekend, see Thomas, and water my roses. I'm sure Ella forgot."

She'd also been pondering Gus's questions about her relationship with Thomas. Why she'd picked him. Did she love him?

Her answer sounded like she was choosing a good motor, not a husband. Not the man she loved so deeply she couldn't imagine her life without him. But why get lost in heady romance? More than one of her friends had crashed and burned on the island of *He's the Love of My Life.*

"Are you going to start wedding planning?" Lucy raised Daffy's left hand so that her engagement ring glinted in the light. "Are you excited? Have you looked at any wedding dresses? Besides these?"

"Haven't even thought about it." Which made an odd confession. "We probably should fix the date first."

"You're so fortunate, Daffy. I've only met Thomas a few times, but he seems fantastic. Good-looking, successful, funny. Has that dimple in his chin." She laughed behind her hand. "When *Finance Today* put him on the cover, I saved it. Hung it in my office. Don't be mad."

"Why would I be mad?"

"Because I have a pinup of your man?" Lucy shrugged with a question mark sort of expression.

"I'll tell him. He'll be thrilled."

"Oh, don't tell him it was me. I'll never be able to look him in the eye. I read that journal every month."

"A financial journal? You're a curator."

"Yes, but I don't want to be stupid with my money. Anyway, Thomas was refreshing compared to their usual covers. Some old bloke with thin hair and cigar-stained teeth." She sighed again and leaned on the gallery railing. "Funny how a few hundred million dollars can turn a frog into a prince."

Daffy laughed. "You're punchy. Go downstairs and eat. Make your spa appointment. I'll see you back here Monday morning. Unless you want a movie night. Then ring me." She collected her things and started for her suite. "I'll be down for some soup."

Before he'd taken off for the weekend, Chef Charles announced the kitchen was stocked with leftovers, soups, and sandwich fixings, along with a fresh loaf of bread and scones. Daffy already imagined a bowl of his amazing wild rice and chicken soup with a slice of warm, buttered bread.

After storing her tools and kit, she collapsed on the love seat in her suite's lounge and closed her eyes, just for a moment. She kicked off her shoes. Removed her jacket. Reached for a pillow to prop under her head.

But instead of relaxing, she rehearsed next week's schedule. Inventorying the remaining dresses, calculating how much work needed to be done to set them up. The newer ones wouldn't require much tending, so the task would go quicker in the end.

Then there was the chair. Daffy bolted upright. What if Ernst didn't come through? She'd need to find another way. Take charge. Mum gave her the dickens for a missing wedding veil. One she'd never seen or touched. What would she say about the chair being destroyed while she'd watched?

It will be all right. It will be all right.

Would she really mind a life in the tower, surviving on bread and water? She'd lose those few stubborn pounds from Christmas. Maybe they'd let her read books to pass the time.

She jumped when a text sounded from her slack's pocket. Let it be Gus. But, no, it was Thomas.

> We were at the pub, missing you. Decided to come up. Ski weekend. The lot of us. Please say you're free.

> Really? When?

> Now, actually.

> Now?

> I'm being spontaneous.

> I'll say you are.

She clutched her phone to her chest. Look at Thomas, trying to be more whimsical. More…romantic? He did say he was missing her. Daffy needed to step up her game.

> I can't ski but I'll be there for lunch and dinner.

A text shot in from Ella.

> Can I borrow your gear?

Yes. And water my roses.

I have been.

Honest? Thank you.

Okay I haven't but I'm sure they're fine.

This changed things. Lifted her mood. She was going to see Thomas, her fiancé. Goodness, she had a fiancé. She'd been working so hard she hadn't realized that she'd missed him too.

Lucy texted next.

If you don't get down here, the soup will be gone. Cranston has gone back for another bowl and the skinny footman, Miles, has a wooden leg. Hurry.

Now she was awake.

"Evening, all." Daffy headed straight for the soup tureen, interrupting a lively debate over the North Dals, Northton's champion football team, and the Capitals, Port Fressa's challenging football team.

"Daffy." Cranston focused on her as she took a seat. "The *King Titus* is missing from the Queen's Library."

Her spoon clattered against her bowl. They never came up with a story for the ole butler. "What? Are you sure? I saw it there Monday evening. Miles, can you pass the butter?"

"I've looked and—"

"Am I late?" Gus to the rescue. "I hear there's leftover soup and warm bread. Miles, good to see you." He clapped his hand on the footman's shoulder.

The staff hurried to their feet. But Gus paid no mind and served himself. With a glance at Daffy, he chose the chair next to her.

"I called Ernst on my way down." He whispered the words as he slid into his seat. "He said to come to the pub tonight."

"Do you think he found this Emmanuel chap?"

"We shall see." Gus glanced around the table. "Did everyone have a good week? Were you discussing the match between the Port Fressa Capitals and the North Dals?"

"We were discussing the missing *King Titus* chair." Cranston peered at the prince over the rim of his wine glass. "It's not in the Queen's Library."

Here we go. Daffy all but buried her face in her bowl.

"The *King Titus*, of course. My apologies, Cranston, but I took the chair to my apartment for safekeeping until the ball. After all, I did find it in an unlocked library."

Daffy spewed her bite of soup.

"Yes, of course, but..." A very pale Cranston worked to collect himself. "No one told me the chair was moved. And I locked the library, sir." His lean cheeks began to redden. "Eventually."

"I'm sorry you weren't informed, Cranston. But Miss Caron and I will be looking after the chair. Thank you for your concern. Your devotion to your duty is admirable." Gus put on an HRH show. "I shall mention you to Her Majesty."

Cranston sat a little straighter. "Thank you, sir."

Daffy focused on her soup, her very delicious soup, controlling her smile and urge to shout, *"Brilliant!"*

CHAPTER
THIRTEEN

GUS

D affy met him by his apartment at nine o'clock. "Ready?"
He locked the door and tucked the key in his pocket.
Zipping up his anorak, he led her to the secret door.

"You were clever tonight. At dinner. Putting Cranston off."

"I couldn't very well tell him the truth, could I? Not without
trying to fix my mistake." He pulled on the book, the shelf opened,
and he tugged the chain of the bare bulb light. "Take my hand
again. The steps are wobbly. If one gives way, don't tumble with
me."

"But I will try and save you." She hovered close, her hand on
his shoulder, gripping his coat. "I'd rather tell the queen about the
chair than how I watched you fall headlong down a dark, secret
stairwell."

Gus activated the torchlight on his phone and waved it over the
steps, illuminating where the glow from the bulb stopped.

"Do you remember the legend of the tower in Brighton
Kingdom? How if a young man rang the Pembroke Chapel bell
at the beginning of the Christmas season, he must win the heart
of his true love by Christmas Eve and marry her Christmas
morn?"

"How could I forget? I cried when I heard the story in primary
school. How poor Prince Michael fell to his death when he slipped
on the stone steps, racing down to meet his true love. What a
horrid story to share with a bunch of eight-year-olds."

"At least the man died nobly. If I fall and burst my head open on the stone below, it will be because I'm sneaking off to meet a man about a chair." He stopped short, bracing his hand against the wall. "Blast, I forgot Hemstead again. Why can't I ever remember him?"

"Because you don't want to, Gus. Shall we go back?"

"Never." He grabbed her hand, liking the feel of her palm warm against his, and continued down the winding stairs. At the bottom, they burst out the hidden door and dashed across the snow-covered grounds toward the woods.

"Can't we go round by the road next time?" Daffy said, untangling her hair from a craggy, broken branch as they paused by the gate. "Out the front door? Down the steps?"

"And be seen? Or be stopped by Hemstead? Never."

"You're so busted, Prince Gus. *Forget*, my eye. You want to escape without him."

"You read me like a book. Let's go." He punched in the security code and escorted Daffy down Centre.

When she slipped on the cold cobblestone, he caught her by the arm, then linked his through to keep her upright. After all, it was the gentlemanly thing to do.

Besides, his old friend was easy to be around. Especially in the Old Hamlet and at Hadsby, which was like living in a pop-up fairytale. The ancient walls of the castle, the rows of quaint shops along cobblestone avenues, ancient street lamps, mentor-friends who spoke in shorthand and mysterious characters who came down out of the mountains. But only when they were called. Would Emmanuel require a pure heart or a drop of blood to accomplish the royal task?

"Do you think we should tell?" Daffy's words broke through his thoughts. "Even if we get the *Titus* repaired. The work should be documented. I pulled the chair's specifications from the Royal Trust files and there have been fixes over the centuries. There are pictures and notes. It was treated for woodworm in the late 1800s. And it seems there was new upholstery about the same time. Maybe the fabric isn't so hard to match after all."

"I'm of the camp what they don't know won't hurt them."

"Don't you mean won't hurt us?"

He laughed, but the sound was brittle. "Maybe. I'm willing to take the fall, but I'm not willing for you to be tangled up in my mistake."

"Too late." He glanced over at her. "We're in this together now, aren't we?"

"I suppose we are." And he was glad.

The trouble with Daffy was she got under his skin. No, it was something more. She seemed to fit with him. He woke up the past two mornings thinking of her. Not romantically, although he would consider...*anyway*, it was more as if he needed, wanted, to see her as soon as possible. And then his day would be right and good.

As they turned onto Wells Line, a sharp cracking fired through the chilled air. Daffy stopped and pulled back on his arm.

"What was that?"

"Ice in the channel." Gus nodded toward the end of the narrow lane. "The blocks floating down from Scandinavia have hit warmer water."

"Can we see it from up here? By the Canal Street barrier?"

"Too dark. But if we climb the Hand of God during the light, we can see miles of ice."

"No, thank you, sir. You go and text me pictures. I've seen the path leading around the cliff up to the cleft." She shivered.

"What if I held your hand?"

"As we both careen over the side?" Her eyes widened at the thought. "Very comforting."

He laughed. "Don't tell me you're afraid of heights."

"I won't. But I am. I can see it now, you helping me up the path. I slip, panic, grab your arm—and over we go, twisting and screaming, down to the rocks."

"Would it be so bad? I'd be the new legend—Prince Augustus of Lauchtenland fell to his death from the Northton Cliffs while holding the hand of his true love." The words came without hesitation. A wild, unanchored confession. A warm flush flowed up his neck to the top of his head. "Ha, ha, um, you know, so to speak."

He had to say something. Otherwise she'd think he was serious. Or perhaps not. But still. Any chance she didn't hear him? He stood at least a foot away. But he couldn't leave "true love" hanging out there, flapping in the unanswered breeze.

Gus leaned to see her face. Her composed expression communicated nothing.

"Let's not fall off the cliff," she said, low and sweet. "I don't want some eight-year-old lass a hundred years from now cry in class when the teacher relays our tragic story. Come on, we're late."

When they entered the Belly of the Beast, Ernst came from behind the bar, patting his broad stomach. "Prince. Sit. Sit. Pints."

"How about hot chocolate instead, Ernst?"

"Stella. Choc," Ernst hollered toward the kitchen. "Ice cracking." He pointed to Gus's chest.

"We heard." Gus held Daffy's chair. "Ernst, did you find this Emmanuel chap?"

Slipping off his coat, he warmed his hands by the fire, shoving—no, deleting—the "true love" comment from his *being*. Why would he say such a thing? Coral and Robbi had scrubbed him of romantic overtures, his verbal poetry, his princely charm. And why did Ernst point to his chest? Right where his heart lived? Weird old geezer.

Gus looked up as another booming crack penetrated the pub's thick plaster walls.

"Yes, Emmanuel." Ernst leaned over the table, arms barely able to fold over his expansive chest. But Stella called him, and Ernst toddled off, calling, "Wife number one."

Daffy made a face and laughed behind her hand. "What did that mean? I can't understand him. Do you think George Lucas visited Dalholm when he was dreaming up *Star Wars* and Yoda?"

"There is a rumor—"

"Hot choc." Ernst set down two large mugs of cocoa. "Emmanuel. Come."

"That's why we're here." Gus ignored the hot drink. "Where is he?"

Ernst pointed to the door. "There."

Gus stared, waiting, then checked with Daffy, who watched Ernst.

"Ernst, is the man invisible? Because I—"

The pub door opened and ashes from the fireplace stirred from the hearth. A man, dressed in a long, woolen anorak from another century and leather boots, stepped inside.

The pub's atmosphere sparked and shifted. Every bleary eye fixed on him. The clanking of dishes and glasses ceased. Even the music from the mounted speakers silenced.

"I'm looking for the prince." The man's voice filled the room as he removed his worn leather hat and shook snow from his boots.

"Welcome, carpenter." Ernst pointed toward Gus's table. "A choc?"

"That'd be fine." The gentleness in his answer matched his commanding size. He moved with sublime grace and his expression, while stern, was kindness itself. His eyes seemed to glow, making their own light. Gus imagined he walked down the mountain without a torch.

Gus stood, offering his hand, all the while resisting the urge to bow.

Emmanuel spoke first. "Your Royal Highness. I'm the carpenter, Emmanuel." He carried the scent of the high forest— snow and rain, sunshine and wind. He turned to Daffy, who was also on her feet. "You must be the princess."

"Me?" Her cheeks flamed with a quick blush. "No, I'm a curator with the Royal Trust. Daffodil Caron." She shook his hand. "We're so hoping you can help us. You see, a very valuable chair, the *King Titus*—"

"I know this chair. Seen it many times."

"Goodness, well, you see, the chair—" Daffy frowned. "You've seen the *King Titus*? Many times? It's only come out of storage twice in the last twenty-five years. Before that, I believe it never left Hadsby."

"And now it is in need of repair?"

She glanced at Gus, who felt her expression. This was no ordinary man. "Have you repaired it before?" she said.

"Indeed, I have."

"But our records indicate the last repairs were—"

"Daffy, let the man sit." Gus pulled out a chair. "We don't care about the past, do we? We care about *now*."

Emmanuel smiled at Gus, taking a seat as Ernst arrived with a mug. "Thank you, my friend. And how's Stella?"

"Kitchen. Sends love."

"Send mine in return." Emmanuel took a sip of hot chocolate. "So, tell me about the chair."

"I, um, sat on it and it cracked." Gus sank down to his chair and cupped his hands around his warm mug. "I wanted to see if I could fix the crack so I—"

Daffy interrupted his story. "He ignored me when I told him to get up and kept moving the chair."

"Then splat. On the floor," Gus said. "Me and the chair."

"I see." Emmanuel glanced about the pub. His attention landed on a man across the room. "Dean Hayden. His new wife is ill. Let me say hello." The carpenter carried his mug three tables over and sat with Dean, whose chin sat on his chest as he listened, occasionally bobbing his head and wiping his cheeks with the back of his hand.

"He's an odd duck." Gus gulped his cocoa. "Do you think he's coming back?"

"I don't know, but Dean seems to need him more than we do at the moment."

Gus watched, sorting through his impressions of this man. Sorting through his feelings for the woman across from him. He just needed to guard himself until the chair was fixed. Until she finished staging the gowns and returned to Port Fressa. And her fiancé. Never forget the fiancé.

The carpenter was another matter. His presence stirred something familiar in Gus. A desire for greatness. Not the kind that came with his birthright, but the kind he earned. The kind that came with doing what was right instead of what was expected of him. Greatness didn't require fame or fortune, but rather a life well lived. Of being honest, true, faithful. Which he would begin in earnest once the chair was repaired and back in the Queen's Library.

"I don't understand him." Gus shook his head. "But I like him."

"I was thinking the same thing. We can trust him, Gus." When she touched his arm, he covered her hand with his, liking that she used *we*. That he wasn't in this predicament alone. Though he should be.

But en garde, mate.

Moments later, Emmanuel patted the man on the shoulder and set his empty mug on the bar with a salute to Ernst. "Until."

Ernst raised his hand in salute. "Not so long."

He paused by Gus and Daffy's table. "I'll come tomorrow morning at eight. Gus, will you help me make the repair?"

"Yes, yes, of course. I'm not handy with these things, but I'll do what I can. I'm better at hoisting beams." He resisted the urge to point to the one he installed thirteen years ago. How much bragging could a man do when he only stood on a ladder holding one end along with four other chaps?

"Meet me at the workshop by the mews."

"Workshop. Mews. Check." How did Emmanuel know about the workshop?

"You and the princess have a good evening. Don't stay out late. Snow's coming. See you in the morning."

Daffy rose from her chair. "Sir, I'm not a…"

But Emmanuel had settled his hat on his head, paused by a red-faced man by the door who shoved him away, and then exited into the night.

"Guess I'll be up early. You'll cover for me?" Gus returned to his seat, reaching for his phone. "I can't tell Hemstead where I'm going."

"You don't need my help to escape him. But what should I say if he asks?"

"Tell him I'm outside. Be as vague as possible." He scanned his weather app. "Did Emmanuel say it was going to snow? Not according to my map. We're in a warming. Tomorrow will be sunshine with a high of ten Celsius."

"Maybe he means in the mountains? By the way, I won't be around in the afternoon. Thomas and my mates are coming up to ski."

Gus tucked his phone away as a bit of chill seemed to settle in his chest. *Double en garde, chap.* "You never said."

"He and Ella just texted this evening. I'm meeting them for lunch.

"You'll be glad to see your fiancé."

"Of course."

"We should go." Gus dropped his payment on the table. "How should I get the chair? I'd like to get it in the morning, only move it once. Will you be up?"

"I'll have to be, won't I? How will you get it to this workshop? What can I do to help?"

Gus assisted Daffy with her coat before pulling on his. "The garden carts. Golf carts really, but the groundskeepers use them for their work. I'll come to your room at seven. We'll take it down our staircase." He arched his brow, smiling. He couldn't help it. They had a secret staircase. "To the garage. But if you really want to help, the wedding ball is giving me fits. The planner emailed the final menu options this afternoon. It has everything on it from squid to tater tots. Now I ask you." Gus followed Daffy to the door. "Good night, Ernst."

"Royalness. Until."

"Squid? Tater tots? You're joking." Daffy tied on her scarf and stepped off the curb, crossing Wells Line.

Gus followed only to have her stop suddenly, whirl around to say something, and land in his arms. There they were face-to-face, their breath intermingling. A subtle tilt of his head, and his lips would touch hers.

"Daffy—"

"Gus, I—" She rested her hands on his chest. "What did you mean when you said—"

Just then her phone rang. Worst luck. A loud obnoxious jingle that pierced the night and killed the moment.

"It's Ella." Daffy stepped away and started up the lane. "Hello? So you're there? Everyone? Good, good. No, I'm too tired…for lunch… I have something to do in the morning."

Hands in his anorak pockets, Gus walked Wells Line a good five feet from Daffy. The waves of yearning for her were frustrating. Tempting his heart. As if he was daring himself to trust her.

But there was nothing honorable in flirting with an engaged woman. Thomas was a very fine fellow, offering her more than Gus could at the moment. He only had friendship to give, nothing more.

When she hung up with her sister, they walked Centre in silence. The air was thin and crisp, seasoned with a fresh chill.

"Everyone made it?" he said after a moment.

"Yes. I'll see them for lunch. Ella went by my place for ski gear and saw a box of my old things Mum found in the garage and dropped by my place. She was laughing at my worn, stuffed toys."

"Siblings," Gus said with a small laugh. "One time John and I—"

Daffy's phone beckoned with a text. "Thomas," she said, tucking her phone in her pocket. "I'll reply when we get to Hadsby. You were saying? You and John…"

"Daff, do you mind me asking? You're not going to the lodge? To be with Thomas?"

"No." She kicked through a lingering drift of snow. "I've been there, done that. Not hopping in bed with a chap until I'm sure. Until it's right."

"Okay. Respect. But he's your fiancé. Sounds like he's right to me. Is he okay with—"

"He didn't really have a choice, Gus. My decision. Which apparently didn't keep him from proposing."

"There you go. The whole cow and milk thing worked for you."

She stared at him through the muted street light, then laughed. "Did you just call me a cow?"

"No... I mean...yes, I suppose I did." He shook his head, daring to laugh with her. "But what I meant was, you set the boundaries, did it your way. If Thomas wanted you, he had to play on your pitch with your rules, not his own."

"Yes, but I was also terrified of being hurt again. The chap I dated at uni was supposed to propose the day we graduated. Instead he broke it off, and a month later moved in with someone else. I now know that I dodged a bullet, but at the time I was devastated."

"Your whole world crumbled. I know the feeling."

"I suppose you do. More than I."

While it seemed no one had endured a humiliation at his level, heartbreak was still heartbreak. Painful and dark, froth with doubts and questions about everything from worthiness to kissing skills.

Daffy reminded him he wasn't love's only walking wounded.

"So Thomas must wait."

"Thomas must wait." A soft silence lingered between them until Daffy spoke again. "Do you want me to look at the wedding ball menu for you? Though I'm not sure why. You've attended dozens of state dinners, royal balls, and garden parties. Just choose something similar. Choose what *you* and John love."

"Choose what I love?" Gus stopped under the corner street lamp and peered down at her. "What if I can't have what I love? Like hamburgers and French fries?" He retrieved his American accent.

"Are we still talking about menus?"

"Aren't we?" He knew he was baiting her as a way to deal with the jealousy he felt when Thomas texted.

"I feel like you're talking about Coral or Robbi."

He turned for the hill leading to the castle gate. "We're talking about a menu. Do you really think John or Holland would appreciate hamburgers and chips? That's what I'd choose."

"For a royal ball? Seriously? Gus, why are you being so weird?"

Weird. Because he felt things he didn't want to feel. "Though I could have an American buffet table. Coral and her husband will be there."

"What? Coral's coming?"

"Yes, she's a friend of Holland's. So is Robbi."

"Are you, I mean, how does—"

"Does it matter how I feel? Or what I want?" Gus dropped the fake accent and pressed the gate's security code. "This ball is not about me. It's about my brother and his bride."

"Tell me you're not going alone." She hurried ahead of him, walking backward up toward the stand of trees. "You must enter the ballroom with a stunning, amazing woman on your arm."

"More stunning and amazing than the two that got away?"

"They don't own the corner on amazing. There are plenty of women who shine as bright as they. Even more, because those women wouldn't have broken your heart."

Gus laughed. "Is that a true qualification, Daffy Caron?" He secured the gate behind them and started toward the trees. "But if I show up at this ball with a stunning, amazing woman, the press will go bonkers. She'll be in the news, hounded and scrutinized, having to defend herself. I'll repeatedly say, 'We're only friends,' which no one will believe. In the end, this amazing woman will feel slightly rejected, which isn't fair. Quite frankly, I'm not up for the drama. Watch out for the limbs and roots."

Well, he'd made a speech and was glad. He meant every word. It was a bit of a relief to summarize his love life with such passionate clarity. Why he was an affirmed bachelor for the time being. He'd preached to his own soul—which was needed.

"You have to move on sometime." Daffy stepped in front of him when they'd cleared the trees.

"Not by the wedding ball. I'll be fine. Dance the opening waltz with my aunt or granny then duck in the Blue Room for billiards with the boys."

"Now you're just being stubborn. Hiding won't be fair to John and Lady Holland. Besides, you need to speak to Coral. Ask her why she ran away. I mean, you said you didn't know."

"I was planning to avoid her."

"But she left for a reason. How can you—"

"Avoid a conversation of how worthless I am? Easy. How I

didn't make her happy? How I failed in some dramatic fashion? Enough for her to justify driving away from the abbey instead of toward it? How my humiliation was worth her...her, what? Freedom?"

"And what if she says something completely different? Something that gives you understanding. What if her reason has nothing to do with you?"

"Impossible. It had everything to do with me. If not, why did she not share her fears with me? Let me help? Be the husband I wanted to be? No, she found some fatal flaw, and if it's all the same to you, Daffy, and the rest of the world, including my family, I'd like to keep some of the dignity and self-worth I regained the past two years. I'll not have it trampled again so soon." He moved past her for the hidden, ivy covered door. "I'm going in. It's cold."

"What if it wasn't you? What if it was all about her?" Daffy was a stubborn lass, no?

He swung around. "The old 'It's not you, it's me' speech?"

"There's truth in that speech, cliché or not." Daffy fell in step with him, their feet splashing through muddy snow pockets. The groundskeepers would lay new sod before the ball, hoping to dry up the ground for guests to take long walks or play a game of bocce. "What if she realized she wasn't ready? Not worthy? Or that she'd be a foreigner in the royal family, living away from home. That must be daunting."

"Then she should've said so. And wasn't her readiness, worthiness, as you say, for me to decide? Not her? She left because I wasn't worthy, and if you don't mind, I'd like to end this conversation."

"What if I ask her?" Daffy's suggestion arrested him.

"Ask her what? Why she left? No, Daffy, leave it." His eyes watered with a sudden dash of emotions and he was glad for the dark stairwell.

"She told *Good Morning New York*. Why not your friend?" Daffy lit the torchlight on her phone, shining it on their feet.

"She told *Good Morning New York* nothing. I couldn't make heads or tails of what she said. Nor of what she told my family.

It's all very mysterious and cryptic. Frankly, I didn't want to know then and I'm not sure I want to know now."

"I watched it. She said something about—"

"Daffy, please. I'm asking as your friend. Leave it be."

"So you don't want to know? Really?"

"In this case ignorance is bliss. Better than being hurt. Besides, what good will it do? She's moved on. I've moved on. Let the past die."

He illuminated the steps with his phone's light and started up. The conversation soured his silly affection for Daffy and reminded him not to get caught up in the romance of the Old Hamlet, of Dalholm's lore of love. Romance was his Achilles' heel.

Despite his attraction to Daffy's forthright charms, he was not ready to move on. So, other than their mutual interest in the *King Titus*, they had no business hanging round together.

He bid her goodnight in the royal wing. "See you in the morning."

She smiled softly. "I'll be ready."

In his apartment bedroom, Gus slipped from his clothes then brushed his teeth. He fell into bed with nothing on his mind but sleep and his morning errand. Not true. Daffy was all over his thoughts. Her bold honesty irritated him. Why did he need to speak to Coral? To hear her justification for leaving? He didn't.

Gus snatched up the remote and powered on the telly. Then after a moment, clicked it off.

In the dark room, his gaze drifted toward the window where Emmanuel's predicted snow fell through the ethereal glow of the castle's lights.

A soft laugh vibrated through him. There was nothing predictable or usual about this trip to Hadsby. And oddly enough, Gus found the notion comforting.

CHAPTER
FOURTEEN

DAFFY

Midnight. And she still wasn't sleepy. Her thoughts churned and turned. All because of her conversation with Gus.

He was so close when he helped her on with her coat. His warmth whispered over her. When she all but ran into him, their eyes met, and for a moment she thought he was going to kiss her. Just the memory of it now made her lips tingle. She'd seen desire in his deep blues.

Then her phone rang. Worst luck. Ella. And what did he mean when he said he'd be like Prince Michael, falling to his death from the Northton Cliffs while holding the hand of his true love.

What true love? Did he mean her? She was the other person in the scenario. And why was he so touchy about Coral? Didn't he realize how amazing he was? He went on and on about the amazing women in his life but failed to recognize his own real worth.

Now the glowing blue digital clock on the other side of the room declared 1:00 a.m. Somewhere in her musings she'd drifted asleep only to be startled awake by her buzzing 6:30 a.m. alarm.

Just when she entered a sweet dream too. She wore an exquisite blue gown with a vast skirt and running through a field toward a golden sunset and the old cracked portico. A relic from another era located on the highest ground behind the castle. Once used as a lookout for invaders from the east.

Daffy sank down under the covers, eyes closed, and willed herself to return to the dream. But it was too late. The slumber fairy had vanished.

The alarm sounded again.

All right, all right.

She kicked out of bed and stumbled toward the bathroom. Gus would arrive soon. After a quick shower, she tugged on her best jeans and warmest jumper, fixed her hair in a ponytail, and brushed on a bit of makeup. Well, she didn't want to scare the poor lad.

After the chair was safely delivered to Emmanuel and his workshop, she'd do some paperwork before heading to the lodge for lunch. To her friends. To her fiancé. To her love.

After her uni boyfriend confession last night, she realized she might be holding back on Thomas. Afraid she'd get hurt. Well, she'd not pull a Prince Gus and refuse to trust.

Today, she'd be all Thomas's. She'd been too flirty with the prince. And frankly, he with her. Her lips had a lot of nerve tingling with the idea of a kiss from him.

Thomas was nothing like the dirtbag from uni. He was the opposite. Proposed in a public place with a very public demonstration of his love and devotion. That should be enough for her to trust him. For their relationship to work, she must go all in.

Fear of rejection was a prison, not a protector. She'd learned young that rejection was a part of life. From inside the walls of Perrigwynn Palace to the man she thought she'd marry.

Looking at you, Rex Childress. And you, Your Majesty, Queen Catherine II.

She'd loved them both. And they rejected her. But it's how she handled the rejection that really mattered.

Turned out, Rex was a pinhead, and Daffy was well rid of him. She didn't miss him at all. But the queen? She'd been like a favorite aunt. A friend, really. She'd invited Daffy to tea or to sit with her in her lounge. She would often reach out and stroke her hair. Then their relationship was over in the span of an afternoon and Daffy was banished.

Today…today she'd not let her past define her affection for Thomas. Or her future. She was going to break out some romance. Stop being the practical girlfriend, the practical couple, and say, "I love you."

In the meantime, there was the business of the chair. When Gus arrived, he slipped inside like some royal secret agent. "I heard voices down the corridor, but no one saw me."

"Let's pack this up and go." But he didn't move. Just stared at her for a long moment. "What?"

He blanched. "Nothing."

"Enough with that routine. Tell me." She patted her face. For first time, she could tell she wasn't blushing. "Is something amiss?"

"No, you just, I'm sorry I was curt with you last night."

"No, I was being pushy. I'm the one who should apologize. I just hate that you think you're worthless because of what Coral Winthrop did."

He smiled. "It warms my heart to hear you say it. And I don't think I'm entirely worthless. I've grown up a bit the last two years."

"If you talk to her I'm sure she'll say something you never imagined."

"Maybe. Shall we get the chair? Did you see it snowed last night?"

"Our carpenter is also a weatherman."

In the dressing room, Gus knelt beside the chair, which was still swathed in the pink blanket. "Hello, mate. Time to haul you to surgery."

Spreading out the blanket, they rearranged the pieces to make their task easier. There were two main pieces. The two right-side legs, and the rest of the chair. The tall, flat back of the chair had snapped from the seat rail but remained held in place by the fabric, which was untorn.

The back right leg was the worst. It snapped in half and broken away from the seat rail, which fractured a section of the back post, which now poked against the purple cloth. The front right leg was partially splintered and needed to be reattached to the base.

"What do you think?" Gus helped her rewrap the *Titus* in the blanket. "It doesn't look so bad, does it?"

"It doesn't look good, either. If it's not repaired properly, we won't have a choice but to confess. Keep an eye on this carpenter. Also, the chair needs to be covered with the blanket and a tarp. Do you know the condition of this workshop? The longer the chair is exposed to the elements, the more damage we risk. Be sure to lock the workshop when you're done."

"I'm not entirely an idiot, Daffy. I'll protect the chair."

"Sorry, I'm just nervous."

"Yeah, me too. I had a nightmare Mum surprised us and came up early for the ball. Ready?"

"Now I'll have the same nightmare." Daffy pulled on her coat and reached for a satchel. "Ready. Try not to bang the pieces about."

"What's in the case?"

"The chair specifications to help you and Emmanuel put it back together. It was last inspected with minor repairs in 1922." Daffy hovered next to him. "If we make it to wherever we're going without being seen, I'll kiss your muddy boots."

"My boots?" He arched his brow and gave a look. The kind that pinged her heart. "Surely you can do better."

"Ha ha. You know what I mean." Why did she say that? Of course she wouldn't kiss his boots or his lips. Not even his cheek.

Gus peeked out the suite door. "Coast is clear. To our secret stairs."

They'd have to walk across the Grand Gallery, but the dresses she and Lucy set up would act as frontline guards, hiding them from the view below.

They entered the hall with the blanket swinging between them like a hammock. Eyes forward, Daffy moved in time with the prince's long stride. Adrenaline turned her legs to jelly, but she pressed on and they slipped through the dresses without a word, then all but ran through the back half of the open gallery.

Now they were in the royal wing where no one but Stern and Hemstead entered, except the weekday maids.

"Where's Stern?" Daffy kept her voice low.

"Gone to see his sister in The Haskells."

"And Hemstead?"

"Breakfast. Oh, he gave me a ticking off this morning for sneaking away last night, but I told him I was working on a surprise for John, and he settled down."

"Yes, but did he believe you?"

"He growled, so I think so." He pulled on the book spine and the bookshelf door opened. They eased themselves down the narrow back stairwell, mindful of their priceless burden, but they went right toward the garage instead of left toward the door to the grounds.

Gus punched in another security code. Daffy stepped inside and stopped short, nearly causing Gus to lose his hold on the blanket.

"Oh my word." There were no less than one, two, three, four... twelve motors. "Who needs twelve cars?"

"People who like motors. Like Dad." Gus motioned to an old car just inside the doorway. "They're in order of year. That's the Starfire #89, built in '04. That's 1904. The manufacturer only made seven, so it's one of the rarest cars in the world. The very first one made is in the Grand Duchy of Hessenberg. Princess Regina found it in Meadowbluff's mews. Four are in museums. Two by private collectors. Dad bought this one from a billionaire getting divorced. He didn't want the true value to be known, so he sold it for one percent of its worth. And no, you can't have it for the Royal Trust."

"We will have it one day, you'll see. And don't forget the *Princess Louisa* wedding gown. It's a rare, priceless gem too. Because of the gown's designer and enduring style. The fashion world is still talking about it a hundred twenty years later."

"In centuries to come, some lass will be flying around Hadsby in a garden cart trying to find a skilled seamstress to repair her carelessness with the *Louisa*." Gus nodded back toward the cars, raising his eyebrow.

Daffy laughed. "Probably. In moments like these, I realize how much of history we don't see. Our sojourn through this life is so short. We only see a small slice of humanity."

"Let's pray we survive our slice." He stopped by a shiny, blue cart fitted with tracks instead of wheels and a bed in the back for hauling. They gentled the chair into the back then Gus trotted off for the keys.

"Here we go."

Into the dawning day, the cart rattled over the fresh snow, crashing down into hidden winter divots.

Daffy held on as he steered toward the mews, giving him a sideways glance, all too aware of how much she loved being on an adventure with him. Even if it involved a precious artifact.

Up and over a small hill, the row of white sheds in need of a spring sprucing appeared. The doors were closed except for the very last one from which emerged a tall, regal Emmanuel.

Daffy stiffened and gripped the satchel. Gus slowed the cart. The man had been nothing but kind when they met at the Belly of the Beast, but here in this moment, he seemed as majestic as the surrounding mountains.

"Emmanuel." Gus stopped the cart. "Thank you for coming. Truly."

"My pleasure. I'll help you carry the chair inside." As he passed by Daffy, he touched her shoulder, a rush of goodwill warming her. "Good to see you."

"We're so grateful."

The carpenter had exchanged his wool anorak for a wide work apron. He was leaner than she imagined, and muscled. A streak of morning light kissed his milk-white hair. And he was fragrant with a rich perfumed oil, like a powdery spice.

"On the workbench." Emmanuel motioned to the wide, clean table.

When they'd settled the chair, Daffy surveyed the shop, which was clean and airy, made of plaster walls and a wide board floor, furnished with two workbenches, a large tool cabinet, a sink, and coffee maker, and in the corner, a shiny, black potbelly stove.

"Can I ask how you got on the grounds? In this shop?" Gus said.

"I was granted permission a long time ago by the Family. Grab an apron, son." Emmanuel peeled back the blanket to inspect the damage. "Your King Titus I was quite a skilled furniture maker. I see a bit of him in you, Gus. Only he didn't let a broken heart derail him. He got back in the fight."

"I take it you are a student of history, Emmanuel. As well as a reader of modern newspapers."

"That, and then some. Now to the task at hand."

"I brought the specifications." Daffy lifted the satchel over her head and set it on the second workbench. "There are photos, details, materials, as well as an inventory of repairs."

Emmanuel inspected the chair's legs. "We can't use gray cedar since the tree is extinct, but ordinary cedar will do."

"How did it break?" Gus leaned to see what the carpenter saw.

"You sat in it," Daffy reminded him.

"I mean, *why* did it break?"

"Time. Even the old gray cedar becomes fragile. If it hadn't been you, Gus, the next person to sit in this chair would've come crashing down."

Gus gave Daffy an "I told you so face."

She smirked. *Whatever.*

Emmanuel set out a plan for the repair. Fix the legs with rod and glue—whatever that meant—and reattach to the seat base. He spoke with assured authority, so Daffy was more than satisfied the *King Titus* was in good hands.

"Well, I should go," she said. "Stand watch at the castle. I'll take the cart."

"I'll drive you." Gus walked her to the door. "Emmanuel, I'll be right back." He grabbed Daffy's arm and leaned close. "He's weird, right? Acting like he knew King Titus. Saying I was like him."

"Who cares? He has a solid plan to fix the chair. Also, you can't drive me and leave him alone with the chair. We trust him because of Ernst. But do we want to leave a priceless chair with him? I think not." She spied the keys in the ignition and sat behind the wheel. "Let me know how it's going."

"I'll text you to come get me."

"Can't." She offered him a small smile. "I'm going up to the lodge."

"How will I get back?"

"Walk. It's only a kilometer or two. Looks like our carpenter doesn't have a motor."

"He probably flew here. With his wings." Gus glanced over his shoulder. "I'll borrow a horse from the mews. The groom can retrieve my trusty steed later. John sent up a dozen for the ball weekend. I am a prince, you know, and princes ride horses."

"You really do read fairy tales, don't you?" She patted his chest. "Text me."

"Have fun at the lodge. Tell Thomas I said hello."

"I will." Their eyes met and her smile faded. Then she pressed the gas, and the cart fired over the cold, white ground toward Hadsby.

CHAPTER
FIFTEEN

DAFFY

L unch at the lodge was scrumptious. Roasted lamb, garlic
potatoes, asparagus with a hollandaise sauce, and warm,
sticky toffee pudding.

Now reclining in the lounge by a roaring fire, a fresh snow
falling, Daffy curled next to Thomas, her elbow brushing his,
relaxing, letting the burdens of the past week fall away.

Forget Gus and the chair. She was with her fiancé. Her friends.
She'd never taken the time—had the chance, really—to relish
being a bride-to-be. To enjoy the idea of Thomas being her man
for the rest of her life.

Her phone buzzed from its perch on the large coffee table.
Thomas reached for it while talking football with Rick.

It was Lucy raving about her massage and oh, they needed to
find a gown for the *Unknown Bride*.

Daffy replied.

> Check. Let's look this week. But let's make
> headway on the existing gowns first.

If need be, the *Unknown Bride* could be fitted with a gown
from Mum's closet. Although, according to tradition, the dress
should be special, symbolizing all future brides. Representing the
hope of love. Preferably, the gown needed a story.

Daffy wasn't sure when the tradition started, but somewhere

through the generations, a special frock was staged during an upcoming royal wedding. Perhaps to give hope to the young lasses longing for a match. Maybe as a way to celebrate the future princess. In the twentieth century, the dress, whatever color or fashion, started going to a deserving woman. It was the equivalent of a royal medal.

After Princess Catherine II married Edric, the Duke of Connought, the *Unknown Bride* was given to a staff member who'd recently become engaged.

Queen Catherine's mum gave her *Unknown Bride* gown to one of her maids to wear at her wedding reception when she married Prince Rein IV.

A memory of the queen flashed through Daffy's mind. The day she found ten-year-old Daffy in her dressing room wearing the blue dress. She squeezed her eyes shut to fade the scene. The queen had been so angry…

"Daffy, are you hearing this?" Rick stretched across the table to tap her foot.

"What? Yes. No. What's going on?" She glanced to where Rick pointed. To Marlow, who told an animated story.

"I'm in the ski lift, you see, and in the distance is this, this pink *thing* sticking out of the snow, flailing." He demonstrated by flopping his arms and body about. "As we glide over I realize it's Blinky, crashed into a snow drift headfirst, her pink ski suit legs sticking straight in the air."

"What?" Daffy turned to her friend. "Are you all right?"

Marlow concluded his story. "From the ski lift it looked just as if a giant rabbit had swallowed cotton candy."

The gang, including Blinky, laughed and toasted her Olympic-level blunder.

"But are you all right, Blink?" Daffy stretched around Thomas to touch her arm.

She was being such a sport, but being the brunt of a joke wasn't always fun.

"Oh gosh, of course." She looked up at Thomas. "I had my hero. He rescued me."

Daffy peered at him. He was blushing. "Just a friend helping a friend," he said.

"You're a good friend, darling." Daffy rubbed her hand over his back, but he didn't look at her.

He wasn't usually so shy with praise, but then he'd never been called a hero before either. Not that she was aware of.

Tonya and Kayle announced their craving for hot chocolate, which sounded good, so Daffy joined in the order. So far, she'd not had much time alone with Thomas. The whole lot wanted to hang together. Gus's inquiry surfaced.

"You're not going to the lodge? To be with him?"

Maybe it was time she took their relationship to the next level. She had his ring. His promise.

"Anyone for more skiing?" Frank glanced at the lads. "Jones? Albert?"

"I'll go." Ella rose to her feet.

"Not me." Leslie Ann sank into her chair, eyes closed. "I'm beat. This piece I'm doing on the queen—"

"We know." Everyone. In unison.

Leslie Ann didn't even open her eyes, but gave them her best snarl. The idea of more skiing led to talk of dinner, followed by the Sunday-morning departure time.

Thomas roped his arm around Daffy and nuzzled her hair, his breath hot on her skin. "What do you think about staying with me tonight?"

She twisted his ring about her finger. "I was thinking maybe I could."

He pressed his lips to her cheek. "I was hoping so."

She searched his eyes. For what she wasn't sure. A hint of his heart. An "I love you."

"Thomas, I know you proposed, but why do you think we're not very, well, verbal? We've only said 'I love—'"

"Did you tell her?" Blinky moved from her spot on the other side of Thomas and plopped on the center table. "Daff, I can get you a great deal for your wedding and reception at Saldings on the Waterfront."

"Saldings?" Very fancy. Very pricey. "We've not really talked about it. We haven't even set a date let alone a budget."

"Blink said if we book now for October we'll get half off." Thomas pulled his arm from around her shoulders and leaned toward the woman in the pink suit with bright blue eye shadow. "She said she'd go with me since you're working. Unless you can get away."

"We can send you tons of pictures. Tom said an October wedding would be perfect."

Tom? Did she mean Thomas? No one ever called him Tom. Not without being corrected. "I've been to Saldings. I know it's beautiful, but I want to get married in our church. We can have the reception there I suppose."

"But Saldings, babe. Imagine the wedding photographs."

"Look, let us talk to her." Blinky patted Daffy's knee. "We'll get back to you."

Us? We? Since when was Blinky in the middle of this relationship?

"October seems perfect, Daffy darling." Forgive her but Thomas, er, Tom, sounded more like he was siding with Blinky than Daffy.

"I agree," she said. "October is a lovely month for a wedding."

"Good. I'll give you a full report." He pulled out his phone and picked a date to tour with Blinky.

This wasn't what she expected, but Blinky was a good friend. And Thomas liked to have things researched, scouted, and detailed. Really, when Daffy considered it, Blinky was doing her a favor.

The hot chocolates arrived and the room split. The lads gathered to talk more football, while the girls talked weddings.

"How's the famous dress display going?" Leslie Ann settled next to Daffy. "Can you get me a press pass?"

"You know I can't, Les. Go through the Chamber Office. And the dress display is beautiful. Thank you."

"But what about your wedding, Daffy? What are your plans?" Kayle's voice was ever sweet as she raised Daffy's ring hand. "I never got a good look the night he proposed. It's beautiful."

"Should be. He spent enough." The lot of them turned to Blinky, who'd squeezed in between Daffy and Thomas. She popped a handful of nuts into her mouth as her wide eyes regarded them.

"How do you know how much it cost?" Tonya spoke first.

"I might have been with him when he picked it out." Blink sank into the couch cushion. "Sorry, Daff, but he needed help."

"It's fine." She waved off the apology. "I think most guys need help with a ring. Just wish I'd known he was even thinking of proposing. When did he go shopping?"

"You mean you two never talked about marriage?" Kayle switched her surprise from Blinky to Daffy.

"Not really but I do like surprises." Daffy smiled. *See, I do like surprises.*

"Blink, what did he say about Daffy when you two went ring shopping?"

"How should I know?" She reached for her cocoa mug. "I can't remember a conversation we had two years ago." She froze, the mug still to her lips, then glanced away.

Daffy looked at the others then Blinky. What did she mean, two years ago? "Darling, you must be mistaken. Thomas and I have only been dating a year."

"Right, right." Blink nodded, her laugh breathless. "That's what I meant. A year. Two? *Pfbbt*, what was I thinking. I'm so bad with dates. Can't remember my own birthday."

"Blink, the other day I was trying to remember when we first met." Leslie Ann angled around Daffy. "Winter of our second year of A-levels?"

"What? And you're a reporter? We met on the first day of our first year, at orientation, and you know it. We ate lunch together. Oh, do you remember seeing Luke Jonas? He had on a blue shirt and—" She stopped, then yawned. "Look at the time. Who's ready for bed?"

"It's two-thirty." Leslie Ann pressed Blinky back in her seat. "Did you help him pick out this ring two years ago?" She used her telly presenter voice.

"Maybe." Blinky winced as she faced Daffy. "I'm sorry. I didn't mean to say anything."

"So far you haven't." Leslie Ann bulldozed right along. "Spill the deets."

"Les, leave her alone." Daffy elbowed her pushy friend. "Blinky, you don't have to tell me any details."

But shouldn't she? Two years ago Thomas dated someone else.

"It's not a big deal. Honestly." She looked toward Thomas, who'd gotten up to demonstrate a football move to the lads. "I mean, the man is gorgeous, right? With a great career and future. Who cares if he bought the ring two years ago?"

Ella joined the debate. "Two years ago he was dating Sorcha Davenport."

"Was he?" Blinky gulped her cocoa. "Hey, how about that time I ended up headfirst in a snowbank? What a sight."

"Thomas?" Daffy's tone stopped his demonstration. "Did you give me Sorcha's ring?"

"What?" He shot a glance at Blinky which told her everything. "Who said anything about Sorcha?"

"Me. My big mouth. I'm so sorry." Blinky reached for Daffy. "Oh, I forgot this part. She never saw it. She broke off with him before he could propose. Right, Thomas?"

Blinky thought she was digging herself out of the hole, but she was only going deeper and dragging Thomas down with her.

"Thomas?" Daffy pulled away from Blinky's grasp.

"Daff, love… Blink, move aside." He shoved in next to Daffy. "Leslie Ann, do you mind? Yes, I *have* had the ring for a while. But I—"

From the back of the sofa, Ella hovered between them. "Ella— you'll be my sister one day, but I don't need your nose in the situation right now."

"A while?" Daffy stiffened at Thomas's touch. "How long? Two years?"

"Something like that, yes." Thomas made a nervous reach for a bag of crisps from the bowl on the table. When he tore it open, fried potatoes flew in the air. "She never saw it. Never knew I had it." He bent to pick up the scattered crisps.

Rick's low whistle underlined the conversation. "Mate, what were you thinking?"

Daffy closed her eyes. Inhaled. Exhaled. "Why didn't you return it or sell it?"

"I told you Sorcha never saw it. Why dispose of a perfectly good ring when I didn't have to?" He held up Daffy's hand. "Darling, the ring is you. Perfect."

She pulled her hand away. Yes, the diamond, the setting were beautiful. But was she wrong to want him to be thinking of her when he'd selected it?

Most of her life she'd been ordinary. Average. Good at sports, but not great. Good in school, but not excellent. She had to work really hard for her high marks. Not the prettiest girl in the room but she could hold her own.

While her parents and family loved her, and she had a lot of stellar friends, her marriage proposal was to be special. About her. In that moment, she should be more than ordinary. She should be the girl who consumed her man's thoughts. The one he serenaded under a proverbial ivy-covered trellis. She didn't need fame or fortune, she just needed to be one man's chosen. His favorite. The girl he couldn't do without.

"I need to go." Daffy shrugged off Thomas's touch.

"Love, wait. Where are you going?" His hand slipped down her arm.

"Daffy, darling, don't blame him. This was my blunder." Blink pulled her around and, gripping her arms, pressed her forehead against Daffy's. "I wasn't thinking."

"But now I must." She wanted to escape the lounge, the watchful eyes, wanting nothing more than to end the three-way conversation with Thomas and Blinky. She needed to breathe.

"Daffy." Thomas refused to let her go, standing between her and her exit to the door. "Maybe I should've purchased a new ring."

"You can say that again." Thank you, Leslie Ann.

"But you, and only you, were on my mind when I proposed. I didn't think of Sorcha at all." He wagged his finger at Blink. "What do you mean outing me?"

Ella swatted at him. "What kind of man gives his girl a ring he bought for someone else?"

"If you must know, the ring was darned expensive. I couldn't return it and I didn't want to sell it. I'd lose a quarter or more of the value." Thomas's repentant countenance turned to one of defense. "What's the quarrel here? Albert, help me out. You're a shrink."

"You are on your own, mate. Daffy, I'm available to talk."

Thomas flared to his defense, a growl in his voice. "If she talks to anyone, it should be me."

"You're the one who gave her another girl's ring," Tonya said.

Around, around, around they went. Daffy sank beneath the weight of it all just waiting for her moment of escape.

"All right, enough." She raised her voice and hands to silence the banter. "This is between Thomas and me."

"Hello, what's happening here?" The entire lot jumped to their feet as a smiling Prince Gus leaned on his skis and into the conversation. "Sounds like a good old-fashioned row."

"Your Royal Highness." Ella curtsied, as did Leslie Ann, Blinky, Tonya, and Kayle. The men bobbed with a curt bow.

Daffy locked eyes with him. What was he doing here? What about the chair? Was it fixed already? Oh, who cared? She was glad to see him. Happy he interrupted the debate.

"Ella, good to see you." Gus winked at Daffy, and the tension in her middle over the ring eased. Well, wasn't he pouring out his princely charm? "Are you missing Florida as much as Daffy and I?"

Daffy and I? Oh, he was definitely having fun at everyone's expense. When he peered at her again, the bothersome blush crept across her face.

"I am." Ella grinned. "Very much."

"Me too." Leslie Ann pushed forward with one of her fake telly smiles. Which meant nothing but trouble. "Your Royal Highness, please join us."

"Thank you, Ms. Parker, but I thought I'd take a run down the slopes." He glanced at Thomas. "You're the fiancé, I believe."

"Thomas Dune, sir."

"Congratulations. You've a good one with this lass."

"Indeed." Thomas hooked Daffy into his chest with one arm.

"She's the best." Gus backed away from the exchange. "Nice to meet you all. I'd better hit the slopes while the light is still good."

When he'd left the lounge, the group collapsed in a collective hush. Daffy reached for her cocoa but the drink had gone cold. But she didn't mind. The prince had somehow come to her rescue. She still needed to sort out the ring business, but Gus's appearing helped de-escalated the situation.

"He's right." Leslie Ann moved to the edge of the lounge area, her gaze following the prince's path. "We're wasting a good afternoon of skiing. I think I'll go for another run myself."

"You said you didn't want to go," Jones said.

"I changed my mind." Leslie Ann picked up her ski jacket. "A final run will be breathtaking."

Right.

"Sit down," Daffy commanded her friend. "You're not fooling anyone. Leave the prince alone. Haven't you done enough damage?"

"I don't know what you're talking about." Leslie Ann tugged on her jacket and hat. "I'm going to ski—get some exercise. Ta-ta."

The woman left her no choice. Daffy fired off the couch and launched from the center table like Superwoman. She flew over the adjacent couch and landed on Leslie Ann like a duck on a June bug. They crashed to the lodge floor with a resounding thud.

"Get off me." Leslie Ann kicked and squirmed, struggling against Daffy's grip.

"Leave. Him. Alone."

Leslie Ann huffed and puffed, her face a deep red. "I *must*...get an interview... There's still a story... I'm the one to get it. Why did Coral Winthrop leave him...at the altar? Nothing on *Good Morning New York*...went on and on about God. Good grief, we get it. Jesus saves." She gave Daffy a final push but Daffy's strength prevailed. "Let me go! How much do you weigh?"

"Daffy, get up. People are staring." Thomas lifted her to her feet while Jones and Rick aided Leslie Ann.

"I thought you're my friend." She straightened her jacket and smoothed her hair.

"Yeah, well you started this in Florida. You promised to leave me out of your shenanigans."

"How am I including you? I saw him for myself."

"Les, if you ever want an in-depth sit down with Her Majesty or any of the Family, you'd better respect protocol." Daffy brushed her hair away from her face. "When and *if* Prince Gus ever wants to talk about his breakups, don't you think he'll choose a presenter he trusts? Who lets him ski without being hounded? You chasing him down the trail—'Hello, Your Royal Highness, *yoo hoo*, a word? Why did Coral Winthrop leave you at the altar?'—won't get you what you want."

"I'm aghast. Insulted. When have you ever heard me say '*yoo hoo*?'"

"Daff." Thomas pulled her close, touching her face as if she had a fever. "Darling, you're flushed. You need to sit down. Maybe take a walk outside."

"She's fine, Thomas. That's her Prince Gus blush. Happens whenever he's around. That's how I figured out he was in Florida." Leslie Ann ran over to the window and stared toward the slopes.

"What do you mean she blushes when he's around?" Thomas said.

"It's nothing. A childhood tic." Daffy reached for her coat and kissed her sister on the cheek. "Love you all, but I'm tired. Leslie Ann, leave the prince alone."

Her mates uttered low goodbyes followed by a soft, feminine "Love yous."

"Wait, Daffy." Thomas caught her in the lobby. "You don't want to stay? Please, love, we can talk." He attempted to kiss her, as if a kiss made everything fine between them. "And, you know, other things." He smiled and arched his brow. "Are you really upset about the ring?"

"I don't know. Maybe. I don't want to be but I need to think." She zipped on her coat, far removed from her earlier thoughts of going to the next level with Thomas.

"You're upset." Thomas took her scarf and tied it around her neck. "I wish you'd stay."

"I really am tired. And I don't want our first night together to be like this."

He drew her in for a hug. "Do I need to be worried about this blushing?"

"No more than I need to be worried about a ring you bought for another woman."

Or that he shopped with Blinky. Or that he wanted to tour their wedding venue with her. Deep down Daffy knew Blinky was just trying to help, but she felt confused and weary.

"Touché." Thomas stepped back. "I'll ring you later. Maybe we can meet in the Old Hamlet for dinner. Just the two of us."

She held his hands in hers. "Thomas, why did you propose?"

He shrugged. "Because we're good together."

"And you love me?"

"I know I don't say it much, but yes, I... I do."

"I love you too." She kissed him, her hand pressed to his chest. But when she pulled away, she could've sworn she felt nothing of his beating heart.

CHAPTER
SIXTEEN

GUS

"Where in blazes were you yesterday? Don't say the grounds—I looked." Hemstead fell into step with Gus as he headed down to the servants' hall breakfast. On Sundays, a local chef came from town to set out a brunch for those living on premises.

"Skiing."

"Your Highness, I need to be with you whenever and wherever you go."

"It was spur of the moment. I forgot."

How long was the protection officer going to buy that excuse? It was just he didn't want a *shadow* as he spied on Daffy. He'd finished the first stages of the chair repair with Emmanuel and, as he left the workshop, the snowy day had given way to a glorious, sunlit afternoon. The golden glints crowning the Highcrest ridge called to him.

Besides, he'd reckoned with something as he filled the splintered chair legs with putty then clamped them to dry—under Emmanuel's supervision. He was filled with Daffy. The sense of her, the idea of her.

He was becoming all too fond of his old friend. It was time for a dose of reality. Not the romantic, fairy-tale atmosphere of Dalholm. Seeing her with her mates, her *man*, would stop his nonsense.

To his surprise, he found her friends in the middle of a row while she sat by listening, looking bored and a bit put out.

"I don't think you forget, sir," Hemstead said. "I think you mean to ditch me."

Gus paused on the stairs. "In all honesty, yes. I rather liked not having anyone off my flank while in Florida."

"A dangerous move then, and even more so now."

"Why? Does the Crown have enemies?" Gus started down, inhaling the scent of warm scones.

"Everyone has enemies. Especially those in power."

"Rather grim look on life, Hem."

"I've been a protection officer for fifteen years, and I assure you that people like you have enemies." Hemstead followed Gus through the Grand Foyer, through the formal parlor, and around the hand-carved column to the downstairs doorway. "I understand you're comfortable in Dalholm. People know you and, for the most part, have let you be. But that's precisely when things go wrong. The hamlet has changed, sir. The New Hamlet is full of career-minded men and women wanting to make their mark. Greed has no gender, race, or creed. I am responsible for your safety. The protocol seems simple. Inform me when you want to take an excursion and I'll be ready in a moment."

"I will try." Gus scanned the servants' hall for Daffy, but her usual place at the table was empty. Did she stay with Thomas? Which was really none of his business, but if anyone asked, she didn't look or act like a woman in love.

In the hall, Cranston sat at the head of the table, reading his paper, along with two hall boys, the two groomers, one maid, and one footman—not Miles—and Lucy.

"Good morning." The staff stood as Gus made his way to the buffet. "Tell me there are plenty of scones left."

"Your Royal Highness," Cranston said. "Are you sure you want to continue dining with us? It's nothing to set a place in the Grand Dining Hall. I think the queen would prefer it."

Gus found the scones. "I, however, would not."

Filling his plate and pouring a cup of tea with plenty of cream, he chose a place across from Lucy.

"How are you?" He snapped open a starched cotton napkin.

She choked and swallowed. "G-good, Your Highness. And you?"

"Have you seen Ms. Caron?"

"This being her day off, she may have slept in."

"Something I wish I'd done."

Lucy smiled. "I'm an early riser, me. Can't sleep in. My mum never let us linger much past eight, even on holidays."

"Now that I think of it, neither did mine." Gus layered his scone with clotted cream and took a hearty bite.

"Your mum, the queen, woke you up in the morning?"

"Not always, but yes, quite often. She wanted us up and about, living life. 'You can sleep when you're dead,' she said."

"Goodness. That's exactly what my mum said." Lucy sat back, her eyes wide, a small giggle escaping. "She'll go bonkers when I tell her the queen said the same thing."

"Mums, eh?"

"Yes," Lucy said with an easy laugh. "Mums."

Hemstead sat two places down with a cup of tea and a plate of eggs and bacon. "What are your plans today, sir? With Stern gone to see his sister, you've no royal duties."

"I've a busy week ahead. I think I'll have a quiet day in my apartment. Maybe read or catch up on a show or two. I never watched telly in Florida."

"Why would you? You had the sun and the beach." Lucy seemed more relaxed with him now that their mums had something in common.

Hemstead brooded for a moment, his heavy brows creased. "About earlier, sir, I apologize for my tone. For scolding you."

"You're doing your job. Think nothing of it."

He sighed, the lines in his face easing. "If you should go out, please ring. I'll be there straightaway."

One by one the staff exited the hall, beginning with Cranston and ending with Lucy, until Gus sat alone.

But he didn't mind. The early March day was bright and blue with the sun falling through the windows. Taking his teacup to the row of double doors behind the dining table, he shoved them open and leaned against the frame. In the distance were the columns of the old portico. He and John used to try to scale those wide, round things only to fall back down to the cracked concrete foundation. The portico used to be a forward fortress, but the walls had crumbled. Now it was a nice place to see and look down on the world. Mum used to take afternoon tea there.

Overnight, most of the snow had melted, except for the stubborn drifts in the shade of the castle. Spring was desperately trying to make its mark on Dalholm.

The season of love. What was the old fable?

"...love blooms from the earth the same as flora and fauna. It perfumes the air... Expect a bit of fairy dust on your heart. Expect to fall in love."

Gus sipped his tea. Despite Daffy's accusation, he'd never been one for fairy tales. But love? He'd chased it hard. And it crushed him. But he'd not begrudge love to others. Like his brother. And Daffy. She deserved love. A passionate, devoted love. A man to cherish her. He stepped farther out and gazed toward Highcrest, barely catching sight of the lodge's rooftop.

Did she stay?

"I see the snow is melting." Daffy appeared next to him, her gentle presence as comforting as if she'd actually touched him. She'd freed her auburn tresses from their usual constraint, and the waves fell around her face and shoulders. She wore a thick pink jumper and jeans. "Please tell me there are scones."

"I believe so." He turned back inside and visually followed her to the buffet. "Lucy thought you'd slept in. I wondered if you'd stayed at the lodge."

Her reach for a plate froze, then released. "No. I came back. Right after we saw you, as a matter of fact." She looked back at him. "You seemed lost in thought when I came in."

"Was I?" Gus settled at the table, finishing his tea with a large gulp. "Ready for spring, I think. And to get this royal ball business finalized."

She eyed him as she sat in her usual spot. "Don't let Coral Winthrop's presence ruin your time with your brother, Gus. Years from now when you reminisce with him, or tell his children what his ball was like, you want to share good memories. Details. Not that you were lurking in a back room because a woman you loved two years ago danced a reel. She's not worth it. No one is. If you ask me, she'd respect you more for moving on than for stopping your life because she made a very bad choice. In twenty years' time you'll be happily married with—"

"From what crystal ball are you getting all of this?"

"—children of your own. Coral Winthrop will be a distant memory. And you know I'm right. No crystal ball needed."

"Have you forgotten the Blues are one of the most documented families in royal history? Being left at the blooming altar will quite literally go down in history. For crying out loud, you've details on a thousand-year-old chair."

"Not a thousand years' worth. Only about three hundred years."

"In this digital age, everything will be recorded, videoed, photographed, and stored until the age to come and then some. And Coral didn't make a bad choice, Daffy. Not for her."

"Then *how* she left. Very poor choice. She agrees. I did hear her say that on *Good Morning New York*." She spread a dollop of clotted cream on her scone. "How's the chair?"

Was it his imagination or was she becoming bolder, more forceful, in her opinions? About him?

"Fine. First phase done. Daffy, why do you care about me this way? About letting go and forgiveness?" Gus folded his napkin in half, then in quarters. "What's it to you?"

"Because I hate to see anyone give another person power over them. And you're my friend."

For which he was entirely grateful. "I've forgiven her."

"Have you?"

In a matter of minutes, Daffodil Caron had gone from lovely and demure to straight up irritating. "She has zero power over me."

"So dragging your feet on ball decisions and declaring your intention to hide all evening is entirely based on...what? Past experiences? Your disdain for the waltz? Your refusal to reel?"

"What about you? Does Thomas have power over you? You didn't look like a blushing bride-to-be last night. You looked bored. *Trapped*." Yes, that was the word. He'd fished for it all night. *Trapped*.

Her expression hardened. "I am not bored, nor trapped. I was rather upset by the argument."

"What was it about?"

"Nothing."

"An argument about nothing? Enough with that routine, Daffy." He pushed away from the table and returned his cup to the buffet. "But you don't have to tell me. I'm going up to Pontus Lake." He paused by the door. Did he ask? Seemed stupid to go to the lake alone and leave her *here* alone. But there were boundaries. On the other hand, she'd just declared their friendship. "Are you meeting Thomas today?"

She glanced over at him. "They all went home. Only came up for the day. Work and family obligations."

"Even Thomas?"

"Ella texted his car was the first to pull out this morning."

"Then would you like to go to the lake?"

She hesitated, finishing her scone. "Pontus?"

"Pontus."

"I've only been twice but I love that place." Daffy rummaged through a cupboard and produced a portable tote. "We'll need snacks."

She wrapped several scones in a napkin and dropped them in the canvas bag, then retrieved two bottles of water.

"I was feeling a bit out of sorts, wondering what to do with my day off. Even considered working. But this is better. How will we get there? Don't say horses. I don't ride. Not well, anyway."

"We'll take one of the carts. Best get our coats. The snow is melting, but the air is still like ice."

Fifteen minutes later he met her at their secret stairwell, remembering halfway down he didn't tell Hemstead. Before he started the cart, he shot the burly protection officer a text.

Visiting Pontus. No need to tag along, chap. Back soon.

CHAPTER
SEVENTEEN

DAFFY

"It's so beautiful here." Daffy snapped a picture of the serene Pontus Lake as it reflected the noon sunlight. She reclined against the stack of rocks smoothed by time and, for a moment, almost believed she was more than an ordinary girl.

From this vantage point, the castle grounds were clear with their rolling hills, rows of trees, patches of flower gardens with Hadsby, a stone fortress, rising above it all, keeping watch.

"Why didn't the queen tear down the eastern portico?" Daffy looked toward the tip of the column, shading her eyes with her hand. "What's it for?" The concrete structure with Greek columns was from the Middle Ages, maybe once used for plays or minstrels.

Next to her, Gus stretched out, eyes closed. "I'm not sure. Mum keeps threatening a family portrait there. But it was a forward lookout in the day. Even the ruins are historical really."

"A family portrait would be lovely there. At the right angle, everyone would seem to be walking on clouds."

"Maybe." Gus locked his hands behind his head and stretched out his long legs. He wore hiking boots with his jeans and faux-fur lined leather jacket. Every once in a while, he'd rake back his loose hair, only to have the wind blow it forward again.

Daffy watched the hair battle for a moment, lost in his presence, in everything that was Prince Augustus. Burnished highlights lit his hair, and his newly trimmed beard accentuated his strong jaw and firm chin. By the construct of his face and body, he was built to take a punch or two. Even emotional ones.

He was the poster boy for the classic Prince Charming. Maybe that's why he tried so hard at love. He was supposed to win.

"You're stronger than you know, Gus."

He shifted his eyes toward her while remaining in repose. "Are we resorting to clichés now?"

"I'm sorry if truths become clichés, but you're not weak. You're not a reject or—"

"There's a new word to add to my self-talk. Reject."

"Only if you add the word *not* in front of it." Daffy faced the water, savoring the breeze. "You know what I'm trying to say."

He patted her foot. "I know. Thank you. I'll bear it in mind."

"I guess it's none of my business."

"Don't friends help friends?"

"Why do I feel a boulder of advice coming my way?"

When she glanced back at him, he was smiling. The one that bedazzled the world. She breathed through the flutter floating through her.

"I'll say only this, Daffy." His smile disappeared as he sat up, propping his arms on his bent knees. "If you're not sure—wait. Be honest. Talk it out with Thomas. Coral and I never talked about whatever bothered her. I was just in go mode. Foot on the gas and driving toward our big fat royal wedding. Robbi and I talked… more like danced, around our feelings. We were afraid of being honest. She didn't want to hurt me. I didn't want to look the fool with another breakup. But then she ran into her ex and had no choice but to tell me she still loved him."

"I am honest with Thomas." The words *I think* hovered. She wasn't honest with him. Nor was he with her. She was sure. Blinky's revelation was proof.

"We should go up to the Hand of God." Gus stood, facing west, in the direction of the channel and the famous cutout in the rocks. "Then you'll really be on top of the world."

"You go. I'll cheer you from the quay."

"Are you really so afraid of heights?"

"Yes." Or sometimes just afraid. Of getting it wrong. Of being selfish. Of being too self-focused. Of believing she had a privilege or right when, in fact, she didn't.

"I'll hold your hand," he said.

"The queen won't thank either of us when I fall and take you with me."

Gus laughed. "I feel a challenge coming on. Get Daffy Caron to the Hand of God by next week or my name isn't His Royal Highness Prince Augustus Carwyn George."

When he was relaxed, truly himself, HRH Prince Gus was almost irresistible. Daffy was grateful for her coat and jumper which hid her tumultuous, traitorous heartbeat.

She blamed the hamlet. The romance of the mountain, the cliffs, the contrast of budding green meadows against blue skies. She blamed the wind, the snow, the shorthand speech of Ernst. It was as if all of Dalholm existed to charm and woo.

She'd not be duped into a fantasy. She had love. In Port Fressa. With Thomas. Who she first fell for in Dalholm. So there.

"I lied." Gus's words broke through her act of mental defiance, so low Daffy wasn't sure he meant her to hear. "About hating her. Coral. Most days I wonder if I'm still trying to fall out of love. How to untangle myself from what I'd planned...envisioned... with every part of my being."

Daffy rose from the rocks and stood next to Gus.

"I was completely and utterly in love." He continued, never looking at her, only toward the Hand of God. "I had zero reservations or qualms about what we were doing. I wanted no other woman and committed my life to hers. I was ready to speak the vows and 'therefore pledge thee my troth.'"

He recited the ancient words with sobriety.

"Then talk to her, Gus. You can't let this simmer. You have to hear her truth. Her reasons."

"Other than me being a reject?"

"Don't make me wash your mouth with soap."

His chuckle was low. "You and what army?"

"I don't know but I'll..." She grinned. "Hemstead."

"Blimey, you got me there. He'd love to punish me for leaving him behind." He'd sent a raging text while Daffy steered the cart over a concoction of soggy grass, melting snow, and muddy rocks. "Know what else?"

"Tell me."

"Coral didn't deserve the whacking she got in the press. She's a truly genuine, lovely, intelligent, witty woman. Caring."

"Which is why you fell in love. Why her leaving hurt."

"So, wise one, how do I move on from what I thought my life was going to be? How do I fall out of love with the expectation? How do I trust myself to love again?"

"If I knew those answers, I'd have my own TV show." She nudged his broad shoulder with hers. "But I'll say this. Just because it didn't work out doesn't mean you can't love her. As a friend. As someone who meant something to you once. Love is free, Gus. We can love whomever we want. We don't need to wait for them to love us back. It's powerful, really, when you think about it."

Gus dropped his arm about her shoulder. "Thomas is a lucky bloke. I won't deny it."

Silence fell. The kind that comes during contemplation. The kind that pulls truth from the soul. They both returned to their respective rocks. Then she said it. No preamble.

"They were arguing over my ring. Yesterday. When you came upon us." Daffy cradled her left hand on her lap. "Blinky let it slip that Thomas bought it two years ago for Sorcha, his former girlfriend."

"Does she have it out for you? How does 'He bought the ring for another lass' just slip out? She wanted to say it."

"You have to know Blink. She speaks first and thinks later. We're all used to her. She's a loyal friend, sweet and kind. Never means harm."

"How did she know Thomas bought it for someone else?"

"She was with him when he made the purchase."

"She was—" Gus put his hand to his ear and pretended to make a call. "Hello, Thomas, this is Prince Augustus. Buy your lass a new ring, mate, immediately. By royal command."

"Stop. It's fine." Daffy swatted his hand. "Thomas Dune is a practical man. If Sorcha never knew the ring existed, why return it? Or sell it for a loss?"

"Dune? Your married name will be Daffodil Dune? Sounds like a pseudonym for a romance author. One whose heroes are bare-chested on the covers."

She laughed. "You sound like my father."

"Doesn't he like your chap?"

"Well enough. But he wants grandchildren, so any man will do."

"Seriously?"

"Not the any man part. But most certainly on the grandchildren. He also wants his daughters in happy relationships." Daffy adjusted how she sat on the rock, but the cold and wet started to seep through her clothes. "He wants to stop worrying about us."

"He's a good father. Now, back to this ring. Why the row among your friends?"

"They thought he should've given me a new ring." Daffy touched the platinum shank with her thumb. "Thomas argued Sorcha never saw it. Didn't even know about it. So why not use it? It was expensive."

"The only person who matters is you. What do you think?" Gus said.

"I think—" If she were to script the perfect proposal—her perfect proposal—it would not include a ring purchased for another woman. "I think he meant well."

"You're letting him off. Come on, Daff. If I'd given Robbi the ring I'd chosen for Coral, what would you say?"

"I'd probably smack you upside the head. Your fiancée deserves a ring that represents how you feel about her. Perhaps a precious heirloom. A family jewel that represented love."

"What's different here then? With Thomas?"

She shrugged, tucking a strand of hair behind her ear. "I guess because—"

"You don't think you deserve a ring he bought just for you."

"What? It's not a matter of deserve. It's practical." She held up her hand. "You can't deny the ring is beautiful. And in twenty years, am I going to care Thomas first bought this ring for his ex-girlfriend? It'll be part of our family lore. A recurring joke. 'Hey, remember the time Dad gave you another woman's ring, Mum?'"

"I don't care about twenty years from now." Gus held her face in his hands. "What about now?"

Her eyes filled, blurring Gus's image, and she pulled away from him. "It's not the ring. I'm...scared. I don't know if...if I want to marry him. *Pledge my troth.* But decent chaps don't come along every month or even every year. I've had two boyfriends in my life. *Two.* Rex and Thomas. Five years in between."

"So you say yes to a *decent* bloke—even when you're afraid and unsure? Does that sound like a recipe for happiness?"

"But I *am* happy. If not, I should be. We can make it work. Lots of couples have doubts in the beginning."

"You need to talk to him. Tell him how you feel. Don't repeat my mistake." Gus scooted on to her rock and drew her close with a one-armed hug. Then he gently pressed a kiss to her forehead. For too brief a moment, a warmth, a sense of right-place, right-time enveloped her. "You deserve every dream in your heart, Daffy."

"Why? Why do I deserve that?" She pushed away from him. This...this...*thing* between them was getting out of hand.

"Because—" His palm brushed her cheek as he swept back her hair. "You're... I don't know..." He looked off toward the hills, a red tint shading his cheeks. "Lovely. In every sense of the word."

Lovely. Prince Gus declared her lovely. Okay, she'd deal with the *thing* between them later. For now, she'd to cling to his compliment.

Gus finally stood and offered his hand. "Feel like a walk along the shore? It's a bit of a climb down this way. You game?"

"You're blushing," she said, reaching for his hand. "Did you catch my disease?"

"I'm not blushing. It's the chill in the wind. The question is why you're *not* blushing. Are you so used to me already?" He laughed but the short burst never reached his eyes. "Because that would make me sad."

"You're either teasing me or flirting with me." Her voice remained a whisper, the words tossed away by a breeze.

"I am. I'm sorry." He released her hand and stepped away. She never felt so cold. "Come on," he said. "To the shore."

As they maneuvered the path down to the beach, Daffy Caron knew one thing for sure. Right here, right now, was exactly where she wanted to be.

"Should we start a contest to see who will go with Prince Gus to the wedding ball?"

–MADELINE AND HYACINTH LIVE!

"We expect to see the prince at the ball but not with anyone on his arm. He's still working his way back to romance."

–LESLIE ANN PARKER ON THE MORNING SHOW

CHAPTER
EIGHTEEN

GUS

B y Monday morning, he'd settled the wedding ball menu, all thanks to Daffy, who'd offered her suggestions Sunday evening via email.

She was just down the corridor, across the Grand Gallery, and down another passageway, but he couldn't see her. They exchanged emails as if miles apart. Seemed odd after being so honest during their lake outing.

But that was the nature of relationships. One needed to let them be. Breathe. And to always stay within the proper boundaries—especially if one was a royal. Daffy may have confessed her doubts about Thomas, but she still wore his ring. Secondhand ring, but there you have it.

The final menu was stellar. In place of squid or tater tots, the ball guests would dine on London broil, saddle of lamb, roasted goose, and wild salmon, along with an herb salad, creamed spinach, wild mushrooms and rice, and roasted baby vegetables.

For dessert, the Port Fressa parfait, a sherry trifle, and chocolate cake for John, since it was his favorite. There would be a fruit buffet with nuts, cheese, and sauces. To drink, wine and champagne from Lauchtenland's The Haskells many wineries, and a fountain flowing with a lemon-lime punch.

All the busywork had kept him from sorting through the excursion to Pontus Lake and the deep heart confessions between him and Daffy.

He'd never told anyone he still loved Coral. He wasn't certain he'd realized the truth until he said it out loud to Daffy. Or how difficult it was to untangle his feelings from their commitment.

He'd spent two years trying and failing. Yet once he confessed, he seemed less burdened. Then Daffy's advice, so on point, so unusual, helped him see everything in a new light.

"We can love whomever we want."

Gus could love Coral. Not like a husband, of course, but as someone he cared about. Past tense. Though it felt a bit like self-betrayal to care about someone who hurt him so deeply, he was actually free to love without expecting something in return.

Knock him over with a feather, but the idea was glorious.

"Did you sort out the menus?" Stern stood when Gus entered the office. "I was just going over your diary... Are you all right, Your Highness? You're..." He pulled a face. "Glowing."

"Glowing? That's something you say to a bride-to-be, Stern, like Lady Holland." Gus picked up his tablet and reviewed his calendar. "I had a good afternoon at the lake. Got some fresh air and sun. Where are we off to this morning? The Youth League? I'm eager to see the lads and lasses in a game of football or field hockey."

"The press will be there." Stern straightened his shoulders, his expression bland. "Reporters for the *News Leader*, the *Dalholm Daily*, *London Times*, *New York Times*, as well as several photographers, and social media outlets. The usual brood."

"Only questions about sports, Lauchtenland's children and what the Family hopes for the future. Nothing personal."

"Your brother's wedding?"

"Yes, they can ask about the wedding and the ball. Anything else, I won't answer." His Daffy-inspired glow gave him the courage to take command. Be who he wanted to be. "Also, I need to be back here by one o'clock. I've something to do."

Stern frowned. "It's not on your diary, sir."

"It's on *my* diary. Not yours. It's all on the level." *Sort of.*

"Yes, sir." Stern reached for his coat. "We should go down. Hemstead and the car are waiting."

"Prince Gus Tackled Big Tech in Dalholm. Today he tackled youth sports. Check out our footage of the prince on the pitch."

—THE NEWS LEADER MIDDAY UPDATE

The prince praises Lauchtenland youth. "Our future is bright." Also toured Smart Life's new facility. Brags on their ingenuity and initiatives. Believes Lauchtenland will become a leader and force in technology.

—@DALHOLM DAILY TWITTER

Prince Gus is lOOking good on the pitch today with Youth League members. Dressed in gray Armani slacks and white button-down, he won the day. Swipe up to see more photos. The last one shows his world-famous smile. You'll swoon, I promise.

—THE ROYAL BLUE EYE INSTAGRAM

"Sorry I'm late." Gus shed his coat and reached for the apron he'd used Saturday. The shop door was open, letting in the cold. But Emmanuel had stoked the potbelly stove with firewood and the hot glow from the firebox warmed the work space.

"Busy morning?"

"I visited the Youth League, then held a short presser. How did our legs turn out?"

"See for yourself." Emmanuel had removed them from the clamp and set them aside.

The putty had filled in the cracks and breaks, but both legs pretty much looked, well, broken.

"Please tell me we're going to refine these. Otherwise, the gig is up."

"All refining, or healing, comes in phases." Emmanuel set two small dowel rods on the workbench, along with the drill. "You can't expect phase one to look like the final product." He popped Gus gently on the arm. "Embrace the process with its pain and ugliness and you'll soon find yourself at a beautiful end."

The old man's words were jovial, almost spritely, but they hit Gus square. A flash of heat washed down his neck and back as their eyes met. Emmanuel wasn't talking about repairing the ancient chair.

"You'll appreciate this." The carpenter rotated the seat and pointed to an intricate carving. "Your ancestor's initials. He was only twenty-two when he conquered the Normans."

Gus leaned to see *THB1066* whittled in the base of the chair. He traced the lettering with his fingertip, his long-ago relative becoming a bit more real.

"I was just finishing uni at twenty-two and destined for the Royal Army." As a prince, he lived in splendor and privilege. His most taxing duty was deciding weekend plans.

"Titus was a brave, bold soul," Emmanuel said. "Loved well too. Like you. Now let's get to work."

Emmanuel explained the next phase, but all Gus could hear was Emmanuel's declaration, *"Loved well. Like you."* He should challenge the man. "How do you know me?" Yet deep down he wanted to believe he loved well. Or could love well. And not fail trying.

"Emmanuel, you seem to know a lot about old Titus. Almost as if you knew him. How do you know he loved well?"

"Ah, well, a man hears things."

"Still, you talk as if—"

Hemstead's text interrupted Gus's thought. Hashtag *trouble*.

Where are you?

On the grounds. All is well.

Where on the grounds?

Gus ignored the request for his location. He'd risk Hemstead's wrath to keep the condition of the chair a secret.

"Where were we?"

"Fixing the chair. We need to fortify the legs."

"I think you were about to tell me how you know so much about my ancestors."

"Let's just say I'm an old man."

Gus started to protest then laughed low. Why press the man? "It's a reason but not a good one."

"Time will reveal all, Gus. Time will reveal all. Now, we're going to use this drill…"

Gus listened and followed the carpenter's instruction, drilling into the first old leg so a dowel rod could be inserted for fortification. Then did the same with the second one.

When the task was completed, Emmanuel set them aside and walked Gus through mending the cracked seat. More putty and clamps.

"Can I ask you something, Emmanuel?" Gus straightened, gripping the putty knife, eyeing where he'd worked the bonding agent into the wood.

"Go."

"Do you think love is free? That one can choose to love, even if it's not returned? Did my grandfather the first King Titus, love freely? You seem to know so much. Tell me."

"Can I ask you something?"

Gus grinned. The old man was quick to turn the tables. "Go."

"Why do you ask?"

"A friend suggested I could love Coral, my ex-fiancée, even though she broke my heart. I assume you know her, at least of her."

"She ran out on you." Emmanuel's gaze was kind.

"Would you love her, forgive her, if you were me?" Gus stared at his putty knife, then applied more of the compound to the seat rail.

"Do you love her?"

"Not like before. I've had a whale of a time moving on, but I've gotten there. I think. I love what we were supposed to be." Gus rubbed his forehead with the back of his hand. "I just don't want to be anchored any longer to her past actions. Don't want to be clamped down the rest of my life." Gus shot a glance at the clamp that once held the chair legs together. Looked positively painful.

"So you're asking if the bonding agent of love can repair the crack in your heart?"

Gus sighed with a low laugh. "That's one metaphor for it."

"Choosing a love that keeps no record of wrong is highly admirable. A better option than love that keeps a tally. You'll always come out short on that road. While you're keeping a record of someone's wrongs, another body is keeping a record of yours. Love as a bonding agent is love as a healing agent."

"Then I should love her. As a friend. Forgive her? Even if she doesn't love me?" Gus applied another scoop of putty. "That will work?"

"Every time." Emmanuel declared Gus had puttied enough and pointed to the clamp. "Gently... Tighten the screw. We'll let it dry a couple of days. We'll have this chair in royal order by the first of next week."

"Just in time for the ball." Gus worked the clamp until the putty and chair bonded, then wiped away the excess. "Have you ever been hurt by someone you loved, Carpenter, but loved that person anyway?"

"Indeed, I have."

"And? Was it worth it?"

"Every single time."

CHAPTER NINETEEN

DAFFY

The week flew by...and Daffy whispered *Thank you* at the end of each day. Staging the dresses consumed her time and distracted her thoughts from Thomas, the dilemma of the ring, and a possible October wedding.

She'd called and texted him a lot this week, trying to get her heart fully on board, sending him pictures of her work to show him another side of herself. But last night's conversation was less than pleasant. He seemed rather rushed and on edge.

"Daffy, is something wrong? You've texted me ten times today. You've called every night."

"Just missing you. Can't I miss you—"

His soft sigh was sweet. "Of course. I miss you too."

But he was at dinner with his boss and a big client, so he rang off as soon as he could. If she'd known he'd had a big dinner, she wouldn't have called.

Then there was the prince. The conversation and laughter from their Sunday outing lingered with her. She thought of him far too often. And yes, she felt guilty. But their time together was, well, magical. Wednesday when she thought she heard him on the Grand Gallery, her breathing shallowed and her hands trembled.

By Thursday morning, she and Lucy staged another eight dresses. The Gallery was a splendid retrospective on Lauchtenland's royal brides. Daffy took her time yesterday to set up the *Princess Louisa*, then stationed it to stand out among the others.

"I wish I knew Taffron Björk." Lucy stood back and surveyed the gown.

"Me too. Or owned one of his gowns. But I don't think any of his gowns remain. What few he made."

Daffy snapped a few photos to send to Mum, who was quite pleased and texted later the same day.

> I showed the queen. She said to tell you that you'd done well.

Daffy sighed and tucked the praise in to her heart.

However, with only seven gowns to go, plus the *Unknown Bride*, her time at Hadsby neared an end. Thus, her time with the prince, which truly was as it should be. Each of them getting on with their lives.

"I want to find something special for the *Unknown Bride*," Daffy said as she staged the wedding veil for *Princess Clemency*, who'd become Lauchtenland's Queen Victoria. She didn't reign as long, but she'd steered the small nation through nineteenth-century modernization and left her mark in Port Fressa's Clemency District.

"Why don't we take a break and shop this afternoon?" Lucy said.

"Good idea. If we can't find what we want up here, we'll have to find an alternative. We don't have time to waste."

So they agreed to go after lunch. Speaking of... Cranston met Daffy in the servants' hall as she entered.

"Didn't you say the *King Titus* was in the prince's apartment?"

"I believe he said so, yes." She picked up a plate, avoiding the butler's piercing gaze.

"The maid tells me she's not seen the chair."

"What is the maid doing snooping about the prince's apartment? She's to tidy his room, bathroom, and kitchen, not open closet doors."

"Why would the *Titus* be in a closet?"

"I don't know. Safekeeping?" She glanced toward the door, hoping Gus would appear. But Hemstead was also missing, which meant the prince was at one of his many engagements this week.

He'd texted her this morning.

> Chair repair going well. How are the wedding dresses?

> Good. You should come see them.

> I will. Busy diary this week.

After lunch, Daffy met Lucy on the path outside the servants' hall. They followed it out the front gate and down to Centre Street.

The day possessed a healing sun, coaxing the life from nature's long winter sleep. In a month, the walkway from the palace to the street would be lined with the white blooms of the dogwood trees.

"Let's try the shops in Old Hamlet." Daffy tugged on her gloves as they walked. "If we can't find anything, we can cross over to New Hamlet. But those gowns will be so modern. I want something timeless and unique."

"How about this? Shop Vintage." Lucy held up the map on her phone, revealing the image of a storefront. "Can't get a more generic name than Shop Vintage, but maybe they have something special."

"Let's hope they do."

Their heels clicked against the cobblestone as they crossed to the other side. "Daff, can I ask you something?"

"Sure." Daffy's phone chimed with an incoming text. From Leslie Ann. She'd sent a picture of the queen in a stunning blue gown with a romantic, flowing skirt, a deep V in the back, and wide, gauzy straps.

Daffy stopped walking. The dress. The one the queen caught her wearing all those years ago. Her fingers trembled slightly as she enlarged the photo to inspect the layers of chiffon and organza that composed the skirt and fitted bodice.

"What are you looking at?" Lucy angled forward to see Daffy's screen. "Now that's a beautiful gown. Let's find one like *that* one for the *Unknown Bride*?"

A second image pinged in. Another shot of the beautiful princess who grew up to be a queen. She wore the same winning smile as her handsome second born. Daffy could almost feel the joy, the happiness as the then-princess walked toward the photographer, her hand locked with a man off camera.

Leslie Ann, what are you up to?

Where'd you find this?

My secret source. Do you know this dress? Is it part of the RT?

What secret source? No, not part of RT. I've not seen it.

"Do you think the queen still has that dress?" Lucy raised Daffy's phone for a better look. "The skirt looks like it's filled with starlight."

"I don't know—" Images from that day in the queen's dressing room burst from Daffy's locked memories.

She'd hidden there during a game of hide-n-seek with the princes. This blue gown was on the floor. She'd tried it on. And got caught. Then banned.

LA, where'd you get this photo?

An old royal reporter. But that's all I'm saying. This is the Q's twenty-first birthday. I want this dress! But seriously, do you know it?

No. Not at all.

So, Daffy had tried on the gown from the queen's twenty-first. She'd never known. Was that why she was so angry? Did she spoil her memories? Did the dress relate to happier, carefree times? The queen's youth? Of first love? Of a life before her father dropped dead of a heart attack making her a queen at thirty-three. Of a time when she was simply the young mother of princes not the mother of a nation.

Daffy read Leslie Ann's next text.

So you've never seen this gown?

No. Who's the queen with?

My source says a friend. Thanks for the help.

Why are you asking? Where'd you get this picture?
Are you working on a story?

Gotta run. Miss ya! Xo

Daffy sighed and stared between the aged shops toward North Sea Channel. *Leslie Ann, you promised.*

"Come on," Daffy said to Lucy as she tucked her phone away, a sour twist in her gut. "We're wasting daylight."

"You okay?" Lucy said.

"I'm fine. It's just my friend, Leslie Ann. Never mind."

They turned down Wells Line without another word. Past the Belly of the Beast down to Canal Street toward the oldest Old Hamlet shops. The heady aroma of fresh bread from a little bakery mingled with the salty sea air.

"Daffy," Lucy said, low and slow. "Have you been keeping up with things on social media?"

"Things?" She glanced at her friend. "Like what? The news? No. My personal accounts? Sort of. Why? The internet is spotty here at night and I'm too tired for a page to load. And there's no time during the day."

"I hear you, but I usually check during lunch and dinner. Please correct me if I'm wrong, if there's something I don't know, but on Thomas's profile, there are a lot of posts with your friend Blinky."

"Really? I don't think they're hanging out more than usual. Though she went with him to Saldings on the Waterfront to check it out for a wedding venue."

"Yes, I saw those but, Daffy, they're like, hanging out. So much so their posts fill my feed. My sister got a puppy two days ago and I just saw her pictures today." Lucy held up her phone. "Maybe you know, but this is what I see."

Daffy swiped through the pictures. Thomas and Blinky at Saldings, thumbs up, smiling, her arm around his neck, his arm about her waist.

Thomas and Blinky huddled together at Pub Clemency, mugging for the camera.

Thomas and Blinky in the background of a photo of Rick and Jones holding up a sign for Albert—*Happy birthday ole chap.* Daffy enlarged the image. Was his hand on her hip?

She handed back Lucy's phone. "What are you trying *not* to say, Lucy?"

"Come on, you saw his hand on her hip. They look like a couple." She flashed the photo where Thomas and Blinky lingered in the background. "It looks as if he is going to kiss her. He doesn't realize he's been caught on camera."

Daffy thumped down Canal Street's steep incline. "Why would he cheat on me when he just proposed? And you don't know Blink well, but she's crazy, exuberant, affectionate. She hugs and kisses people all the time. Sits on the lads' laps without asking. She's a flirt! Look at her other social media sites and you'll see her hanging on lots of guys. But she's also a loyal friend who'd never betray me."

"Here's another one." Lucy shoved her phone under Daffy's nose again. "Blinky's Insta."

Daffy glanced at the shot of Thomas standing on a street corner under a gorgeous seaside sunset, staring toward the horizon. The caption read Friends Forever.

"So? They're friends."

"One more." Lucy showed Daffy a dinner scene. Two plates. Two glasses of wine. A candle. Dinner...okay... Daffy looked closer. The city lights in the background were from Thomas's living room window. That was his dining table.

She scrolled to the time stamp. Last night. Right after Daffy called and he claimed to be dining with a client.

"So they had dinner together." Daffy walked on. "I've eaten at the pub with Gus."

Lucy tucked her phone into her coat pocket. "Well don't get me started on *him.*"

"Do you have something to say, Lucy?" Daffy pulled up again.

The wind slicing up the hill from the channel wrapped her in a dewy chill. "Started on what?"

"You're in love with the prince." Lucy spoke with bold confidence. "It's all over your face every time he enters the servants' hall. Plain as day. You blush."

Betrayed again by her silent affections. "That doesn't mean I love him. Please, tell me no one else notices."

"Maybe one of the maids, but not the men. Daffy?" Lucy's voice softened. "Are you in love with him?"

"I don't know. I don't know." Being asked point-blank forced her to be honest "I'm engaged and—"

"Are you? Maybe in word but not deed."

"What does it matter? Gus has sworn off love. We're just friends. Nothing more. Good friends who are comfortable together. Honest with each other. We could talk all night. He told me something Sunday afternoon he'd never told anyone." At the bottom of Canal Street, Daffy spotted the Shop Vintage sign and headed that way. "And I confessed to him I wasn't..." She drew in a deep breath of the salted sea air. "I wasn't sure about Thomas."

"Daffy...*really*?" Lucy squeezed her hand. "Isn't it good news he might not be sure about you either?"

"For him maybe. He'll have Blinky but I won't have Gus. Oh, what a mess." Daffy dabbed the mist from her eyes. "Let's see if we can find the gown."

But Lucy didn't move. "I feel horrible I brought it up."

"You should."

"Really? I'm so sorry." Lucy hurried after Daffy.

"It's all right. Forget it. Let's just do our job and find a gown for the poor *Unknown Bride*?"

"For what it's worth," Lucy said, "I see how Prince Gus looks at you and—"

"Don't say it." Daffy swung around to her colleague and friend. "Gus and I could never... I'm not a princess. I can't be a princess. The queen would not allow it."

"What do you mean? Not allow it?" Lucy made a face.

"Never mind. Dress. Shop. Now." If she started even the smallest explanation, Daffy feared the whole blooming thing would spill out. And she could not risk it. Even with the prince she worried she might fall into a contemplative moment and reveal her secret. What she knew about the queen. But just imagining the shock on his face was enough to buy her silence.

Yet there were those moments when she wondered. Had she heard right? In eighteen years, there's been no proof. And she'd been a mere child. Eavesdropping. Surely, she misunderstood. Twisted the details.

They arrived at the shop without another word of love and princes. Lucy was bold but respectful and let the topic drop.

A lone bell attached to a Christmas ribbon clattered against the glass. The broad floor boards creaked beneath their feet, and the shop's fragrance was timeless, a perfume of generations past.

"Hello?" Lucy glanced around with a twist on her lips. "Look at this junk."

"One man's junk is another man's treasure. I know, I know—a cliché, but it's true." Daffy kept her voice low. "Luce, you're a curator for crying out loud. Open your eyes, See the potential."

Daffy wandered deeper into the large, open showroom. In the back appeared to be living quarters, as would've been the norm when the shop was built three hundred plus years ago.

To her right were shelves of knickknacks, books, china sets, dolls. On her left, center tables arranged with antique toys, bolts of cloth, old pictures, handkerchiefs, tea towels and washrags.

Lucy moved through to the opposite side to peruse the racks of dresses, shirts, and slacks. She picked up a pair of scuffed women's wedges.

"Who would wear these? They look as if they marched in World War II."

"There are people with a gift to see beauty in old things. And we should be two such people."

"We're also trained to recognize junk." Lucy dropped the shoe to the floor with a thud and wiped her hand on her coat.

"Hello, hello, I didn't hear you come in. Welcome. I'm

189

Adelaide." A tiny, sweet-faced woman with white Brillo-pad hair above sparkling eyes appeared from the back. "May I help you?"

"Sorry to have disturbed you." Lucy shot Daffy a pointed look. "We were just going."

"Actually, we're from the Royal Trust and staging royal wedding dresses at Hadsby. We came to see if you had something special to represent the *Unknown Bride*."

Lucy pointed to the rack of gowns. "But your inventory will not suffice."

Adelaide ignored her and focused on Daffy. Rather intently too. "You say the gown is for the royal wedding gown display? The *Unknown Bride*?" The woman, who seemed to have stepped into some sort of glowing spotlight, popped her hands together. "Good, good, good. I have just the thing. Are you Daffy?"

"I am. How did you know?"

"Be right back." The woman dashed around a corner and returned moments later with a large, pale blue box tied with a white ribbon. "This." She set the box on the cashier's counter and stepped back. "This is what you're looking for."

Daffy shot Lucy a glance. Might as well look. Lucy nodded, adding a slight eye roll.

"Did you know the tradition of the *Unknown Bride* was to find a bride for a young prince Blue?" Adelaide's story swirled in the air. "Now I understand it's to be donated to a lass of lesser fortune. Isn't that delightful? But in the old days, the *Unknown Bride* gown was for the girl who'd become a princess."

"We thought no one knew the origins." Lucy had softened but still had one foot out the door.

"Well, you lose details with each century, don't you? But I remember when—" She stopped, a winsome smile on her lips. "Listen to me go on. Why don't you open the box?"

Daffy reached for the tied ribbon, one eye on Adelaide. "Have we met?"

"I don't believe so."

"Have you ever been to Perrigwynn Palace?"

"Not recently, no."

"How did you know my name? Did Prince Gus come by here? Mentioned me? Or Ernst?"

"I've not seen the prince. Nor have I had the pleasure of meeting Ernst."

"Please open the box so we can go." Lucy leaned near to whisper. "She gives me the willies."

Daffy ignored her. "Then why does it feel as if we've met."

"Perhaps you know me through Princess Corina."

"Yes, yes, of course." Daffy swerved to Lucy with her arms wide. *See*. "When I first joined the trust as Mum's administrator, before grad school, Princess Corina loaned the Trust a Pissarro painting from her collection for the History of Art Tour. We got to talking and she told me about this wild, *angelic* woman who helped her become a princess."

"You can't be serious." Lucy oozed pure skepticism. "This is that woman? She's having you on, Daffy. Corina became a princess because she's rich, beautiful, and married a prince."

But Adelaide did look a bit angelic. "Are you Princess Corina's Adelaide? You fit her description perfectly."

"I might be. Now open the box." Adelaide cupped her hand beside her mouth. "This gown was sewn by a local tailor, a nice man, Taffron Björk."

Lucy's laugh bounced around the small shop as she turned a full circle. "Okay, joke's over. You've read up on the Trust. Seen something on social media. Where are the hidden cameras?"

"There are no cameras."

"Adelaide—if that is your real name—Björk has been dead for seventy something years," Lucy said.

"Did I say otherwise? Taffron was commissioned to sew this gown for the princess before he died. And now Emmanuel has asked me to give it to you—"

"Emmanuel? The carpenter?" Daffy paused as she lifted the box lid trying to connect the crazy dots of this encounter. "Why would he want you to give me a dress?"

"If you want to know, you must ask him. Now, come on, open, please. I'm so excited."

Lucy leaned forward as Daffy looked inside to find a blue chiffon-and-organza gown with a fitted bodice, V-cut in the front and back, and a shimmer like the night stars.

The exact same gown in the picture Leslie Ann sent. The exact same gown Daffy had tried on in the queen's dressing room when she was ten years old.

CHAPTER
TWENTY

GUS

D affy was a million miles away. Sitting across from him by the Belly of the Beast's grand fireplace, she was here only in body, not spirit.

She answered his questions with a single word or a shrug as she hovered over her plate of ribs and parsley potatoes.

"What's going on?" he said.

She raised her gaze from her plate of food. "What do you mean?"

"You're quiet."

"Oh, sorry." She forced a smile. "Long day."

He'd debated extending her an invitation to dine. Were they getting too close? Tempting the Dalholm spell of love and romance? If rumblings of doubt shook her confidence about the man she'd agreed to marry, he had no business playing the nice-guy friend. Because no matter what, he'd shine in comparison just by being sweet. And being royal. And that wasn't fair to anyone.

Besides, Gus had no intention of ending his commitment to bachelorhood anytime soon.

Yet, there he was on his way out—still sans Hemstead—choosing the front stairs for once instead of the secret passage, when he thought of Daffy and walked through the Grand Gallery, past the parade of wedding gowns to the guest suites, and knocked on the Princess Charlotte door. He'd missed her this week. Wanted to see her. So he promised himself he'd behave. Not flirting. Be friendly, but aloof.

Seems he didn't need his little self-speech. They were dining together but somehow separate.

Ernst hovered and fussed, told a story or two, adding his own boisterous laugh for emphasis, glancing between Gus and Daffy. But she barely cracked a smile.

In between bites of ribs and potatoes, and gulping from her wine like a parched Viking, she scrolled through photos on her phone.

Gus leaned to see. "Wedding ideas?"

"What?" She turned her phone facedown on the table. "No, just, you know, catching up with people."

"Funny thing about social media. It can be such a façade. People only posting what they want you to see. Writing what they want you to believe. All smiles and giggles. Until one day when you pass by the profile of an old uni mate to learn his ten-year-old marriage to the love of his life is over. Of course, neither one posts anything honest, letting us know, at some level, what happened and how they came to move on. Instead we see photos of holidays and gatherings without each other. Eventually one of them posts they're in a new relationship and we shake our heads."

"If you're trying to be cynical, it's working. If you're trying to say loving someone can be challenging and difficult, you're right. If you're trying to say love is not worth it, then you are wrong."

He winced at her soft rebuke. "I only meant—"

She leaned over her plate and whispered through clenched teeth. "I get it. You're not going to fall in love. Beat another drum, lad, beat another drum."

"I wasn't trying to make a point about me." But wasn't he? "I'm sorry if I came across—"

"Don't." She held up her hands, surrendering. "I'm the one who should apologize. It's been a weird day. How's the chair?"

He tried to keep up with her sudden changes and answered her question. "We've fixed the legs and seat-rail. Emmanuel is extremely slow and methodical. And he talks. A lot."

"Really?" Daffy sat up straighter, her eyes intent on him. "What does he talk about?"

"Stuff. He's full of sage wisdom. And while I can't really pinpoint any one thing he's said, other than his intimate knowledge of my ancestors, I feel wiser when we part ways. Refreshed."

Even more so than after all his time in Florida. More than any time he could remember, really. The sensation wasn't so much mental, as it was emotional. Even spiritual.

The spring in his step, the hum in his heart as he went about his day. The hope... Yes, that was the word. Emmanuel imparted hope. And a chap could never have too much hope.

"Has he ever said anything about a dress? About a woman named Adelaide?"

"No. Like I said, I can't remember anything specific. Just Emmanuel going on about this, yakking about that." If asked, Gus would admit the old carpenter was becoming a friend. Like Ernst, only with whole sentences. "Why do you ask? Who's Adelaide and where's the lass who panicked over my recklessness with the chair?"

"She's still here. Just taking a break from it to worry over something else."

"Daffy, I can see something is troubling you. If it's me, then say so. If not, say what it is. Perhaps I can help."

Gus ripped open one of the packets of towelettes Ernst kept on the table and passed one to Daffy. "Here, this will help."

She smiled softly. "Will it?"

He was about to give a quippy reply when Hemstead charged into the pub, a mad bull pawing the ground for his prey.

Oops.

Gus rose from his chair with a small wave. The man fired visual darts as he chose a table near the front, making a racket with the chair, and resituating the table. Hearty ole Ernst greeted him with enthusiasm and a pint.

"Do you know this dress?"

Gus sat back down as Daffy flipped over her phone to show him a beautiful picture of his much younger and clearly celebrating mum. She held a chap's hand but he was off-screen. Must be with Dad because she looked so in happy and in love.

"I've seen a *lot* of gowns in family photos, public and private, but never this one. Nor this photo. Where'd you get it? Is it part of the Royal Trust?"

"No. Leslie Ann sent it to me."

"There's a reliable source." He shook his head, waving away the mention of the woman. "What does she want with it?"

"She found it, I think, researching a story she's doing about your mum or royal weddings. I'm not sure. She wanted to know if the dress was part of the RT." She placed the phone on the table again. "When your mum, the queen, caught me in her dressing room, I was wearing *this dress*. She was very upset. Her maid led me downstairs by my ear—"

"The dress in this picture?" And he could believe that about Mum's maid, Hilda. She didn't muck around.

"Hilda told Mum I'd crossed a boundary, entered the queen's private quarters without permission. The queen was very upset. Mum gave me the dickens and I felt so bad I went back up to apologize. The butler, Greenly, let me in the apartment. He didn't know what happened. Said the queen was in her room. So I went down the hall to knock on her door but it was ajar. She was on the phone. Still very upset. I heard everything she said. I didn't know what she was talking about exactly, but I heard her side of the conversation." She paused, her eyes clouding, her lips pressed together. "Hilda found me again."

"Blimey. Poor you. Where was I?"

"Still hiding? Playing a video game? I don't know. Anyway, things became truly ugly. Everyone yelled at me."

"What was the conversation? Something of national security? What would that have to do with the dress?"

Daffy gazed toward the low-flickering fire. "I'm not sure, but was her conversation something of national security?" She peered at Gus. "Yes, I believe so. I truly do."

"Like what? Can you remember?" Gus raced through memories for some eighteen-year-old security issue. But he'd been a kid himself. Mum would not have shared government business at the family dinner table.

"No." Her answer came swift and low. Somehow, he didn't believe her.

"Why'd you hide in Mum's dressing room? It's in the heart of her bedroom."

"I knew John would never find me there."

"Brilliant. John and I never messed with Mum's things."

"I hid against the wall by the door, covered by dresses. Then I heard you screaming and running from him." She laughed—a sound he'd never tire of hearing—and pressed her hand to her heart. "I held my breath until I thought I'd pass out. My pulse was pounding so hard. When I thought the coast was clear, I started to sneak out. But the queen's gowns... They are beautiful. That's when I saw the blue gown on the floor, discarded without care. The crystal chandelier in the dressing room made the dress sparkle. I had to try it on."

Gus sat back, listening, looking back through his memories. "And Mum caught you."

"She dismissed me with a look. She might as well have strung me up in the castle courtyard."

"Mum has a way about her, I'll grant you." He raised his pint, as if saluting the queen. "She must, if she's to be an effective queen. So is this the secret you alluded to in Florida? Nothing more than catching you in a discarded frock? Doesn't seem like much of a secret."

Daffy reached for her wine goblet. "I guess not. I overreacted."

"But you heard a phone call." Gus tilted his head, narrowing his eyes. "Seems there's something you're trying hard not to say."

"The ribs were delicious, weren't they?"

"Daffy..."

Ernst popped by just then with his staccato gusto. "Friends. More?"

"Not me." Daffy patted her middle. "Do give Stella my regards. Delicious."

"Pudding?"

Gus avoided puddings. No need to return to his Prince Pudgy

days. But the Beast did have a splendid apple tart. When he suggested it, Daffy heartily agreed.

"I'll be up a half stone by the time I go home," she said.

"But good." The cherub proprietor tapped his finger on his nose.

"Ernst." Gus nodded toward Hemstead. "The man by the door. Serve him whatever he wants and add it to my bill."

"Righty-o."

"You should really stop running off without him," Daffy said. "You're disrespecting his job."

"I'm what?" Gus sat up, chest puffed.

"You're disrespecting his job. He's hired to protect you, Gus. But you treat him like the annoying friend from down the road."

"I just..." Her rebuke struck home. "Just...don't want a shadow. Someone always on my flank, watching my every move."

"He's watching your back. Who wouldn't want someone, wherever he went, on his side? Buck up, chap, and accept what he's here to do. Stop being a child."

Gus snapped his napkin from his lap and wadded it up. Was it too late to cancel the apple tart? He gulped from his pint.

"I'll try to do better."

"Don't try. Just do."

Another swallow of beer, rather than his pride. "So, what did you do today? I played another round of football with the young five- and six-year-olds in the Youth League this morning."

"Got kicked in the shin, I'm sure."

"Hard, too." He laughed. "But they are earnest in their efforts."

There was a little girl among the pack who'd so captured Gus's heart that for the first time, he wondered about being a father. What would it be like? Seems Dalholm was raising all sorts of buried desires.

"Lucy and I went dress hunting. For the *Unknown Bride*." Daffy launched into a story of an old shop above the quay. Shop Vintage. "When this woman with spinning eyes handed me a box—"

"Spinning eyes?"

"Yes, with light. And very vibrant. Unique."

"The eyes are the window to the soul," Gus said.

"She gave Lucy the creeps, but to me she was so sweet. Surreal." Daffy lowered her voice. "She's the same woman Princess Corina says helped her when she returned to Brighton Kingdom looking for Prince Stephen."

"Princess Corina? How do you know?"

"The princess described her to me when she visited Perrigwynn during the History of Art tour."

"Did this Adelaide move from Brighton Kingdom to Lauchtenland?"

"I didn't think to ask her about her personal story. Corina said she never saw Adelaide again after she married Prince Stephen. You'd have to hear her tell the story. It's wild. Anyway, there I am talking to this Adelaide and—"

"This magical woman handed you a box."

"With this dress inside." She showed him the photograph again. "I had chills all over. It was creepy yet sort of divine. Then she said Emmanuel told her to give it to me."

"Emmanuel? The carpenter?"

"I guess. Do you know of another one lurking about in Highcrest Mountains?" She shivered and ran her hand down her arm. "The dress is for the *Unknown Bride* but she kept going on about the tradition being for the next House of Blue princess. I think she was confused."

"I wouldn't know. Though I heard Granny once say the gown for the *Unknown Bride* gown was to be blue."

"For the House of Blue?" Daffy said. "A little on the nose, but I get it."

He laughed. "I guess so. Did you put the dress in the gallery?"

"Not yet. It needed minor tending. But oh, Gus, it's as beautiful as I remember. As it was in this photograph of the queen."

He took her phone and studied the image. "When was this taken?"

"Her twenty-first birthday."

"Can't be Dad's hand she's holding. Mum graduated Yale before she met Dad. Talk about a whirlwind romance. Met, married, and conceived John in like eight months." He handed back the phone. "Mum was a beauty."

"Still is." Daffy tucked the device away. "Adelaide told us the gown was designed by Taffron Björk, the same designer of the *Princess Louisa*."

"Which means?"

"Björk died nearly forty years before the queen would wear this gown."

"Perhaps the person who had the gown before gave it to Mum? Or she acquired it through, say, one of her designers?"

"A designer giving the Princess of Lauchtenland another designer's gown. A dead one to boot? I doubt it." She looked weary to him. Like more than the dress weirdness bothered her. "Even so, how did the gown end up in a box in a vintage shop?"

"Mum often gives her gowns to charity or for auctions."

"True. Then the person who bought the blue gown donated it out of hand? It doesn't make sense. Unless the person didn't understand the dress's value. Still, I can't quite piece together why Adelaide gave it to me. Or why Emmanuel had anything to do with it."

"I have no idea but I'm starting to think we've been tricked. Emmanuel is no ordinary man. No ordinary carpenter."

Chapter
Twenty-One

Coral

A lot had changed in the last two years. Since she'd gathered her courage and ran from Clouver Abbey without a word to the man waiting at the altar.

She'd joined a story society that had nothing to do with books and everything to do with hearts, and healing, and true human stories. She'd made new friends, rescued her company from ruin, and fallen in love. From a prince to an Uber driver—who would have ever guessed? Her American version of the would-be princess and the pauper.

The haunting of what she'd done to Prince Gus had eased, even faded some, but in the deepest parts of her being, she knew their story was not done.

Gus refused to talk to her after, well, everything. She'd kept silent until an appearance on *Good Morning New York* a year ago. Even then, she spoke mostly of her new faith. So when Lady Holland called and invited Coral and her new husband, Chuck, to the wedding—a personal, heartfelt invitation—she'd accepted. Of course she wanted to celebrate her friend's wedding, a friend who was also a business associate. But Holland was marrying into the Family Coral fled.

But oh, this was her chance to right things with Gus.

When the official invitation arrived two months ago, she and Chuck began earnest, nightly prayers for Gus, for Coral, and an opportunity for repentance.

And now she and Chuck were leaving New York on Monday for three weeks. A week in CCW Cosmetics' London and Port Fressa offices, after which they'd go on vacation, launching their two-week delayed honeymoon with a royal ball and wedding.

The timing was a bit off. Chuck had just won a bitter custody battle with his ex-wife. This was their first weekend with the seven-year-old twins. Coral was now a stepmom. Wow! As much as the notion warmed her heart, it panicked her. She'd read ten books on the matter already.

"Did you see the quarterlies on our *fabulous* preteen lip gloss?" Coral had been staring at her computer screen lost in thought when Lexa Wilder entered with her tablet in hand. "Pink Coral still leads the tweenie market."

"Thanks to your genius ad campaign. You're a marketing guru—and a brilliant CEO."

Who knew that the same story society where she'd met her husband would be where she'd find Lexa, now one of her best friends, and CCW's CEO?

"I don't know about brilliant but thank you. By the way, it's three o'clock. Didn't you want to leave at three?"

"Is it three already?" Coral glanced at her watch, reaching for her handbag and laptop case. "The car will be waiting. Lexa, I'm so nervous yet so excited."

"Your first weekend as a stepmom. You'll be amazing. The kids are going to flip over their bedrooms."

"You should've seen Chuck last night. He woke up every hour to make sure nothing had changed. Like the paint peeling off the wall or the beds collapsing." Coral laughed at the image of her big teddy bear of a man sneaking out of their room with his phone flashlight aimed at the floor.

After the custody decree gave him possession of his children again, he spent a week emailing Coral bedroom designs from

Pinterest. Who knew the burly man even knew what Pinterest was let alone opened an account.

"Text me an update when you can. By the way, is everything set with the London and Port Fressa offices for your trip? Do you want to stop in Paris again? You were just there last quarter so—"

"No. After the wedding we'll be on vacay for two weeks."

"Are you ready?" Lexa quirked an eyebrow. "To see him? Can you believe he spent a year tending bar on a Florida beach?"

"Believe it or not, yes." Coral started out the door. "I just want closure, Lexa. I want to say how sorry I am."

"Don't worry. God will open the door."

"I've rehearsed my speech to him so many times, but when it comes time, I wonder if I won't just fall apart." Her eyes filled. "If I could do it all over again—"

"Don't fret over what you cannot change. Just have faith. Believe God for what He can do, not what you can do. Aren't you always telling me to leave the outcome to God?" She smoothed her hand over her baby belly. "You encouraged me so when I was terrified of losing this child."

"Listen, don't preach my own words to me. Those are for you. I'm allowed to wallow in pity and worry."

Lexa laughed. "We'll debate that lie later. For how, get going. Don't be late for your first weekend with the twins."

"Right. I leave you in charge. See you in three weeks."

Coral and Lexa walked down the marble-and-stone center staircase. "By the way, we posted the corporate curator job," Lexa said. "In-house curator to design and oversee the CCW Cosmetic museum. We already have a dozen resumés."

"Good. Let's not settle. Wait for the one right for us. I'd love to take credit for this, but again, your genius took over."

"I think a museum will build company pride, help the staff lay hold of what we're about and who they're working for when they see the history of the company." When they got to the street exit, Lexa offered some final advice. "You're Coral Winthrop Mays, owner and president of one of the world's oldest and most successful cosmetics companies. Prince Gus is a lowly HRH." She squeezed her hand. "Make him listen to you."

"When you put it like that, I almost believe I can. Nevertheless, I'll leave the outcome to God."

Coral slipped into the back of the waiting black sedan. All she wanted was a chance to say she was sorry. She didn't expect his forgiveness. She'd not make excuses or point the finger.

She'd hurt someone she loved and all she wanted was to whisper, "I'm sorry. So very sorry."

DAFFY

By Friday evening she was spent. Not so much with staging the wedding dresses—only three remained as well as the *Unknown Bride*—but with the mystery of the blue gown. Adelaide. Emmanuel. The chair. Gus.

The pictures of Thomas and Blinky on social media and the instilling of doubt.

But when she talked to Thomas this morning, he'd been kind and loving, even a bit romantic. He said he missed her and ended their brief call with, "I love you."

She was certain Blinky was just going bonkers with pictures. She fancied herself a talented amateur photographer.

By Friday afternoon, the events of the past month tumbled down on her like too many boxes of shoes stuffed onto a closet shelf. She had to break away. Find her norm. Her city. Her people. Her calm, steady life with its predictable job and predictable routine was out of sorts. And Daffy Caron intended to sort it out this weekend.

She booked passage on the four o'clock Northton Express to Port Fressa, packed a small bag she'd purchased at a quaint little shop in the Old Hamlet, and left Hadsby. Training home in a surprisingly empty third-class car, Daffy stared out the window as small villages, meadows, and farms zipped past, waiting for the moment of relief. Waiting for the clang of, "You're doing the right thing."

Instead, her heart pulled her backward. To Dalholm and Hadsby. To the prince. Was she cheating herself of a final weekend with him? Yes, and being sad about it was totally and completely wrong.

Upon arriving home, she planned to sort her snail mail, water her dying roses—she felt sure Ella forgot—and take a long soak in her deep, porcelain tub. Then she would fix herself up, fluff out her curls, and head to Pub Clemency to surprise her mates.

As the train sped down the track, she assessed her life since being conked in the head with a green Frisbee. Seriously, how could she question Thomas and Blinky's relationship when her own heart teetered on the brink of unfaithfulness?

She blushed and yearned for the prince. If by some wild dream-come-true miracle Gus actually *chose* her, the queen would never approve. Daffy refused to live her life under the critical scrutiny of her mother-in-law. Especially Queen Catherine II.

Furthermore, as if she needed a furthermore, Gus was a committed bachelor. For the time being anyway.

Further, furthermore she was engaged. Engaged! Daffy held up her ring hand and stared at the clear and perfect diamond Thomas originally bought for someone else. That's it, she'd stepped into a Jane Austen novel.

Either way, going home was prudent. Even necessary. A wise move to save her future and her heart.

Unlocking the door of her flat, she dropped her bag to the floor and collapsed in the overstuffed chair she'd found at a rummage sale. Home. Peace. Quiet.

"I've missed you, flat." The Princess Charlotte, while beautiful, had nothing on *her* place, with the eclectic furnishings, handwoven rugs, and art from local artisans.

But she didn't have time to lounge. With only an hour to get ready, she needed to utilize every minute. The lot of them usually met at eight, so Daffy planned a grand entrance around eight-fifteen. No one, not even Ella, knew she was home.

Her mail went straight into the rubbish, and her roses were one day from joining the mail. Nevertheless Daffy watered them one last time, and as she set the vase on the counter, two petals fluttered to the floor.

Tossing them in the bin, she spotted the box of things Mum brought round from the garage and read the attached note.

"Dad found this while cleaning the garage. I found that old diary of yours in here. That being said, you're getting married. Don't keep junk. The less you take to your new place the better. You'll accumulate closetsful by the time it's all said and done. Live lean. It makes life so much simpler."

Love, Mum

(You'd never know we had the big cleanse of '09. How could we have collected so much stuff in such a short time? I blame your father. Really I do.)

Daffy dropped the note. Mum found the diary? But it'd been missing for so long. Shoving the box contents around, she dug to the bottom, looking for the leather book which held her story, her young dreams.

But it wasn't there.

Daffy pulled out a framed photo of her with Nana and Papa and set it on her kitchen island.

"Miss you both."

Then she dug out three empty frames. They used to hold photos of that lying snake, the cheater Rex Childress.

Ah, her stuffed bunny. Poor thing. She slept with it every night until well past thirteen. Daffy tucked it under her arm to put on her bed when she went in for her bath.

She removed books, ribbons, theater tickets, and a pair of socks she stole from a chap at uni—what in the world?—but not the diary.

Daffy read mum's note again. "I found that old diary of yours in here."

She must have meant she didn't find it because it wasn't here. Not even close.

Well, she had Bunny. Daffy set the pink, stuffed toy against her pillows and apologized for abandoning her. Then she soaked in the tub and tried to imagine everyone's reaction when she showed up at the pub. She'd missed Thomas. Well, a little. No, more than a little. She missed his familiar scent. The strength of his embrace, the taste of his lips on hers.

Choosing her finest night-on-the-town clothes—black slacks with a tailored white blouse, Jimmy Choo heels, and her leather coat—Daffy hurried through the Clemency District under blooming cherry trees and glowing street lamps.

Once inside, she gazed toward their table, expecting to hear a burst of laughter. But the pub overflowed with patrons and she couldn't get a clear look.

From the stage, two women sang a classic standard, "Dream a Little Dream," and mesmerized the patrons.

Daffy passed their favorite server. "Are they here, Gypsie?"

"Well, look at you. Where you been?"

"Working in Dalholm. Hadsby Castle."

Daffy squeezed between the tables, nodding at familiar faces. But when she arrived at the large table in the corner by the windows, it was occupied by strangers. Four chaps and three ladies.

One of them peered up at her. "Can we help you?"

"No, thank you. I just thought my friends were here tonight."

"Sorry, love, but we've had this table the last two weeks. Hope we didn't displace you."

"Of course not." She backed away. "First come, first served. Sorry to have disturbed."

Where was everyone? Out on the street, she texted Thomas.

Where are you?

Home. Ring you in a bit?

Sure.

Little did he know that she'd knock on his door in a few minutes, fall into his arms, and kiss him like a woman in love. She'd repent of her wedding details' hesitation and dive into the ideas she'd contemplated while soaking in a bubble bath.

At his building, a nervous shudder had Daffy pulling her leather jacket closer. Riding the elevator to his fifth floor, she pictured his corner view of the city and the port. A lovely place to start married life. They could let her apartment.

At his door, she rang the bell, resisting the urge to call out, "Thomas, it's me."

Hands in her coat pockets, she shivered again and danced around just a bit. After a few minutes, she knocked and rang the bell again.

He had said he was home, right? Daffy checked his text to be sure. Ringing the bell again, she was about to call through the heavy steel door when the door jerked open.

"What in blazes—" He stepped back, grabbing at his open shirt. "D-Daffy?"

"Surprise!" She sprang toward him, ready for his open arms. But instead, he drew the door half-closed and blocked her entrance.

"What are you doing here?"

"What does it look like?" His question was as good as a physical shove. "Surprising you." What was wrong with him?

"Love, that's fantastic, but...but I'm rather busy." Behind the door, music blared, then faded. An interior door thudded closed.

"Busy with what? Thomas, who's here?" Daffy pushed against the door but Thomas remained steady. Immovable.

"I said I'd call you later."

"But I'm here now. Thomas, what's going on?"

"Let her in, Tom."

He glanced into the flat. "I don't think—"

"Blinky?" Daffy ducked under his arm to find her friend in the living room, dressed in a very tight cocktail dress, her bouffant hair in a Marilyn Monroe mess.

Daffy buckled, reaching for the nearest chair. "Do I need to ask?"

The scene said it all. Tapered candles flickering from the dining table in the windowed corner. Soft music in the background. Blinky dressed to kill. Thomas staring at his feet while he buttoned his shirt.

"We didn't mean to fall in love, Daff. Believe me." Blinky's typically high, fast voice was low and slow. Thomas walked around Daffy to stand beside Blink. "But—"

"You started spending a lot of time together." Daffy closed her eyes as the light in the room dimmed, vanishing into a black hole that beckoned her. "I saw the pictures you posted."

"It was nothing at first, I promise." This from Thomas. "I didn't know I could fall for someone so fast."

Daffy clung to her handbag as if it could hold her steady, help her survive sinking through the airless room. "So, you're in love?"

"We didn't mean—"

"You're in love?" Hearing it spoke left her weak. "W—what happened?"

"We went to Saldings on the Waterfront and had a blast, but it was all for you. Truly." Blinky's smile wavered.

"We started talking about wedding venues and texting, then we discovered we had a lot in common."

Blinky forced a laugh. "The wild child and the buttoned-up CPA. Who'd have guessed?"

"If you didn't love me, Thomas, why did you propose?" She glared at Blinky. Why didn't she excuse herself so she and Thomas could talk?

"I thought it was time. I adored you, and we got on so well, but now I think we're actually too much alike."

The first tear always burned the hottest. Daffy caught the drop with the back of her gloved hand. But somewhere inside of her, a loud, resounding clang sounded.

"This is the right thing."

"I'm sorry you found out this way, Daff." Thomas started to reach for Blink's hand then stopped and stepped toward Daffy. "This is actually our first official date. We talked about everything tonight. What was happening between us. What this meant for you."

"Looks like you were up to something more than talking." Daffy pointed to Blinky's hair.

"We might have, um, gotten, um, carried..." Blinky cleared her throat as she patted down her messy locks. "Daffy, you're one of my best friends. I'd never intentionally hurt you."

"Then there's nothing more to say." Daffy removed her glove, slipped Thomas's ring from her finger, and set it on the nearest end table. "When you propose to Blinky, *Tom*, buy her a new ring. Give this one away. Or make it into a necklace."

Thomas intercepted her as she made for the door. "I am truly sorry, love. Please believe me."

Daffy reached up and brushed his hair aside and straightened his unbuttoned collar. "I know." Why did tears insist on falling? "I should go."

Thomas drew her into a hug and kissed her forehead. "Maybe, in time, we can be friends."

"Maybe." She reached for the doorknob.

"Daffy?" Blinky, this time. "You might consider that you're in love with the prince. The way you defended him at the lodge…"

Daffy remained facing the door. "I didn't want Leslie Ann to get to him."

"You jumped over a large couch and tackled her. And I saw how you looked at him."

"Let's not try to change the focus of *this* conversation, all right?"

Daffy left without another word or backward glance. She'd just crossed the lobby when Blinky called her name and marched toward her like a familiar friend, not the woman cheating with her fiancé.

"I'm going to say this, whether you want to hear it or not. The prince has to get over Coral and Lady Robbi sooner or later. Why not you?"

"I'm afraid he's planning on later. Much later. And there are a lot of reasons, royal reasons, why *not* me."

"What reasons? They're rubbish." Blinky squeezed Daffy's hands. "As for later, Daffy, darling, make him change his mind."

CHAPTER
TWENTY-TWO

GUS

"Hello, love—what are you doing here?" Gus stopped working on a chair leg when a slight shadow fell in the workshop Saturday afternoon. *Daffy.* He blew a breath to shift his wild bangs from his eyes. "Lucy said you went home for the weekend."

The news had affected his mood, like clouds moving in to block the sunshine. Daffy had said nothing of going home during dinner Thursday. But she didn't owe him any explanations. Spending the afternoon with Emmanuel in the workshop was a blessed distraction.

The two of them had swapped stories, sharing the crazy antics of their friends. Gus thought he'd topped the older man when he recounted the time Sorrels jumped from their third floor bedroom window to hide from the headmaster, using a sheet as a parachute.

"Broke his leg in two places."

Then the carpenter regaled him with a story of a mate who attempted to walk on water.

"Are you serious? Was he drunk?"

"Very serious and very sober. I thought he had the faith for it. I told him to give it a go. But in the end..." Emmanuel shook his head. *"I suppose I shouldn't laugh. It wasn't so funny at the time. But looking back..."*

And now, Daffy inched closer, her countenance somber. "I was home and now I'm here. How's the chair? We need it done soon."

"It's coming along nicely." He motioned for her to inspect his handiwork. With Emmanuel's help, he'd attached the legs to the seat and was about to sand and stain. "We'll have to redo all the stain, but we found a proper match."

The carpenter gave a silent nod to Daffy and lifted his teacup.

"Will it be ready when the guests arrive?" She ran her hand over the now-smooth leg. "I wonder if King Titus really fashioned this Doric column, or if someone put these legs on later. This style was used widely in the sixteenth and seventeenth century."

"I wish we could know." Gus glanced at Emmanuel. "Don't suppose you know, do you?"

He shrugged. "I know what you're doing is good. Let's keep going. Daffy, are you all right?"

"Of course." But she looked as if she'd lost her best friend. "Emmanuel, do you know a woman named Adelaide? She said you told her to give me a box holding a blue gown."

"I know Adelaide well. I thought you'd like the dress. Doesn't it fit your needs?"

"It does. We're using it for the *Unknown Bride*. But I find it odd that the gown once belonged to Queen Catherine II."

"All the more reason you should use it."

"Yes, but how did Adelaide get it? And why did you tell her to give it to me? How did you even know I would go to Shop Vintage? Why do you care?"

"Adelaide and I are old friends. I told her if you visited to give you the box. And I care because that's who I am."

"Was the dress yours to give? It was a Taffron Björk, so it wasn't made yesterday or in the '80s. Did you purchase it somewhere? Donate it to Shop Vintage?"

Gus regarded Daffy. What was going on? She was visibly tense and drilling ole Emmanuel as if he were on trial.

"Daffy, do you need all the answers now? Let them come when they come." The carpenter touched her shoulder. "Peace." Then he finished his tea and set his cup in the sink. "Gus, why don't we call it a day? We'll finish next week and return the chair to its rightful place." Emmanuel settled his wide-brimmed hat on his head. "Gus, a word?"

Excusing himself with a glance at Daffy, Gus wiped his hands on his apron and met the man outside the shop door. A light spring rain dripped over them from budding tree limbs.

"What are you going to do?" the carpenter said.

"About what? The chair? Return it good as new, or well, *old*, and never sit in it again."

"And Daffy?"

"Daffy? What do I—" He looked through the shop where she inspected the chair and read from the Royal Trust folder. "She's engaged, mate. And I'm not looking for a relationship. We're friends, nothing more."

"Are you?" Emmanuel tipped the collecting water from his hat. "Until Monday."

DAFFY

Sunday morning Daffy stood among the gowns and the sunlight falling through the skylights and pooling down the Grand Gallery.

The gowns moved in color from a rich burgundy to cream, to white, with the brilliant blue sheen of the *Unknown Bride* shimmering at the end of the line.

"Surveying your work?" Gus approached, his hair shiny and loose about his face. He wore jeans, work boots, and a thick pullover. No denying the flutter her stirred in her heart.

"They look so stunning in the light. The *Princess Louisa* especially. The pearls look like tiny moons." She smiled at him before looking away, surprised by a spring of tears.

Gus had carried her home in the cart after he closed the workshop, asking if she wanted to dine at the pub. But she'd declined. Stayed in her suite and ate popcorn, watched the telly, and cried when she felt the tears. Even if breaking with Thomas was right, it still stung.

She threw kernels at the flat-screen when Leslie Ann came on announcing her Royal Special airing on *The Rest of the Story* Sunday night, the 30th.

Then she'd cried again and talked to the walls. Told Thomas and Blinky what she thought of them, indulged in ice cream she found in Chef Charles's kitchen, and at last, slept.

When she woke up the next morning, her head was clear. She could admit the truth. Thomas wasn't the one for her. She should've had the courage to tell him just that, not wait to discover him with Blinky. Wasn't she a strong, independent woman?

Yet the real conundrum was facing the rest of the truth. The challenge Blinky presented to her.

"You might consider that you're in love with the prince."

Yes. To the blazes, yes! Out of the frying pan into the fire. Worse than being engaged to the wrong man was being in love with the impossible one.

"Is this every lass's dream?" Gus's question pulled Daffy from her internal wrestling. "A garden of wedding dresses?"

"Not every girl, but most. We're going to stage a couple of the grooms' suits. Just to create an atmosphere."

"Was this your dream? Staging wedding gowns and overseeing the secret repair of an ancient chair? Ratting around in dusty, royal antiquities for a living?"

"I love history and *antiquities*, so yes. But I'm also interested in corporate curating, acquiring art and collectibles for banks, businesses. A lot of companies are doing this now to give the work environment culture. There's also a new trend in older companies of restoring and preserving their history through documentation, film—corporate museums where old products and technology and photographs are on display. But Mum offered me a job before I graduated, so I said yes." A tear escaped and slid down the side of her cheek. She wiped it away before Gus could see. "I'm starting to think this is my lot in life. Settling. I'm content with good-enough instead of waiting for the best. I took the first job offered. Accepted the first man who proposed."

"We all settle, Daffy. We all make choices to keep us safe."

"Not you. You turned your broken heart into an engagement."

"Which didn't work."

"Which you turned into a year as a bartender in Florida. Gus, you take risks."

"Is that what you call it?" His laugh twisted around her. "I call it hiding. But I've learned my lesson. And what's this about the first man who proposed? Your uni boyfriend? Didn't he miss his chance?"

She turned to him. "The first day we were in Floridana Beach, I stood on the shore thinking how ordinary I was, so average. Run of the mill. I never do anything that scares me or challenges my fears. I didn't even try for a corporate curator position. I said yes to Mum because it was easy. Because it was what she wanted. And I do have an affection for the House of Blue. Then Thomas proposed. I accepted him but I should've said, 'Mate, you've barely told me you loved me.'"

"Daffy, what happened?"

She held up her left hand to show a bare ring finger. "He's in love with Blinky."

"The lass with blue eyeshadow up to her eyebrows?"

Daffy snort-laughed, batting back tears. "Opposites attract." She walked through the dappled light toward the blue gown. "We'll be done on Tuesday but I want to see the chair, so I'll stay until it's done. I'll have to make up an excuse but—"

Gus touched her shoulder and turned her to him. "Love, are you all right?"

"I am. Embarrassed more than anything. Angry I didn't demand more of myself, of Thomas. But at least we realized it in time."

"He's an idiot. I knew it when you said he gave you another woman's ring."

"I'll tell him you said so."

"Please do." Gus hugged her close and she felt, heard, the rhythm of his heart. "Want to get out of here? Do something crazy?"

"Like what?" And yes, double yes.

"You have to say yes first."

"How crazy?"

"Yes or no, Daffy?"

But wait. She'd only fall harder for him if she ran around the hamlet with the handsome, impetuous prince. Especially now that the barrier of being engaged was removed. Could she be such a glutton for punishment?

"I'll get my coat." She dashed toward the guest wing. "By the way, that's a yes."

He flashed his famous smile. "See you at our stairs."

"Yes, *our* stairs."

Ducking into Princess Charlotte, Daffy caught her reflection in the gilded framed living room mirror.

"You're mad to go off with him." The confession made her smile. "But you only live once, so why not?"

She figured they'd head toward the lake. Maybe climb the rocks. Or maybe jump in the cold mountain water, clothes and all. Now that'd be crazy.

Instead of her coat, she tugged on her thickest jumper and exchanged her flats for her trainers. Phone in her hip pocket, she made her way to the secret stairs.

They escaped by their usual route. Through the hedges, across wet and muddy grounds, and through the woods. When they hit Centre Street, Gus started toward Wells Line.

"Don't tell me we're going to the Belly of the Beast." She calmed her breathing. "That's not crazy."

Their footsteps harmonized as they rounded the corner toward Canal Street. But there, Gus stopped.

"You know, you never seemed like a *blushing* bride. He was not an attentive groom."

"I know, and maybe I'd have come to my senses before the wedding, but part of me thinks I'd have settled. We'd have had a good life, done well."

"The trouble is—" He brushed his hand over her cheek. "You don't know how extraordinary you are."

She felt her Prince Gus blush claim her cheeks, her nose, her eyes.

"Ah. There's my royal blush. I've not seen it in a while. You've gotten used to me and—"

Daffy stepped back with a sober rebuke. "Gus, don't. Don't flirt with me. Tease me."

He peered toward the channel. "Do you want to go on?"

"And do something crazy?" She started down the Canal Street incline. "Stop me."

They headed toward the quay, through the narrow lanes of small houses built by Dalholm's first settlers.

"Are we taking the ferry to London?" While she loved the idea, it would take the day to go over and back.

"Come on, you'll see." He grabbed her hand and tugged her through the swirling, gusting wind to the pedestrian path, away from the slow-moving line of disembarking cars.

About halfway across the quay, revelation dawned. The Hand of God. "Oh no, Gus, I'm not going up there." Just like that, he'd stopped her. Five minutes ago, she believed nothing could. But climb the steep path to the cleft in the rock? No. Nope. No.

"You said you were up for something crazy. Now's your chance, Daffy. I know you can do this. Climb to the Hand of God with me." He started forward again, his hand clamped around hers.

"It's not safe. The wind is vicious." Daffy hurried to match his strides. "Look at those clouds. It's going to storm."

Dark blue cumulonimbus clouds roiled along the morning horizon, promising a storm.

"It's beautiful up there when it storms."

They were almost to the rickety footbridge when she finally broke free of his hold. "Gus, I can't."

"Yes, *you can.* I know it. I see everything you want to be. Do this and you'll know it too. You can be a corporate curator. You can wait for the man who will love you with his whole heart. Climbing to the Hand of God will teach you who you really are, Daff."

"And if I slip on the rocks and plummet to my death?"

"At least you died doing something thrilling."

She gaped at him before sputtering a laugh. "What if I take you with me?"

"I'll try to hit the rocks first. Soften the blow." Gus gazed toward the looming cliff. "When Coral left, I sailed the Mediterranean alone. It was something I'd wanted to do but had been too afraid to try. That journey started my healing process, Daffy."

When he faced her again, he caught a twisting, curling lock of her hair with his finger. "One night I was caught in a storm, which was my worst nightmare about sailing. I was terrified. But I didn't give in. Didn't give up. I steered the ship through. In the morning, I was spent. But the sunrise never looked so beautiful. I'd conquered. I'd overcome. That's when I knew I could go home again and start living."

"And then... Robbi."

"An ordeal that drove a new nail of doubt through me. Like you and Thomas, I knew it wasn't right, but the fact that she broke it off—"

"And not you." She pressed her hand to his chest. "I feel you. I do."

Someone blasted a car horn. "Prince Gus! Hello! Over here!" A woman aimed her phone and snapped a picture.

"That'll be on social media in sixty seconds," he said as another car horn sounded. Then another. He took Daffy's hand. "Let's go."

"Wait." She pushed her heels into the sidewalk. "If I climb up there, what are you going to do that you can't do now? I'm not going unless you put something on the line too."

More car horns. A few motors stopped so people could get out for a better shot.

"Your Royal Highness..."

"Prince Gus! Over here."

"Can I get a selfie?"

"*Now* I wish I had Hemstead." He tried to move toward the footbridge, but Daffy leaned back, anchoring in.

"Come on... I want...a mutual deal. What scares you, Gus?"

"At the moment, you. Do you want to be mobbed?"

Overhead, thunder cracked.

"Tell me. Come on." Another crack of thunder and a flash of lightning.

"We have to go." He was too strong for her and pulled her forward. Daffy ran with the prince as a few of the spectators followed. This was madness.

As they approached the footbridge, several of the quay officers noticed them and intercepted the gathering crowd, ordering them to their motors.

"You're holding up the schedule. All of you, get on now. Leave the prince be."

Across the footbridge, which was as rickety as Daffy imagined, Gus cut through tall waves of grass to find the narrow path up and around the sheer North Sea wall of granite.

There was no room for error. A wall of rock to her left. A straight drop to the rocks on the right. Not even a blade of grass to grab on the way down.

"Daffy." Gus framed her face with her hands. "Keep your eyes level and on me. Don't look to the right or the left. Fear is the most perilous part of the journey."

She had no reply. Only fear pulsing in her ears.

Releasing her, he swung two fingers from his eyes to hers. "Eyes on me. Understand? If you slip, drop to your knees and lean forward."

She nodded. Her mouth was dry. Her legs shaking. But she followed as Gus started up. With her first step, she slipped, yelped, and dropped to one knee, gripping the path with her fists.

"Eyes on me," Gus commanded without stopping, without looking back. "You won't fall if you look ahead."

"That's exactly how I'll fall." She stood and dragged her left hand over the sharp, damp rock face. "How will I know where to step?"

"Because you're following me. If I fall, stop walking."

"And be the one to tell the queen you're dead. I'll get sacked for sure."

"Good, you can pursue your dreams."

Unless the very climb itself killed her. Nevertheless, Daffy trained her gaze on Gus's broad back.

"You won't fall if you look ahead."

Each step forward was an act of her will. An act of trust. But the higher they got, the easier she breathed. "If I fall, tell my parents I went down singing."

"What song?" Gus's words floated back on the wind. "You know they'll ask."

"Just listen. You'll hear it when I'm going down, arms and legs flailing."

"Then be sure to sing loud."

Her laughter eased the tightness in her stomach, tossing it away over the edge. Fine. Let those emotions fall away. In fact, the higher they climbed, the more her confidence grew. The view was incredible.

"You never said what you were going to do that scared you, Gus."

"I'll tell you…the top." The wind garbled his words.

"It has to be real," she hollered back. "Not wear a pink tie with a lime-green shirt."

"…do that…for fun."

"You have to talk to beautiful Coral Winthrop when she arrives for the wedding." Daffy cupped her hands around her mouth. "That's what you have to do, mate of mine."

As they rounded the curve in the cliff, the path narrowed. Daffy had to push against a continuous wind. The cold sank through her jumper, causing her to shiver. Even so, her legs burned and trembled from the steep grade. "Gus, I'm not sure—"

"Don't quit." He continued around the rock face.

Watch Gus. The wind tangled his dark hair. She stepped on a sharp rock, twisting her foot, but she muffled her cry and forged ahead.

"Almost there."

Thank God.

In mere moments, the incline leveled off and the climb seemed over all too soon. Ducking under a curved tree trunk growing out of the rocks, the two of them emerged into a half circle cut in the stone, flowing with grass and flowers.

Gus ushered her forward. "The Hand of God."

"Wow…just wow. It's beautiful." Worth every fear and perilous moment of the climb.

In this space, the wind behaved like a gentle breeze, teasing the wildflowers. Four reaching pines bent over four large stones.

"We're standing in the palm?" she said, turning a slow circle. She wanted to take it all in. Store it in her heart forever.

"If the trees are the fingers, yes."

To the right was a whitecapped North Sea tossing and turning toward the curve of the horizon. The storm clouds rumbled and rammed together.

But in the midst of it all, there was peace. The Hand of God, carved by wind and rain into the rock wall, was a place of refuge.

"Pretty amazing, isn't it?" Gus spoke in a hushed, reverent tone.

"More than I imagined." The climb, the struggle, now seemed part of its awe and wonder. "I've seen pictures, but not one of them did this justice."

With a swell of courage, she moved closer to the edge, arms wrapped around her waist, and faced the world.

"An investor came in a few years ago and wanted to construct a suspended walkway to attract tourists. Set up a souvenir shop by the quay, hire tour guides, exploit our little natural wonder. But the hamlet council walked out before he could finish his pitch."

"I'm glad. The climb should be something a person decides to take on her own." She met his gaze. "Take the risk."

"Kind of like a big life metaphor right here in Dalholm." Gus sat on the edge of God's palm, dangled his feet over the side, and patted the flat rock next to him.

Using his shoulder as an anchor, Daffy sat, dropping her legs next to his. Two hundred feet above the crashing waves below, there was nothing between them and the end of the world but a breathtaking view of a rolling blue-green sea and the coming clouds.

Daffy inhaled the pure air. "Now that I'm here, I'm not sure I want to leave."

"It does sort of put your troubles behind you, doesn't it?"

They sat in silence. Comfortable. Content. And then—

"So, Prince Gus, what is your scary thing? I think you should talk to Coral and—"

With a hesitant touch to her face, he turned her to him and kissed her, exchanging the first awkward touch with one more determined. One more certain.

His hand slipped around her waist as he pulled her to him. She gripped the sleeve of his jacket and kissed him back, sharing her affection, welcoming his passion.

When he at last raised his head, her freed lips fired the first traitorous question that came to mind. "What was that?"

"What? No good?"

"Um…very good." Daffy touched her cold hand to her warm, tingling lips.

"Kissing you was my scary thing." He pulled his arm away and brushed her hair from her eyes. "I've wanted to kiss you since Florida. When I hit you with the Frisbee." He lifted her up and moved back from the edge to sit on a small grassy rise. "I don't want to accidentally push us off if I kiss you again."

"If?" She laughed. "Blinky said something to me as I left Thomas's flat." Dare she confess their conversation? "That I was in love with you. There, that's my *truly* scary thing."

His gaze returned to the channel. "The next part is the scariest. What do we do? I don't want to hurt you, and I don't want to be hurt again. Or humiliated."

"If you think I'd hurt and humiliate you, then why did you kiss me?"

"Because I love you." His lips found hers again as he worked his hand through her hair. "I—I can't believe I'm saying it, but I do. Love you."

Daffy held his coat collar in her fists, his warmth melting the ice in the air around her. "I love you, HRH Prince Gus of the House of Blue. I will not hurt you. I won't run or hide or confess I love someone else."

"No, I don't believe you would." He kissed her once, then twice, caressing her with his affection. "But to be fair, are you ready for a life with me? Being analyzed and criticized? Do you know the *News Leader* is on record as saying whenever they need to increase sales, they post a ludicrous story about the Family, especially me, and boom! Back in the black."

"Forget being analyzed and criticized. Gus, are you inviting me into your world?"

"I'm saying I want to be with you. And if you want to be with me, you need to know everything that comes with that choice. I'm not a simple bloke who works at a financial firm, or argues cases in court, or sacks your groceries." He brushed his hand along her cheek. "I've been debating with myself the whole way here. Should I? Am I ready? Then I look at you and I know, if I don't wake up and step up, I'll lose you. Here you are, miraculously free just when I think I might be ready. What are the chances?"

"Feels rather divine."

"It does but you're...not blushing." He traced his finger along her jawline and down her neck. "Is that a bad sign?"

"Keep touching me like you are and I'll blush like you've never seen me blush." She cradled against his chest and wrapped her fingers around his. "I think I've loved you for a long time, Gus. I know being a royal comes with its distinct trials, as well as privileges. But I'm all in, Gus. If you want me."

His laugh was so rich and warm. "You hear that world? She loves me!"

"Hear that world?" she hollered into the wind. "*He* loves me."

Their voices bounced against the rocks, and "loves me" echoed around the Hand of God, through Daff and straight to her bones.

"So now what?" she said when he'd kissed her again. And again. His lips were soft and inviting, but firm, like he knew what he was doing. "Do you think the queen—"

"Wants me happy. Whatever happened eighteen years ago needs to be let go. Buried."

"Should I talk to her?" And should she tell him the rest of the story? Oh, this was a pickle she never thought she'd face.

"We can talk to her together."

Okay. Together. That worked.

But for now, she'd live in this glorious moment. Daffy closed her eyes and retreated. *He loved her.* She'd never imagined this outcome twenty-four hours ago.

Going home for the weekend was, in fact, a marvelous decision.

However...back to the queen. In truth, Daffy wasn't a hundred percent sure what she'd overheard that day. And memories were tricky, changing with time. Words and images faded, got intertwined, moved from one year to the next, even one person to another. Hearing something outside the queen's bedroom door while she cried was not a reliable tale.

If she told Gus her story, she'd raise questions she couldn't answer. And she'd implicate the queen in something that was more than likely not true.

Besides, it wasn't her secret to tell. Nevertheless, in this moment, sitting in the Hand of God, the world at their feet and the very real possibility of a future together ahead of them, keeping the secret felt like betrayal.

Okay, self, shut up. If the relationship moved forward to marriage, she'd talk to Mum. Get her advice.

"We should go. You're shivering." Gus shrugged out of his coat and held it open for her. "I was wondering if you'd be free for this fancy wedding ball I'm hosting?"

"I might be. Do you have a date for me in mind?"

He scooped her in his arms and kissed her, turning in a slow sway as the wind played a zither melody through the rocks and trees. The distant, booming thunder crashed in time with her heart and she would never be the same. She'd encountered true love in God's hand.

Gus breathed in and stepped back. "I'll make a fool of myself kissing you." He planted another one on her lips, laughing, and already, his touch was a familiar taste. "Daffodil Caron, will you go to the royal ball with me?"

"My, my, Prince Gus." She batted her eyes and fanned her face. "This is so out of the blue, but of course I'll go with you."

He swung her around with a shout. "It feels so good to be free."

Setting her down, he bent for another bold kiss. He wasn't kidding about making a fool of himself. But who was she to stop him?

"Gus, seriously, do you want to go public? Are you ready? We just now figured out how we feel."

"I'm ready. But if you're not, we can—"

"If you help me, I'll be ready."

"Always." He squeezed her hand. "I'll never let you go. But, darling, did you see the number of phones aimed at us down below? Trust me, we are already public." Another kiss. This one more graceful and full lipped, depositing more than he took.

"You're a good kisser," she whispered.

"So are you. Looking forward to a lifetime of these." They stood on the edge of the path, ready to go down. "We should go slow though. Get to know each other as a couple."

"I agree. But know this, Gus Blue. I'm not going anywhere." It was her turn to draw him close. Seal her pledge with a kiss.

The storm echoed over the channel and released the first drops of rain. With a yelp, they hurried to the path. Climbing down, Daffy kept her gaze on Gus. Her foot never slipped. As they crossed the footbridge, the storm unleashed its fury.

"Let's head to Hadsby," Gus called over his shoulder.

Running through the deluge, hand in hand toward Centre Street, they passed the Belly of the Beast and headed up the incline to the castle. But as they approached, Gus slowed his pace. A motor sat inside the gates and the royal standard flew above Hadsby's turret.

"The queen," she said. "The chair."

As the words left her mouth, the queen's protection officer stepped through the gates. Gus dropped Daffy's hand. "Your Royal Highness, we were just about to search for you."

"We'd gone for a walk." Rainwater dripped from the edge of his hair and beard. Reaching back, he took Daffy's hand again. "We need to get inside."

The sturdy man nodded, first at the prince then Daffy. She tried to smile as she wiped rainwater from her eyes.

"Her Majesty would like to speak to you," he said. "Now."

"Wedding ball is two weeks away. Royal reporter Leslie Ann Parker shares her thoughts on which designer Lady Holland chose for the big night. Stay tuned."

—STONE BRUBAKER ON THE MORNING SHOW.

"Madeline and Hyacith Live! Another royal wedding ball is upon us but will we actually see a wedding? Stay tuned for thoughts from royal experts around the world. Also, was Prince Gus the first prince jilted at the altar? We're live in five."

—MADELINE AND HYACINTH LIVE!

OMG! I just saw Prince Gus at the port in Dalholm. Who's he with?

—@STEFWITHANF ON INSTAGRAM

Prince Gus was at the quay today with this woman. Anyone know her? Are they a thing?

—FACEBOOK POST FROM ANDREA FULLER

Now Trending on Twitter: Prince Gus

Does Prince Gus have a new love? My sources identify her as Daffodil Caron, a member of the Royal Trust.

—@ROYAL WATCHER ONE

CHAPTER
TWENTY-THREE

GUS

Stern handed him a towel, accompanied by a look that matched his name, as Gus entered his apartment. Mum stood in the lounge, hands at her side, her head tipped with curiosity.

"This is a surprise." He ran the towel across his face and through his hair, gathering his thoughts. "Did you say you were coming up early?"

"Your father wanted a weekend away before all the fun begins. I was able to clear my diary for a few days, so I joined him. The child case has worn me to bits. The images are forever embedded in my brain. I thought between Hadsby, Dalholm, and seeing my son, I'd gain a fresh perspective." Mum gave him the once-over. "You're soaked."

"I climbed up to the Hand of God." *Don't be a shy man, out with it.* "Daffy and I climbed. Got caught in the rain." The residue of their kisses still buzzed through him. From the moment his lips touched hers, he fell into a deep pit of love. Best part? He felt certain she loved him as much.

"Daffy? Caron?" Mum made a face. "That seems rather odd. Have you spent a lot of time with her?"

"Why would it seem odd, Mum? We're childhood friends. We're living in the same castle."

"A rather large castle. One could go days without seeing someone from the guest wing. Isn't she engaged?"

"As a matter of fact, they broke it off. And I've been dining in the servants' hall. Didn't fancy eating alone." He handed the damp towel back to Stern. "Where's Dad?"

"Raiding the downstairs kitchen, where else? He loves Chef Charles's cooking. He'd bring him to Perrigwynn if he had a prayer the man would move. Besides, I want to see the wedding gowns on display and check out the *King Titus*."

"The gowns are in the Grand Gallery. I saw them this morning. Daffy and Lucy have done a splendid job." He held himself in check, trying to sound objective about his newfound love while his heart skipped and tap-danced to an inner love song.

"Shall we go see them together?"

"Give me a moment to change out of these wet togs." When he escaped to his room, Gus sent Daffy a quick text.

> Going to see the gowns with the queen. Meet you there in five.

He thought Daffy might already be in the Grand Gallery when they arrived, but for the dresses, it was empty. "I'll get Daffy. She's in Princess Charlotte."

The moment she opened her door, he wanted to push inside, take her in his arms, and tumble into the nearest chair, kissing her, as his heart and body melted with desire. This beautiful woman loved him? Let Coral Winthrop tell every ugly truth about why she left. He'd discovered the wonder of Daffodil.

"Did you get my text? The queen wants us to join her in the Grand Gallery," he said as if nothing at all boiled beneath the surface.

"No, I didn't. Why does she... Is something wrong?" Daffy looked down at her trackie bottoms and sock feet. "I can't go out there now."

"You look beautiful." No, she *was* beautiful, her bare face sporting nothing but the mark of his kisses and the cold wind. She was sexy without trying. "Come on."

"*I can't.* The Royal Trust must always appear before Her Majesty in uniform. Anything else is a breach of protocol. My boss could reprimand me. Even sack me, if she had a mind to."

"Your mum is your boss, and your prince—me—is telling you to come and see the queen. Now, who do you mind?" He leaned down so his lips almost touched hers. "Me or your boss?"

"Gus?" Mum stood at the head of the guest corridor. "Where is Daffy?"

"She's just here."

"Tell her to come."

"I'm not dressed, Your Majesty."

"You mean to tell me you're standing in front of my son *naked*?" The queen's voice spiked high.

"Good grief, Mum. She's in trackies."

"We'll wave protocol for now." Mum motioned for them to follow her to the Grand Gallery.

With Daffy beside him, he gained a deeper sense of purpose. He belonged to someone. The *right* someone. He wasn't alone.

Daffy raised the lights by the switch on the wall and spotlighted the gowns as the rain drummed a continuous beat against the skylights.

"Daffy, please walk me through the display."

"Yes, Your Majesty." Daffy curtsied, then stood just off Mum's left shoulder. "This is your wedding gown. Designed by—"

"I'm really more curious about the blue gown at the end." Mum moved ahead. "Can we start there?"

"Yes, ma'am."

"Can you explain this?" Mum flicked her hand toward the dress, then waited, arms folded. "Is this some sort of joke?"

"No, ma'am. This is the dress for the *Unknown Bride*. Lucy and I—"

"Where did you get it?"

"A vintage shop. In the Old Hamlet."

"Surely you recognized it."

"I did, ma'am, yes. In fact, finding it was very surreal. There was this woman, Adelaide, who gave me a large box with the dress inside. She acted as if I was expected. I was very surprised. How did it get there?"

"I've no idea but take this down." Ice weighted Mum's words. "Now. And throw it away."

"Throw it away?" Daffy said.

"Mum, what's going on?" Gus stepped between his mother and the woman he loved. "What's wrong with this dress?"

"A-Adelaide had it, Your Majesty." Daffy's voice trembled as she stumbled with a defense. "She said Emmanuel told her to give it to me."

"Emmanuel? Well…" For a moment, the queen seemed to soften. But only a moment. "I said *take it down*." Then her expression lost all light. "Burn it."

"Wait—burn it?" Gus said. "Mum, isn't this the dress you wore to your twenty-first birthday? You're typically very sentimental about—"

"I know when I wore it." She clenched her hands into fists, then eased her fingers open. "Just please, take it down. Find another dress for the *Unknown Bride*."

"Yes, ma'am." Daffy looked at Gus. For what? Help? Guidance? He was as flummoxed as she.

He offered the smallest of nods. *It'll be all right.*

"Come, both of you. Show me the *King Titus*." Mum turned for the Grand Stairs and the Queen's Library.

Daffy clasped her hand to his, lowering her voice to an insistent whisper. "What are we going to do?" Then, "Ma'am—begging your pardon, but I'll stay here to remove the dress, as you requested."

"Agree. Mum, I can show you the chair." If at all possible, he wanted to leave Daffy out of the mess with the chair. At least to the queen. He motioned to her. *I've got this.*

"You can do that directly after. Daffy, you represent the Royal Trust, do you not? Now where is the *King Titus*?"

DAFFY

A job sorting rubbish at a recycling center wouldn't be *so* bad, would it? After all, she appreciated *old* things. Although old, used, *gross* things would present a challenge.

Still, a job was a job.

To her surprise and relief, the queen asked no questions as Gus led her down to the garage and helped her into the cart's passenger seat.

"This ought to be interesting," she said as the prince steered out of the garage.

Jostling along in the folding rear seat of the cart, she plotted how she could "bounce off" at the next rut—*Gus, hit them all*—and pretend to be hurt while urging them, "Leave me to die. Go on without me."

But the path to the workshop became smooth as the old white clapboard structure came into view.

When he pulled up to the workshop's open door, Daffy leaned to see if the carpenter was inside. If there was a God, Emmanuel would appear to help smooth the waters. And bonus, explain about the blue dress. Finally, a silver lining on this thunderous day of wild emotions.

The queen stepped out with a pressed, firm expression, her blue eyes narrowed with suspicion.

"Gus, once again, explain to me why we've taken a joyride in this dreary, cold, wet rain?"

"Mum, funny story," he said, taking the queen's hand as she maneuvered around a small puddle.

Daffy stepped up behind him and raised to whisper in his ear. "If I get sacked, you better get me a job with your friend in Florida. At that pub on the beach."

"You won't get sacked." He spoke low, out of the side of his mouth. "Besides, what happened to corporate curating?"

"This. Right here. What's about to go down will end my career."

"What are you two going on about?" The queen ducked into

the workshop, her shoulders shivering, shaking raindrops from her coat.

Gus joined her with a backward glance at the door's dangling lock. Daffy trailed in with slow steps.

"I'm not sure how to begin." He seemed to search his memory. "You see, Daffy was in the library and—"

"Don't start with me." Sorry, but she'd not be the anchor to this tale of disaster. By her expression, the queen was already blaming her. But this time she was not a gullible, assuming ten-year-old. "I was merely checking to see where Cranston had placed the chair."

"Right." Gus wagged his finger at her. "Daffy was doing her job but I, however, was just back from the pub. Drunk."

"Go on." The queen's gaze fired a thousand cannons. Daffy moved next to Gus and patted his back. Might as well face the firing squad together. After all, they were in love.

"I might have had a few pints. Ernst was very chatty that night—"

"Ernst?" The queen huffed. "The expert on the Dalholm shorthand speech chatty? He could've told you his life story in ten minutes."

"I had more pints than I realized. Anyway, as I headed to my apartment, I saw the light on in the library. I went in. Long story short, I sat in the chair—"

The queen gasped. "You broke the *Titus*?" Sharp cookie, the queen, seeing the picture before it was completed. But then again, this was a paint-by-numbers sort of tale.

"It was an accident. I heard a crack, so I moved the chair about, thinking I could locate the weakness."

"Where you were, Daffy? You're the Royal Trust person on-site."

"Mum, she was yelling at me to get out of the chair. But I was too inebriated to listen. I scooted the chair forward—"

"*Stop.*" The queen raised her hand as if about to issue a royal proclamation. "I've heard enough. The chair broke. How bad was the damage? Where is it now? Why are we here? Honestly, Gus, you are such a child at times."

Hey, now wait a minute. Daffy stepped in front of the firing squad. "We found a skilled craftsman, Your Majesty."

"Yes. Emmanuel." Gus crossed around the bench to turn on the overhead lamp. "He helped me fix the chair."

"You...met Emmanuel? In person?"

"Ernst found him for us." Gus glanced at Daffy then his mother. "Why? Did he help you fix the chair too?" He smiled and laughed, but only a little. "Did you break it? Like mother, like son."

"No, I did not break it. I'm not stupid." She peered at Daffy. "You say Adelaide gave you the dress by Emmanuel's command?"

"I don't know about command but yes, she said he wanted me to have it. I'm not sure why a carpenter would—"

"Where is the chair?" Queen Catherine raised her chin, her jaw taut.

"Here." Gus moved to the corner where the chair had been carefully preserved in cotton and covered with a canvas. But the ancient artifact was not there. He dropped down, searching, scouring the small space, flinging the coverings over his head as if the chair might magically appear. But all his searching produced was a cloud of dust and a dew of perspiration.

"Gus, where is my chair?" The queen was not messing around.

"It was here, I promise you. Two days ago. I pieced together the seat and legs." He knocked over boxes, peering into cupboards much too small to hold the *King Titus*.

Daffy focused on breathing, feeling as if she was alone on the cliff's pathway and one wrong step away from plummeting to the rocks. Falling, falling, falling.

"Are you telling me someone stole the world's most known and valued chair?"

"No, impossible. Emmanuel, Daffy, and I were the only ones who knew the chair was out here. And he'd never take it."

The queen shot a glance at Daffy. "And you? Did you take it?"

"Mum," Gus said. "Of course not. She was the one helping me fix it. She hounded me about even sitting in it."

"Then where is it?"

Seconds ticked off as Daffy searched for her voice. "Ma'am,

we'll find it. His Royal Highness is right. Emmanuel is very kind. Very knowledgeable. In fact, he talked as if he knew the first King Titus personally."

"I know all about Emmanuel. What I *don't know* is the location of my chair." The queen approached Daffy, wielding her finger like a sword. "You are dismissed. Gather your things and go."

"What? Mum, that's not fair." Gus stepped ahead of his mother. "Daffy had nothing to do with this."

"Precisely. Had she done her job, one of the world's most valuable historical pieces would not be lost."

"I took command of the chair once I broke it. She wanted to report it but I talked her into waiting."

"So she purposefully did not do her job? She is dismissed."

"Mum, I will find the chair."

"Yes, you will, Augustus. But Miss Caron is still dismissed. I'm sorry, Daffodil, but you have let me, the Family, and your country down."

"Oh, ma'am, I am so, so sorry." She held onto the workbench and tried not to weep.

"Mum, please, that's rather harsh. This is my doing, not hers. Sack me if you've a mind to sack someone."

"I would if I could. You've let me and your country down as well. You should've known better."

The queen exited the workshop, head high, spine stiff, without another word. Gus trailed along behind Daffy and tried to fasten the lock—not that there was anything valuable to protect—but the steel piece just dangled there.

"What's wrong with the lock?"

"I'm not sure," Gus said, low, over her shoulder. "But she'll calm down. I'll take care of this."

"I doubt she will. And she's right. I should be sacked." Daffy fought the rise of shame.

"This isn't how I envisioned our first evening as a couple in love," he said.

"How can you still love me? The queen will never accept me as your girlfriend now, let alone anything more."

"But I do. I love you. This doesn't change anything."

"What are you two going on about? Shall we get on? It's wet and cold. Gus, you've a chair to find and Daffy, you've luggage to pack."

Love was a magical wonderful thing that healed a lot of wounds. But in this moment, love was a fantasy.

Riding in the jump seat, Daffy gazed toward the cliff and the Hand of God. She could just barely see the tip of His "fingers."

Their true love confession seemed long ago and faraway, even silly and frivolous. Their magical afternoon ended in disaster. How could she climb out of this one? More royal security statutes? She'd never be allowed near the palace again.

A stony royal silence serenaded the ride back to Hadsby. She'd never be a part of this family. *The Family.* It was one thing to face the public, with their criticism and scrutiny, but it was another entirely to break a family—royal or not—apart. She'd not do it. And because she loved him, she'd not allow Gus to do it either.

GUS

"Ernst." Gus burst into the Belly of the Beast. "Have you seen Emmanuel?"

After a pretty good row, Gus had given in and agreed to drive Daffy to the train station to catch the six o'clock to Port Fressa. She'd packed in mere minutes and almost ran from the castle.

"How can this be?" He'd stood in the doorway to her bedroom as she'd packed. *"We confess our love to one another, and three hours later you're leaving on the heels of this stupid argument."*

"We attempted to deceive the queen. We should've been honest about the chair."

"This is my fault. I thought I was protecting you."

"And yourself." She dumped clothes from a drawer into her suitcase. *Didn't bother to fold them.*

"I'll make it right, Daffy. I won't stop until I do."

Their goodbye at the train station was nothing for the movies, or even a short novel, but he was able to hold her for a few brief moments. Tangle his fingers in her hair. Kiss her soft lips.

"I do love you."

But she'd not returned his sentiment, and the feelings of old stirred deep in his belly and whispered, *"Here we go again."*

"Yer Royalness," Ernst called. "Come. Oh, problem?"

"Emmanuel." Gus landed at the bar where Ernst dried a tray of mugs. "Immediately."

"Not seen." He pushed Gus down on a stool and filled one of the glasses.

"Tell me where he goes. Even better, where he lives. I'll find him."

"Can't."

"What do you mean, 'Can't?' How'd you find him the first time?"

"Word out."

"Please, my mate, word out. Again. It's urgent. Very, very urgent."

"Give twenty-four. Forty-eight."

Two days? Gus dropped his forehead to the old, scarred planks of the bar. "I don't have twenty-four hours, minutes—not even seconds." His very heartbeat seemed to count the time he raced against. He raised up, his hand around the pint glass, too weak to lift it, too full of angst to drink it. "Ernst, find him. There's a Queen's Medal in it for you. I'll see to it myself."

Ernst propped his wide girth on the bar. "And princess?"

"Princess? What are you talking about?"

"Daffy. Pretty. Hair." Ernst waved his broad hand about his head.

"Why do you call her a princess?"

"Because you love her."

"You know?"

"Ernst see."

Gus swilled his pint. "I do love her, but the queen is angry. We... I lost the *King Titus* chair and now Daffy is sacked and on

her way to Port Fressa. I think she's changed her mind about me."
Of course she had. This was his lot in life. The Love 'Em and Lose
'Em Prince.

His phone buzzed from his pocket. Let it be Daffy from the
train telling him she was all right. That she believed in their love.

But it was an incoming message from Helene. A picture of
Adler holding her lime-green Frisbee.

> I miss u. Come play wiff me.

> Miss you too, Adler. Tell your mom to teach you to
> spell.

Helene answered with a simple, Ha!
Another text came in. This one from Hemstead.

> I don't know where you've gone but I don't care. I
> resign.

Great. Perfect ending to a rotten day. With a solo sip of his
pint, so as not to offend Ernst, he reminded the proprietor to "word
out" for Emmanuel and headed back to Hadsby.

He gathered the staff and interrogated them, beginning with
Cranston, who assured him the chair was in Gus's apartment.

"I don't even have a key, sir."

Stern was clueless. And not surprised when Gus announced
Hemstead had resigned.

"If you don't mind me saying, it's time to remember who and
where you are, sir," Stern said when they returned to his apartment.

"You sound like Daffy." This should've been a night of dining
with the woman he loved, not fighting with the world and fearing
for his heart.

After shoving down a cold meat pie he'd carried to his quarters
from the kitchen, Gus ambled to his parents' apartment and
knocked.

Dad let him in with a grumble. "She's on the phone. Still quite
angry."

"Do the words, 'It was an accident,' mean nothing?"

Dad held up his hands. "Save your case for her. You know she has to process. But she's extremely disappointed in you and Daffy."

"Daffy is innocent. I did all the breaking and deceiving." Gus sat in the nearest chair and slumped forward. "Ernst is the only man I know who can find the carpenter. He's on the task."

"Is the carpenter Emmanuel?" Dad's attention flicked back and forth between Gus and the telly before he pointed the remote at the screen. "Your mum knew him when she was young. What's this?" Dad leaned forward. "Leslie Ann Parker is doing a story on your mum? Next Sunday night. On LVT-1."

His father's attempt to mimic the announcer's voice almost made Gus laugh. Almost. Reporters never got the story right. They exaggerated, found untrue details from clandestine "inside sources" and spoke them as gospel truth.

"I'd think Ms. Parker would want to report on John and Holland. The ones getting married."

"Who knows with Ms. Parker."

Gus caught the last of the commercial. "...join me, Leslie Ann Parker, on *The Rest of the Story* as I take an in-depth look at our queen with never before seen photos and a story that just might change history."

Change history? The woman was reaching. "What aspect of Mum's life could possibly be hidden? Or change history. Other than her private life within palace walls, every major and minor move is documented. They'd have had a crew in your wedding night suite, if the law still required."

"Good heavens." Dad switched to the game show he and Mum watched Sunday nights.

Gus eased to his feet but stopped at the sight of the blue gown Mum demanded Daffy discard, even burn, draped over a wingback chair.

"Dad, what's this doing here? Mum told Daffy burn it."

"Burn it?" Dad didn't look away from the telly screen. "I don't know. You'll have to ask her."

"You should've seen her. She went mad when she saw it on the *Unknown Bride* mannequin. Gave Daffy quite the ripping."

"Doesn't sound like her."

Gus stood as Mum entered the room. "Glasgow Towns and Morwena Caron have been made aware."

"Who's Glasgow?" Gus said.

"A member of the Royal Trust in charge of textile restoration, including furniture pieces. He and Morwena will quietly inquire about the chair." Mum sat next to Dad but fidgeted, curling her legs over the cushion, then sitting up straight, feet planted. "I assume the thief will issue a ransom note. Make his demands. The whole world will know our failure."

"If we must tell the world, Mum, I'll do it."

She gripped the end of the couch arm, her fingers white. "I keep it in storage for twenty-five years, and when I bring it out, my own son turns it into a trampoline."

"I sat in it. I didn't jump."

"Why didn't you listen to Daffy?"

"I was drunk. And then I was a bullheaded man who said, 'I can fix it. Hush, let me listen.'" With a sigh, Gus knelt next to his mother, his queen. "I am truly sorry. I will find the chair."

"How? How will any of us find it? It's lost. Taken."

"You said yourself that we should expect a ransom note."

"Or the chair will be sold on the private market and we'll never see it again. Forever lost." Mum stood to pace, her bare feet leaving imprints in the plush carpet. "A thousand years of rulers, and the *Titus* lost on my watch."

"We'll be infamous together, Mum. You for losing the chair. Me for being the only prince in recorded history to be left at the altar." He glanced over at the dress. "Do you want me to take *that* to the incinerator?"

"No." Her sharp words caused Dad to look away from the telly. "I'll... I'll find something to do with it."

"I can take it back to the vintage shop. Daffy said it was down by the quay."

"I said I'll deal with it. Edric, do you mind watching alone? I have a headache."

Dad muted the telly and reached for Mum. "Love, it's going to be okay. Historical things get lost, damaged, burned up in fires, given away, traded, and stolen. We could have a regular Robin Hood in these woods, taking the chair to sell and give the money to the poor. But whatever the case, life and the world will go on."

"Thank you, Edric. But not helping. I hope this noble marauder informs us of his intent. I'd be more than happy to give him any amount of money in exchange for the chair."

Gus gathered his courage. No more deception. "Mum, I don't think you should've sacked Daffy, but she has other career aspirations, so maybe she'll make lemonade with her lemons. Also, I want you to give her a good reference."

For the first time since he'd know Catherine, Queen of Lauchtenland—his mum—she seemed frail. Even a bit broken.

"All right. I'll tell Morwena."

"There's one more thing." Here goes. "I'm in love with Daffy. I know you have some angst toward her from the past, but it's time to move on. I've asked her to the ball and she said yes."

Now for real courage. To make sure Daffy didn't change her mind.

CHAPTER
TWENTY-FOUR

DAFFY

"**I** know you're in there. *Open up.*" Ella's voice pressed through the door. "We know you broke up with Thomas. We know you got sacked."

Her sister's muffled pronouncement of all the disastrous events shot Daffy just a wee bit lower.

"Then you know to leave me alone. Besides, it's almost midnight. Don't you have to work in the morning?"

"Not if you need me."

"I don't." Daffy burrowed into the couch cushions and pulled her favorite blanket up to her nose. Her body ached as if she'd crawled up and down the mountain path to the Hand of God. Her heart churned like the stormy sea she and Gus had watched together.

Gus.

"Daffy?"

"Go away." She needed to think, process.

Friday she broke up with Thomas. Sunday morning, she declared her love for Prince Gus. In the afternoon, she was sacked for something she didn't do but was, in truth, her responsibility. The queen was right to let her go.

And now…now she needed to figure out what happened next. But before she accepted, once and for all, that her dreams of a life with a prince had been nothing more than that—a dream—could she please have a quiet moment to replay the scene at the Hand of

God? To kiss Gus over and over in her mind? To succumb to the chills of his whispered *"I love you"*?

Lucy had called, wanting to know what happened. Daffy gave her the Dalholm shorthand version. *"Chair. Lost. Sacked."* Told her to find any gown for the *Unknown Bride.*

"So that Adelaide lady had no idea what she was talking about?" Lucy dug for further explanation but Daffy answered in again in Dalholm-speak.

"Queen. Dress. Hates." She was beginning to see the wisdom of her northern countrymen.

"Daff?" Ella knocked again.

"Sleeping."

"I can hear the television."

Daffy hit mute. The show she wasn't really watching had gone to commercial and Leslie Ann entered her living room by way of the air waves. She strolled through some wooded, hilly countryside. What was she saying? Daffy raised the volume. "…this year's most fascinating documentary."

"Daff, I'm coming in. I have ice cream, and it's melting." The lock clicked. The door creaked open.

"What kind of ice cream?"

"Your favorite." Heavy footsteps echoed on the hardwood, stopping just over the threshold. "Chocolate peanut butter."

"Okay, but one bowl and you're out of here, sister." Daffy kicked off her blanket and tugged at her trackies. "What's everyone saying about me and Thomas? No one has texted or— Gus. W-what are you doing here?" She smoothed her hair, tugged down her short, tattered T-shirt.

He scooped her into his arms with a fast and furious kiss heating her surprise into desire.

"I had to see you. I hated how we parted so I borrowed one of Dad's motors." He held her by the arms, his forehead against hers. "You didn't say you loved me, and the old Gus, you know, the one from before Florida, felt a bit wobbly."

"I'm sorry but was feeling so blue…so confused, but you… here…makes everything better." She pressed a quick kiss to his lips and reached for the ice cream he held. "And this seals the deal."

"Ella said it would." He sighed as with relief.

"You called her?" Daffy linked her arm through his, loving his nearness, and steered for the kitchen.

"I needed someone to tell me where you lived. Help me surprise you." He sat at the island, his famous smile dispelling the gloomy atmosphere.

A smile aimed at her. For her. Because of her. How she loved how handsome he was—his high cheeks, curious eyes, and how his full lips were surrounded by a whisper of whiskers. Mostly she loved the heart he carried beneath his sculpted chest.

Setting out two bowls, Daffy filled them with ice cream. When she handed one to Gus, he grasped her wrist, his warmth radiating along her arm.

"This crazy day doesn't change anything for me." Huskiness deepened his voice.

"Are you certain?" Daffy joined him on the other side of the island, sitting in one of the inexpensive tall chairs she'd found online. "The queen is not my fan."

"She will be. When she knows the truth. I told her to get over her old grudge."

"What did she say?"

"What could she say? And she's going to give you a good reference for a new job. Unless you want to return to the Royal Trust. Then I'll fight for you."

"I'm not sure what I want." She took a small bite of ice cream. "Does she know you're here?"

"Does it matter? I'm not sixteen. Besides, she's more concerned about the *Titus* right now than the fact I'm in love with you. But tonight, she looked spent. Almost wrecked. She didn't even watch her usual Sunday night program with Dad. Something more than the chair is bothering her. Maybe it's the child case she's hearing."

"Those details should wreck us all."

"Know what else is odd, Daff?" Gus dug into his ice cream

then waved his spoon about with a look of contemplation. "The blue dress was in their apartment. I asked if she wanted me to carry it out and she said no. Not an 'Oo, I'm not sure.' Or the 'I don't know' sort of no. More like a bullet. 'No!'"

"Maybe she realized her sentiment for it." Daffy skimmed a small taste of chocolate peanut butter ice cream. The cold, sweet treat brought up childhood memories. And now, helped her create new ones.

As for the dress, she had no idea if the gown was connected to the frantic phone call all those years ago, but the chain of events was suspect. She remembered the queen going on about "sixteen something or other" and how "she *something*" and "wearing it," her voice rising and falling. She also heard the words "Trent" and "daughter."

"What are you thinking?" Gus devoured another large spoonful of ice cream. "It must be serious. You're not eating. And you have a wrinkle, right here." He gently pressed his thumb to the crease in her brow, then caressed her cheek and down her neck.

"I guess the reality of this weekend is hitting me. Lows to highs to lows." She drew his palm to her lips. "I love your hand against my face."

"I'm disappointed though. You're still not blushing. I'll have to think of another way to see that pink rush over your cheeks."

"I'm sure you will." She rather looked forward to his attempts at making her blush. In fact, he was off to a good start. "So, what about the chair. Do you think Emmanuel stole it?"

"No. But after I dropped you at the train station, I went to the Belly of the Beast."

Daffy savored her ice cream as Gus detailed his conversation with Ernst, hoping to rouse Emmanuel sooner rather than later.

"I was going to fight for your position then I realized this was your chance. Do the job you've always wanted. You made the perilous climb to the Hand of God, why not go for your dream job? You possess the courage to forge a new path."

"I've been thinking the same thing. Trouble is, most of those sorts are in London."

"I see." Gus paused. Cleared his throat. "Well, London is not too far. Easy to travel on weekends. Even week nights."

"And... America. New York."

"New York? I see." His spoon scraped the bottom of the bowl. "That's a bit farther than London."

"In fact, your old love has an opening for an in-house curator at CCW Cosmetics." She made a face. "I might have looked to see what was out there. CCW opened a new position for a curator to create a museum of the company's history from scratch. It's a dream opportunity."

"Foiled again by Coral Winthrop." There was no humor in his words. "D-do you want me to speak to her?"

"Yes, but not for me. For you." Daffy slipped from her stool and held his face in her hands. "I'm not going anywhere without you. Promise."

"I won't stand in your way."

"You think I'd want any job more than you? More than the life we'd build together? Something meaningful and lasting. A dream career is rewarding, but a home and family with my dream *man* is what makes my world go round. Not that we're getting married or anything but—"

His kiss made her breathless. Sliding from his stool, he pulled her against him, his arms tight around her back, as if he couldn't get close enough. His kiss was rushed and passionate, then after a moment, softened, and their breathing fell into the same rhythm.

Daffy locked her arms about his waist, sliced open her heart, and poured her love into him.

He stepped...she stepped...until somehow how they tumbled backward and toppled over the rummage sale chair.

Laughing, Gus raised up, his face inches from hers. "You didn't finish your ice cream."

"Let it melt." She grabbed him for another kiss and rolled onto the floor, landing with a thud.

"This was way better than the scene I imagined in *My Life with the Prince*."

"Your life with the prince?" Gus raised up on one elbow. "What's this?"

"Guess it's okay to confess now. Back in the day, I kept a diary, well, more like a novel, of what it would be like to be your girlfriend. Only you were Romeo and I was Juliet. I know, not very original. But I was ten."

"Where is this book?" He glanced toward her bookcase. "I want to read it."

"Lost. Thrown away in my family's big purge of '09."

He traced his finger along the collar of her jumper. "Then we'll have to write new chapters. Where everything is real." Gus kissed her forehead, then her cheek, moving down to her neck, returning to her lips—his kiss seeking…searching…and finally finding her soul.

CHAPTER
TWENTY-FIVE

GUS

They stayed up all night talking, reminiscing, catching up on each other's lives, asking the hard questions. Children. Pets. Finances. Chore list. All the practical things of joining two lives.

Gus was a talker. Had to get out what bothered him. Even if he talked to himself. He wanted the listener to hear, understand, then offer encouragement or advice, or tell him to get over himself.

"With Coral then Robbi, I didn't want to talk about issues. I thought it made me appear weak. But I'd fill up and eventually download on my mates. Poor lads at Pub Clemency heard more than they ever wanted. After Coral left, they practically screamed at me to talk to her. But I couldn't cross that hurdle. Robbi was easier because, well, I knew it was right."

Daffy, on the other hand, was a brooder. Had to walk away, think about things. Not just about what bothered her, but almost any decision.

As dawn slipped across the dark, sleeping city, Gus rose from the pallet they'd made on the floor, where they stared at the city lights reflected on the ceiling, and offered to make breakfast.

"My omelets are infamous." He moved about the kitchen as if it were his own.

"For what? Are you going to poison me, Prince Gus? Then say I'm on the lam with the chair?"

He peered inside the refrigerator. "Well that was the plan but it seems you're void of eggs."

She came around the island and kissed him. "I have milk and cereal. Get two bowls from that cupboard."

She set out the milk. He found the spoons. How easily they chatted and moved about. As if they'd been together for years.

"You realize after the ball, we'll be official," he'd said, pouring milk over a large pile of toasted oats. "We're already all over social media, shots of us talking on the quay. So here we go."

"What was it the Duchess of Sussex said? She knew it wouldn't be easy, but she thought it would be fair. I'm ready for whatever, in my head anyway. But like I said at the Hand of God, if you stand by me, help me, be with me, I'll ride whatever storm comes our way."

The slightly stale cereal was the best he'd ever had. That's how it was when you shared with someone you love.

While Daffy loaded in the dishwasher, Gus checked his email and read the text messages he'd ignored all night.

"Did I tell you Hemstead resigned?"

"Why am I not surprised?"

"They're sending me a new chap. Ollie." Gus tucked his phone away and met Daffy in the kitchen. "I should go." He bent for a long kiss. "I don't want to but I've a final meeting with the planners this afternoon." He glanced about for his coat, spying it in a pile by the front door. He wasn't sure how that happened. "The ball setup begins next week and we don't want any surprises. Guests start arriving as early as Tuesday."

"Will you miss me?"

"Every moment." Gus stole another kiss and wrapped her in a tight embrace. "I love you."

She pressed her head against his chest. "Me too, Gus. Me too."

Daffy assisted him with his coat then straightened the collar. "Are you looking forward to the ball?"

"Very much." His slow kiss was ripe with passion. "Because you'll be there."

"When should I go up? I'll need to book a room—"

"You'll stay at Hadsby. In the guest suite on the royal wing." Gus lingered by the half-open door. "I'll ring you tonight. As for when you come up, I'll leave it to you, but tomorrow works for me. What's on your diary today?"

"Sleeping. Not that I can. I feel like my life has fallen into place and I don't want to miss a minute of it. In reality, I need to redo my résumé, unpack, return some things to Thomas. Leslie Ann and Ella want to meet for tea later. Oh, her piece on the queen runs this coming Sunday night. Are you going to watch?"

"We don't tend to watch shows on the Family. But because she's your friend, and only because she's your friend, I'll half tune in. Though I can't imagine she's come up with anything new. Mum's been documented to death."

Their goodbye kiss lingered, and he knew he'd propose sooner rather than later. But they were ready.

He had Great Granny's engagement ring from 1933. A six-carat diamond in a gold filigree setting. Very art deco. Daffy would love it. It was so old, it was in style. But then, didn't she deserve her own ring? One selected just for her? Now he understood why he'd never considered Coral or Robbi for Great Granny's ring.

Maybe he'd hint around, see what she'd prefer. But would that spoil the surprise? Ella might know. Or even Leslie Ann. Ridiculous thought. She'd announce it on the telly for another "scoop of the decade."

All good thoughts while speeding up North One toward Dalholm. Parking the motor in Hadsby's garage, Gus tossed the keys on their hook and bounded up the stairs. He paused in his office to let Stern know he was up and about.

"Just a quick shower and I'll be ready."

"Very good, sir. The queen was asking for you."

"The queen?" Gus picked up his tablet and scrolled through, looking for a break in his week to go back down to see Daffy. Maybe Thursday afternoon. "What does she want?"

He was booked on Friday with the Dalholm Home Restoration Society. He was eager to see their work restoring the hamlets' historic homes.

Saturday, John and Holland would arrive. He should invite Daffy for the weekend, let her ease into things before the ball. And ease Mum toward the idea Daffy was his true love.

True. Love. An unbelievable realization. Yet oh so nice. The usual twang of doubt, of hesitation, barely registered. Before Daffy, he had no desire for a relationship. Five weeks later, he was calculating the best engagement ring.

"Perhaps there is a God."

"Excuse me, sir?" Stern said.

"Nothing. Talking to myself. Well, I best get on. I'll see you in a few minutes. Can you ask housekeeping to ready Royal Guest One?" The room should be ready for Daffy whenever she wanted.

But first, a quick visit to Mum.

"You wanted to see me?"

"Yes." She looked very much like herself. Composed, in command. "We've found the chair."

"Where?" An immediate weight lifted. Yes, there was a God. "What happened? Did Emmanuel come round?"

"Hemstead found it in the workshop and took it to Perrigwynn. Then he resigned."

"How did he get inside?"

"He broke the lock. That's why the door was open when we arrived. He observed you heading in that direction several times and decided to investigate.

"He didn't need to break any locks."

"He might have pretended that lock was your head," Mum said with a laugh.

"Perhaps. I was rather used to my freedom in Florida."

"Which kept me awake at night." Mum poured a cup of tea and offered it to Gus. "When Hemstead found the chair, he felt it his duty to protect it. I'm grateful."

"Why didn't he ring, tell me he'd found it? He had to know it was there because of me."

"After the way you treated him, I'm sure he felt he'd not get a square answer. Anyway, the *King Titus* is at Perrigwynn, where Glasgow Towns will finish the restoration. He said it was in very good condition and the work done so far was excellent."

"You're welcome." Gus set his tea aside. "However, since I caused the damage, I should pay for the repair."

"The Trust will pay, but you might make a large donation. Ease your guilt." Mum refilled her teacup, smiling as Dad entered, dressed for a day of hiking.

"We looked for you at breakfast," Dad said to Gus, declining Mum's silent offer of tea. "Chef Charles made his famous eggs Benedict. Darling, are you sure we can't get him down to Perrigwynn?"

"I was in Port Fressa. With Daffy." Gus glanced at his watch. He needed to shower. "I must run. Meeting with the planners."

"You drove to Port Fressa last night?" The cordiality evaporated from Mum's voice.

"I couldn't leave things unsettled. She was sacked on my account." He made his way to the door. "You may have thought I was having you on last night, but I *am* in love with her. She with me. We'll be attending the ball together."

Mum's cup rattled against her saucer. "You've only known her a few weeks."

"I've known her my whole life."

"As children. Gus, this is rash and foolish. Have you not learned your lesson?"

"Dad, a little help here. Back me up."

"Gus, are you sure? This isn't another rebound, is it?"

"A two-year rebound from Coral and one from Robbi. No, it's not a rebound. I wasn't planning on this at all. In fact I was dead set against it. But, Mum, Daffy is real and honest. She tells me like it is and I can tell her anything. Mum, you were the one who told me not to give up on love. Well, here I am, giving it another chance."

"Then, congratulations." Dad popped him on the back and leaned in for a shoulder hug. "I look forward to meeting her again. As my son's future bride, perhaps."

Gus's phone chimed with a fifteen-minute reminder. "That's it, I have to go." But he hesitated. "Mum, I know about Daffy trying on that blue dress. How angry you were at her. How you changed security protocols afterward."

"What?" Dad said. "Surely not. That's the reason you changed them when the boys were young?"

"She was a nosy ten-year-old. Had no business running around the palace. I stand by those changes. What else did she say?"

"Why don't I remember this?" Dad decided on a cup of tea and moved to the trolley. "This will warm me up before my hike."

"That was it, Mum" Gus said. "What else should she say? I guess this was the big secret she hinted at in Florida but really, what was the big deal? She snuck into your room and tried on a gown."

"Do you expect an answer?"

"I expect if you have anything to say about her, say it now. Otherwise accept her like you did Coral, Robbi, and Holland. I'm inviting her for this weekend, by the way, and she'll stay in Royal Guest One."

DAFFY

The week flew by. Daffy uploaded her résumé to various museums and galleries. To her delight, she found two Port Fressa companies looking for a corporate curator. One for art, the other to "curate" a training database, but she thought she'd give it a go.

Gus called and announced the chair had been found and that his mum was no longer angry. Hemstead was both culprit and savior, depending on how one looked at the situation.

Her phoned chimed with Gus's texts throughout the day and calls at night. He shared wedding ball details while she updated him on her life. Sleeping in, job hunting, and meeting friends she'd not seen in ages for lunch. Also, of her goal was to have a job by June, if not sooner.

He surprised her Thursday with a mid-afternoon visit, carrying in a load of groceries to cook his other infamous specialty. Spaghetti with a homemade meat sauce.

They talked until the wee hours again, falling asleep on the couch. She woke at three in the morning curled in his strong embrace and listened to his breathing, resisting the urge to wake him and ask, "Is this real? What's happening between us?"

He left Friday just before her first phone interview. It went well, or so it seemed.

Gus wanted her at Hadsby for the weekend, but she'd volunteered to work the kids' art show at the Metropolitan Art Gallery.

Sunday she would train up to Dalholm for the week of festivities. And the beginning of a new, real life chapter of *My Life with the Prince.*

So far only her parents and Ella knew the truth about her romance with the prince. They'd agreed to keep it that way until after the ball.

Leslie Ann texted and called, wanting to know what was going on with the prince, but Daffy managed to evaded her.

In the meantime, Mum fussed about the impact on *her* life when Daffy met her earlier in the week for tea.

"My phone is ringing off the proverbial hook. Aunt Blithe, my mum, my sisters, your dad's family, the girls in my book club, the RT staff, all wanting to know what's going on, and why I didn't tell any of them. I've never said 'I don't know' so much in my life." Then she sighed. *"But I always knew you two had a connection."*

Yet when Mum stopped by the flat Friday night, she was somber.

"You look worse for the wear. Can I get you some tea?" Daffy said.

"No thanks, love. Your dad and I just ate." Mum slipped from her coat and lowered into the rummage sale chair with a sigh. "I love this piece."

"Then it's yours when Gus and I get married... I mean, if we get married."

Mum's smile was brief. "You're not at the pub with your mates?"

"Steering clear for a while. In case Thomas and Blinky are there." Daffy sat on the edge of the coffee table, facing Mum.

"I can't get over how quickly everything changed for you. Last week you were engaged to Thomas, this week you're in love with Gus." Mum squeezed her hand. "Your eyes say it all. You do love him. I'll say it now, you never glowed with Thomas. I told your dad perhaps you weren't a glower, but you are. I see it."

"I've blushed over him for years." Daffy touched her cheeks.

"I told you! No one believes their mother. You'll learn, when you have kids, how smart I was." Mum sighed, glanced about, admiring Daffy's flat, making small talk.

"Mum, say it." Daffy squeezed her hands. "Whatever's on your mind?"

"Oh Daffy, I'm not sure I should. I've gone round and round in my head since we met for tea. You know I'm thrilled for you, but I don't want you to get hurt."

"Why would I get hurt? He loves me. I love him." Daffy moved to the couch and curled up with the pillow Gus had used, leaving behind his familiar scent.

"You know why, Daff. Don't lose sight of reason in the clouds of romance. The queen is not going to let you waltz in to her family with a secret the size of the one you're harboring. It's too risky. Too easy to let slip. Gus will be your husband. How can you not tell him?"

"I'm not even sure I have a secret, Mum. Eighteen years is a long time. Memories are tricky."

"Not this one, Daffy. You're talking yourself out of it because you love Gus. But one day, out of nowhere, the words will come out of your mouth. When you think it's safe, or you'll think he already knew. Ten years, twenty years from now."

"I won't care then, will I?" She tossed the pillow aside and went to the window. "I'm not sure I remember what I heard that day."

Beyond the window, the city scene was so pretty, spreading like a white and amber fan that glowed through the darkness. The spiral of Clouver Abbey, which survived a German bombing raid, spiked toward the heavens, held the bells that chimed every hour.

"I remember as if it were yesterday. But since you told me about Gus, I've done some digging in my memories and I wanted to check what you wrote in your diary. On those torn out pages you tucked into the cover's little pocket."

"I'd love to reread those pages but, Mum, the diary was tossed in the great purge of '09." When Daffy told Mum what she'd heard, Mum urged her to write it down, get it off her mind and heart, then forget it. Looking back now, Mum must have suspected the story carried some element of truth.

"If you ever need to talk about it, come to me. No one else."

"It's in the box I dropped off." Mum rose up, glancing about. "Where is it? Didn't you read my note?"

"I did and there was no diary."

"Yes, there was." Mum headed toward Daffy's room. "Is it in here?"

"Mum, I took everything out and it wasn't there." Daffy retrieved the box from the closet and dumped the contents on her bed. Picture frames, ribbons, mementos and a pair of gent's socks.

"What am I missing?" Daffy shoved the contents around, finding nothing that resembled a brown leather book with lined pages.

"You didn't find it?" Mum anchored her hands on her hips, furrowed her brow, and twisted her lips. "I am positive—wait, maybe it was in one of your dad's boxes. Or, well…" She made another face. "One of Ella's boxes."

"Ella." Revelation slowly dawned. "She was here while I was away." Daffy pulled her phone from her pocket and tapped out a text.

> Did you take anything from the box Mum brought over?

"Why would she take your diary?" Mum said.

"We talked about it in Florida. Leslie Ann wanted to read it."

"Ella wouldn't take it without asking, would she?"

"What do you think?"

"Oh mercy." Mum exhaled and sat on the edge of the bed.

Daffy paced back into the lounge, around the dining table, and back, waiting for a reply. Mum met her in the middle of the room.

"Do you know if Ella's at Pub Clemency?" Daffy said.

"Not sure." Mum didn't pace, but stayed in one place, hands clasped together, her fingertips white.

Finally, a reply pinged in.

Yeah, why? Gave it to LA.

What? Daffy looked at her mother, a sick sensation rising. "She gave it to Leslie Ann."

Mum dropped again, this time down to the rummage chair.

You said she could have it if you ever found it.

I never.

You did. On the beach. What's the big deal?

The words on her phone screen blurred as the floor beneath her feet began to tilt.

"Mum... Ella gave the diary to...to Leslie Ann."

"I heard you the first time. Please tell me that somehow the queen's secret was not in the back of the book."

"Of course it was. You told me to write. Then I tore out the pages, I can't remember why, and tucked them away. My heart is pounding." Daffy moved toward the kitchen, tugging at the material around her neck. The air was thin. She couldn't fill her lungs. The recessed kitchen lights seemed to blink and wink, fading and brightening, making her world spin. "What are we going to do?"

"Call Leslie Ann. Ask her."

"But what if she didn't read the diary yet? She has better things to do than read my pre-teen musings. If I ask her, she'll read it for sure. But wait, she's not said anything to me. So maybe she's not read it. What if I just ask for it back?"

"Do you have a key to her place?" Mum was on her feet, inflated with hope.

"Blast it, no." Clutching the edge of the counter, Daffy rode a wave of spiking adrenaline. "We could just go over there?'

Then a scene flashed. The commercial where Leslie Ann stood in a green meadow. One that looked like pictures Daffy had seen of America.

"The commercial." Now panic rode up and staked a claim. "Where she's in a sunny, green setting. Couldn't be Lauchtenland—we're still fighting winter. And wasn't she off the show on a special assignment last week? Mum, what if Leslie Ann went to America? To where *he* lived. Was it Tennessee?"

Yeah, she remembered everything she heard that afternoon.

"Surely not. That's a long way to go for a bio-documentary on the queen. And the show airs this weekend. She'd have been working on this story for months."

"Not if the story is now about the queen's love child. Her secret baby. Who was raised in America by her father."

"I… I need to sit down again." Mum stumbled back to the chair.

"I should've burned those pages. Why…*why* did I keep them?"

"You were a girl. I'm the one who should've gotten rid of them."

"Mum, this will destroy the queen. This will destroy *everything*."

Daffy charged through Pub Clemency, bumping into patrons standing in the aisle, around crowded tables. A quick call to Ella informed her the mates had all gathered.

"Excuse you, lass."

"Excuse you too." She was in no mood. No mood.

There they were. At the table in the corner under the window. Her weekly Friday night friends. People she loved and counted on. Marlow and Tonya. Frank and Kayle. Rick, Albert, Jones. Ella and Leslie Ann. Only Thomas and Blinky were absent.

"Daffy! You're here." Tonya waved her over. "Scoot over, Jones, let her in by you. Ella said you weren't coming."

"I'm not staying, darling, but thanks." Daffy leaned over the round table, her gaze fixed on Leslie Ann. "Did you read it?"

"What?"

"Answer me and don't lie. Did you read it?"

"Daffy," Ella interrupted "You told me—"

She flashed her palm. "I'll deal with you later. Les, did you read it? All of it?"

"Every word. Even those juicy pages tucked away in the pocket." The smirk from Florida hovered on her lips. "Brilliant. You were brilliant. I give you credit by the way. In the documentary."

"Credit?"

"You were my credible source. My journey to the truth began with you and your diary."

The sounds of the pub faded under Daffy's steam of anger. "Why? Why would you do such a thing? Is your idea of success tearing others down? Destroying lives? Look at you. You have everything. Beauty, brains, fame—and it's not enough. You have to be the best, or rather, your twisted version of the best. Best story, scoop of the decade, the century, the millennium. Ah, you make me sick. Truly."

"Hey, you two, what's going on?" Albert stood and invoked his shrink voice, which made no impact.

Leslie Ann reached for an appetizer. "It's my job, Daffy. I'd do it again."

"Do you hear yourself? Since when did it become your job to ruin people? Shame them? To stick your blooming nose where it doesn't belong? The diary was my private business. At the very least you could've talked to me. Even better, the queen."

"You said I could read your diary. How was I to know you'd penned a slam-bam ending?"

"It wasn't *the* ending. It was *a secret*. Nothing to do with my stupid story. Does your producer know what you're about to do?"

"Yes, and we're ready. By the way, what *is* going on between you and the prince."

Ignore her. "Did you go to Tennessee?"

"Watch the piece. I need the ratings. It's my first time on *The Rest of the Story*. Relax, you weren't the only one who helped me.

Remember Sinclair Posey? Royal reporter in the '80s and '90s. He gave me lots of leads and information. But oh he was so jealous I get to break this one."

"You and I, Leslie Ann, are through. Done. Delete my name from your contacts. We're no longer friends."

"Daffy, no. Come on." Kayle was always the peacemaker. "Leslie Ann, is this story worth your friendship?"

"Ask Miss Arrogant here. I'm good. She's the one drawing a line."

Their eyes met. Steel clashing with steel. Trembling, vision blurring, Daffy stalked away from the table then swung back around.

"In the process of building your big career of tearing down people's lives, you're ruining mine. Gus and I *are* in love but there will be no hope of a future now. Thanks. Thanks very much."

"You're what?" Leslie Ann shoved way from the table.

"You heard me. Want a scoop, LA? Here you go. Prince Augustus was in love with a royal curator, Daffodil Caron, until her *stupid* diary landed in the hand of her *stupid* friend and ruined the queen's life. Now he no longer speaks to her."

She left the table of gaping mouths and burst from the pub in a shudder of tears. Mum stood outside under the street lamp and Daffy fell into her arms.

"You know what you have to do now, love?" Mum stroked her hair.

Daffy wept and nodded.

"Want me to come with you?"

"No, I'll do it. No use dragging you down with me."

CHAPTER
TWENTY-SIX

GUS

"Hello, gorgeous." He gathered Daffy in his arms when she reached the top of the Grand Staircase and kissed her. "I thought you weren't coming until tomorrow. How'd you get out of your volunteer gig? Not that I mind."

"Mum took my place." Daffy's voice was low, if not cold. When he bent to see her face, she glanced away. "I drove up in Dad's little blue car."

"You all right, love?"

"Tired."

"Where are your things?" He glanced behind her, expecting to see a footman in tow.

"Um, I didn't bring anything."

"Why not? You're staying the week, aren't you?" He stepped away with a sense of déjà vu. Her tone and posture mimicked Coral's and Robbi's. The old struggle renewed. But no, this was a new day. A new season. "Tell me straight up. Have you changed your mind? Returned to Thomas?"

"No, never. I've not changed my mind."

"You love me?"

She nodded.

"And this makes you unhappy?"

"Gus." Daffy raised her head with a deep inhale. "I need to speak to the queen."

"Now? I think she's gone hiking with Dad."

"As soon as possible."

Gus settled her in her the guest suite, though since she didn't have luggage, it was only a matter of showing her around and giving her the lock's passcode.

She offered monosyllabic answers to his questions and stared away from him more than at him. He suggested a walk over the grounds, but she didn't bring the right shoes. She raised her foot and pointed to her thin-soled trainers.

"Darling, I wish you'd tell me what's wrong."

A tear dropped from her eye to her hand. "You'll know soon enough."

"Tell me now. Let me help."

"I'm not sure I can say it twice."

The hour they waited for Dad and Mum to return might as well have been a trip around the moon. In slow motion. Gus ended up watching the telly, sitting on the couch alone, just to keep himself distracted, to keep from freaking out.

How could she still love him and be so aloof and cold? No probing for a hint of her mission worked, so he waited.

When they were called to the queen's lounge, Dad, Mum, John, and Holland were all present. Daffy appeared both pale and green, hunched over as if she might be sick. He placed his arm around her shoulders, but she shrugged him away. Her eyes glistened with ebbing and flowing tears.

"What is it?" Mum spoke into the silence that had stretched on too long. "You have us here, so you might as well say it."

"Perhaps, ma'am, I should speak to you first. In private."

"We've no secrets." Dad's voice was gentle, but firm. "Go on, Daffy. And relax. You're among friends."

"Yes, we've done away with firing squads and sentences to the tower." John's laugh added a bit of lightness to the room, but only for a moment.

Holland chimed in, complimenting Daffy on the beauty of the wedding dress display.

Still, Daffy did not speak nor move from her position in front of the telly.

Mum stood. "Perhaps I should talk to her in my office."

"Sit, Catherine." Dad again. "Daffy, just tell us. Gus, do you know what this is about?"

"Not a clue."

Daffy raised her chin with a long inhale. "When I was friends with the princes, I wrote a story. *My Life with the Prince*. It was all pretend. Just pretend. A sweet journal of how our love affair began." She glanced at Gus and his heart nearly broke for her. He wanted to sweep her away and remove the thorn she bore. "When we were children. Of course, I had no idea I'd actually fall in love with him one day."

"You two are in love?" Holland sat up, glancing at Gus then Daffy. "Since when? I'm thrilled."

Daffy held up her hands. "Let me get this out. Most of you know the story of the queen finding me in her dressing room."

Gus glanced toward Mum. She sat straight, her hands clasped in her lap, her ankles crossed just so.

"I tried on a blue dress. Which I found again, quite oddly, at the Shop Vintage by the quay. We were going to use it for the *Unknown Bride*."

"And I requested she change it."

"You told her to burn it, Mum," Gus corrected.

"Why would you want to burn it?" John, more than curious.

"But Mum rescued the ole thing herself," Gus said. "Where is it?"

"Anyway—" Daffy's raised voice reined in the scattering questions—"I was sent downstairs. I felt horrible for overstepping my bounds." She glanced at Mum for half a second. "I loved you. All of you. I thought we were friends, even family. But I realize my error. I was young and silly."

"You were her friend," Dad said. "Catherine, tell her how you adored her. I think you told me at one time she was like a daughter to you. She reminded you of someone."

"Edric, hush. I really think I should talk to Daffy in private." Mum stood but Dad urged her back down.

"I want to hear this."

"Me too," John said.

Mum hesitated, then returned to her chair.

"I came back upstairs to apologize," Daffy said. "But the queen was on the phone. I started to leave, but then decided to wait until she'd rung off. I heard things. I wrote them down in my diary. Which I thought was lost. Thrown out. A few weeks ago, Mum found it. Put it in a box of old things she left at my flat. My sister Ella saw it, gave the diary to Leslie Ann Parker. Sinclair Posey filled in the details I didn't know."

"I don't understand." Holland shook her head. "What did you hear?"

"Your Majesty, do you want to take over the story?" Daffy started for the door.

"Stay." Mum trembled as she pushed up from her chair. "What...*who* Daffy is referring to is my daughter... Scottie O'Shay. Her father is Trent O'Shay. An American. I met him at Haxton. I was talking to him the day Daffy overheard. Now if you'll excuse me."

Her words dropped into the room like rocks cast across a lake, sending ripples over the smooth surface.

"Catherine—" Dad stood, his voice deep and commanding. "You have a *daughter* we know nothing about? When? How?"

But Mum disappeared into her room and Dad followed, intent on answers, their voices hushed, then loud, behind the closed door.

"Wait." John turned toward Daffy. "We have an older sister— and you've known for how long?"

"Eighteen years." Her answer was firm. As if she was resolved to her fate.

"And you never said a word."

"If your mother didn't, why would I?"

"But now Leslie Ann Parker is going to tell the entire world?" John paced, a bull seeing red. "We...we haven't even begun to process this. What of her, this Scottie? Does she know?"

Daffy shrugged. "Leslie Ann will tell us tomorrow night."

"Gus." John snapped his fingers. "Can't we invoke some sort of gag order?"

"Are you kidding? No. Besides, Mum is the champion of the free press."

"So we're just to watch her be humiliated? Why would Leslie Ann do this?" John faced Daffy again. "And why would you give her the ammo?"

"John, love," Holland said. "I don't think Daffy intended to arm Leslie Ann. Her sister found the diary. She gave it to Leslie Ann."

"Why did she even write it down?" The more John talked, the more his words fanned his temper.

Daffy pressed her lips together and Gus wanted to hold her, but he was trying to understand everything himself. "I was told writing things down in my journal would keep me from saying them out loud."

Dad returned, retrieving his phone. "I'm calling the doctor. John... Gus—one of you call your mother's secretary. And Lord Bellish. He'll convene her privy council. We'll need to get ahead of the tsunami."

"Is she all right?" Holland stood beside John, her hand on his arm.

"Overwhelmed." Dad looked as if he'd stepped in front of the Northton Express. "Did you know, Gus? Any clue? I can't take it in. Thirty years of marriage and she never said a word."

Gus shook his head. "None. Except—" He faced Daffy who'd retreated to the shadows near the main exit. "You weren't lying, that day on the beach. Mum did have a secret."

"You were so angry with me... I wanted to fire back. But I couldn't actually tell you. I'm so, so sorry."

"This is why you didn't bring luggage."

"Yes."

"You're not staying?" He didn't think he'd argue with her over it. The family needed space.

"No."

"Then you should probably go." He needed to process, be there for his mother.

Having been where Mum would soon be—humiliated, scrutinized at a level no one should endure—he understood what was needed.

His family had circled around him, even when he was too stubborn to accept their comfort and advice. Mum, however, would be the opposite. She'd want everyone near. And in the days ahead, she'd have a story to tell.

On the verge of a glorious wedding week, one secret threw their joy in a tailspin.

"I'm sorry, everyone. Truly." The door clicked as Daffy exited.

Gus dropped to the nearest chair, head in his hands.

"You can't go on with her now, Gus." John's directive was firm. "Daffy is a liability. Especially as long as she's friends with Parker. Mum will never trust her."

"What? Surely you can't shoot the messenger." Holland intervened with sweet grace. "That poor lass just stood in front of the Royal House of Blue and warned of a coming storm. She's a hero, if you ask me. Brave. Gus, go after her."

He stared toward Holland, but he didn't see her. He saw the faces, heard the voices, of *that* day in Clouver Abbey—his parents, his brother, his mates.

"Go after her!"

"What happened?"

"Did you have any idea?"

"Win her back!"

Move. But his feet remained planted, anchored between the past and the present. *Go!* In the distance, Holland and John debated.

"...let her walk out of here feeling as if she launched a world war."

"Let her go. It's over...see it in her eyes...not want to be in this family."

"Seriously...narrow minded?...thought better of you."

As they argued, Gus sorted his thoughts. Why wasn't he charging out the door to catch her? This was not her fault. She never intended for Parker to read her diary. Still, betrayal was betrayal. Those who sat in the getaway car were as guilty as those robbing the bank.

If he went after her, what would he say? Where were his loyalties most needed? With the family, the House of Blue, or with her?

"I will not hurt you. I won't run or hide or confess I love someone else."

A *clank* rattled through him. The sound of breaking chains. Of love conquering fear.

Out of the apartment and down the corridor at top speed, he raced through the Grand Gallery and down the Grand Stairs. Bursting across the foyer and out the main door, he skidded to the edge of the granite portico.

"Daffy!" He jumped to the ground, stumbling and rolling through wet grass, and scrambled toward the castle parking.

Little blue car, be there. *Be there.* But the car park was empty. He dropped into a squat, head down. After a breath or two, he reached for his phone.

Waiting for her to answer, Gus gazed west, toward the channel, the cliffs, and the Hand of God. Overhead, the conflicted sky warred between sunlight and a coming storm.

His call landed in voice mail.

"Daffy, ring me. *Please.*"

Her father's old blue motor was probably no match for Dad's Aston Martin. Why not chase her down? Go for it. Gus exhaled, cleared his head and shook the slimy ropes of past rejection from his mind, his body, his soul.

"I heard you wanted to see me."

Gus swerved round to see Emmanuel approaching, his winter anorak exchanged for a brightly colored, thick wool sweater. "Where've you been?"

He'd stopped wondering how the man retained access to the castle grounds.

"Busy. Tending business."

"The chair was stolen. I wondered if you'd taken it."

"If I wanted to take it, I would've long ago. I'm not a thief, Gus."

"I know. Hemstead, my former protection officer, went to the workshop to see what I was up to, broke the lock, saw the chair, and took it to Perrigwynn."

"Then the matter is resolved." Emmanuel stood next to Gus and gazed toward the horizon. "What do you think, rain or shine?"

Knowing what he knew? "Rain. A big, fat blooming storm."

"I'll go with sunshine." Emmanuel pointed toward the gold ring around the blue clouds. "If not today, after the storm."

"That's like picking both teams to win." Gus laughed and faced the big man. "Why did you help me? With the chair? You didn't even quote me a price. I don't know how much I owe you."

"Nothing. I'm your friend."

"A relatively new friend."

Emmanuel cut him a sideways glance. "Still, my friend."

"Yet I can't even find you without Ernst putting out 'the word.'"

"Yes, you can." Emmanuel touched Gus's chest. Just over his heart. "If you ask. Don't you know?" With a final glance, the carpenter started down the portico's tall stone stairs. "I've some folks to see at the Belly of the Beast. See you around, Prince Gus."

"What do you mean, you're in my heart? If I ask what? I don't understand."

"You will." Emmanuel carried on down the pebble-and-stone concrete poured path to the main gate and out to Centre Street. "Tell Coral I said hi."

"What? Coral? Emmanuel, come back."

The man was mad. Loony. But the skitter of chill down Gus's arm gave him pause. *Emmanuel.* He'd look up the name after he chased down Daffy. He'd just arrived in the garage when John texted.

Mum wants to talk to us. Come now.

CHAPTER TWENTY-SEVEN

DAFFY

Nothing felt right. Not the scenic three-hour drive back from Dalholm. Not her beloved apartment with its picturesque scene of a modern yet ancient Port Fressa wrapped in the lights of Clemency Avenue.

Everywhere she looked, she saw Gus. Falling over the secondhand chair as they lost themselves in a kiss. The couch where'd they'd snuggled and talked until falling asleep in one another's arms. The pillow which still held his scent. If she sat still long enough, she could almost catch the tones of his laugh...

Now it was all shaded with the shame of the secret, anger, and sadness.

Gus had not come after her as she exited Hadsby. Oh how she'd wanted him to chase her down the Grand Stairs and scoop her into his arms, but such fantasies were for her diary, her *Nonexistent Life with the Prince.*

She didn't blame him. His first loyalty was to his family.

She tried to watch a show, but Saturday afternoon television wasn't all that entertaining. Or it could've been her restlessness— which made everything darker. Sadder. And LTV-1 channel kept advertising Leslie Ann Parker's Sunday night documentary.

After a cup of tea and wandering about her place with no aim for the hundredth time, Daffy grabbed her keys and returned Dad's motor.

She arrived in time for pudding, and for a moment, the day was shut out, conquered by the comfort of her parents' home.

But the conversation turned to the secret baby, what Daffy knew, how and when, and the possible ramifications of Leslie Ann's exposé.

Sitting at the banquette in Mum's warm, bright yellow kitchen, pretending to enjoy a slice of Mum's yummy pumpkin cake, Daffy remained a foreigner in her own world. But the cake wasn't yummy after all. Instead it tasted bland and dry, and Mum's usually strong coffee was like water.

Dad's phone pinged with a text and she jumped, thinking it was hers. But it wasn't. She'd left her phone at home, shoved under a couch cushion. Gus had called but she wasn't ready to talk to him. No matter how she imagined the conversation, it ended with goodbye.

On top of that, she and Dad didn't even use the same text tone.

She had to get over this. Move on. Brooding changed nothing. Life was too short to wallow. But oh, how was it possible the queen's secret daughter business burned Daffy twice? She didn't mean to hear about it back then. She didn't mean for Ella to give Leslie Ann her private diary now.

"What'd the queen and king consort say when you told them?" Dad returned to the yellow table with the yellow seat cushions, holding another slice of cake. "By the way, you did the right thing, love. Giving the Family a heads up. I'm proud of you. Brave, that's right, what you did was brave."

"They said nothing really. Lady Holland was the kindest, but the princes were shocked, as was the king consort. Her Majesty was upset, of course, in an eerily calm way. She was the one to say she had a daughter, not me. I merely set the stage."

"Gus hasn't rung?" Mum refilled Daffy's coffee.

"Yes, but I've not listened to his messages.

"Why not? You love each other." Mum again.

"For all of five minutes. I can't expect him to choose me over his family. He's better to break with me now and support the queen. I'm sure that's how the conversation will go." Daffy pressed her hand over her middle, all the sadness and tension building into a solid rock.

"You're such a martyr, Daff." Ella finished her last bite of cake. "The poor little girl who got kicked from the palace. 'Woe is me, I deserve the dungeon.' Fight for him. Stand with him *and* the queen. Did you even give him a chance?"

"You weren't there, Ella. You don't know. For your information, he agreed I should go. Didn't try to stop me. I'm quite sure they all hate me. Especially the queen. This is probably her worst fear come to life. Thanks to me, my little sister, and my friend, Leslie Ann."

"Then make her see truth. No one likes a perpetual victim." Ella dropped her plate into the sink with a clatter. "Remind them I gave away the diary. That all you wanted was to apologize when you overheard the call. Is there no justice anymore?"

"You know, I wonder if this disaster isn't a blessing," Daffy said, holding her coffee without taking a sip. "A sign I'm not right for the Family. I'm not House of Blue material. Finding myself the victim far too often. With them I'm usually in the wrong place at the wrong time. Thank you, Ella. You've opened my eyes."

"Mum, Dad, talk to her." Ella leaned down in front of their father. "Why is her glass always half empty?"

"Ella, you cannot deny my bad luck with the Blues," Daffy said. "Best to be free of any lofty notions of making a go with Gus." She gulped her coffee and reached for her cake, which tasted rather yummy this time round.

You should at least call him," Ella said. "What if he's waiting for you to respond?"

"I don't think he is."

"You're such a martyr." Ella sighed as she dropped down to her seat. "What about Leslie Ann? Are you really breaking with her? She is one of your closest friends."

"Was. And yes."

"Are you going to forgive her?" Ella said.

Daffy added a bit more cream to her cup. "Eventually."

"I still can't get my head round it." Dad leaned forward, arms on the table. "You heard the queen say she had a daughter?"

"In so many words. Just how she went on and on about how this girl—*she*—who was turning sixteen and something about a cotillion. Which I had to look up later. Anyway, she said she'd not seen her since she was a baby. It was hard to understand everything because she cried the whole time, telling some bloke named Trent that she missed her. I remember his name because of a chap in my class at school. She asked if he was a good father." An old memory surfaced. "Mum, I just remembered. The queen also asked if the girl wondered about her. If she did, what did he say?"

"That's right. I remember you telling me."

"I'm sure I wrote it down."

Dad rocked back in his chair with a low whistle, propping his coffee cup on his chest. "Just goes to show you that you never really know about people. Morwena, you don't have a secret child, do you?"

"I was a virgin when we married, so you know I don't. Do you?" Mum's stern face made Dad smile.

"You know I don't." He winked at Mum. "Daff, you're a sharp cookie. Figuring all that out and only telling your mum. I'm proud of you. Most kids would let it out sooner or later."

"If Gus and I had gone on, become engaged, I would've had to tell him, don't you think? Either way, the question is moot now."

"Why'd you write it in your diary? It wasn't even a diary, it was a romantic fantasy novel." Ella reached over and took a bite of Daffy's cake.

"Mum suggested it."

"I'd moved to the Royal Trust by then so Daffy went to the palace on her own." Mum picked up the story. "When the new security protocols came down, I didn't think it had anything to do with her. Then she told me what happened."

"We talked about it, love," Dad said. "Decided it had more to do with the princes growing up, increasing their friend circle, than Daffy's free rein."

"But why ban Daffy for what she might have heard? Why not say she was talking about a niece or a friend's child? And, Daffy, you know I'm so sorry." Ella added yet another apology to the one she'd uttered with tears.

"I know." Daffy stretched across the table to squeeze her sister's hand. "Leslie Ann isn't, I don't think."

"Six months or so after the new security protocol, I finally had a moment to speak to the queen." Mum sat forward, cupping her coffee. "I asked if Daffy was not allowed in the palace. We'd been keeping her out but I wanted to confirm the rules applied. She said yes, and we left it there." Mum looked at Dad then Daffy. "Remember when the queen used to say you were like the daughter she never had? She was extremely fond of you."

"Maybe that's it," Dad said. "You reminded her she had a daughter."

"Somehow the blue gown is involved," Daffy said. "The queen was very angry when she saw me in it."

"So why'd she sack you for the chair?" Ella said.

"It was my job to protect it."

"But the prince broke it."

"My gut?" Dad always came round with the calm, wise point of view. Which Daffy desperately needed now. "I think she's been afraid for eighteen years you'd spill the beans. If you're out of sight, you're out of mind. Then she arrives at Hadsby to see you all cozy with her baby prince.

"Partially right, Seamus," Mum said. "Though I'm quite sure any other curator would've been sacked over that chair as well. Prince or not. Daff, I can speak to the queen if you like, ask her to reinstate you, but—"

"Would you do it for any other curator?" Mum shook her head. "I didn't think so. Believe it or not, working at the Royal Trust is not my dream. I'm looking into corporation positions. I might even accept a position abroad." She made a face at Ella. "In America."

"You wouldn't dare."

"Watch me." Daffy's bold declaration made her sit a bit taller. Raise her chin.

That started a rousing conversation about jobs and careers, higher education and families, but in the end, the news of the queen and her daughter was too much to leave behind.

"I feel like Leslie Ann is holding the whole country captive. Weird to think how one person can change a nation." Daffy glanced at her watch and slid out from the bench. She was tired. Ready to end this day. Reaching for her coat, she ached for a long soak in her tub, a short glass of wine, and an early night in bed. "Thanks for the cake and coffee, Mum."

"Are you leaving? You just got here." Mum stood to kiss her cheek. "We were going to watch a movie."

"I'll knock off before the opening credits." She kissed Dad's cheek, then Ella's. "Oh, I forgot. Dad, I'm painting my bedroom tomorrow. What kind of paint should I buy?"

"Got just the thing." He wrote down a few top brands, along with the best brush and roller. "Be sure to get a drop cloth." He peered into her eyes. "You okay, love?"

"I will be." She held up his note. "Thanks for this."

"Call if you need anything." But he wasn't talking about painting, was he?

"Seamus, drive her." Mum nudged him forward.

"No, I'll take the bus. From my stop it's a nice safe walk to my place." She mustered a smile from the door. "Don't worry, okay?"

"Daff, I am truly sorry." Ella's eyes brimmed with tears. "I feel like I've ruined your life."

"No, you didn't." Daffy embraced her sister. "I love you and forgive you."

"I promise not to give away any more of your diaries."

"Well, that would be lovely if I had any more diaries." Daffy kissed her sister and parents good night and headed for the door. "Thanks for the pudding, Mum."

Tomorrow she'd start over. Reboot into her new life. Run to the paint store for the supplies Dad jotted down. Spend the day painting, windows opened, blasting an oldies station so loud the neighbors would bang on the walls. The spring air would clear away paint fumes, along with any memories and any lingering scent, real or imagined, of Prince Gus.

Monday, she'd touch base with the businesses where she'd submitted her résumé and set up profiles on a few more online employment sites.

The world was her job pool. She'd go wherever, whenever. Make a fresh, exciting new start. And move far, far away from the coming tsunami. The queen's secret baby was sure to be the story of the year if not the decade.

Proud of yourself, Leslie Ann?

Poor Prince John and Lady Holland would be overshadowed by the stories to come. The constant chatter and musings on telly talk shows around the world. Wedding? What wedding? And what of Scottie and Trent?

What an incredible choice the queen had to face. Even in the hip '80s, the Crown Princess was not to have a child out of wedlock.

So, see, everyone had burdens to bear. Some more weighty and public than others, but heartbreak crossed all social and economic barriers.

Disembarking the bus, Daffy started toward her flat, but the lights of Pub Clemency beckoned. Cutting across the street and through a fragrant stream of night-blooming jasmine, she entered the warm atmosphere with its laughter and clinking glasses, music and wood smoke.

She smiled at the waitress as she made her way to her usual table. She didn't anticipate it being empty on a Saturday night but—

She stopped. Indeed, it was not empty. Thomas and Blinky canoodled while sitting with a couple she didn't know.

Turn around before they see you. She wasn't ready for this scene.

"Daffy, over here. Join us." Did Blinky have no sense of propriety? Really? Was she so unaware as to call Daffy over?

Spinning round for the door, Daffy left the pub and hurried home, her thoughts numb and cold. When she arrived at her building, she noticed the twinkle lights in the courtyard.

Crossing the lobby, she stepped into the fragrant garden and chose a bench under a cluster of trees. Jazz music floated from the open window of a ground floor apartment. With an exhale, she closed her eyes and listened, releasing her anxious thoughts on the rising vibe of the music, and on every craggy, dissonant note.

GUS

"Daffy, open up. I know you're in there." Another insistent round of pounding. "Please. I went by your parents'. They said you'd gone home."

A door creaked open behind him and a man with weekend scruff on his cheeks peered out. He looked to be a member of Clemency Street high finance.

"Your Royal Highness." He gaped, then bobbed a bow. "Are you looking for Ms. Caron?"

"Have you seen her?"

He turned aside. "Darling, do you know if Ms. Caron is home?" Then to Gus, "She's been out of town lately."

"Don't reveal her habits to a stranger." The wife, another soul with a weekend look, but who bore the distinct air of the educated and careered—lawyer, perhaps—peered into the hallway. "Your Royal Highness." When she curtsied, she fell against her husband. "She's out. I saw her in the elevator a few hours ago."

"Did she say where she was going?" He glanced at his watch. It was nearly nine. Where would she be this time at night? "A friend's? Her sister's? Pub Clemency?"

"No, I'm sorry."

"If you see her, please tell her to ring me." This exchange would be on social media the moment he rode down in the elevator to the lobby, but good. He wanted Daffy to know he was coming for her.

"We will." The wife moved in front of her husband. "Are you two an item? Is she really the lass in the photos?"

"As a matter of fact, I'm in love with her." He walked backward, arms wide.

Go ahead. Share that with whom you will.

Next he tried Pub Clemency—which was jammed to the walls and rafters. The air was thick with sights, sounds, music, and the scent of the roaring fire. But no Daffy.

"Your Royal Highness." The owner came around the bar. You know, Gus actually preferred "Yer Maj" and "Yer Royalness." "How can I help? Your usual table?"

"I'm looking for someone. Gorgeous woman with auburn hair, about yea high." He raised his hand next to his neck. "Stunning blue eyes, the kind you can fall into and get lost. Oval face. Seen her?"

"About a dozen of them tonight. Are you looking for one in particular?"

"Daffy Caron. She comes in on Friday night—"

"With her mates. Leslie Ann Parker is one. Now she's a dish. Haven't seen Daffy in a while. Gypsie?" He stopped the passing waitress. "Have you seen Daffy? The lass who sits in on Friday nights with Ms. Parker, the presenter."

"She was just here. Came in, looked back thataway, and left."

Gus looked where the server pointed. Thomas was there. With Blinky and another couple. That explained why she didn't camp out for a spell.

He thanked the owner and pulled out his phone. *Daffy, answer, please.* The call went to her voice mail, as all his others had.

DAFFY

"Thanks for this." She shook her pillow into a fresh cotton case. "I was dreading going up to my place."

"You're lucky I heard the music from the courtyard or I'd never have found you."

Daffy dropped down on the thin mattress of her sister's foldout couch. "There's a metaphor in there somewhere."

In the middle of her jazz music therapy, Ella interrupted, joining Daffy on the bench, announcing the family was helping her paint tomorrow.

"And we'll watch Leslie Ann's telly special together."

"Leave me out."

"Daffy, you can't bury your head about this. You need to make sure she's telling the truth. Not adding to it, giving you more credit than you deserve, if you know what I mean."

Then her little sister dragged Daffy to her place for a sisters' slumber party. Which was perfect because Daffy needed to be sure she'd forgiven her sister. And Ella needed the same assurance.

Ella laughed and curled up next to her. "Mum's going to bake bread and puffs while you, Dad and I paint. She thinks she's perfected the recipe this time."

"That's what she said the last time. Goodyear Tires called, wanted to know how she invented a new kind of rubber."

Ella flopped back with a laugh. "Didn't Nana break a tooth?"

"Yes, and she was so angry." Daffy pressed her hand against the pinching sensation in her abdomen. "Ella, I can't watch the show. Just imagining it—thinking about what Leslie Ann will say—it makes my heart pound so hard. The poor queen—"

"I wish the queen understood what a gem you are, Daff." Ella linked her arm through Daffy's. "If it's too much, you and I will go down to the courtyard and listen to the jazz music."

She smiled and wiped away a tear. "You know the worst part? I really love Gus. We'd found each other. I would never hurt him. Never humiliate him. Yet here I am, the lynch-pin to a story that will hurt his mother. Humiliate the whole Family."

Ella motioned to Daffy's bag. "Why don't you see if he's called? Even better, call him."

Daffy raised her hands. "Can't. No phone. Remember?"

"Then use mine." Ella jumped from the sofa bed and snapped her phone off the charger. "I have his number."

"How'd you get his number?"

Ella extended the phone. "He called me, remember?"

The pinch in Daffy's belly sharpened. "What can I say? What can *he* say?" She heard the words in his bass voice. *"Then you should probably go."*

"I'll call him tomorrow." She tossed the phone back to Ella.

"Fine. Then I'll call him."

"Ella, no, don't." Daffy launched from the bed and tackled her sister to the floor with a thud. "Give me that phone."

Ella waved her hand up, down, back, forth, until Daffy caught her arm and yanked the phone away. "This is my life, my relationship. Let me handle this my way."

Sitting up, Ella brushed her hair out of her face. "You never go to the gym. How are you so strong?"

"How do you know I never go to the gym?"

"Do you?"

"No."

Ella jumped up, tugging her pajama bottoms into place. "I'm not letting you give up on him."

"It's not your choice. Or mine. He won't choose me over his family." Daffy crawled back to her pillow. "You should've seen Prince John's face, Ella. Like someone smacked him with a cricket bat."

"But, Daffy," Ella said, sliding onto the bed next to her sister. "You love Gus and he loves you."

"Oh, Ella, what am I going to do?" She pressed her hands to her face. "I love him so much it hurts."

CHAPTER
TWENTY-EIGHT

GUS

Maybe it was stupid. Even a bit over the top, but he returned to Daffy's flat one more time after Pub Clemency. He knocked softly. No need to disturb finance guy and lawyer girl across the hall.

Taking out his phone, he scrolled past the missed calls and messages from his new and even more frustrated protection officer, Ollie, and rang Daffy again.

He made a face, lowering the device as he heard a chime from beyond the door. Perfect. She was either inside, refusing to answer, or she'd left her phone behind.

Gus slipped down the wall to take a seat on the floor. Head back, eyes closed, he'd wait. She had to come home sooner or later. Or go out.

The hard floor reminded him he had a lovely apartment a few miles away at Perrigwynn, but he'd remain camped, not willing to miss her coming or going.

For the first time in his life, he wished he had social media accounts. He had a secret Instagram for posting pictures he took of the beach. And Adler. He followed a few uni friends, but no one knew he was the man behind the @name.

If he were active on other accounts, he might know where she went. He'd discover her friend circle. He could stalk her.

Ella. Of course. When he popped by Daffy's folks' place,

they said she and Ella had recently departed. Maybe they were together.

He searched his recent calls only to remember he'd called Ella from his Hadsby office. How could he be so last century?

All right, back to Plan A. Shifting his position, he made a bed of the wall and floor. He'd slept on worse during his stint in the Army. And Daffy was more than worth a hard night's sleep.

Because when she finally came home or stepped out her door, he'd be here, waiting, heart in his hand.

DAFFY

After breakfast, Daffy and Ella spent a bob or two at the paint store, loaded down Ella's tiny sports car, and headed to Daff's place.

"Thanks for last night. I actually slept well." Daffy balanced her share of the supplies in her arms as they rode the elevator up to the fifth floor. "Now I'm ready to update and refresh." Today was a new day. A good day. The first day of her rebooted life. "Do you like the gray paint we chose?"

"It'll look smashing with a white trim. Let's do my place next."

Arriving on Daffy's floor, the sisters started down the hall and around the corner. Mum texted about then and Ella paused to answer.

"Dad and Mum are on their way," she said, adjusting the weight of her bags. "Mum had to get a special flour for the puffs."

But Daffy was focused on the lump of man outside her door. "Gus?"

He sat forward, eyes opened. "Oh, hello." He pushed to his feet. "I knew you had to come home or go out sometime."

"What...why...what are you doing?"

"Waiting for you." He waved to Ella. "Hello."

"Your Royal Highness."

The Lasslos from across the hall peered out. "He was out here all night, Daffy." Tessa wore a slinky robe that revealed too much of her store-bought assets. "I offered to let him sleep in our guest room, but he refused. Wanted to wait for you."

"Can we continue this discussion inside your apartment?" Gus lowered his voice and nodded to her door. "Thank you again, Tessa and Will, for the sandwich and milk. I do appreciate it."

Daffy fumbled to unlock the door. Ella reached to help. "I don't know why you'd sit up all night. What if I'd gone off to London or Florida?"

"Then Tessa would feed me more sandwiches and milk. I might have to start paying a squatter's fee to your co-op."

Daffy unloaded her things in the middle of the floor. Ella excused herself for the bedroom. "I'll start setting up."

"What's going on?" Gus said. "Can I help?" This was not at all how he imagined things would go. But Daffy seemed to be processing.

"We're painting my room."

"I love to paint. I'm great with a brush."

"Gus, what are you doing here?" Her eyes teared up when she briefly looked his way. "Do you want some tea?"

"That'd be lovely." He took a seat at the island while Daffy filled the kettle.

Ella came out and announced she was going down to meet their parents. "Text when the coast is clear."

"There's no coast," Daffy said.

"Thank you, Ella. Say a prayer for me." Gus seemed rather full of himself.

When the door closed behind her, the silence between them echoed. Daffy retrieved one of the bags from the lounge and took out a box of scones. Back in the kitchen, she arranged them on a plate, trying to plump up the one that was smashed.

"I know why you're here. At least I think I do. It can't work, Gus. *We* can't work." Might as well lead off. Address the elephant in the room. "I won't come between you and your parents. Not that I could. I won't be a point of contention in House of Blue."

"This isn't about my family or the House of Blue." Gus walked around the island toward her. "It's about you and me. Do you love me?"

"You know I do." She stared at her feet as a tear dropped to the tile.

"Then come to Hadsby. To the ball. Let's face it together."

"Gus, I don't belong. I will never belong. You're pretending because you don't want another broken heart. Though I'm sure our brief relationship caused nothing more than a scratch." She stepped back and raised an invisible barrier between them. "Every time your mother sees me, she'll think, 'There's the girl who exposed my secret.' Have you talked to her? Did she tell you what happened with that chap, Trent?"

"I was supposed to meet with her, but I drove down here instead. John texted a summary. Pretty typical story. Fell in love, conceived a child, but the relationship couldn't work." Gus pinned her between his arms, her back against the counter. "But I care more about you and me in this moment. Daffy, after Coral left, everyone said, 'Go after her,' but I refused. If she didn't want me, I wasn't going to chase her, make a fool of myself as I begged her to take me back. I didn't want to hear her reasons for running. Hear how I failed her. Hear how I came up short. My heart was too broken. When you told us about Leslie Ann and the likelihood of the whole world knowing, for a second, I—I was that man again. The one standing alone at the altar. I knew exactly what Mum would face. I knew exactly how she felt. Humiliated. Mixed up. Ashamed. I thought, 'We must surround her. Be there for her. Protect her.' Everything I needed two years ago but refused to accept. My pride…"

"Exactly my point. You must be there for your Mum. She will not want me at her dinner table. I'll just remind her of the pain. Besides, who knows what is to come? What will transpire with your new sister? What will happen with my career?" She fought a losing battle with the tears. Gus brushed the dew from her cheeks with a tender touch. "I don't know what LA will say in her piece about me or the diary, but we must be prepared. I'm not playing the pity card, I promise. But let's just face it now. We're not meant to be. I'm not Blue material."

She jumped when the kettle whistled. Gus released her, shoving aside his overnight, glorious mess of hair. His blue gaze remained clear and determined. He was not fighting fair. Not at all.

She filled their cups and set out the cream and sweetener. Taking a scone each, they wandered round to the stools.

He bit into his scone with a nod of thanks. "I was hungry."

"Mum's going to try to make puffs today," Daffy said. "Last time she did, we could've used them to replace the tires on Dad's motor."

Gus laughed, spewing crumbs. "I hear it's an easy recipe."

"Precisely, but my mum can make dough, grease, cinnamon, and powdered sugar into a hard, chemical compound."

His laugh was so strong and lyrical. Daffy grabbed onto the melody and pressed record. To make a memory.

"I want you to come to the ball," he said.

"Thank you, but no."

"Too late. You already said you would. I won't let you off. You're a woman of your word, are you not?"

"Gus, when that story airs tonight, the world will explode. It may rival what happened with Coral. There is another royal child of our sovereign. Your family won't see each other or me the same. I'm not sure I see me the same."

He pulled her stool toward him and lowered his forehead to hers. "I see you the same and more. Know what Holland said?"

"I can only guess. Did it have a B-word in it?"

"Yes—*brave*. She lauded you for standing in front of the Royal Family and telling them something devastating. You showed courage." With the pad of his thumb, he caressed an escaping tear. "'Gus, go after her,' she said. It took me a second to get myself together, but I'm here. I love you. Daffy, I let one woman walk out of my life without a backward glance. I'm not doing it again. Not when that woman is you."

"Coral Winthrop was a loss." Daffy sniffled. "Beautiful times ten. Smart. Rich. Influential."

"Daffy, stop." He made a face and she felt the sting of disappointment. She was playing the martyr and her prince didn't find it sexy. "You know how you said you probably always loved me? On the drive down here, all I could think was how I wanted to tell you everything. How I couldn't wait to introduce you to Coral and Robbi." His hands circled her waist. "Ask your thoughts on how we could support Mum. Tell you how you've lived in my heart since our first video game marathon."

"Where I beat you."

"If I recall, my controller arm was broken."

"Excuses will get you nowhere, Blue."

His kiss was sudden, tasting of tea and scones. Of life. She hooked her hands on his muscular shoulders and surrendered. She'd take what he offered because she may never be here again.

Gus broke away and pulled her close, his breathing labored as he held her. "The silver lining of Coral leaving is I found my soul mate. I feel rather lucky. Blessed. Like the Divine cares about me. You cannot let us go because of Leslie Ann Parker's actions. Because Mum hid a secret as large as the Hand of God. That's on them, not you."

"Maybe…but my footprint is on the path. I don't want to ruin the ball for John and Holland. For your mum. She's going to have enough to deal with. She doesn't need me reminding her of it all."

"Then I won't go."

"Gus, you must. It's your brother. You cannot shirk your responsibility."

"So where are we then? What? Just forget that we love each other?"

"Take a break. Let this blow over. See how we land. But, Gus, I won't be at that ball. Based on what happens tonight, I may never leave my apartment."

He released her and drank his tea. Ella texted that it was starting to rain and they were coming up. They greeted Gus and talked too loud about the rain and Mum's puff attempts.

Dad and Ella set up in the bedroom while Daffy walked Gus to the elevator. Instead of leaning in for a kiss, she offered her hand. "Good luck. Have fun."

But he held her and kissed her until she rose up on tiptoe and stepped into the elevator with him just as the doors slid closed.

"Leslie Ann Parker dropped a royal bomb last night with her piece on The Rest of the Story. Recap on our YouTube."

–LTV-1

"Are you KIDDING!? The Queen's Secret American Baby? The House of Blue has entered a romantic novel cliché."

–THE LAUCHTEN LOUD!

"Queen, Privy Council, PM Discuss Succession. Can It Be Challenged?"

–THE NEWS LEADER

"The Morning Show's Leslie Ann Parker is all guts. Wow!"

–LAUCHTENLANDTWEET

"Maddie, I never. Did you? Queen Catherine II has a love child."

–MADELINE AND HYACINTH LIVE!

"Queen to release a statement today at 3 o'clock."

–THE CHAMBER OFFICE

"Our requests for an interview have been denied so far. But we'll keep trying. Until then, we wish the Family all the best as they walk through this together."

–TAMMA TUCKER NEWS AT NOON

"Wishing Prince John and Lady Holland all the best joys of this season, especially in light of recent news. Can't wait for the ball and the wedding!"

–LOYAL ROYALS BLOG

"Prince Gus set to host wedding ball for his brother. Will he go stag? Or has he found love again with Daffodil Caron, the girl on the quay?"

–THE TALK MAG

CHAPTER
TWENTY-NINE

CATHERINE

She was glad to wake up in Hadsby Castle Monday morning. Perrigwynn and the surrounding city were buzzing with the news.

Queen Catherine II's love child.

She suspected the media would swarm Hadsby and the hamlet by the end of the day.

For thirty-five years she'd believed there was no option but to keep her secret. No one must know. She was a Crown Princess. An example to young women and men. The leader of a proud country.

She had goals, plans, and dreams. An educational path to follow. Yale Law followed by a rotation of legal internships throughout Lauchtenland courts. Then a term at Haxton to study economics. Another to study agriculture.

Since she was eighteen, Dad included her in meetings with his privy council, the Prime Minister, church leaders, and business executives.

Then there were dances and dinners, parties and holidays in Switzerland and the south of France.

When Dad passed her the crown, she'd be ready. But she had years and years to be a princess. Why, she'd be a grandmother herself by the time Dad went to glory. Until then, she'd make Dad proud by honoring her royal position and duty.

Then Trent O'Shay waltzed into her life...and captured her heart, mind, soul, and strength. For all her education, no one had ever schooled her in the blinding euphoria of love.

Her twenty-first birthday was the highlight of her life. So grown and mature, so she thought, she gave herself that night to the man she loved.

Confessing her pregnancy was the hardest thing she'd ever done. Until she placed Scottie in Trent's arms to raise her on his own. Then they vanished from her life and left a wound she had yet to heal.

Last night, watching that uppity blonde Ms. Parker tell *her* story, HRH Queen Catherine Amelia Louisa Charlotte, her whole life came screaming into focus. By the end she was angry she'd not dealt with this long ago.

Monday morning broke with rain, but for Catherine II, Regent, freedom beamed its brilliant light through her soul.

The secret was out. The burden she'd carried for so many years, lifted. Even the little pains in her back were gone. Was it any wonder?

Shoving her musings aside, she sat up, kissed her sleeping husband and wrapped up in her robe. The secret had locked her down, limited her ability to love. Because if she loved a hundred percent, Edric would've stumbled upon what she never wanted him to know.

How modern she thought she was in the '80s—but a baby out of wedlock came with a stigma. A royal baby shook governments. She should've just gone public. Endured the criticism and backlash. But the king insisted they deal with the matter quietly and discretely.

Escaping to the conservatory where the rain beat a steady rhythm against the tile roof and large windows, Catherine lit the gas heater on her way to the front right corner. Pulling back the carpet, she knocked on a loose floorboard and reached inside for the small photo book where she kept three baby pictures in the plastic sleeves.

John, Augustus...and Scottie.

Curled under a blanket in a wide, mohair chair, she turned on the lamp and studied their sweet baby faces.

Three babies in four years. She developed a soul of steel to manage it all. Scottie's baby picture was the only one she possessed until Trent sent her a photo of "our" girl a few months before her sixteenth birthday—which was a big deal in America.

The image of the beautiful young woman she'd given life to but did not know had sliced her heart, and she'd retreated to weep in private. That's when she discovered poor Daffy Caron in her dressing room in the blue gown.

Catherine looked between the photo of Scottie and John. Now that the truth stood in the light, she could see the similarities in her children's cherub faces. Scottie and John had the same eyes. She shared a chin with Gus. Minus the whiskers.

"It's cold in here." Edric wandered in with a shock of dark bedhead, his hands tuck in his robe pockets.

"I just lit the heater."

He perched on the edge of the couch with a sigh. "Another rainy day. I was hoping to hike."

"The meteorologist assured us the weather will clear by midday."

He smiled. But not much. "What's in your hand?"

Catherine snapped the photo book to her breast, so used to hiding the truth. After a moment she offered it to her husband. "Baby photos. All three."

"She's a pretty little thing." He glanced at Catherine. "Is this your only one?"

"Until right before she turned sixteen. I'd asked Trent not to send me anything. No photos, updates, or anecdotes. We'd made our decision, and playing long-distance Mum would only cause me to doubt."

When she met Edric, she'd told him of Trent. The one-paragraph version. *"There was a chap. I loved him, but he went back to America."*

"The boys seemed to take it in stride," Edric said, handing back the photos. "John's worried about succession, though I wonder if he's not a bit relieved. He has an out, should he want one."

"Why would he? He's been raised and trained for this. Holland will be the perfect partner. Besides, I determined the patent letters. He is my successor. If he wants out, Gus is next up."

Edric moved to the window. "Do you want to see her?" He spoke to the glass, not his wife.

"The question is, does she want to see me? I couldn't tell from Leslie Ann's story if Scottie even knows." She nor Trent made an on-camera appearance. "If so, this must be terribly unsettling for her."

"What about him? Trent."

"Do I want to see him? Not particularly."

Edric returned to the couch. "Why didn't you ever tell me, Kate?"

"To let her go, I had to let it *all* go. I felt I was doing what was best for her, for the Family—"

"All hail the House of Blue."

"Don't. You know what a tenuous throne we sit upon. We're a lasting royal family despite our detractors and enemies. In 1986, the monarchy was stronger than ever. I was part of that and had a duty to fulfill."

"After we were married? Why not share with me?"

"I don't know." Catherine set the baby book on the end table. "I selfishly wanted you to see me as I was before she was born."

"Oh, Kate—"

"Room for me?" Gus hesitated then entered, joining his father on the couch. "I want Daffy to come to the ball, but she won't because she feels she betrayed you."

Catherine focused on her younger son. "She's a smart girl."

"No, Mum, she's brave. She kept your secret for eighteen years. It'd still be a secret if her sister hadn't found the diary and given it to Leslie Ann. Let's put the blame where it belongs. On—"

"Me," Catherine said. "I know. I should've been honest with you all." She passed the book of photos to her youngest. "Your sister's baby picture. You have the same chin. While Ms. Parker handled her discovery poorly, I am the one who hid the truth from my husband, my sons, my country."

"So why does Daffy have to bear the shame alone? The guilt?" Gus lingered over Scottie's picture. "She looks sweet."

"Should we invite Scottie to the wedding?" Edric said. "Meet her?"

Catherine shook her head. "Let's not stir the waters. We can call Trent later, see how things stand with the American side of things." She tossed off her lap blanket. "But for now, you chaps must excuse me. I've an errand to run."

DAFFY

Her flat smelled of paint mingled with the fresh dewy air of spring. The weakening rain released the city, allowing a streak of sunlight to break in.

Daffy raised another bedroom window and scooted her bed into place, careful of the newly painted wall. The apartment literally rocked yesterday with music, laughter, and Mum's baking.

Her puff recipe came out like chewing gum this time.

"Morwena." Dad tossed the entire lot into the trash bin. "Just follow the recipe. Don't change it."

"Where's the fun in that?"

Ella came up with the Daffy 3.0 slogan. "New career, new you. Maybe a new country."

Sunday evening they had ordered pizza and watched *The Rest of the Story*. It was all Daffy could do to sit still and not shout at the telly every time Leslie Ann opened her mouth.

As they thought, the ambitious presenter unleashed the hounds. She actually began the piece holding up Daffy's diary, *My Life with the Prince*, and credited her with exposing this royal scandal.

With all the drama of someone who believed she was a legend in the making, she dragged out the story for twenty minutes, interviewing former royal reporter Sinclair Posey, who knew the queen as a princess more than anyone else in the media.

Her trip to Tennessee was just for show. Trent O'Shay refused to be on camera, and she never contacted Scottie, who was out of the country. Standing in the middle of Hearts Bend's main street, Leslie Ann recited unnamed sources, each who suspected, wondered, or once heard Scottie was the daughter of a princess, but no one knew for sure.

She'd produced Scottie's birth certificate, which proved nothing other than her mother's name, Belinda O'Shay. LA claimed the woman never existed. If she did, she found no evidence.

Nevertheless, social media blew up. The hashtag #queenssecretbaby nearly broke social media.

Now the hunt was on to get a face-to-face with Trent and to find Scottie. Leslie Ann created a firestorm.

"For what it's worth, Daffy,"—Mum clicked off the telly as the family sat in silence—"you're right not to go to the ball. You'll only keep the story alive and the attention off Prince John and Lady Holland. They deserve their day. I admire your wisdom and courage. The effects of what Leslie Ann revealed are just beginning."

"Do you think it has succession ramifications, Morwena?" Dad began collecting the used plates and empty pizza box.

"I doubt it, but I suppose someone could make a case for it."

Ella arched her brow. "Like an American girl named Scottie?"

Yes, the firestorm had just started.

But for Daffy, Monday was the beginning of Daffy 3.0. Maybe all was not lost with Gus, but they had a steep pathway to climb.

She'd tossed and turned most of the night, wondering if she'd given up too soon. If she should've said yes to Gus. Was she forgetting how she'd embraced courage during their trek to the Hand of God and not giving in to fear?

Then Mum's encouragement that she was being wise, even courageous, with the choices she was making now, spoke through. Let the Family deal with the fallout.

Twice she almost texted Gus. At one in the morning, then three. But then she played out the scenario of going up to Hadsby, facing the Family, the guests, the press—and she put aside her phone.

By mid-morning she'd reached out to the companies who had her résumé and began creating new online profiles.

A knock sounded on her door, followed by the chime of the bell.

"Daffy." A soft call bled through the door. "It's Catherine."

Daffy jumped up from her desk in the corner by the windows. Catherine? The queen? She reached for a hair tie and corralled her wild mane on the way to the door. When she opened it, the Queen of Lauchtenland stood in the hall with a box in her hand.

"Your Majesty." Her sock slipped across the floor when she curtsied.

"May I come in?"

"Yes, please." Daffy stood aside, then peeked in the hall to see a protection officer surveying the perimeter. "Would you like a cup of tea?"

"That would be lovely." She set the box down on the coffee table, along with her handbag. Dressed in jeans, which she never wore in public, and a jumper, the queen appeared serene. At peace. The wide, colorful headband wrapping up her dark tresses represented the people she ruled and served.

"Your place is lovely." She crossed to the windows, her posture erect, but not imposing. "The night view must be spectacular."

"It's why I bought the place. I apologize for the paint fumes, but we freshened up my room yesterday."

"We?"

"Mum, Dad, Ella." Daffy's hands shook as she set out the remaining scones. Was that a spot on the plate? She retrieved a new one and set the dirty one in the sink.

"I always loved your family." The queen joined her at the island. "We watched your friend's piece last night."

"She's not my friend." Daffy set out two cups, the loose tea, cream, sweeteners. "And I am sorry. So, so sorry. I wish I could rewind the past few weeks but—"

"No, I'm the one who is sorry. Deeply sorry." She paused for a moment, looking away briefly then back again. "Daffy, I treated you cruelly. I blamed you for things you had nothing to do with. I banned you from the upstairs out of fear and shame, worried your pure heart would say what my prideful one could not. That I had a child out of wedlock. That I gave her away to the man I loved, her father, and never looked back. That I put my royal duty above her."

The queen pressed her fingertips to her trembling lips, her eyes brimming with tears.

"I'm not sure any of us would've chosen differently, ma'am. You were in a precarious position."

The queen nodded. "Perhaps, but I should've been honest. I've learned the hard way that the truth sets us free...but there is often pain in the process. I could have avoided so much pain...for so many of us...if only I'd been honest."

"Have you talked to her?" Daffy stood on one side of the island, the queen on the other.

"Not yet. I wanted to speak to you first. I'm not sure Scottie even knows. Trent's not called so there's a bit left to untangle."

"Is she in line to the throne?" Daffy reached for the steaming kettle and filled their cups.

"Patent letters dictate the firstborn of the married crown, prince or princess. We're not entirely modern. There is value in legal marriage."

"So what now?"

"I'm not sure. My secretary tells me every major news outlet in the world wants information. The Chamber Office can barely manage the requests for interviews and statements, everyone trying to discover the whole truth. I pray sweet, little Hearts Bend is not being overrun. Ms. Parker, for all her bold reveal, left a lot of unanswered questions."

"What about you, Your Majesty? Your family? What about *the* Family?" One private, one public.

The queen sat where Gus did yesterday, fixed her tea with cream, and selected a scone. "The boys are shocked. Still struggling to take it all in. Edric feels more betrayed than he's prepared to admit, but I'll give him time. I understand. He believed we had a completely open and honest relationship."

"Will you meet her?"

"I'm not sure. She's a grown woman in her thirties with a very American life. The House of Blue is a life all its own. I wouldn't expect her to change for us, but I'd like her to know the truth. She grew up thinking her mum died. I'd like her to know I loved her."

"Trent O'Shay never married?" Daffy stirred cream into her tea but never drank. The conversation required her attention.

"No. Which, I must admit, surprised me. I anticipated a call from him one day to say he'd found someone and she was ready to adopt Scottie. He was charming and handsome. Quite funny. Certainly swept me off my feet, and then some." She blew softly over the surface of her tea. "Can you forgive me, Daffy? For everything. Banning you. Shutting you out. Sacking you. I was really angry at myself all those times. Not you. If you'd like, please rejoin the Royal Trust."

The moment was so simple. So peaceful. So healing. No more needed to be said.

"Your Majesty, I understand. All is forgiven. As for my job, thank you, but I'm Daffy 3.0 now." At the queen's quizzical look, she explained. "Reinventing myself. Going for a different angle on curating. I only joined the Trust because Mum said she needed me. Maybe in a small way, I'd hoped to see you now and then. And Gus."

"I suppose my unreasonable response in sacking you has a silver lining." The queen patted Daffy's arm and smiled. "We're friends again?"

"Yes, ma'am, please." Their embrace was mutual and heartfelt. There were tears by the time they let one another go.

"I brought you something." The queen retrieved the box— large, white, beautiful—and set it on the island. "I want you to have this."

Daffy dusted crumbs from her fingers and raised the lid. The blue dress rested inside, wrapped in tissues. The one from Shop Vintage. The one from Adelaide and Emmanuel.

The one the queen wanted destroyed.

"I don't understand. You said—"

"A lot of stupid things." The queen held her teacup against her palm. "I wore this to my twenty-first birthday celebration."

"I saw a photo. You were so beautiful."

"Trent and I conceived Scottie that night. The gown I loved quickly became a symbol of everything I had to leave behind. I'd convinced myself Trent and I could overcome all the obstacles in our way, but the reality of a baby ended my pie-in-the-sky notions. There was no time to play house, have secret rendezvous in New York between semesters. No time to pretend I wasn't the future queen of Lauchtenland and he wasn't heir to his family's corporation. I stayed hidden in Tennessee until Scottie was born then Trent took her home and I headed to Yale. His family made up some story that Scottie was from a fling and the woman didn't want to raise her." The queen's voice softened, her gaze clouding. "Our fathers had it all worked out, you see. Trent's father wasn't willing to lose his heir, nor was mine. The plan was for Scottie to be adopted by a good family, but Trent's mother stepped in and put an end to it. Trent would raise his daughter. She was a force to be reckoned with. Made my father cower."

"Did you ever see her? Scottie?"

"Not after I went to Yale and gave myself to my studies, my mission, my destiny. I convinced myself it was right for everyone—me, Trent, my daughter, the Family—to let her go. In the '80s, unwed mothers weren't as accepted as they are now. In Lauchtenland, a royal baby out of wedlock was unheard of. Not that it didn't happen in our long history. It was just swept under the rug. Same as mine."

"You were strong." Daffy clasped the queen's hand. "You shouldn't beat yourself up for it."

"I wonder…If I were truly strong, I'd have stood up to my father. I'd have kept Scottie. People would've been shocked but gotten over it." The queen offered Daffy a brief smile and motioned to the dress. "Anyway, I packed this away thinking I'd get rid of it one day. But it took me a long time to get over Trent. By the time I left Yale and met Edric, I was ready for the next chapter."

"So why was the dress out in your dressing room that day?"

"Trent had contacted me for the first time in years. Tried to send me a photo of Scottie, informing me of her upcoming sixteenth birthday party. Oh, it made me so upset. I spent so many years trying to forget, to hide. Trying not to let Edric discover my secret. You need to know, Daffy, Edric is the love of my life. I love my sons with all my heart. But there was a curiosity about Scottie. Because technically I remained her mother. Had she been adopted, I'd have had an easier time of it, but she wasn't. When Trent sent a picture and I was so overcome, I retreated to my room to cry, and there you were."

"Trent and Scottie..." Daffy sought the correct words. "...they were like an alternate universe."

"Exactly. Thank you. I've been searching for an analogy." The more the queen shared, the more her countenance softened. "Along with the photo Trent asked if he could tell her the truth. I refused. He went on to say she was having a ball for her birthday party. Told me she was fascinated with royals, especially Princess Diana."

Daffy made a face. "That had to sting."

"A little, I'll admit." Queen Catherine laughed. "But I wonder if she'd not started to figure things out. Come across something about Trent and me. If we'd had the internet in the '80s, she would have. Of if she happened across an old collection of People magazines. Nevertheless, Trent and I had managed to keep our relationship mostly out of the public eye. Together we agreed to keep Scottie in the dark. Her grandmother didn't want her to leave Tennessee, so she was a bulwark for our plan."

"You retrieved the dress to send to Scottie? For her ball?" Daffy glanced at the dress box. So why did she have it?

"I had ideas that Trent could say he bought it for her. Or that it was from an old aunt or something. The gown is so magical and timeless, I thought she'd appreciate it. And if she wore it, I'd be there with her. Then I realized what I was risking, even in the smallest way, and decided against my plan. I tossed the dress into the dressing room."

"Where I found it."

"When I saw you, for a moment, I thought you were Scottie. My heart and mind were so wrapped up in her."

"So you threw me out?"

The queen laughed. "I suppose I did, yes."

"I couldn't resist. The dress was—is—stunning. I felt like a princess." Daffy's confession came easy in the light of new things. "Every little girl dreams of being one. Especially me, being so familiar with the Family, the palace."

The queen shook her head and glanced away. "I dreamed of being an ordinary girl."

"Well, there you have it. The grass was always greener on the other side."

"I did love you, Daffy. I'm sorry for the way I treated you. Especially after you overheard my call. But I had to protect the secret." The queen squeezed Daffy's hand again. "While I'd have never chosen Leslie Ann Parker's way of telling my story, it needed to be told. At least to my husband and sons."

"So why did you bring me the gown?"

"I want you to have it. To wear to the wedding ball." The queen tipped up her cup to finish the last drops. "My poor son has been through enough heartache. He loves you, very much, and I will not stand in his way." She set her cup in the sink and with glistening eyes added, "I think you're perfect for him, Daffy."

"But I betrayed you. And—"

"You certainly did not. Your friend betrayed all of us. More than once. No, Daffy, you and I must stand together for the truth. I am incredibly grateful—you cannot know how much—that you kept my secret all these years. Something I should've never allowed to rest on your shoulders. I so regretful of my actions against you. So please, put me *and* my son out of our misery. Come to the ball."

"Oh, Your Majesty, thank you." In an instant, she was ten again and free to embrace the queen who was more like a dear aunt than her sovereign. "I do love him so very much. I think I always have." Daffy tore off a paper towel for the queen to dry her eyes. Then one for herself. "But are you sure I won't be part of the media circus? I don't want to steal Holland and Prince John's moment."

"Oh come now, Daffy, we girls are made of sterner stuff. Besides, circuses are fun."

"Not the kind we're about to face." The queen's sentiments touched her and upon second thought, a trial by fire might heal their wounds.

"Who cares? I'm pretty sure Holland's up for it. Let's show the men what strong women they married. Or will marry." The queen's wink was downright salty.

The truth really did set one free. Daffy turned to the box and lifted out the dress. "Do you think it will fit?"

"Since Emmanuel gave it to you, I'm almost certain it will."

"Yes, about that..." Daffy held the gown in front of her. "How did this end up at Shop Vintage?"

"Ah, well there's *that* part of the story. I also found the dress at the shop. Only it wasn't called Shop Vintage in '85. But it was a rather unique boutique. Magical, the locals said. I was to have a designer gown for my birthday, but this beauty..." The queen motioned to the chiffon skirt. "It captured my heart. Just like Trent. That's when I met Adelaide. Flash forward to *our* incident after which I shipped the dress back to the shop."

"So, Adelaide sold you the dress too?"

"Gave. Just like you."

Daffy dropped down in her chair, the skirt cascading over her lap. "This is so confusing. If it was given to me for the *Unknown Bride*, why was it given to you? Who and what is Adelaide? How does Emmanuel figure into the story?"

"Don't you know, Daffy? Emmanuel, God with us?"

"And Adelaide?"

"Angels also walk among us."

God? Angels? "So this is a divine setup? But why me? Why you?"

"Because the real tradition of the *Unknown Bride* was for a future House of Blue princess." The queen touched Daffy's shoulder and peered into her eyes. "You are that bride. I believe it.

But you don't need a title or a crown to be a princess. You only have to believe. A princess is about honor. Respect. It's about trust, loyalty, and duty. It's about living by your values, even when they cost you. About putting others first. I know from your mum that you are all of these things, love. It just worked out a prince fell in love with you. I knew the day I saw you in the gown eighteen years ago you'd marry my son. Then you heard the secret and well…we've gone over it enough. But, Daffy, you don't need me or Gus to make you a princess. You are loved by God and that alone makes you royalty. As for me, the dress was to remind me of who I was and am. Even I needed to know my calling was sure."

"I feel rather overwhelmed." Daffy laugh-cried. "And I'm going to a royal wedding ball."

"Oh, I'm so delighted. Mission accomplished." After a quick embrace the queen sat with a mischievous glint in her eye. "But first, we need to have a bit of fun. Just a *wee* bit. Payback for Gus for breaking the *Titus*."

"Your Majesty, how scheming of you." Daffy leaned in. "What do you have in mind?"

CHAPTER
THIRTY

GUS

What a miserable week. The media descended on Dalholm like a nasty blizzard, lining Centre Street with photographers, videographers, and wired reporters.

They roamed the shops and every side street. They booked the hotels in New Hamlet and filled the pubs.

They hounded arriving guests or anyone who dared step onto the grounds for air or a visit to Old Hamlet, shouting things like, "What can you tell us about the queen's secret love child?" Or "What does the king consort think? The princes?"

Some focused on the event at hand. "Have you seen Lady Holland's wedding dress? Can you confirm the designer was Bray-Lindsay?"

Others shouted toward the heavy castle walls for Prince Gus to confirm he had a new love.

Social media and the news were full of video clips from Gus's conversation with Daffy on the quay, of ball guests like the band members of Meant 2 Be, singer-songwriter Edward Tucker, and Prince Stephen and Princess Corina of Brighton Kingdom arriving at the castle.

A royal ball was going to be somewhat of a media storm, but the secret baby angle added hail, thunder, and lightning.

On top of the bounty-hunter media types, the formal, age-old press arrived from America, England, France, Australia, Ireland, Brighton, and well, everywhere.

But the melee of media was nothing compared to missing Daffy. No amount of persuasive words or actions convinced her to join him at Hadsby this weekend.

He'd sent flowers. Cards. Texts. They talked every night about the madness in Dalholm, her adventures in creating Daffy 3.0, music, television, movies, news, sports, even their love for one another. But she refused to attend the ball.

"Is this what I have to look forward to when we're married? Sheer stubbornness?"

"Who says we're getting married?" She sounded serious, but he heard the smile in her voice. At least he hoped so.

Last night she'd regaled him with a story of being chased by paparazzi. "Are you the lass in the photo with Prince Gus?"

Several reporters had rung up, wanting to know about her girlhood diary. How they got her number, she didn't know.

"They have their ways, Daffy. Trust me."

The press mess in Dalholm, along with her experiences in Port Fressa, only strengthened her resolve to avoid the ball. She feared she'd be the teeny tiny firecracker that would blow up the tinder box.

Gus hated to admit it, but she was probably right. Did he want the start of their relationship under such scrutiny and craziness?

However, he was not willing to give up so easily. He confronted Mum the Wednesday before the ball. "Ring Daffy and invite her to Hadsby. Please."

Mum remained steadfast. "If she wants to stay away to avoid further scrutiny, respect her decision. Frankly, I think you should get over this little crush, but you're a grown man, so I leave you to it."

Gus steered clear of her for a day and a half to guard against saying something he'd regret.

Then Thursday Mum's secretary announced a family portrait out on the old eastern portico Saturday night before the ball. Mandatory. Even Holland protested the evening.

"Your Majesty, won't we be too busy? We'll have formal photos after the wedding."

"Surely we can spare a few moments for a private family portrait while dressed in our finest." Mum poured a coffee and sat in her favorite chair. Dad listened in, telly remote in his hand. "I've always wanted one on the portico and now I shall have it."

"Mum, the portico is a hundred meters from the castle." John stood beside his future wife. "We'll be dressed for the ball. The grounds will be soggy from all the rain. The portico foundation is cracked and old. It will snag Holland's gown."

"I'll have a runner put down. Edric, the coffee is good. Would you like a cup? As for the photo, we'll drive out and back in the carts. I want a group shot, then one of your dad and me, then John and Holland, and then Gus."

"To what end?" He was with John and Holland on this one. "Mum, we have a thousand family portraits. We'll have wedding photographs. We don't need one Saturday night. At least not on the portico. And not one of me, alone." The image of him posing by himself while his parents, his brother and his fiancée snuggled would make Daffy's absence all the more pronounced.

"We do if I say so."

Mum was not afraid to use her I'm-the-queen card. Even Dad had to discern if he was confronting his wife or his queen.

Perhaps there was an underlying reason for this sudden family portrait. To focus her heart on her husband and sons instead of the mistakes, or rather decisions, of the past.

Mum seemed over the initial shock of her exposure. At dinner the other night, she'd had an air about her that Gus had never seen—deeply calm and at peace. Nevertheless, the topic of his unknown sister had been put aside for the ball week. Yes, decisions had to be made. But in due time.

For now, it was fun to enjoy a castle full of guests with their lively conversations, laughter, and music.

Friday afternoon at two, the official weekend began. Dressed in a suit and tie, hair styled and beard trimmed, HRH Prince Gus of Lauchtenland, House of Blue, stationed himself in the marble-and-gold Grand Foyer.

One by one, he greeted guests, who were then ushered by a

footman into the Grand Drawing Room where they were greeted by the queen and king consort, followed by the bride's parents, Lord and Lady Cunningham, and the beaming bride and groom.

Those already on the premises came down the Grand Staircase to blend in with those arriving by the front doors.

Greeting was fun, really, seeing old friends, laughing at a quickly shared memory. But in the back of his mind, he knew the moment would come when Coral would walk through the doors with her new husband.

This was when he ached for Daffy the most. She reminded him this morning of the opportunity to face his past, discover the truth, and go forward with a clean slate.

"Whatever she says, love, we'll face together."

"Daffy, please, come to the ball. I need you with me."

"No, you don't. I am sure this is where I need to be. Please don't ask me again. And remember, If I climbed the treacherous path to the Hand of God on a blustery, stormy day, you can listen to Coral."

A ruckus at the doors nabbed him from his thoughts. Gus slapped hands with his mates Turner, Lute, and Charles Larrabee, who promptly began plans for a rugby match.

The line moved quickly until Gus spotted his friend and fellow spare heir, Prince Stephen of Brighton Kingdom, who arrived with his beautiful wife, American heiress Corina.

Stephen came at Gus with a low rugby tackle, and Gus juked to the left, spinning, pretending to run across the marble foyer with a ball tucked in his arms.

"Still don't have any moves, I see." Stephen laughed as their hands clapped together for a brotherly embrace.

"And you're still as arrogant. Corina, how do you put up with him?"

"Someone has to do it." Her brilliant smile reflected her genuine heart, and her polished, regal voice still carried a Georgia accent.

"By the way, chum, Nathaniel wants a bocce ball rematch. Said you're going down." The Brighton Kingdom prince rolled his eyes. "I said, 'Whatever.' He and Susanna arrive tomorrow morning and I think he'll challenge you straightaway."

"Bring it on. How many times does he have to lose to crown me champion?" The king of Brighton Kingdom possessed no skill in the ball and jack game. "By the way, Charles Larrabee wants a rugby match. He'll be angling for you to be on his team."

Stephen used to play the sport professionally. One of the best players to ever come out of Brighton Kingdom.

Through the centuries, the Blues and Strattons, leaders of North Sea Island countries, were friends and allies. In John's and Gus's younger years, the families summered together in the south of France. Skied every other winter in Jackson Hole.

"How are you?" Stephen leaned in close, his words for Gus alone. "I saw you spent time in Florida. You should've rung. I'd have introduced you to Corina's family."

"I was hiding. But I'm good. More than good. We'll talk later."

Stephen popped him on the shoulder. "Anytime."

"Stephen, darling." Corina appeared at his side. "Come meet a friend of mine from America."

The brotherly look of spare heirs passed between them as Stephen headed away.

Next Gus welcomed Holland's sister and her husband. Then Edward Tucker arrived. John was a huge fan, and the African American singer-songwriter had graciously agreed to a concert later tonight.

More guests trailed over the foyer's marble floor. Family. Friends from uni. One by one, Gus relaxed, laughed a bit easier, enjoyed the vibrant atmosphere. He'd just reminisced with his cousin Winifred about being caught in a Dalholm deluge when he turned to see the golden mane and vibrant eyes of Coral Winthrop.

His breathing quickened with his pounding heart. Next to her, a giant of a man blocked the light of the open door. Gus glanced away. His foot twitched and a hot vise squeezed his torso. The voices in the foyer seemed to soften, and the light of the chandelier faded.

The moment of truth had arrived. *Steady, mate.* They're just another couple. She's a friend of Holland's. Don't look eager. Or anxious. Don't avoid her either. Just, relax. Be cool.

Words. He needed words. What should he say? *"Hello, Coral? Run out on anyone lately?"*

Suddenly she stood before him, her gaze locked with his. She smiled and reached for the big bloke's hand. He whispered in her ear, and her shoulders relaxed as she nodded.

Coral. His Coral. The woman he wanted to marry. The one who filled, then broke, his heart. Gus braced for the cannon fire of anger and heat of resentment.

Sour words lined up, ones he'd stored up for this moment, should it ever come, ready to march through his lips and shame her the way she'd shamed him.

Every speech, every spitting word he'd delivered while driving in his car, showering, or mopping a greasy floor at the Captain's Hideaway was polished and ready for action. Of course, he'd filled himself with nothing else. Nothing forgiving or redeeming.

"Coral." His tone was cold. Hard.

"Your Royal Highness." She offered her hand, bowing low into a deep curtsy. The kind one offered in surrender, in humility, head bowed so her chin nearly touched her chest. "Thank you for having us." Her soft voice barely reached his ears.

Just like that, every barricade crumbled. His eyes filled and after a moment, he cupped his hand with hers. She raised up, her heart swimming in her eyes. A sob broke through her chest. "I'm so, so—"

"Coral." Gus enveloped her in the tightest possible embrace, cradling her head as her cheek fell against his shoulder. Her soft weeping watered his dry, cracked ground.

"I am so, so sorry. I never, ever wanted to hurt you. Never." Her repeated repentance filled his ears, his heart, his soul.

"Shhh, Coral." Together they swayed side to side. "Of course not, of course. It's all right, love, it's all right. I forgive you. I forgive you."

Headlines flashed across his memory.

Panicked Princess.

Princess-Almost Is Pathetic.

Prince Augustus Barely Escapes Mad Heiress.

Bye, Bye, Miss American Pie.

How did he not see? She'd suffered every bit as much as he. Pieces of buried conversation came to mind.

"What do you think about God? Our wedding vows are full of pledges to Him."

"I think nothing of Him. Those vows are a thousand years old. Just tradition."

"Gus, do you believe in a higher power? In God?"

"What? No. I believe in myself. I'm my own higher power."

"I thought we could read the Bible."

"You read. Give me the Twitter version."

"Do you forgive me?" He spoke the words low, the urge to justify himself gone. "For not coming after you? For not hearing, not listening?"

"No, no, you must forgive me. I was so wrong and foolish."

"Yes, love, but now I realize, so was I."

The foyer guests no longer mattered. How long they held each other weeping and healing, letting go, whispering deep sentiments didn't matter. Moment by moment, they were healing each other and finding freedom through the simple gift of forgiveness.

CHAPTER
THIRTY-ONE

GUS

They agreed to meet in his apartment that evening after Cranston rang the dinner gong. From now on out, Hadsby reverted to the old ways.

The dressing gong rang an hour before dinner, allowing guests time to change into suits and ties, and dresses. Nothing fancy. No one had a lady's maid or a valet. Though Gus noted a few personal stylists sneaking around the back stairs.

After dinner, the women adjourned to the drawing room to talk, play cards, and sip hot wine, while in the dining room the men swapped stories over port and cigars. Those who hated cigar smoke broke away for a game of billiards.

He actually enjoyed this old-fashioned tradition. It fostered an anticipation of returning to the company of the women.

The archaic rituals faded in the mid-twentieth century, but even in the age of instant communication, the old way fostered quick friendships. By Saturday night's ball, the guests would be fast friends.

In his apartment, Gus took a moment to unwind after the three-hour meet and greet. He wanted to process before meeting with Coral and Chuck. Wanted to unpack the foyer reunion.

Chuck was a bear of a man with a tender heart. Coral had chosen well, and Gus liked him. That made him laugh. Six weeks ago, he still resented her. Deeply. Maybe even hated her. And now? She was his friend.

He owed so much to Daffy and the power of true, sincere love. Being with her conquered his fear. He could not genuinely love her while resenting Coral—which held him locked in the past.

Fear of the truth. Fear of rejection. Fear of not measuring up. But right here, right now, a warm peace had replaced the zings of anxiety. He noticed when he spent time with Emmanuel, peace rose within him. The old carpenter was a mystery, to be sure.

When they arrived, Coral greeted him with a kiss, while Chuck shook his hand. She'd changed into a red dress, which she wore well. Another reason he'd fallen for her.

Chuck, blessed chap, was a wall of muscle squeezed into a shiny designer suit. He appeared both amused and uncomfortable.

"I'd say nice place you got here but makes me sound like an idgit." Chuck sat with an *oomph!*, his pronounced New Jersey accent confident and loud.

"Darling." Coral motioned for him to stand.

"Oh, sorry, still learning the protocol." The Uber driver stood, straightening his jacket.

"No protocol here." Gus motioned for them to sit. "I spent a year in Florida as a barback named Pete George. Can I get you something to drink?"

"None for me, Your Highness, thank you." Coral perched on the edge of the couch cushion.

"Same here." Chuck exhaled as he unbuttoned his jacket. "Thanks for seeing us, um, Your Highness."

Gus took a water from the mini fridge. "Call me Gus or I'll call you Mr. and Mrs. Mays."

"I didn't want to assume." Coral exhaled with a glance at her husband and sat back under his arm.

"I'm too new to all of this royalness to assume. So you'll have to forgive me," Chuck said. "American bull in a China shop coming through."

"Do you by chance play rugby, Chuck?" Gus took a sip of water. "If so, you're on my team."

Charles had texted a presumed match in the morning. Stephen and Gus would be captains.

"Played football in high school. American football anyway. Anything involving a ball, running, and tackling, I'm in."

Crikey, Gus liked the guy. Not only his eagerness to knock some heads on the pitch, but how he supported his wife. How he'd helped her heal.

"I'd say this is long overdue, eh?" Chuck got the ball rolling with a blast of honesty. He glanced at Coral, then Gus, adjusting his tie. "Might as well break the ice."

Coral laughed. "All he's heard since we arrived was how nervous I was."

"Had a bit of that going on myself." Gus met honesty with honesty. But now that they'd wept through forgiveness, she didn't seem like the evil witch he'd fabricated to pay for his pity party.

"How'd you two meet?" he said.

"At a library, if you can believe it." Coral spoke first. "One that belonged to my great, great grandfather. Five of us received odd, mysterious invitations to the Fifth Avenue Story Society. We thought it was a prank at first, but it turned out to be rather divine. We became fast friends, helped each other through some trials. Turns out we were all a bit stuck in life."

"I never thought she'd fall for a dolt like me, but God had other plans."

God? So the Almighty was still part of Coral's equation.

"Now all of us in the society are married." She angled toward Gus. "I'm a stepmom now. Can you believe it?"

"You'll be a smashing mum." There was no reservation in his words.

"My kids love her, which ticks off my ex, so it's a bonus for ole dad."

Yes, sir, he and Chuck were going to be good friends.

"What about, um, you? Anyone special?" Coral's question came with a bit of awkwardness.

"You knew about Robbi."

"I did."

"I went to Florida after we split, which was more mutual than our parting. I lived in a large five-bedroom beach house with a gourmet kitchen. Totally wasted on me, as you know, but I worked at a pub pouring drinks. Never partook myself but loved chatting with the lads on the barstools. I took up running and lifting, lost a few stones, and tried to move on." He anticipated embarrassment over his second romantic failure, but it felt good to talk about it. "While in Florida, I ran into a childhood friend from here. Accidentally hit her in the head with a Frisbee. Since then things have become serious."

"I look forward to meeting her. Will she be at dinner?"

"She won't be here this weekend. Or at the wedding. She's the girl with the diary *My Life with the Prince* that launched the whole debacle about Mum. I assume you know about all that mess."

"I'm afraid there wasn't much chance to miss it. Plus, Chuck hears all sorts of tales in his car. He knew I was the Panicked Princess the moment we met. So, you love the girl behind the diary?"

Gus explained everything from his childhood friendship with Daffy to the mishap of Leslie Ann Parker possessing the diary.

"I wanted her here this weekend, but she felt her presence would only add fuel to the fire. Since the queen agreed, as well as John, we let it go. We'll wait, take up publicly when things settle down."

"It's true then? You have a sister?"

"We do. Mum's still sorting things. We'll see what the coming days bring. She's not even sure the lass knows. Her father has not reached out."

"Gus—" Coral hesitated for a moment—"can I tell you what happened? With me? With us?"

"It's time. I need to hear it. Please, don't hold back. I'm not afraid of what you have to say. I've learned the last two years that hiding from the truth only makes things worse."

She exhaled and began. "Do you remember talking about our wedding vows? How we were pledging before God to love and serve Him, to represent Him to the people. Every vow we made was in the name of the Father, Son, and Holy Spirit. Three entities I knew nothing about. How could I possibly vow to them?"

"Funny, I hadn't until we met in the foyer. I recall now we first talked about it here, at Hadsby, on a ski weekend. Didn't we agree it was nothing more than a formality? An old tradition?"

"We didn't actually agree. *You* said it was nothing more than tradition and dismissed me in the same breath. I wasn't settled on the issue at all. I started reading and researching the meaning and purpose of the vows and our role as royal Blues, leaders in the Church, and what exactly all that meant. Lauchtenland has a steep Christian heritage, Gus, a remarkable history of charitable and missionary work. Next thing I knew, I was up all hours reading the Bible. If I was to vow my life and service to you and God, as well as Lauchtenland, then I wanted to know Him. The more I read, the more enthralled I became with a man named Jesus, who died for me. As the wedding neared, I began wondering if we were on the same path. I tried again to talk to you. But—"

"I wasn't interested."

"No. Then you said the one thing that terrified me. You said you were your own master and there was no higher authority than yourself. You felt like a...a rogue ship, alone on a tempest sea. I couldn't get it out of my mind, my heart. I wanted us to have a God to trust, plead with for help, to act as a guide, even a judge between us if we argued."

"You said all of that? Out loud?" He'd blocked out those specifics.

"I did, at least I tried, probably not as plainly." Coral gripped her husband's hand. "I talked about our family heritages, how we both had money, fame, status, and advantages that would be fabulous for children, but what about their spiritual health? Our spiritual health?"

"You got nowhere with me."

She nodded, her eyes clouding. "That's when the fear of God gripped me. This sort of reverent awe. I knew I couldn't live without Him as my friend and judge. I wanted a relationship with Jesus. My love for Him overtook me. I wanted to run after Him with a man who would love Him too. The fear of God was so powerful I feared nothing else, even running out on a global wedding."

Gus stilled. "Are you saying God told you to leave me?"

"No, not at all. At least not the way I did. But we needed to see we were not on the same page. Maybe some could make religious differences work, but I was so gripped I knew I was not one of them. Being both zealous and immature was not a good recipe. I delayed breaking off with you because I wasn't totally sure. I kept telling myself everything would work out. That I just had cold feet. My mother was sure I'd be fine once I started down the aisle."

"I remember you wanted us to read the Bible and pray together. Which I rejected."

The more Coral explained what had happened—the reason she hadn't married him—the more tenderness grew inside of him. He'd never given her a chance. He was arrogant, full of himself, and king of the world with Coral Winthrop by his side. He didn't need God.

"When did you know you'd not marry me?"

"Probably for a month, but the night before brought everything into focus. I was up all night battling with myself, with God, reading my Bible, and praying. Though one can never truly hear God from a place of anxiety. I mean, we had a wedding planned with fifteen hundred guests from around the world."

Beside her, Chuck exhaled. "We had two hundred guests and I nearly sweat through my tux."

"Caterers and wedding planners worked for months on two receptions. We'd paid for flowers and gifts. Our honeymoon was booked. Television crews and the media had been on-site for days. Above all, I loved you and your family."

Coral stood, hands clasped at her waist, her expression somber. "I woke up that morning in such a state. I had no peace no matter how much self-talk and pumping up I did. I went for a run at six. Gus, I don't run. I ate breakfast. I took a long bubble bath. I stared at my gown. Oh, I loved that gown. But peace just would *not* come. I wasn't excited. I dreaded every moment of getting ready. I put my dress on, and instead of feeling like the princess I was about to become, I felt like a prisoner. Finally, I cleared the room.

No one stayed, not even my mom. And I prayed in earnest. 'Jesus, I'm all Yours.'" Her lips twisted. "That's when the peace came and I knew I would not walk down Clouver Abbey's aisle. I also knew He would take care of you. I truly did.

"I should've come to your room and told you. But I was too afraid. I'll live with my foolish decision forever. I humiliated you and the House of Blue. In fact, when Lady Holland called to invite us to the wedding, I was sure she was joking."

"Mum forgave you quicker than I."

"But now you have and I'm so grateful." Coral knelt beside him, hand on his arm, and peered into his face. "You've broken my last chain."

"Do you forgive me? For not listening? For not caring enough to hear your heart? For not coming after you? For not allowing you to explain?"

"A hundred times over." Coral kissed his hand, humbling him once again.

"In the sum of all things, you ran because you fell in love with God?"

"You know, you have something in common with Him." Coral returned to her seat by her husband.

"With God?" Gus shook his head. "I can't imagine."

"He's a prince. The Prince of Peace. Emmanuel, God with us."

"Emmanuel?"

"Yes, God with us."

Gus stood with an explosion of realization. *Emmanuel?* Was it possible... *No.* How? Why? Oh, now he had so many questions.

Then the old carpenter's fiery eyes flashed before him and HRH Prince Augustus laughed. The joke was on him, wasn't it? God bowed low to spend time with him. All those workshop sessions he'd been in the company of the Lord.

Emmanuel, God with us.

"The Grand Dining Hall of Hadsby Castle was resplendent with the Royal Blue china on display and a dinner of London broil, garlic potatoes, asparagus, and a chocolate cake pudding. Wine from The Haskells, port, and champagne were served along with platters of locally sourced cheese and fruit."

—WHAT'S ON THE TABLE BLOG

"We're told the guests are out riding today. Lady Holland is an avid equestrian. The queen and king consort drove a cart down to the mews to watch the guests ride out on a cold but sunny morning.

"Spectators report Lady Holland raced off with Prince John. Watchers were surprised to see Coral Winthrop Mays, the American heiress who left Prince Gus at the altar, on a white mount along with her new husband, an American cowboy sort of chap, riding alongside, gripping the reins with white knuckles, his horse on a steady course for a stand of trees."

—LESLIE ANN PARKER, THE MORNING SHOW

"I was treated to a tour of the wedding gowns with Royal Trust curator, Glasgow Towns. They were stunning and so well designed. I'm told the staging was orchestrated by Daffodil Caron, whom I believe was responsible for the shot-heard-round-the-world. Her diary exposed Queen Catherine II's secret child. The Unknown Bride gown was a stunning silver organza with lace, and we're told it will be donated to the local foster foundation for a lass aging out of the system. It was thrilling to see the Princess Louisa. We've heard so much about it. But let's begin at the beginning, the first gown to be preserved..."

–SYDNEY FRITZ, NEWS AT SIX, LTV-1

"That's right, Farley, we're on-site at Hadsby, about to enter the Queen's Library to see the King Titus. We'll be back live in sixty seconds, after these words."

–PERRY COPPERFIELD, CABLE NEWS PF

CHAPTER
THIRTY-TWO

DAFFY

F riday afternoon, Daffy met Mum for lunch, then went shoe
shopping. Mum went *ga-ga* over a pair of Christian
Louboutin's and insisted on buying them.

"Cinderella would've worn these."

After which Daffy kissed her goodbye and ran all over the
Clemency District hunting for one special item before returning to
her flat to pack.

Saturday morning, Dad, Mum and Ella arrived to see her off
and inspect her suitcase.

"Do you have everything?" Mum snooped through Daffy's
case, rearranged her socks and underwear, then moved to the
closet to see if there was one more item she might need or want.

"Who's going to do your hair?" Ella inspected two pairs of
shoes. A pair of Wellies and a pair of boots. "You should take
these. You never know."

"I have Wellies and trainers." Daffy tossed the shoes on the
floor of the closet. "I'm doing my own hair. Mum, that jacket was
hideous when I bought it. I meant to take it back but never got
round to it." Daffy closed her suitcase, putting the end to her
family's attempt to overpack. "I've got everything I need. My
gown. My Louboutins. Clothes for Sunday. I'll be back Monday
evening."

She had an interview with an art gallery Tuesday morning,
another on Wednesday afternoon with an old Port Fressa family

firm—Trumpeters, makers of fine furniture. They were very interested in her corporate curating ideas.

Dad stepped in from the living room. "Daff, love, we should get going in case there's traffic."

He'd insisted on driving her up to Dalholm in Mum's *Range Rover* so the dress could lie flat. The queen texted to come round to the delivery entrance and sneak up to the servants' quarters on the third floor. She had the old butler's room prepped for her.

> "He'll never expect you to be there. Besides, all the suites are booked. Even Royal Guest One. Sorry, love."

Daffy didn't mind. She preferred those old spaces. In the 1950s, the family modernized and added bathrooms to each room of the servants' quarters. She'd be perfectly comfortable.

Mum handed Dad Daffy's suitcase, while Ella carried the gown, carefully cleaned by an expert at the Royal Trust, Alice.

"Well, have fun." Mum squeezed Daffy against her bosom with a weepy sigh. "I'm so proud of you."

"Me too, sis." Ella hugged her next. "If you meet any eligible bachelors, get their number for me."

"All right, she's just going up to Dalholm for a ball, let's not break out the waterworks." Dad could always be counted on for leveling things off.

"Dalholm." Mom whispered the word. "What a perfect place to say, 'I love you.'"

"Didn't you fall in love with Thomas in Dalholm, Daffy?" Ella, really, this was not the time.

"Morwena," Dad said. "I tell you that I love you and you say to hush."

"Hush and drive safe. You've plenty of time." Mum opened the door and Ella passed Daffy the garment bag. "Are you just going to hide out when you get there?"

"Until five, when Gus goes out to the eastern portico for a family photograph."

"Then what?" Ella and Mum walked with Dad and Daffy to the elevator.

"I run toward him, unless it's raining, which it shouldn't, and he scoops me in his arms, kisses me, and I swoon."

"Crikey, that sounds like a line from *My Life with the Prince*."

Precisely. Leslie Ann returned the diary by messenger along with a note. *I'm sorry for hurting you. I don't want our friendship to end.*

After a day, Daffy responded with a text. Let's talk next week.

After her conversation with the queen, she didn't see any profit in holding a grudge. But she would let Leslie Ann know how she hurt everyone for her own gain and broke her promise to leave Daffy out of her future stories.

Gus called last night and they'd talked for three hours. One hour was his recap of his conversation with Coral and Chuck, how healing and freeing it was, and how he wished he'd done it long ago.

"Also, we need to talk about Emmanuel."

"I know. We do."

The other two hours Gus needled, pleaded, and begged her to come up to the ball. But she claimed plans she could not get out of without letting a lot of people down. But oh it was torture hearing the disappointment in his voice. She almost broke and told him twice. But the queen had been insistent so once again, she kept a secret.

"Not a word. He'll survive. Next time he'll listen to you when you tell him not to sit in a chair."

"Thanks for driving me, Dad." Daffy buckled up in the passenger's seat.

"My pleasure, love. I'll be walking you down the aisle to this chappie one day. Might as well drive you up to get the ball rolling." He laughed. "Get it? I said, 'Get the ball rolling.'"

"You're a regular riot, Dad." Daffy touched his arm as he pressed the ignition button. "Do you like him? Prince Gus? Forget the fact that he's a prince. But for your daughter?"

"I don't know him all that well, but I've watched him handle himself through the Prince Pudgy years, to the fame of his smile, through the shame of being left at the altar, and I'd say he's a good man. Upstanding lad. And if he's the reason for that light in your eyes, then he has my vote."

"Me too." She held her daddy's hand until they hit North One highway toward Dalholm, toward her prince and the rest of her life.

GUS

Just do the math.

If he left now, he'd be in Port Fressa by one o'clock. Okay, in the Aston Martin with light traffic, he'd be there by noon.

Give two hours to talk Daffy into coming, another hour to get her things together—he hoped she had a ball gown—and head back to Hadsby by three.

Two hours back Aston Martin time, he'd be on the portico for Mum's photo shoot no later than five-fifteen. Perhaps, five-thirty.

Gus glanced at his watch. If he was going to do this, he needed to leave now. Of course, he could put on his tuxedo to save time. But, no, it would be wrinkled by the time of the ball.

He'd just have to shorten his convincing time to one hour. And thirty minutes to pack. If she didn't have a gown, she could borrow from Coral. Fifty bucks she brought more than one. And to his eye, his ex and his true love were about the same size.

Gus mimed holding Coral, then Daffy. Yeah, sure they were the same size. Give or take.

Down the back steps to the garage, he grabbed the motor keys, checked the petrol level, and with one final consideration, opened the bay door and fired down the drive.

No one would miss him this afternoon. Just about everyone went riding or hiking. Several were in their suites reading or resting for the big night.

John didn't want to risk injury, so the rugby match was postponed until tomorrow. Prince Stephen cheered the delay, as he wanted more time to woo Chuck Mays over to his team. Poor slob, he didn't stand a chance. Gus had Chuck locked in.

Shifting into high gear, he turned up the radio and flew low down North One through the villages and hamlets to win the heart and presence of his true love.

DAFFY

One would think she was aged or infirm—or both—the way Dad drove up North One, slower than molasses. Apologizing for every pothole. It took forever to get here.

But now that she was settled in her cozy room on the third floor, she was grateful for their time together and that she only had to kill three hours instead of four, when she'd surprise Gus on the portico.

She turned off her phone in case he called. Her silence would up the tension and increase the element of surprise. Also, in the off chance he cruised by the servants' quarters, she didn't want her phone giving her away.

Restless, she paced the generous space, gazing out the window, three stories from the ground. She tried to come up with a hairstyle, but she wasn't good at twists and braids, so she decided to wear it down, let her curls do the talking.

But what if the women were wearing updos? Did it matter? Would she look out of step? Daffy fell back on the single bed's thick mattress.

"Emmanuel, help."

She'd been inspired by her conversation with the queen and retrieved her old confirmation Bible from the bottom of her bookcase, intending to read a few chapters before bed. She also looked up the man named Emmanuel, God with us. Why didn't the queen just tell her flat out? Emmanuel was Jesus, the Christ.

If God was with her, she wanted to know Him. She'd listened intently when Gus talked of God being the impetus for Coral running. Then he brought up Emmanuel, and she knew they'd begun the same journey.

Still on the mattress, she drifted away, the emotional rollercoaster of the week taking its toll. The next sound she heard was someone knocking.

"Daffy? I'm here to help you get ready."

"What?" She unlocked the door to see a slight, pretty woman on the other side. "I'm Coral Winthrop's stylist, Choko. She asked me to help you get ready."

"Coral Winthrop? How does she know I exist?"

"The queen told her who you were and why you're here. May I come in?" She carried a large black case full of beautification magic. "I love your hair. I'm envisioning a fab updo. What do you think?"

"Yeah, if you think you can tame this mess."

"Oh, I've tamed far worse." She pointed to a chair. "Let's do your makeup first, then hair. Last, we'll slip on the dress. Is that the one you're wearing? Gorgeous."

GUS

Worst luck. Daffy wasn't home. It was then he remembered she had a volunteer engagement. He'd forgotten, worst luck.

And now she wasn't answering her phone. What was the purpose of mobile communication if he couldn't speak to the woman he loved whenever he wanted?

Were his surprise visits always destined to fail?

He called Ella. She didn't know where Daffy had gone. Next he stopped by her parents' home. Her mother didn't know either. But she sniffed a lot and her eyes watered. When he asked if she was okay, she choked, nodded her head, and hugged him.

Now he was late heading north. At a traffic light, he texted John.

> Stall Mum for me.

> Where are you? We looked for you all afternoon.

> On my way from Port Fressa. Came down to convince Daffy to attend the ball.

> Are you serious, mate? You're going to be late for the photograph. And Daffy, the woman responsible for Mum's humiliation? Think of us, will you? Someone besides yourself.

> She's not responsible and you know it.

> Just get here. Other than my wedding, this is a big day for me and my little brother has gone mad.'

Agree. Mad with love. Once again, he flew low over North One, aching for Daffy. Aching for the chance to share this glorious night with her.

He'd spend the evening in the bachelors' corner, dancing with old ladies who wore sensible shoes.

No offense, Aunt Astrid and Lady Weatherby.

DAFFY

Five-fifteen. Daffy started for the door then turned back for the bag on the bed. With a shaky breath, she exited the butler's room. Choko had turned her into a mini version of Coral Winthrop, which was fantastic, with her hair pinned up in swirls and braids and adorned with flowers. Her makeup had never been so flawless.

The gown swirled and swished against her legs and sang to her, chiming to the rhythm of her Louboutin heels in the hall.

When she whisked through the servants' hall, someone whistled. Another wished her luck. Probably Miles. She burst into the glorious April sunset, the brilliance clinging to the edges of the advancing dusk.

Prince Gus, the man she loved without reservation, would be waiting on the portico. She kicked into a run, but two steps in, the long grass caught her heels. She should've driven one of the carts like the queen suggested.

But she wanted to run toward Gus. Wanted him to catch her up in his arms. Not help her out of a gardener's cart.

However, her plan was problematic. She'd free one shoe only to have the other one catch. Her next step landed her in a patch of damp dirt, and both heels sank up to the soles.

With a growl, she kicked off her shoes, gathered the front of the skirt and ran, the bag swinging from her hand, her shoes from her fingertips. Up a slight incline toward the portico which rose on the horizon. But even from the distance, she could see Gus was not there. Nor was the rest of the family.

"Gus?" She stepped on the cracked portico surface where a wide red runner had been stretched. "Your Majesty?" Had this all been a joke?

She dropped her shoes on the concrete. Scanned the grounds and searched toward the small forest and down the other side. Acres and acres, much beyond her line of sight.

"Gus!" He could be anywhere. Inside Hadsby, gone for a walk. Down to the Belly of the Beast to see Ernst. "Your Majesty? Prince John?"

She didn't want to believe it, but the queen had turned the tables. Instead of getting Gus, she was getting Daffy. But it didn't make sense. Was the conversation in her flat a farce?

One last visible sweep through dewy eyes, and Daffy dropped down to the porch, shoes by her feet, the bag containing a green Frisbee tossed to the red runner.

GUS

"Where you've been?" Mum's assistant met him outside his apartment. "They're waiting for you."

"On an errand."

"Better have been a good one. Go. They've already taken the carts to the portico. Her Majesty is not pleased."

Nothing like being reprimanded by your mother's secretary. He thudded down the secret stairs and out the side door, pushing through the hedge and around Hadsby's high, ancient stone walls.

Picking up his pace, he left Hadsby's shadows and merged into the white gold light of a Dalholm sunset. His shoes slipped on the dewy grass. Nevertheless, he quickened his pace.

The scene was beautiful and Gus conceded Mum's need for a family portrait might be justified. But blast, why didn't Daffy answer her phone? He must've called her five times on his way home. For the life of him, he couldn't recall the event she was working.

Coming around the northeast side of the castle, he spied the family on the portico, along with the waiting photographer.

Gus picked up his pace. "Sorry I'm late." When he got to the concrete-and-marble structure with its Greek columns, the family merely stared at him. "What? I've apologized for being late. Let's do this."

"We're waiting for one more." Mum motioned to someone behind the column.

Daffy came around, her bare feet sticking out from the hem of the blue gown. Mum's blue gown. Sunlight laced through the swirls of her auburn hair.

"I heard you needed a date for a very important ball. Also, I brought you this." With a quick flip of her wrist, she flung a lime-green Frisbee straight for him. And he did not duck. The blame thing thunked him on the side of his head.

"Gus!" She ran toward him. "Are you all right? You were supposed to—"

He captured her in his arms and found her lips, savoring her touch, her presence, her surprise. Everything about her unlocked the rest of his freedom.

Behind him the family serenaded them with catcalls, whistles, and applause. Still he refused to let her go. He kissed her again then, with a laugh that welled up from deep within him, he released her, only to twirl her around.

"Surprise," Daffy said.

"I thought you weren't coming."

"I made her keep the secret, especially since she's so good at it. Next time, son, do not sit in my rare, valuable chair."

How good it felt to laugh. "Lesson learned."

Gus bent for the Frisbee and, with Daffy on his arm, turned to his family. "I know there's more to the story, but let's do this. Family photo. We've a wedding ball to attend."

Mum motioned for them to face the photographer, who hurried from behind a tree and across the grand lawn. Holland shivered with each gust of the wind, but Daffy, so beautifully flushed and blushed, cradled next to Gus, warm and smiling.

She stunned his heart.

The photographer was useless getting them to pose normally, so with each couple standing askew, laughing, the photographer captured the present and future House of Blue.

The image from that day was framed and hung in Perrigwynn Palace's main hall. It was that year's House of Blue Christmas card. And in time, the most favored photo of the family as well as the public.

Everyone was happy and in love, as was only right and true in the hamlet of Dalholm, where love bloomed like flora and fauna. Where Emmanuel walked among them. God with us.

"He's a true prince. His Royal Highness Prince Gus lands on his feet in love. More after this."

–*STONE BRUBAKER, THE MORNING SHOW*

"Okay, is Daffodil Caron not the cutest? I love her for the prince."

–*LOYAL ROYALS BLOG*

"Daffodil Caron attended the ball in the same gown the queen wore for her twenty-first birthday bash. I think we're going to see a lot of her in the future."

–*@ROYALWATCHERONE*

"The Morning Show announced a new royal reporter, Melissa Faris. Leslie Ann Parker will join the police report every morning at six."

–*THE NEWS LEADER*

LET'S END
HERE...

DAFFY

She ran with Gus down the familiar path toward the trees, the summer leaves lush and green, through the gate and down the cobblestones of Centre Street.

Since their portico kiss, they'd fallen completely, unreservedly in love. With each other and Emmanuel. What a cool chap, this Lord of all, God with us.

She'd landed a fantastic position at CCW Cosmetics as their corporate curator. Finding something in common, Coral and Daffy interviewed one another as they passed on the ballroom floor, sharing questions and answers back and forth, as they twirled and turned. Most unusual interview ever, but after a phone conference with Coral's CEO, Lexa, Daffy was hired the next week.

She flew to New York in May to meet the staff and learn the history of her new employer as well as develop curating ideas. She'd work out of the Port Fressa office with trips to New York as needed to launch the final project.

Gus arrived the last week of her trip to play a bit of tourist and attend church with the Mayses.

They dined with Chuck and Coral that evening, talking well into the night about faith and God, trust and love, forgiveness, and Gus and Daffy's literal sighting of Emmanuel.

But now they were on a weekend holiday at Hadsby with the family.

"This way." Gus grabbed her hand and led her down Wells Line toward Canal. He'd been busy too, launching new charitable initiatives in concert with tech corporations and working with schools to teach about health, love, and faith.

And the Frisbee? Framed. Hanging in his office.

He was also becoming an uncle. Prince John and Lady Holland had secured the next heir to the throne. Due sometime in late January, early February.

That's why they were gathered at Hadsby. To celebrate.

Gus drew Daffy into the Belly of the Beast. "Ernst."

Did the chap ever leave? Ever take a holiday?

"Yer Maj! Princess." He came around the bar with his thick arms wide, embracing them without reservation.

"Sit. Stella!"

"Later, I promise." Gus smiled. "We're on our way somewhere."

Daffy looked around at him. "We are? I thought this was our destination."

"I had another in mind. But wanted to pop in to say hi to Ernst and Stella. Have you seen Emmanuel lately?"

"Here and there. Dom Watson lost his wife of sixty-seven years last month. Came in here to drown his sorrows. Emmanuel sat with him all night. He was a real comfort. Dom's actually traveling to see his kids."

"Give our love to Dom. Hope we see him while we're here."

"Wait a minute." Daffy stepped around Gus. "Ernst, you just spoke in whole sentences."

Ernst huffed. "My friend, I've a degree from Haxton. Do you think I was born in this pub?"

Now that was the surprise of all surprises. Astounded and laughing, Daffy dashed from the Belly with Gus and down the steps to the quay.

She pulled him to a stop. "We're climbing to the Hand of God?"

"Why do you think I told you to wear boots?" Gus grinned. "I wanted to see the view on a summer day."

She raced ahead of him to the footbridge, no longer afraid of heights and of the perilous climb. Love was with her. This time she led Gus up the steep climb to the cleft in the rocks.

"Keep your eyes on me." Her words were bold. "Don't look—"

"To the right or the left. Don't look down." Gus's hand rested on the middle of her back. "You lead, I'll follow."

The summer growth covered large portions of the path. Daffy led Gus over a fallen branch, under a trunk growing out of the cliff, around rocks, climbing higher and higher.

But this time the sun had warmed the breeze. As Daffy grabbed onto a tree branch to pull herself to the next level, the spectacular view of the calm sea-blue water widened before her, meeting the blue horizon at some faraway point.

At last they broke into the clearing and stepped into the nook known as the Hand of God. The grass was long and lush, woven with wildflowers.

"It's like our own personal garden." Gus turned a half circle.

"When we're here, I think it is."

"I climbed up when I visited last week." He took her hand, pulling her alongside him. "I sat with my legs over the side for the better part of two hours. Just thinking and well, praying."

"What did you think and pray about?"

"You. Me. Our lives. How when we first climbed up you were terrified and brokenhearted about Thomas. When I thought I was all cool and Coral, but I wasn't. Didn't even realize the truth until she curtsied in front of me and said, 'Your Royal Highness.'"

"We've returned here as slightly different people. Not arrived, but on our way."

"On our way. Yes." He reached in his pocket and slowly bent to one knee. "Your first proposal was a surprise in a loud, noisy pub with everyone watching and a ring intended originally for another. So what I hope to be your second—and last—proposal comes with you standing in a quiet garden on top of the world, only the seagulls and God watching. The ring I'm offering was purchased with you and just you in mind. It's not even from the

Family vault. I shopped, alone, and selected a ring that most reflected your heart." Gus lifted the lid to reveal a diamond set in platinum surrounded by sapphires, rubies, and emeralds. "The sapphires for your eyes, the rubies for your hair, the emerald for the life of your heart."

"Gus, I—" Her tears spoke a better word.

"Daffodil Daisy Caron, will you marry me?"

"Yes, of course, I'll marry you." She dropped to her knees in front of him, not caring at all about the soggy wetness. "Finally I'll be able to write the true tales of *My Life with the Prince* by Daffodil Caron, House of Blue."

"Her Royal Highness, Princess Daffodil." He slipped the ring on her finger, then raised her up, cupped her face in his hands, and sealed their pledge with a kiss.

They stayed in the cleft for a long time, talking, dreaming, planning. Kissing. She liked the idea of an October wedding after all.

When they climbed down and walked hand in hand up the quay steps, motors honked, people called out their names. They paused to wave and give by passers a quick photo op.

"How about one of Stella's meat pies and chips?" Gus pointed to the pub.

"Food. Good."

With a laugh, he grabbed her to him and kissed her temple. "I love you."

"You'd better. With all your heart." Then something stirred in Daffy. As they started up Canal, she looked back, toward the Hand of God and there, on top of the rocks, stood Emmanuel, his long anorak flapping in the breeze.

He raised a single hand in wave, then stepped down and disappeared.

And Daffy knew. She was more than an ordinary girl and Emmanuel was the reason why.

Being married to a royal would have its ups and downs, but with Emmanuel, God with us, she'd never be alone.

"Ernst will be over the moon I finally made you my princess."

"You know, I think he already knew. Emmanuel probably told him."

Gus paused outside the pub and took her in his arms. "I'm never going to let you go."

"Nor I you."

His kiss lingered, and when he opened the door to the pub, following Daffy inside, he called out, "Ernst. Princess. Finally! Chips on me. Stella!"

THE END

THANK YOU TO...

Kristen Painter and Leigh Duncan. Let's see where the fairytale leads. Your friendship and counsel are treasures.

Robbi Grey for brainstorming Prince Gus and Daffy's "meet cute."

Erin Healy for reading the first, very ugly draft. As always, your editorial skills put me on the right path.

Susie May, whom I called after every scene toward the end. "Okay, now where do I go? How about..."

Beth Vogt for combing through this story line by line and all the brainstorming in between. Above all for your faithful friendship.

Barbara Curtis for additional, fabulous line edits and proofing. Lianne March and Lisa Jordan for stellar proofing. Any remaining mistakes are mine.

Amy Atwell for brilliant production support.

Kristen Ingebretson for the gorgeous cover.

Louise Lee for the fabulous audio edition. I'm glad we met.

Debb Hackett for being so kind and patient when I messaged constantly about British terms. While Lauchtenland is a made-up country, I wanted a British feel. In the end, the language is a blend of American and British, but Debb kept me straight on the British way.

My husband for saying yes to this writing journey with its ups and downs, twists and turns. Much love to you always!

To all the readers who asked for more royals, thank you for inspiring me! I hope you love Prince Gus and Daffodil Caron as much as I do.

RACHEL HAUCK is an award winning, New York Times, USA Today, and Wall Street Journal bestselling author.

Her book The Wedding Dress was named Inspirational Novel of the Year by Romantic Times Book Reviews. She is a double RITA finalist and a Christy and Carol Award Winner.

Her book Once Upon A Prince, first in the Royal Wedding Series, was filmed for an Original Hallmark movie.

Rachel has been awarded the prestigious Career Achievement Award for her body of original work by Romantic Times Book Reviews.

A member of the Executive Board for American Christian Fiction Writers, she teaches workshops and leads worship at the annual conference. She is a past Mentor of the Year.

At home, she's a wife, writer, worship leader, and works out at a local gym semi-enthusiastically.

A graduate of Ohio State University (Go, Bucks!) with a degree in Journalism, she's a former sorority girl and a devoted Ohio State football fan. Her bucket list is to stand on the sidelines with Ryan Day.

She lives in sunny central Florida with her husband and ornery cat.

For exclusive content and insider information, sign up for her newsletter at www.rachelhauck.com.